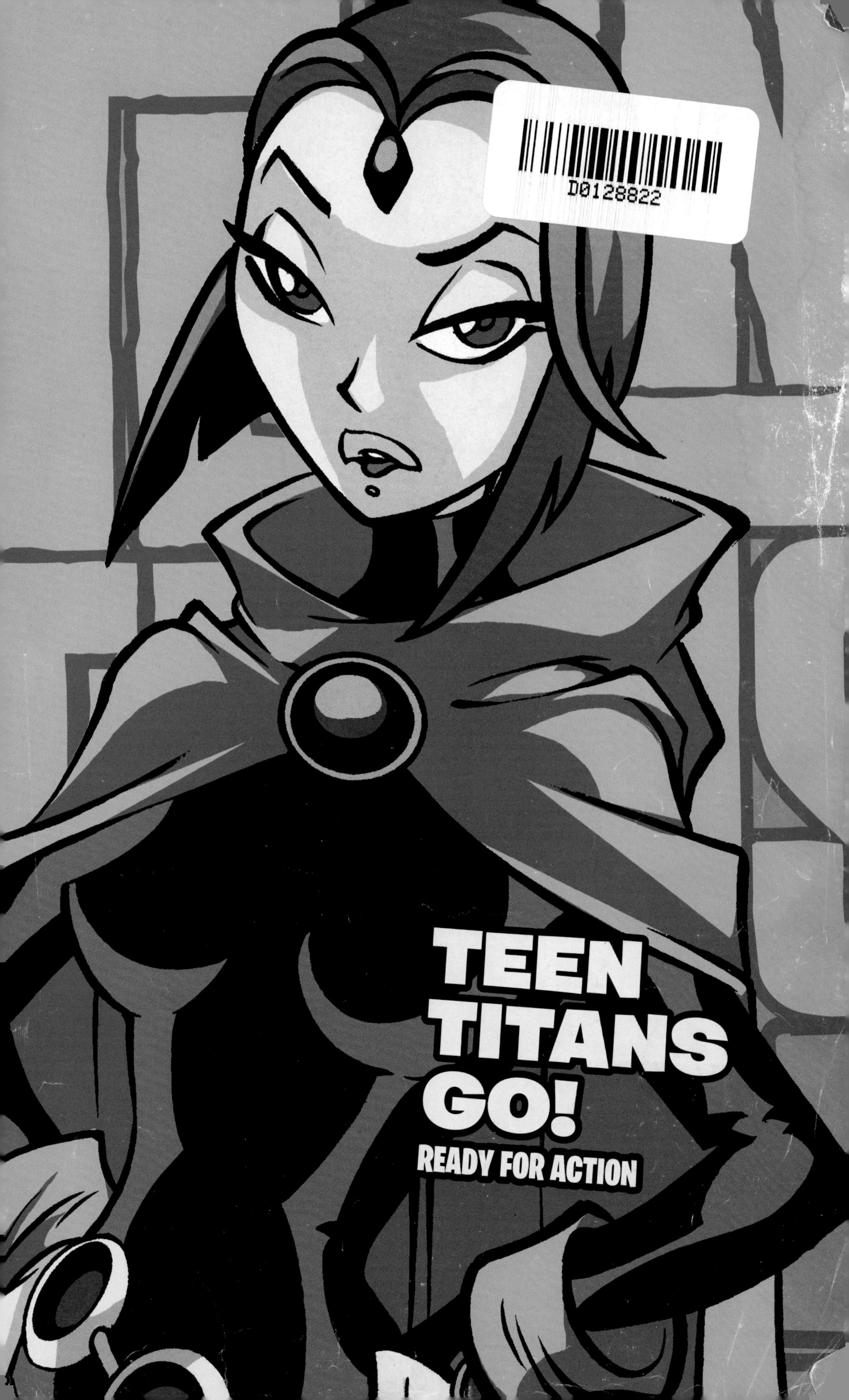
TEEN
TITANS
GO!
READY FOR ACTION

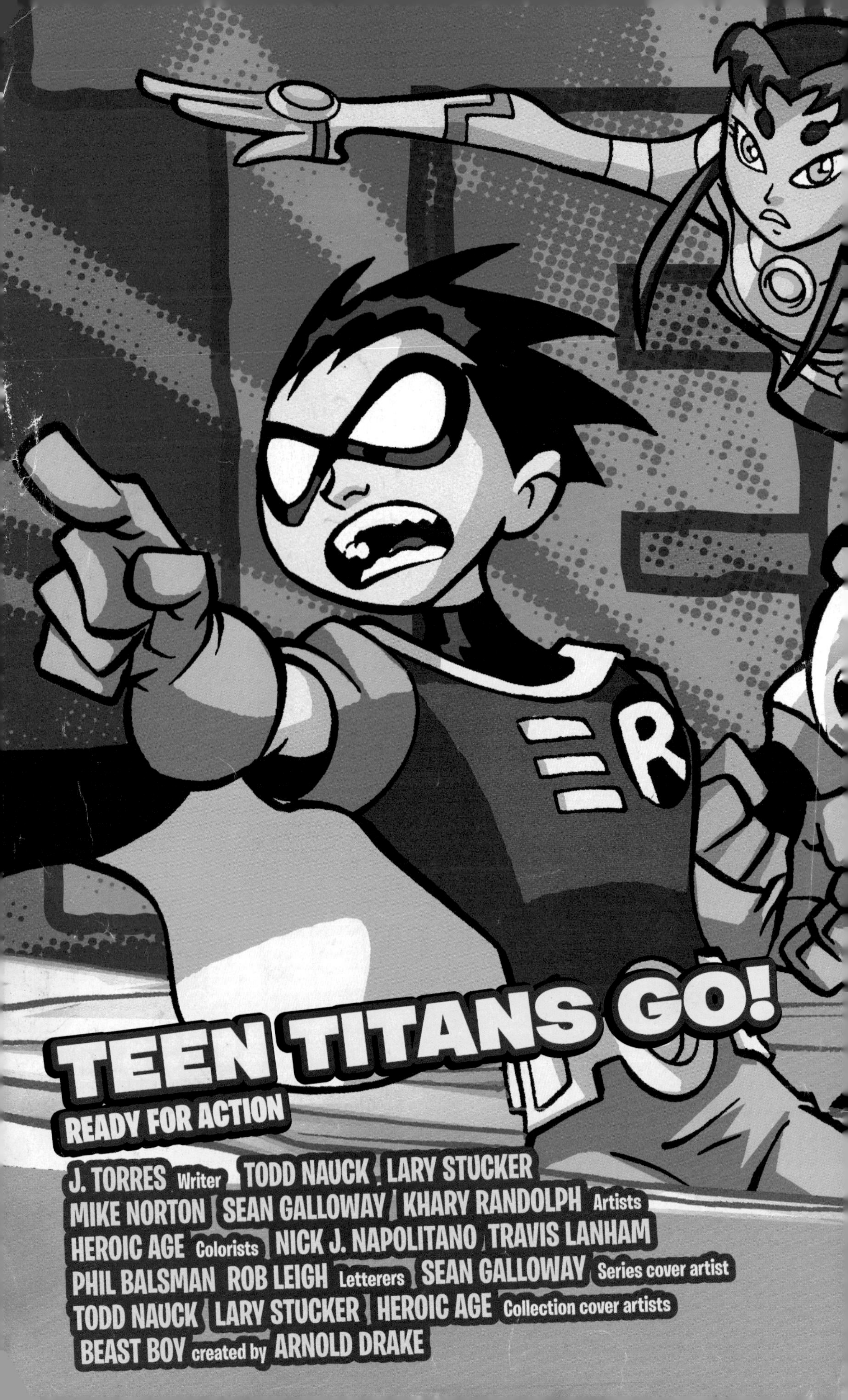

TEEN TITANS GO!

READY FOR ACTION

J. TORRES Writer TODD NAUCK LARY STUCKER
MIKE NORTON SEAN GALLOWAY KHARY RANDOLPH Artists
HEROIC AGE Colorists NICK J. NAPOLITANO TRAVIS LANHAM
PHIL BALSMAN ROB LEIGH Letterers SEAN GALLOWAY Series cover artist
TODD NAUCK LARY STUCKER HEROIC AGE Collection cover artists
BEAST BOY created by ARNOLD DRAKE

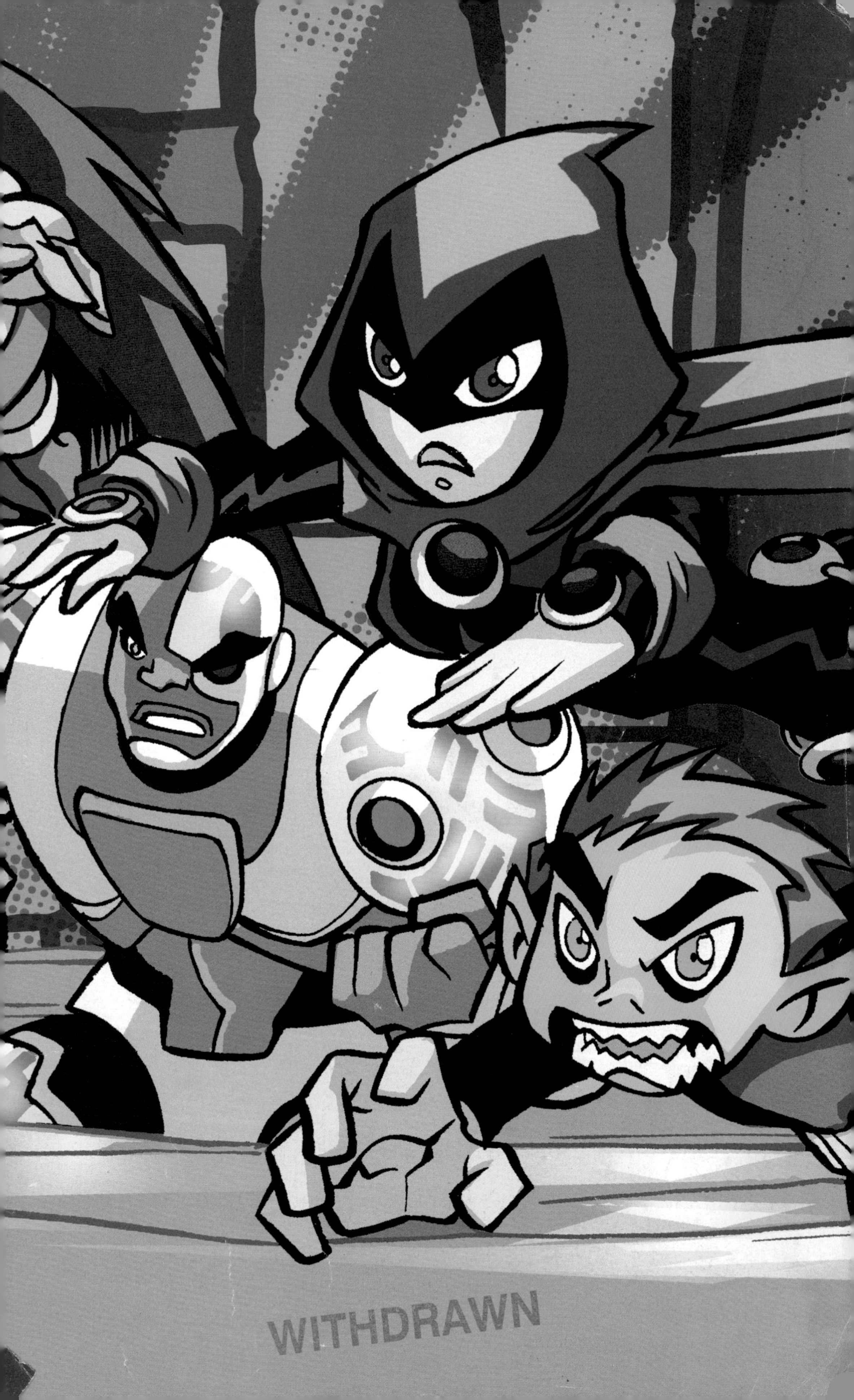

TOM PALMER JR. Editor – Original Series
JEANINE SCHAEFER Assistant Editor – Original Series
JEB WOODARD Group Editor – Collected Editions
ERIKA ROTHBERG Editor – Collected Edition
STEVE COOK Design Director – Books
LOUIS PRANDI Publication Design

BOB HARRAS Senior VP – Editor-in-Chief, DC Comics

DIANE NELSON President
DAN DiDIO Publisher
JIM LEE Publisher
GEOFF JOHNS President & Chief Creative Officer
AMIT DESAI Executive VP – Business & Marketing Strategy, Direct to Consumer & Global Franchise Management
SAM ADES Senior VP – Direct to Consumer
BOBBIE CHASE VP – Talent Development
MARK CHIARELLO Senior VP – Art, Design & Collected Editions
JOHN CUNNINGHAM Senior VP – Sales & Trade Marketing
ANNE DePIES Senior VP – Business Strategy, Finance & Administration
DON FALLETTI VP – Manufacturing Operations
LAWRENCE GANEM VP – Editorial Administration & Talent Relations
ALISON GILL Senior VP – Manufacturing & Operations
HANK KANALZ Senior VP – Editorial Strategy & Administration
JAY KOGAN VP – Legal Affairs
THOMAS LOFTUS VP – Business Affairs
JACK MAHAN VP – Business Affairs
NICK J. NAPOLITANO VP – Manufacturing Administration
EDDIE SCANNELL VP – Consumer Marketing
COURTNEY SIMMONS Senior VP – Publicity & Communications
JIM (SKI) SOKOLOWSKI VP – Comic Book Specialty Sales & Trade Marketing
NANCY SPEARS VP – Mass, Book, Digital Sales & Trade Marketing

TEEN TITANS GO!: READY FOR ACTION

DC Comics, 2900 West Alameda Ave., Burbank, CA 91505
Printed by Vanguard Graphics, LLC, Ithaca, NY, USA. 4/7/17. First Printing.
ISBN: 978-1-4012-6899-2

Library of Congress Cataloging-in-Publication Data is available.

MIX
Paper from
responsible sources
FSC® C016956
FSC
www.fsc.org

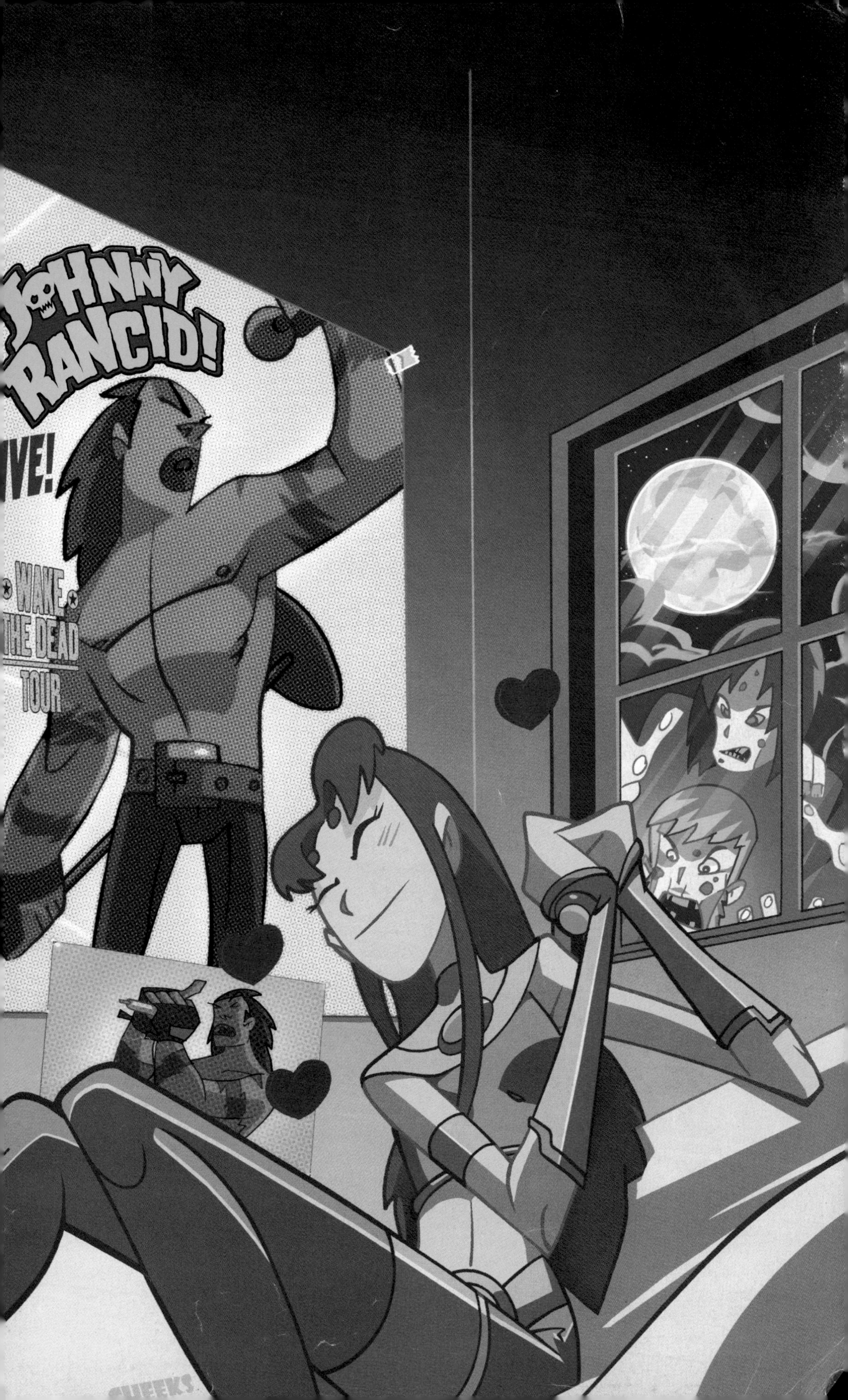
JOHNNY RANCID!
WAKE THE DEAD TOUR

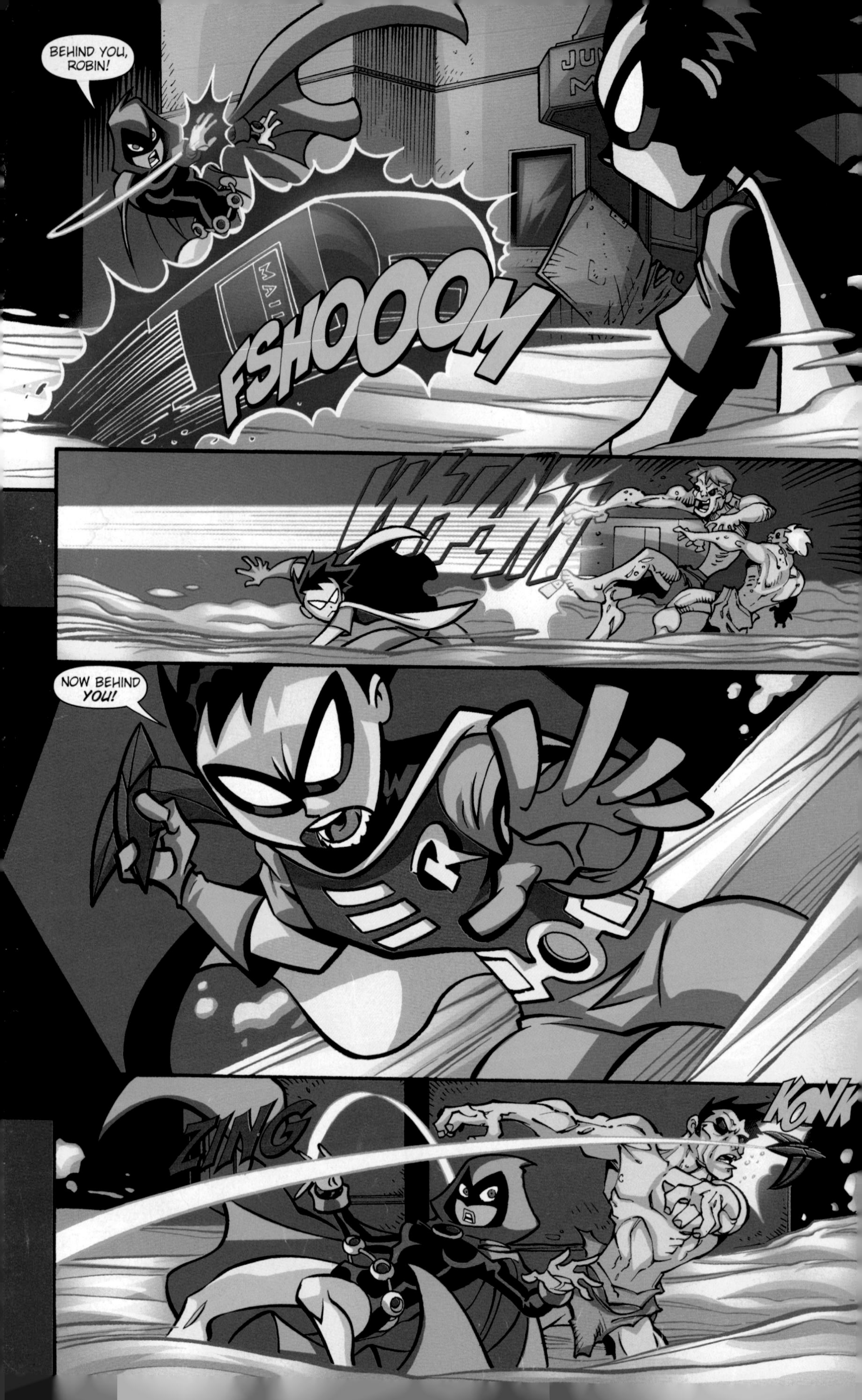

BEHIND YOU, ROBIN!
FSHOOOM
NOW BEHIND YOU!
ZING
KONK

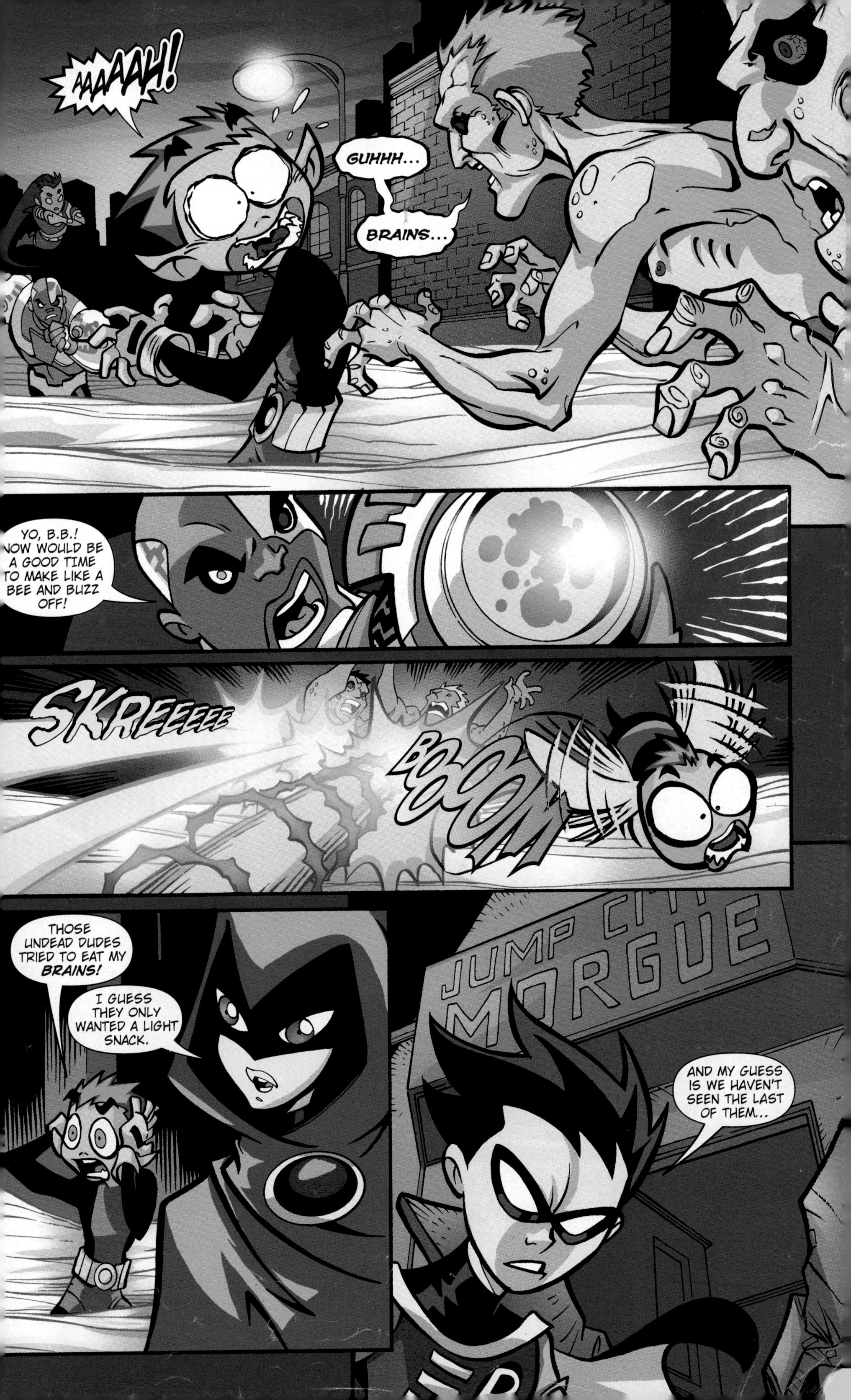
AAAAAH!
GUHHH...
BRAINS...
YO, B.B.! NOW WOULD BE A GOOD TIME TO MAKE LIKE A BEE AND BUZZ OFF!
SKREEEEEE
BOOOM
THOSE UNDEAD DUDES TRIED TO EAT MY BRAINS!
I GUESS THEY ONLY WANTED A LIGHT SNACK.
AND MY GUESS IS WE HAVEN'T SEEN THE LAST OF THEM...

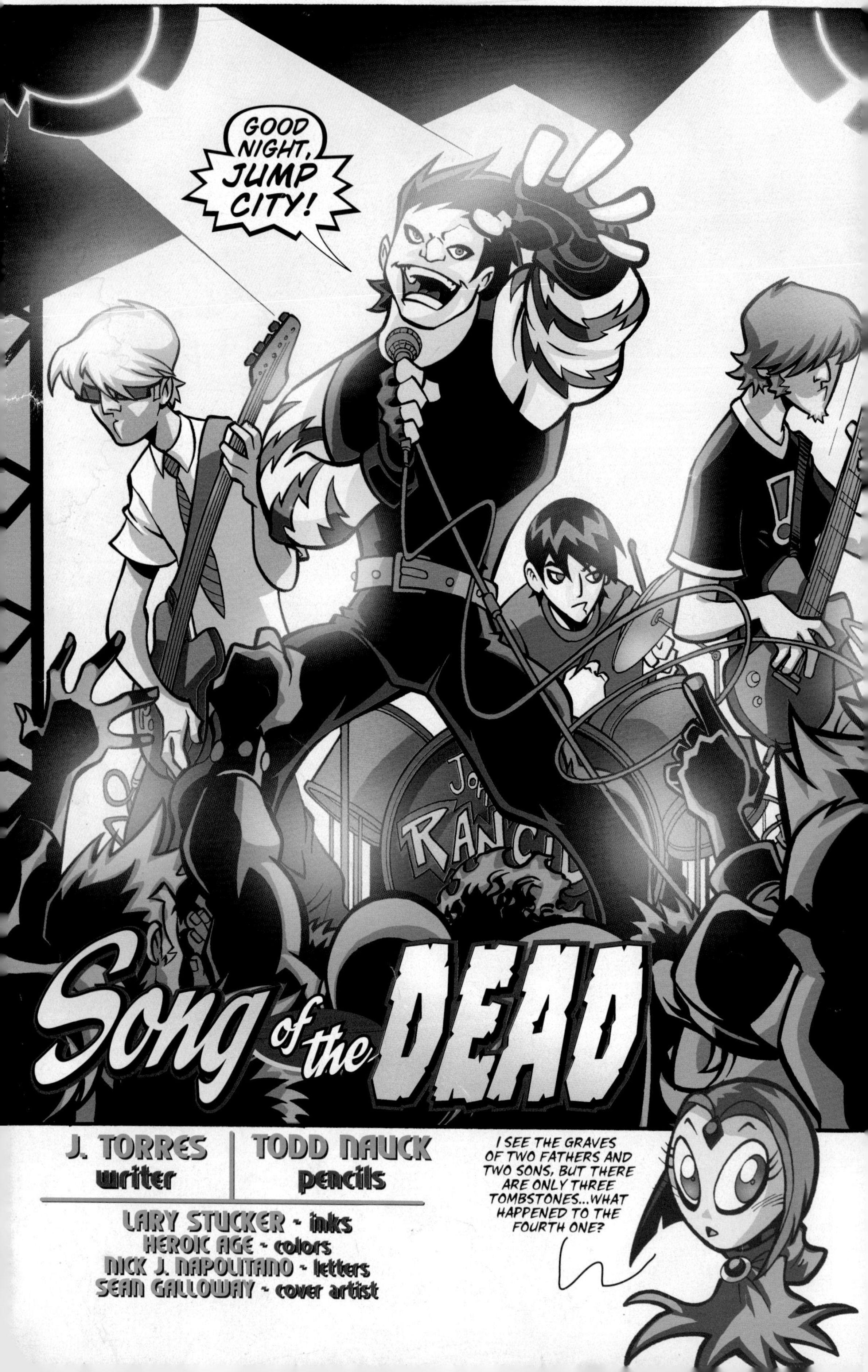
GOOD NIGHT, JUMP CITY!
Song of the DEAD
J. TORRES writer
TODD NAUCK pencils
LARY STUCKER - inks
HEROIC AGE - colors
NICK J. NAPOLITANO - letters
SEAN GALLOWAY - cover artist
I SEE THE GRAVES OF TWO FATHERS AND TWO SONS, BUT THERE ARE ONLY THREE TOMBSTONES...WHAT HAPPENED TO THE FOURTH ONE?

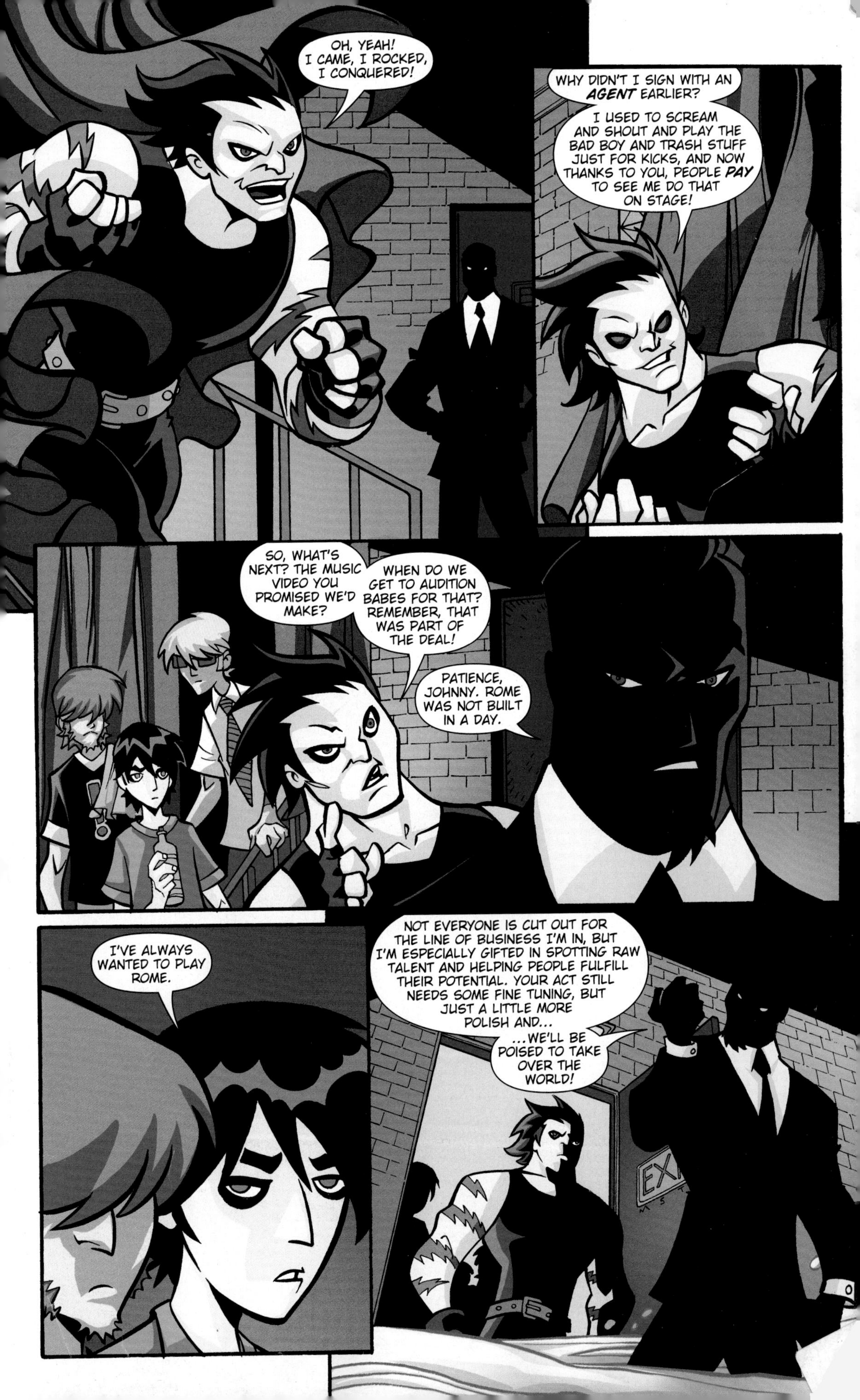
OH, YEAH! I CAME, I ROCKED, I CONQUERED!
WHY DIDN'T I SIGN WITH AN AGENT EARLIER?
I USED TO SCREAM AND SHOUT AND PLAY THE BAD BOY AND TRASH STUFF JUST FOR KICKS, AND NOW THANKS TO YOU, PEOPLE PAY TO SEE ME DO THAT ON STAGE!
SO, WHAT'S NEXT? THE MUSIC VIDEO YOU PROMISED WE'D MAKE?
WHEN DO WE GET TO AUDITION BABES FOR THAT? REMEMBER, THAT WAS PART OF THE DEAL!
PATIENCE, JOHNNY. ROME WAS NOT BUILT IN A DAY.
I'VE ALWAYS WANTED TO PLAY ROME.
NOT EVERYONE IS CUT OUT FOR THE LINE OF BUSINESS I'M IN, BUT I'M ESPECIALLY GIFTED IN SPOTTING RAW TALENT AND HELPING PEOPLE FULFILL THEIR POTENTIAL. YOUR ACT STILL NEEDS SOME FINE TUNING, BUT JUST A LITTLE MORE POLISH AND...
...WE'LL BE POISED TO TAKE OVER THE WORLD!

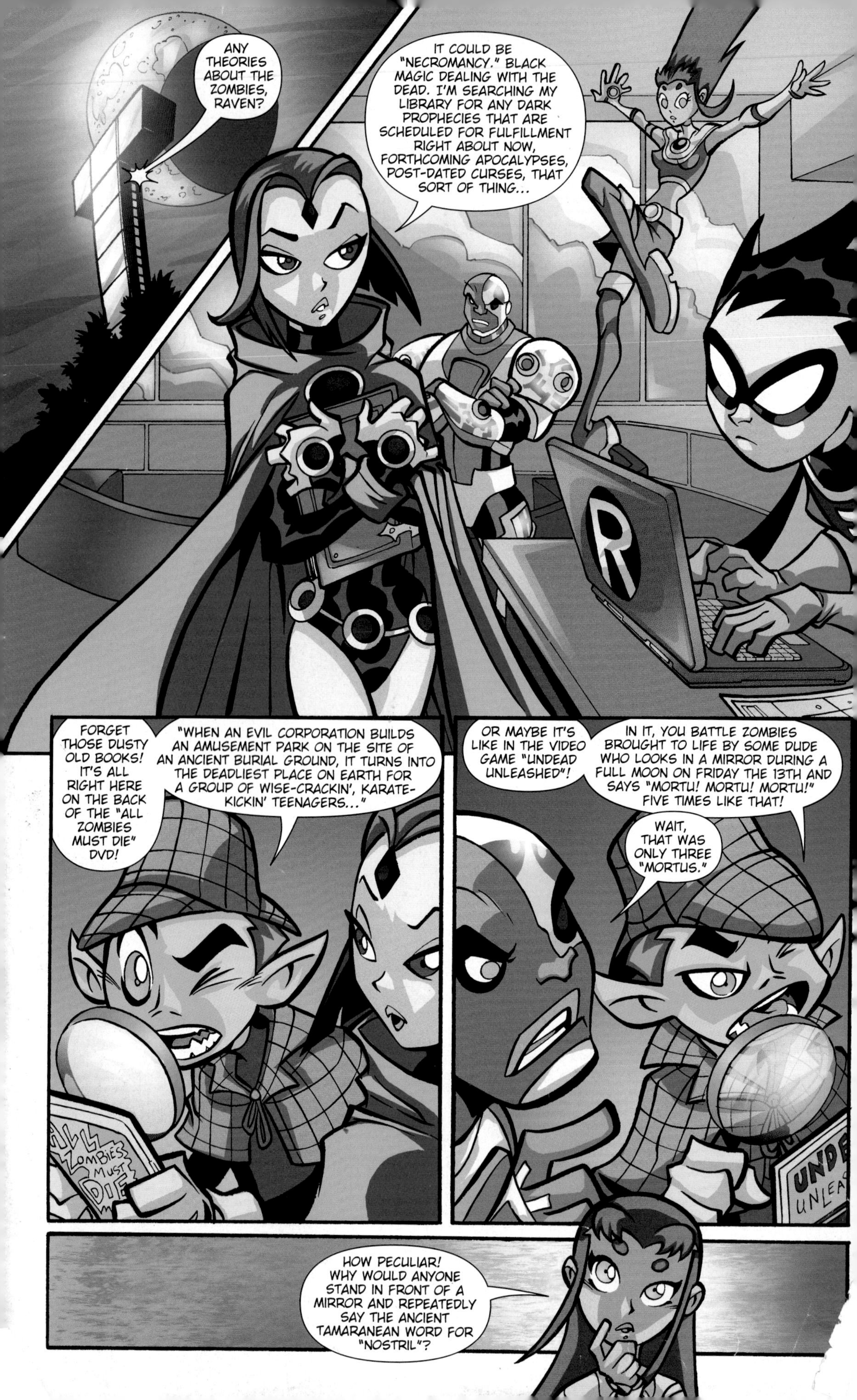
ANY THEORIES ABOUT THE ZOMBIES, RAVEN?
IT COULD BE "NECROMANCY." BLACK MAGIC DEALING WITH THE DEAD. I'M SEARCHING MY LIBRARY FOR ANY DARK PROPHECIES THAT ARE SCHEDULED FOR FULFILLMENT RIGHT ABOUT NOW, FORTHCOMING APOCALYPSES, POST-DATED CURSES, THAT SORT OF THING...
R
FORGET THOSE DUSTY OLD BOOKS! IT'S ALL RIGHT HERE ON THE BACK OF THE "ALL ZOMBIES MUST DIE" DVD!
"WHEN AN EVIL CORPORATION BUILDS AN AMUSEMENT PARK ON THE SITE OF AN ANCIENT BURIAL GROUND, IT TURNS INTO THE DEADLIEST PLACE ON EARTH FOR A GROUP OF WISE-CRACKIN', KARATE-KICKIN' TEENAGERS..."
ALL ZOMBIES MUST DIE
OR MAYBE IT'S LIKE IN THE VIDEO GAME "UNDEAD UNLEASHED"!
IN IT, YOU BATTLE ZOMBIES BROUGHT TO LIFE BY SOME DUDE WHO LOOKS IN A MIRROR DURING A FULL MOON ON FRIDAY THE 13TH AND SAYS "MORTU! MORTU! MORTU!" FIVE TIMES LIKE THAT!
WAIT, THAT WAS ONLY THREE "MORTUS."
HOW PECULIAR! WHY WOULD ANYONE STAND IN FRONT OF A MIRROR AND REPEATEDLY SAY THE ANCIENT TAMARANEAN WORD FOR "NOSTRIL"?

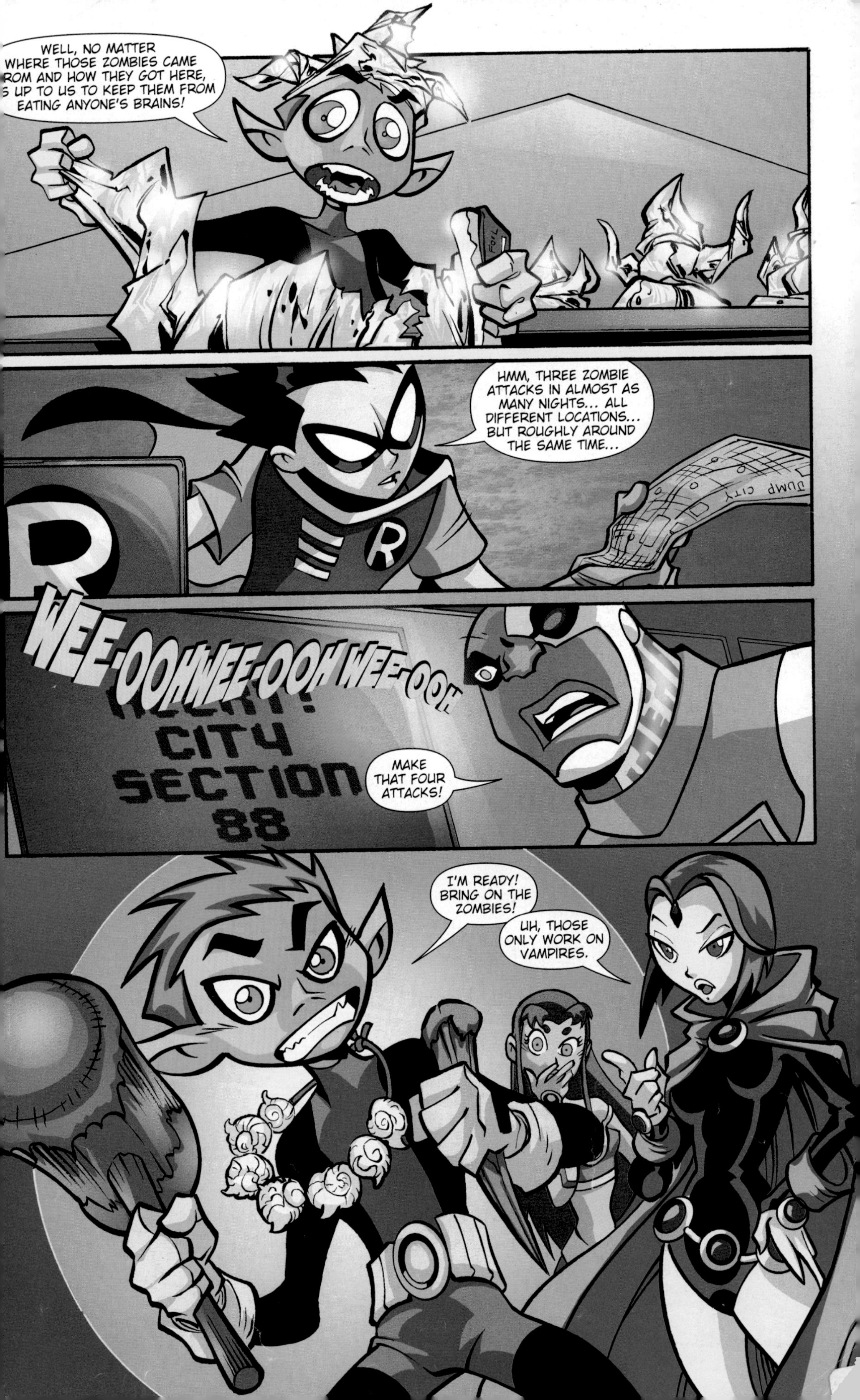

WELL, NO MATTER WHERE THOSE ZOMBIES CAME ROM AND HOW THEY GOT HERE, S UP TO US TO KEEP THEM FROM EATING ANYONE'S BRAINS!
FOIL
HMM, THREE ZOMBIE ATTACKS IN ALMOST AS MANY NIGHTS... ALL DIFFERENT LOCATIONS... BUT ROUGHLY AROUND THE SAME TIME...
JUMP CITY
WEE-OOH WEE-OOH WEE-OOH
CITY SECTION 88
MAKE THAT FOUR ATTACKS!
I'M READY! BRING ON THE ZOMBIES!
UH, THOSE ONLY WORK ON VAMPIRES.

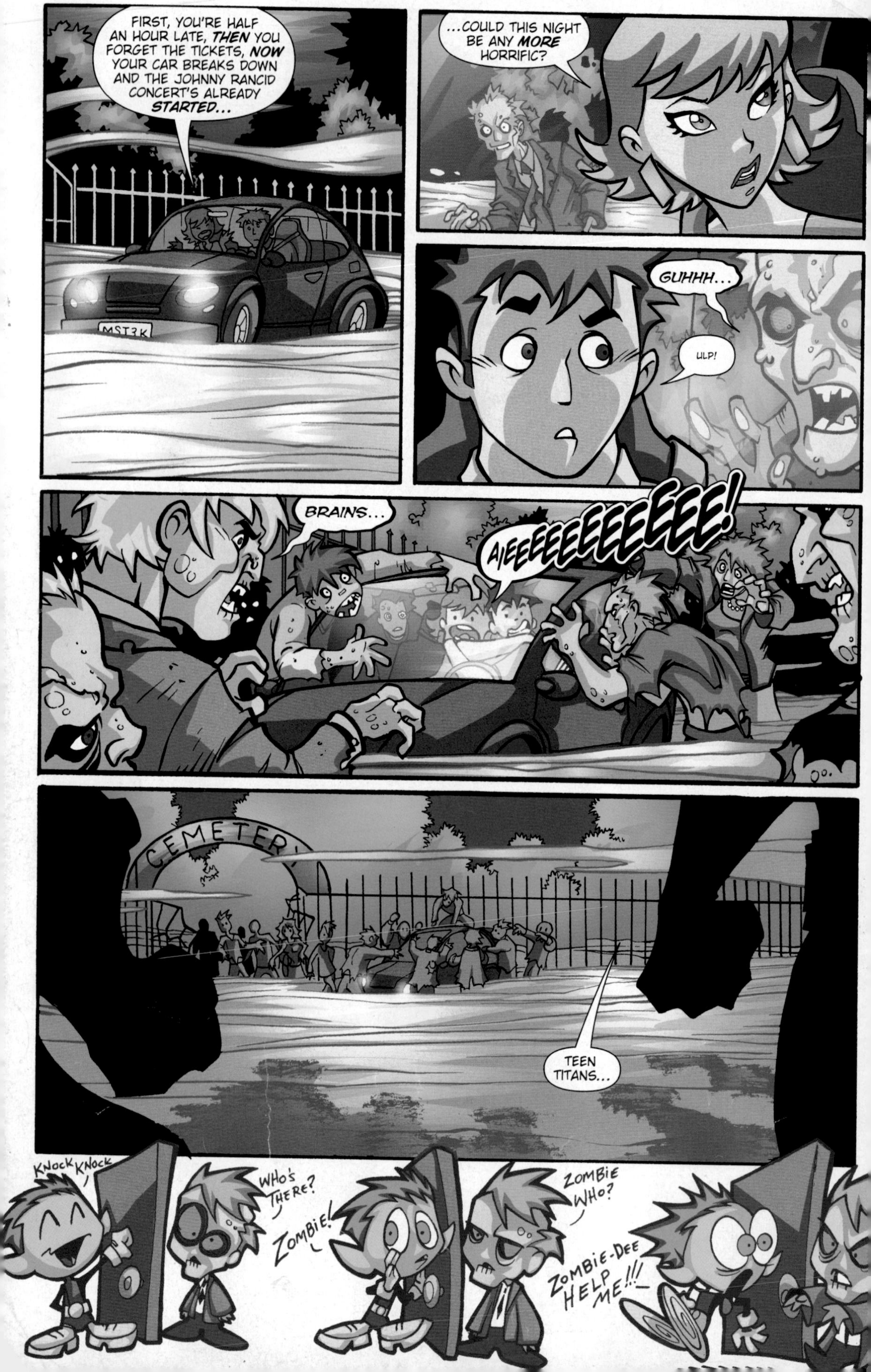
FIRST, YOU'RE HALF AN HOUR LATE, THEN YOU FORGET THE TICKETS, NOW YOUR CAR BREAKS DOWN AND THE JOHNNY RANCID CONCERT'S ALREADY STARTED...
MST3K
...COULD THIS NIGHT BE ANY MORE HORRIFIC?
GUHHH...
ULP!
BRAINS...
AIEEEEEEEEEEEE!
CEMETERY
TEEN TITANS...
KNOCK KNOCK
WHO'S THERE?
ZOMBIE!
ZOMBIE WHO?
ZOMBIE-DEE HELP ME!!!

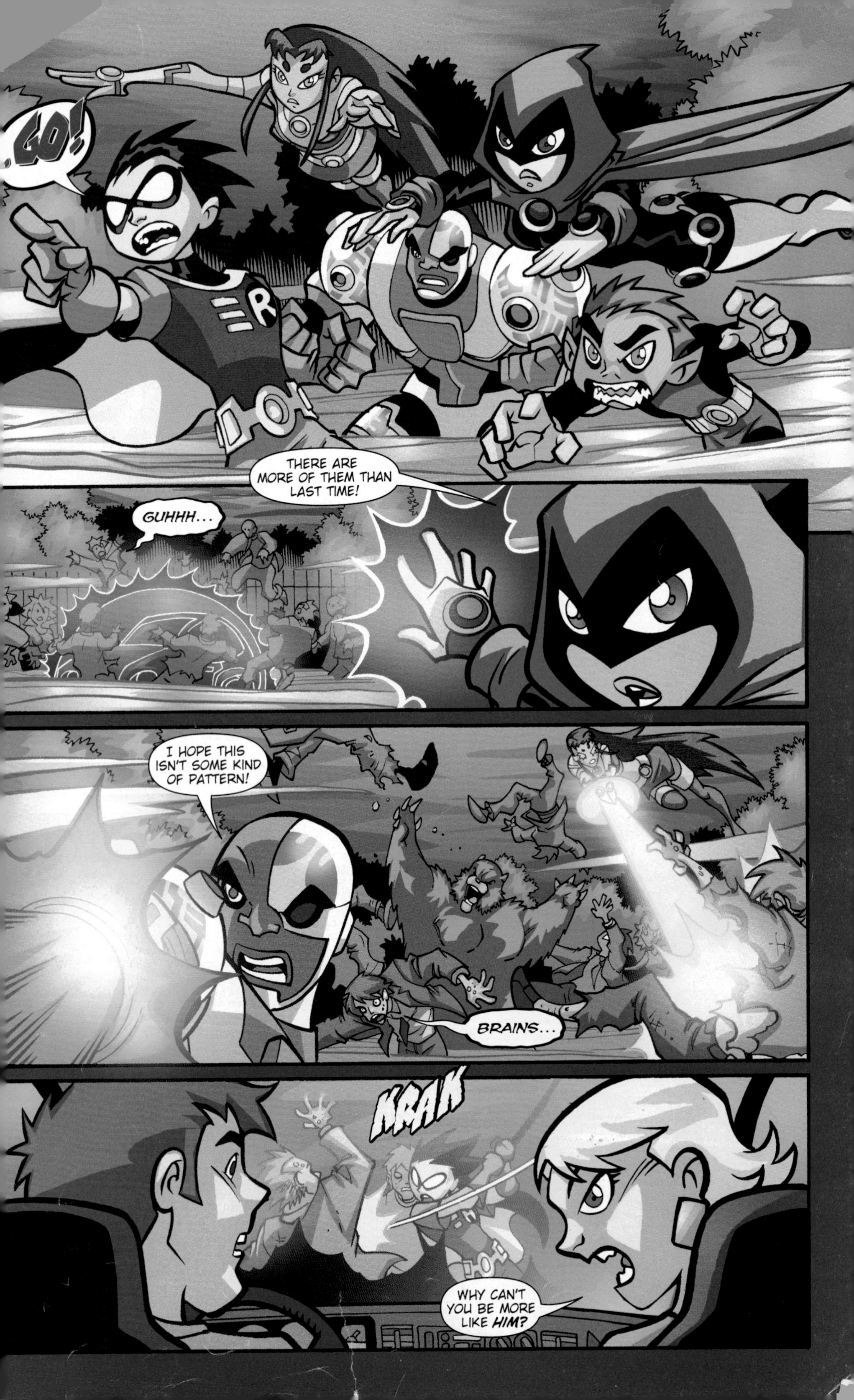

..GO!
THERE ARE MORE OF THEM THAN LAST TIME!
GUHHH...
I HOPE THIS ISN'T SOME KIND OF PATTERN!
BRAINS...
KRAK
WHY CAN'T YOU BE MORE LIKE HIM?

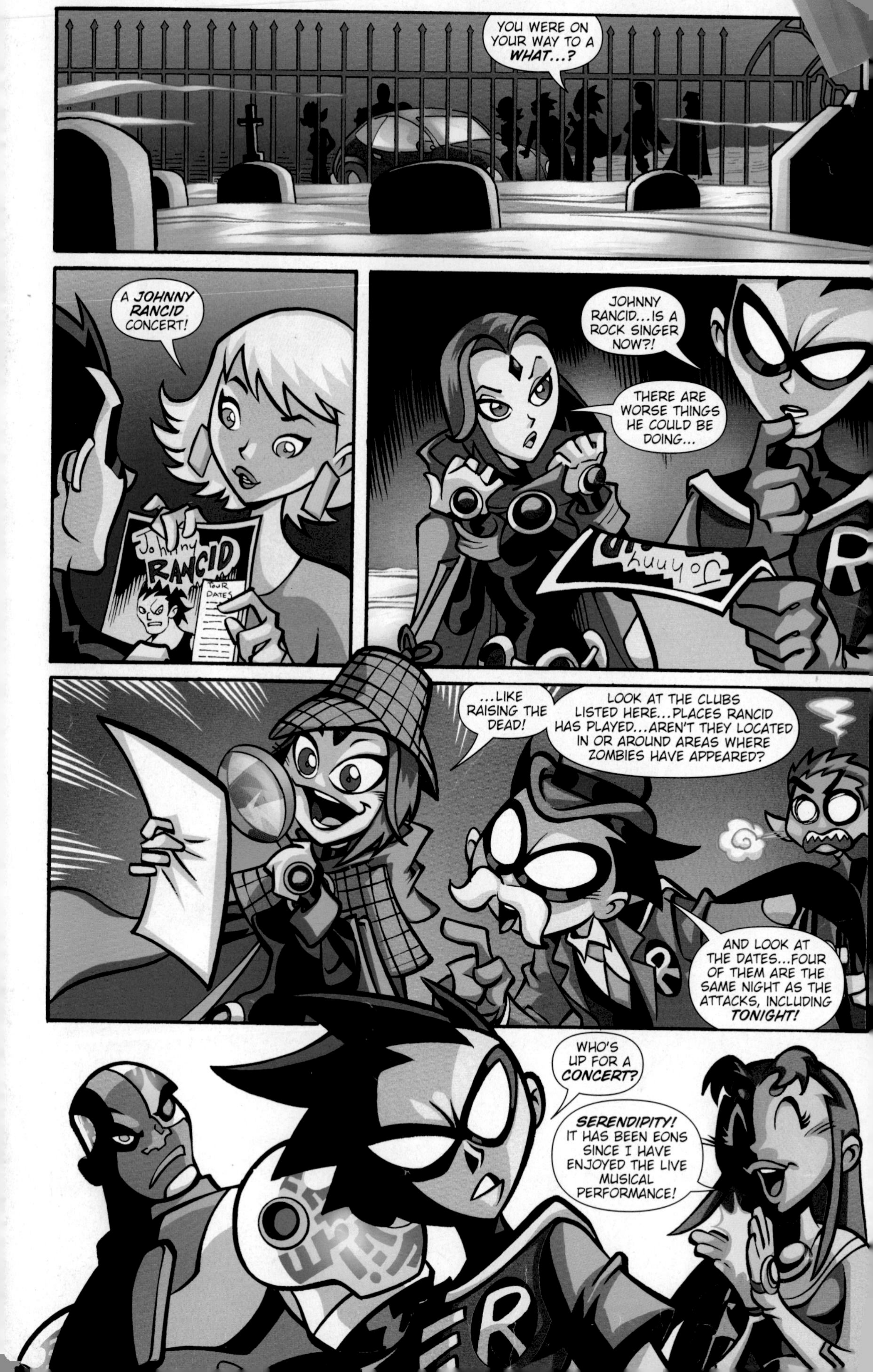

YOU WERE ON YOUR WAY TO A *WHAT...?*
A *JOHNNY RANCID* CONCERT!
JOHNNY RANCID
TOUR DATES
JOHNNY RANCID...IS A ROCK SINGER NOW?!
THERE ARE WORSE THINGS HE COULD BE DOING...
...LIKE RAISING THE DEAD!
LOOK AT THE CLUBS LISTED HERE...PLACES RANCID HAS PLAYED...AREN'T THEY LOCATED IN OR AROUND AREAS WHERE ZOMBIES HAVE APPEARED?
AND LOOK AT THE DATES...FOUR OF THEM ARE THE SAME NIGHT AS THE ATTACKS, INCLUDING *TONIGHT!*
WHO'S UP FOR A *CONCERT?*
SERENDIPITY! IT HAS BEEN EONS SINCE I HAVE ENJOYED THE LIVE MUSICAL PERFORMANCE!

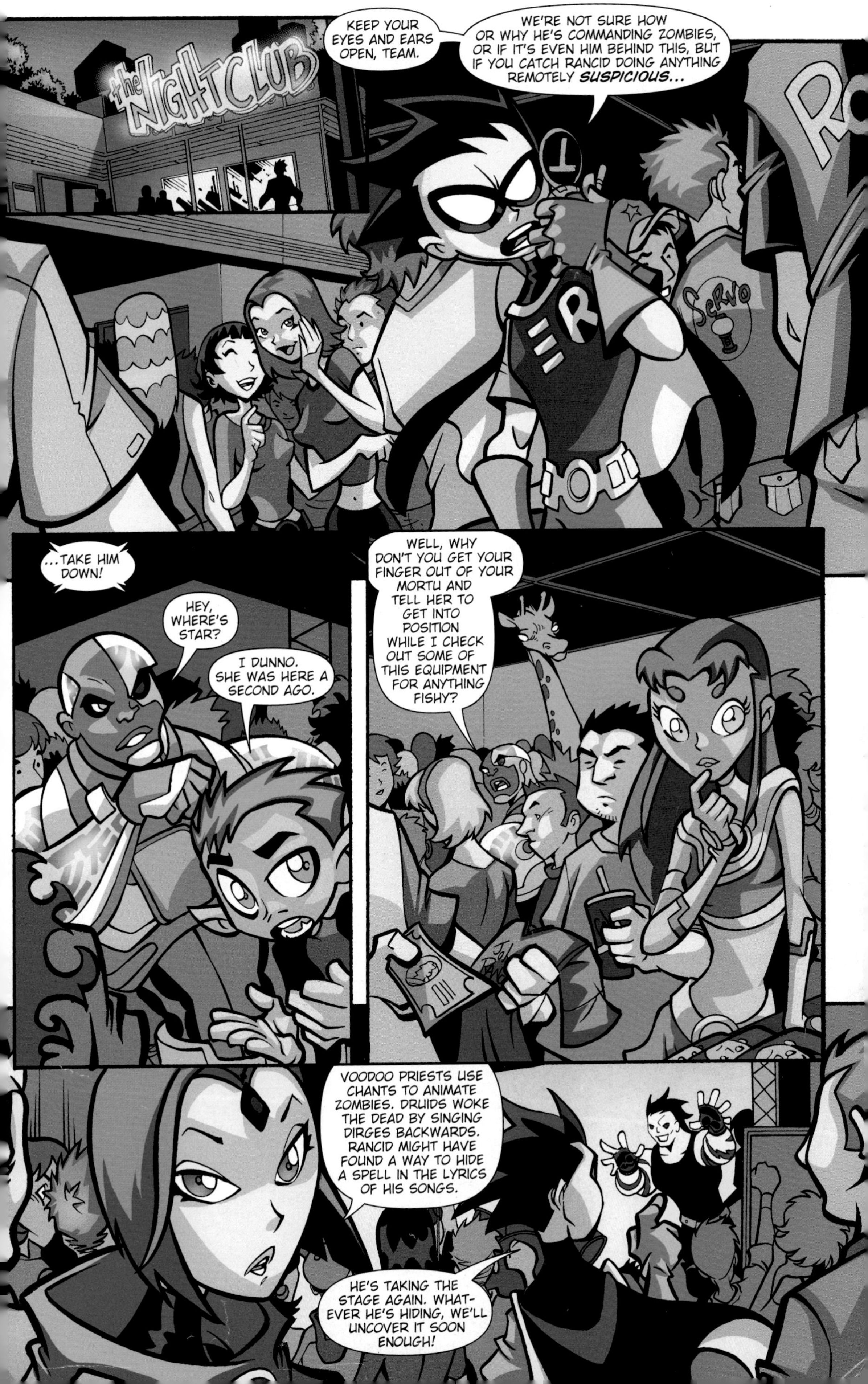
the NIGHTCLUB
KEEP YOUR EYES AND EARS OPEN, TEAM.
WE'RE NOT SURE HOW OR WHY HE'S COMMANDING ZOMBIES, OR IF IT'S EVEN HIM BEHIND THIS, BUT IF YOU CATCH RANCID DOING ANYTHING REMOTELY *SUSPICIOUS...*
...TAKE HIM DOWN!
HEY, WHERE'S STAR?
I DUNNO. SHE WAS HERE A SECOND AGO.
WELL, WHY DON'T YOU GET YOUR FINGER OUT OF YOUR MORTU AND TELL HER TO GET INTO POSITION WHILE I CHECK OUT SOME OF THIS EQUIPMENT FOR ANYTHING FISHY?
VOODOO PRIESTS USE CHANTS TO ANIMATE ZOMBIES. DRUIDS WOKE THE DEAD BY SINGING DIRGES BACKWARDS. RANCID MIGHT HAVE FOUND A WAY TO HIDE A SPELL IN THE LYRICS OF HIS SONGS.
HE'S TAKING THE STAGE AGAIN. WHATEVER HE'S HIDING, WE'LL UNCOVER IT SOON ENOUGH!

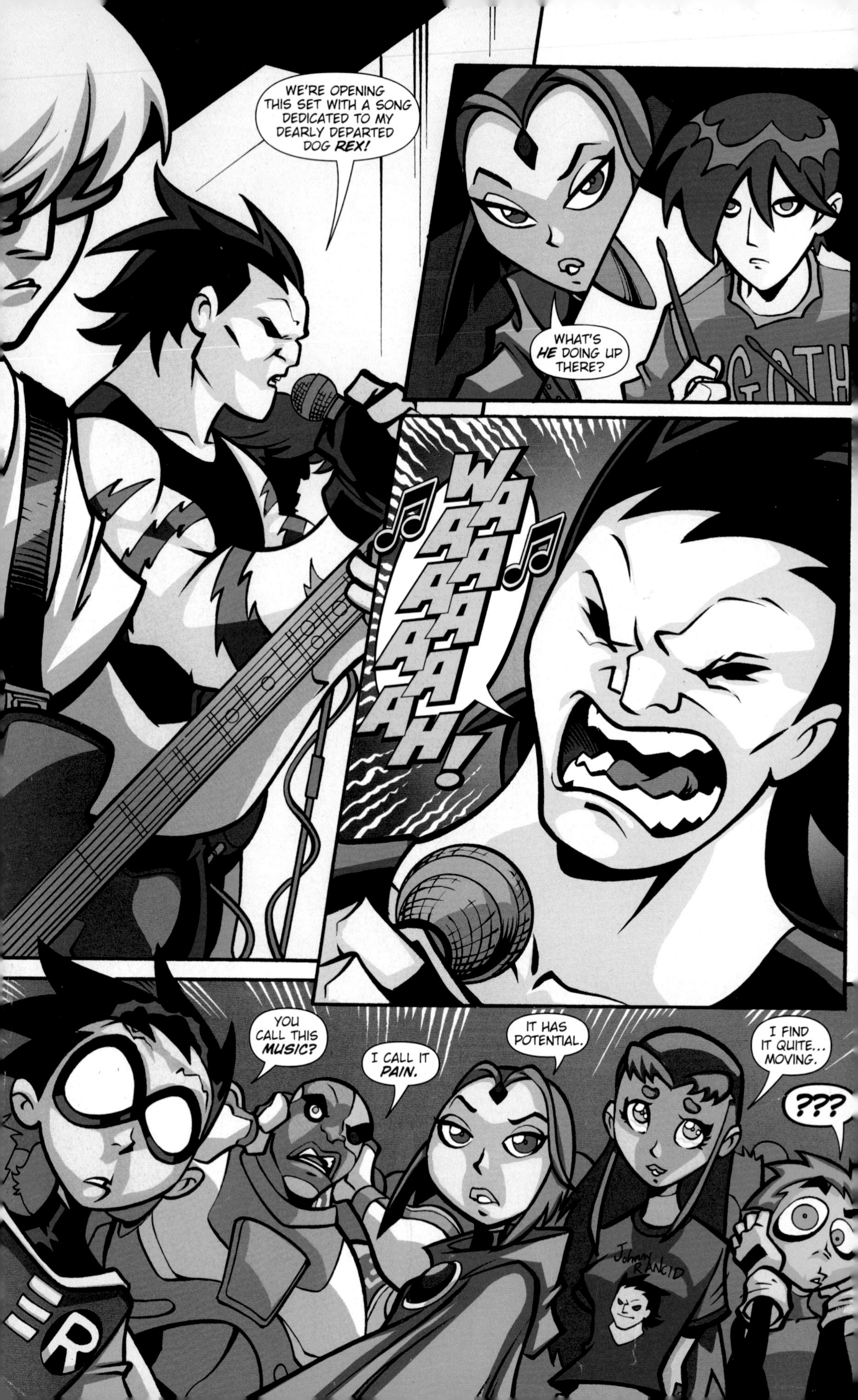
WE'RE OPENING THIS SET WITH A SONG DEDICATED TO MY DEARLY DEPARTED DOG REX!
WHAT'S HE DOING UP THERE?
GOTH
WAAAAAAAAAAAH!
YOU CALL THIS MUSIC?
I CALL IT PAIN.
IT HAS POTENTIAL.
I FIND IT QUITE... MOVING.
???
Johnny RANCID
R

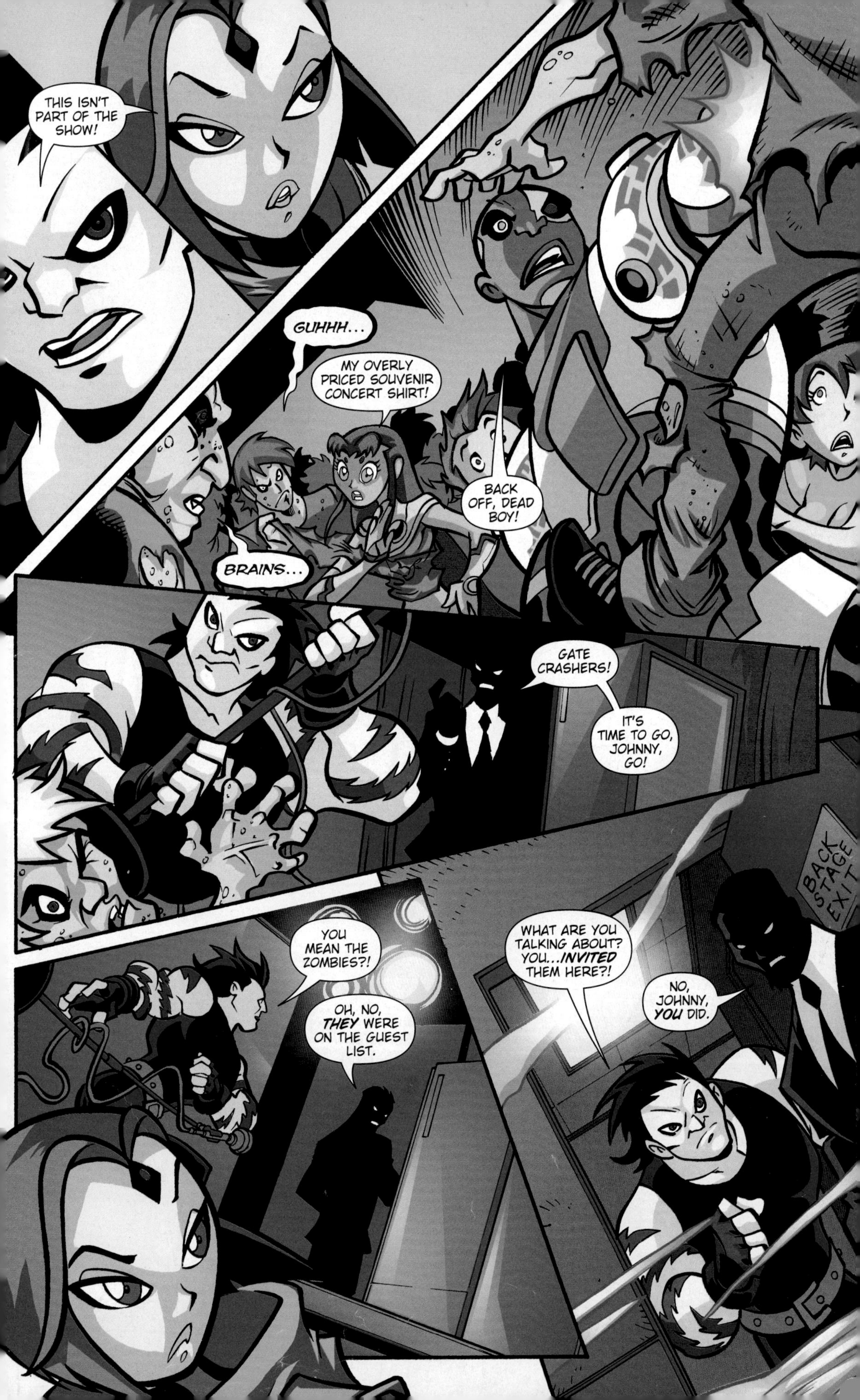
THIS ISN'T PART OF THE SHOW!
GUHHH...
MY OVERLY PRICED SOUVENIR CONCERT SHIRT!
BACK OFF, DEAD BOY!
BRAINS...
GATE CRASHERS!
IT'S TIME TO GO, JOHNNY, GO!
BACK STAGE EXIT
YOU MEAN THE ZOMBIES?!
OH, NO, THEY WERE ON THE GUEST LIST.
WHAT ARE YOU TALKING ABOUT? YOU...INVITED THEM HERE?!
NO, JOHNNY, YOU DID.

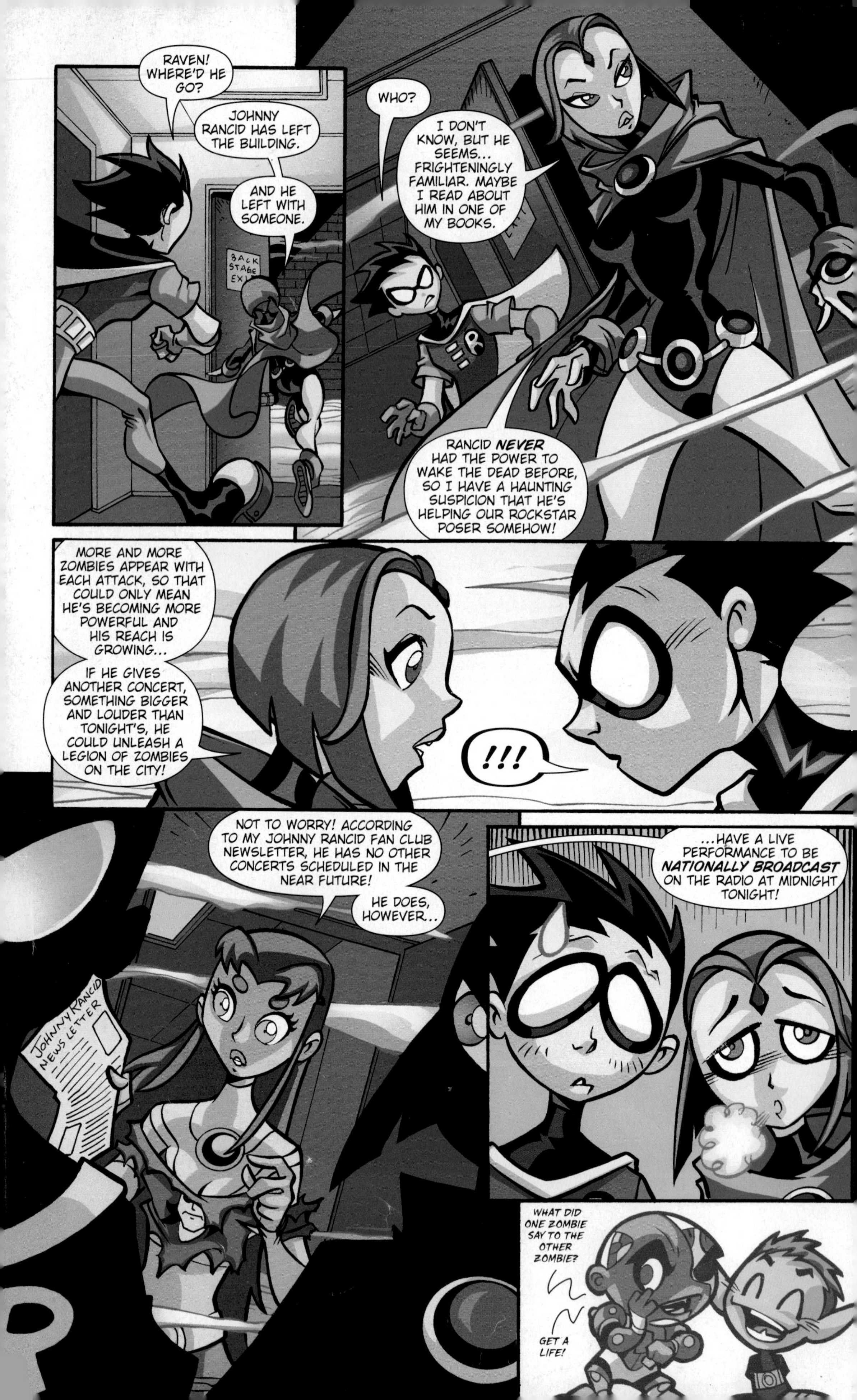
RAVEN! WHERE'D HE GO?
JOHNNY RANCID HAS LEFT THE BUILDING.
AND HE LEFT WITH SOMEONE.
BACK STAGE EXIT
WHO?
I DON'T KNOW, BUT HE SEEMS... FRIGHTENINGLY FAMILIAR. MAYBE I READ ABOUT HIM IN ONE OF MY BOOKS.
RANCID NEVER HAD THE POWER TO WAKE THE DEAD BEFORE, SO I HAVE A HAUNTING SUSPICION THAT HE'S HELPING OUR ROCKSTAR POSER SOMEHOW!
MORE AND MORE ZOMBIES APPEAR WITH EACH ATTACK, SO THAT COULD ONLY MEAN HE'S BECOMING MORE POWERFUL AND HIS REACH IS GROWING...
IF HE GIVES ANOTHER CONCERT, SOMETHING BIGGER AND LOUDER THAN TONIGHT'S, HE COULD UNLEASH A LEGION OF ZOMBIES ON THE CITY!
!!!
NOT TO WORRY! ACCORDING TO MY JOHNNY RANCID FAN CLUB NEWSLETTER, HE HAS NO OTHER CONCERTS SCHEDULED IN THE NEAR FUTURE!
HE DOES, HOWEVER...
JOHNNY RANCID NEWS LETTER
...HAVE A LIVE PERFORMANCE TO BE NATIONALLY BROADCAST ON THE RADIO AT MIDNIGHT TONIGHT!
WHAT DID ONE ZOMBIE SAY TO THE OTHER ZOMBIE?
GET A LIFE!

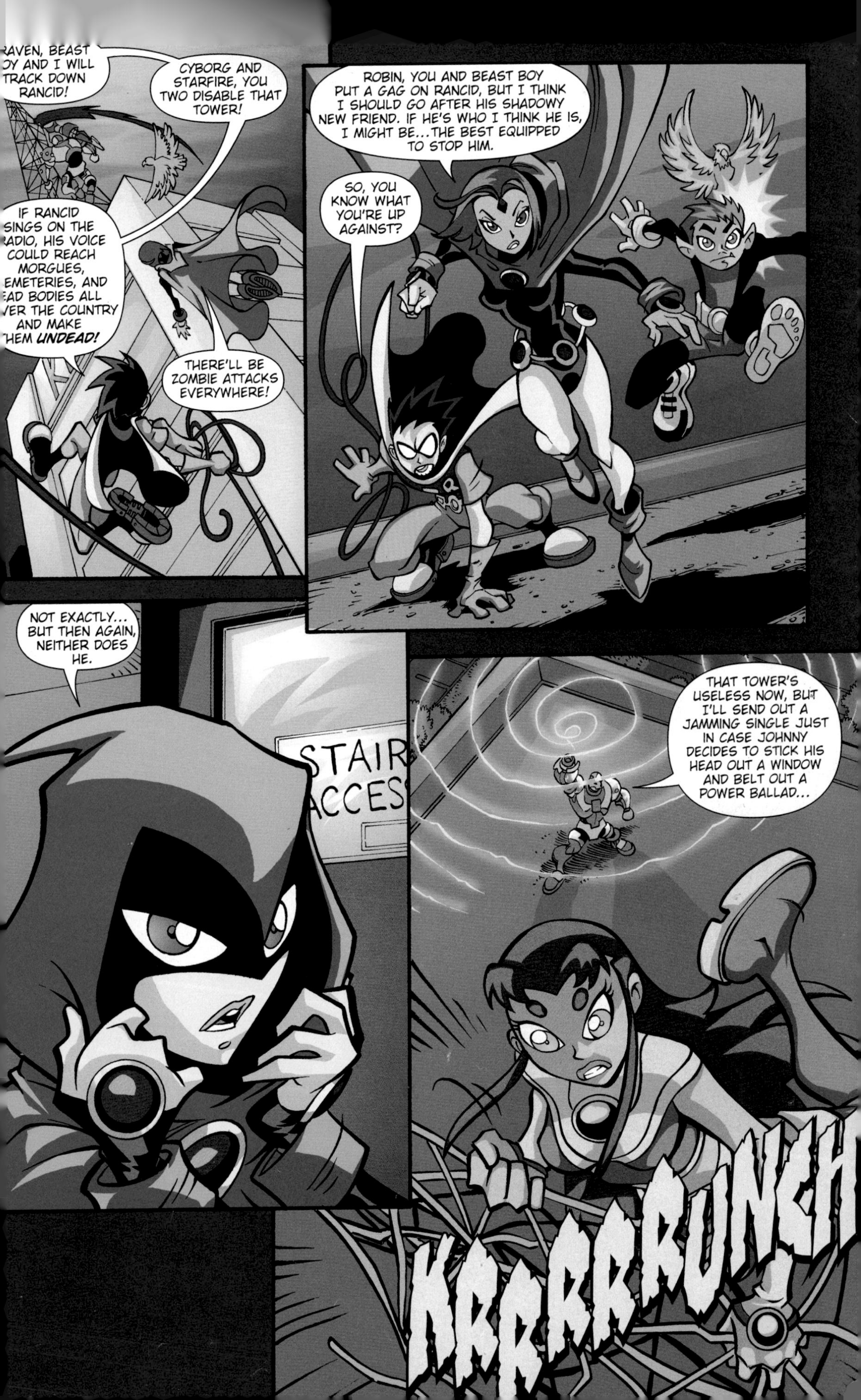

RAVEN, BEAST OY AND I WILL TRACK DOWN RANCID!
CYBORG AND STARFIRE, YOU TWO DISABLE THAT TOWER!
IF RANCID SINGS ON THE RADIO, HIS VOICE COULD REACH MORGUES, EMETERIES, AND EAD BODIES ALL VER THE COUNTRY AND MAKE THEM UNDEAD!
THERE'LL BE ZOMBIE ATTACKS EVERYWHERE!
ROBIN, YOU AND BEAST BOY PUT A GAG ON RANCID, BUT I THINK I SHOULD GO AFTER HIS SHADOWY NEW FRIEND. IF HE'S WHO I THINK HE IS, I MIGHT BE...THE BEST EQUIPPED TO STOP HIM.
SO, YOU KNOW WHAT YOU'RE UP AGAINST?
NOT EXACTLY... BUT THEN AGAIN, NEITHER DOES HE.
STAIR ACCES
THAT TOWER'S USELESS NOW, BUT I'LL SEND OUT A JAMMING SINGLE JUST IN CASE JOHNNY DECIDES TO STICK HIS HEAD OUT A WINDOW AND BELT OUT A POWER BALLAD...
KRRRRRUNCH

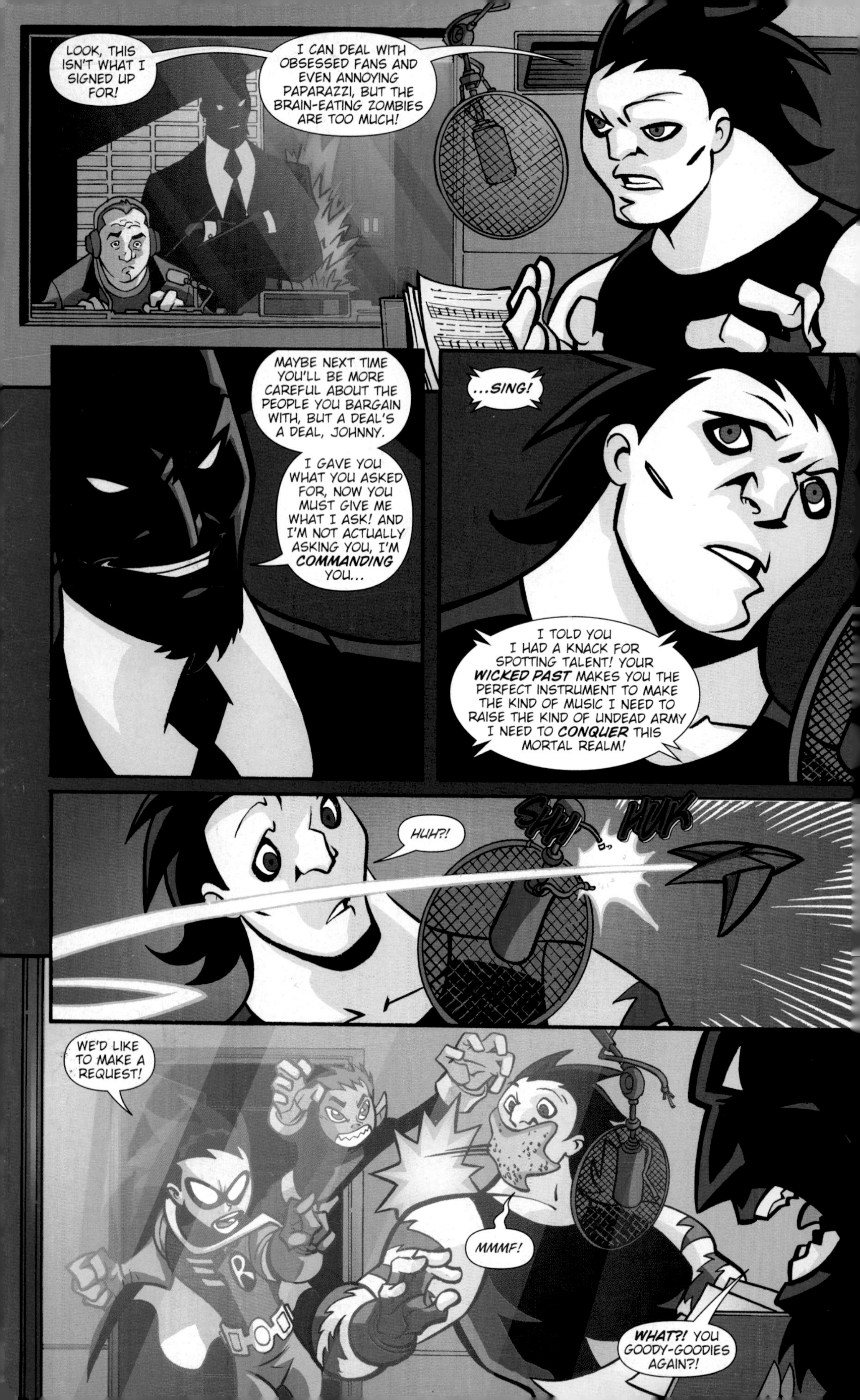
LOOK, THIS ISN'T WHAT I SIGNED UP FOR!
I CAN DEAL WITH OBSESSED FANS AND EVEN ANNOYING PAPARAZZI, BUT THE BRAIN-EATING ZOMBIES ARE TOO MUCH!
MAYBE NEXT TIME YOU'LL BE MORE CAREFUL ABOUT THE PEOPLE YOU BARGAIN WITH, BUT A DEAL'S A DEAL, JOHNNY.
I GAVE YOU WHAT YOU ASKED FOR, NOW YOU MUST GIVE ME WHAT I ASK! AND I'M NOT ACTUALLY ASKING YOU, I'M ***COMMANDING*** YOU...
...SING!
I TOLD YOU I HAD A KNACK FOR SPOTTING TALENT! YOUR ***WICKED PAST*** MAKES YOU THE PERFECT INSTRUMENT TO MAKE THE KIND OF MUSIC I NEED TO RAISE THE KIND OF UNDEAD ARMY I NEED TO ***CONQUER*** THIS MORTAL REALM!
HUH?!
WE'D LIKE TO MAKE A REQUEST!
MMMF!
WHAT?! YOU GOODY-GOODIES AGAIN?!

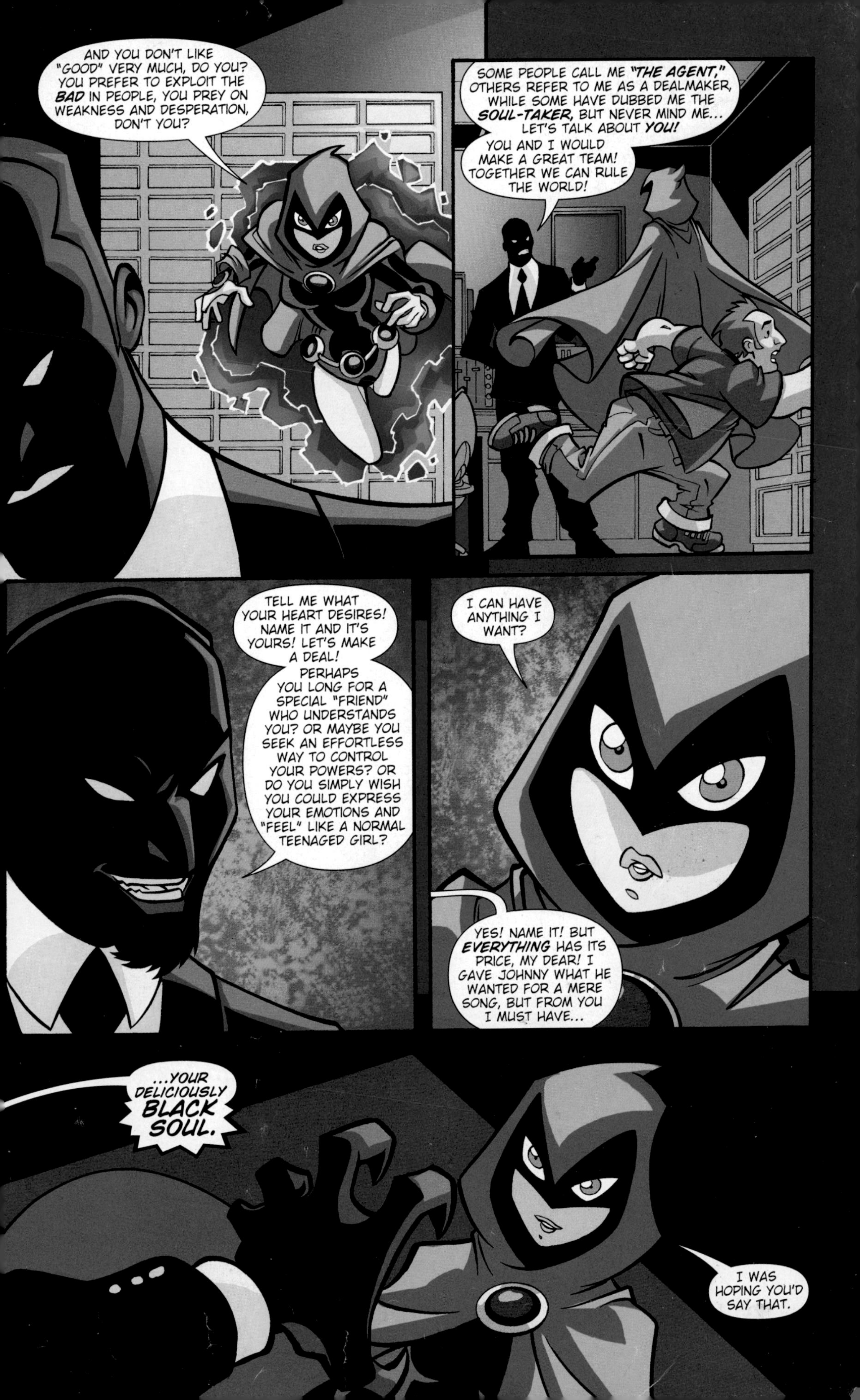
AND YOU DON'T LIKE "GOOD" VERY MUCH, DO YOU? YOU PREFER TO EXPLOIT THE BAD IN PEOPLE, YOU PREY ON WEAKNESS AND DESPERATION, DON'T YOU?
SOME PEOPLE CALL ME "THE AGENT," OTHERS REFER TO ME AS A DEALMAKER, WHILE SOME HAVE DUBBED ME THE SOUL-TAKER, BUT NEVER MIND ME... LET'S TALK ABOUT YOU!
YOU AND I WOULD MAKE A GREAT TEAM! TOGETHER WE CAN RULE THE WORLD!
TELL ME WHAT YOUR HEART DESIRES! NAME IT AND IT'S YOURS! LET'S MAKE A DEAL!
PERHAPS YOU LONG FOR A SPECIAL "FRIEND" WHO UNDERSTANDS YOU? OR MAYBE YOU SEEK AN EFFORTLESS WAY TO CONTROL YOUR POWERS? OR DO YOU SIMPLY WISH YOU COULD EXPRESS YOUR EMOTIONS AND "FEEL" LIKE A NORMAL TEENAGED GIRL?
I CAN HAVE ANYTHING I WANT?
YES! NAME IT! BUT EVERYTHING HAS ITS PRICE, MY DEAR! I GAVE JOHNNY WHAT HE WANTED FOR A MERE SONG, BUT FROM YOU I MUST HAVE...
...YOUR DELICIOUSLY BLACK SOUL.
I WAS HOPING YOU'D SAY THAT.

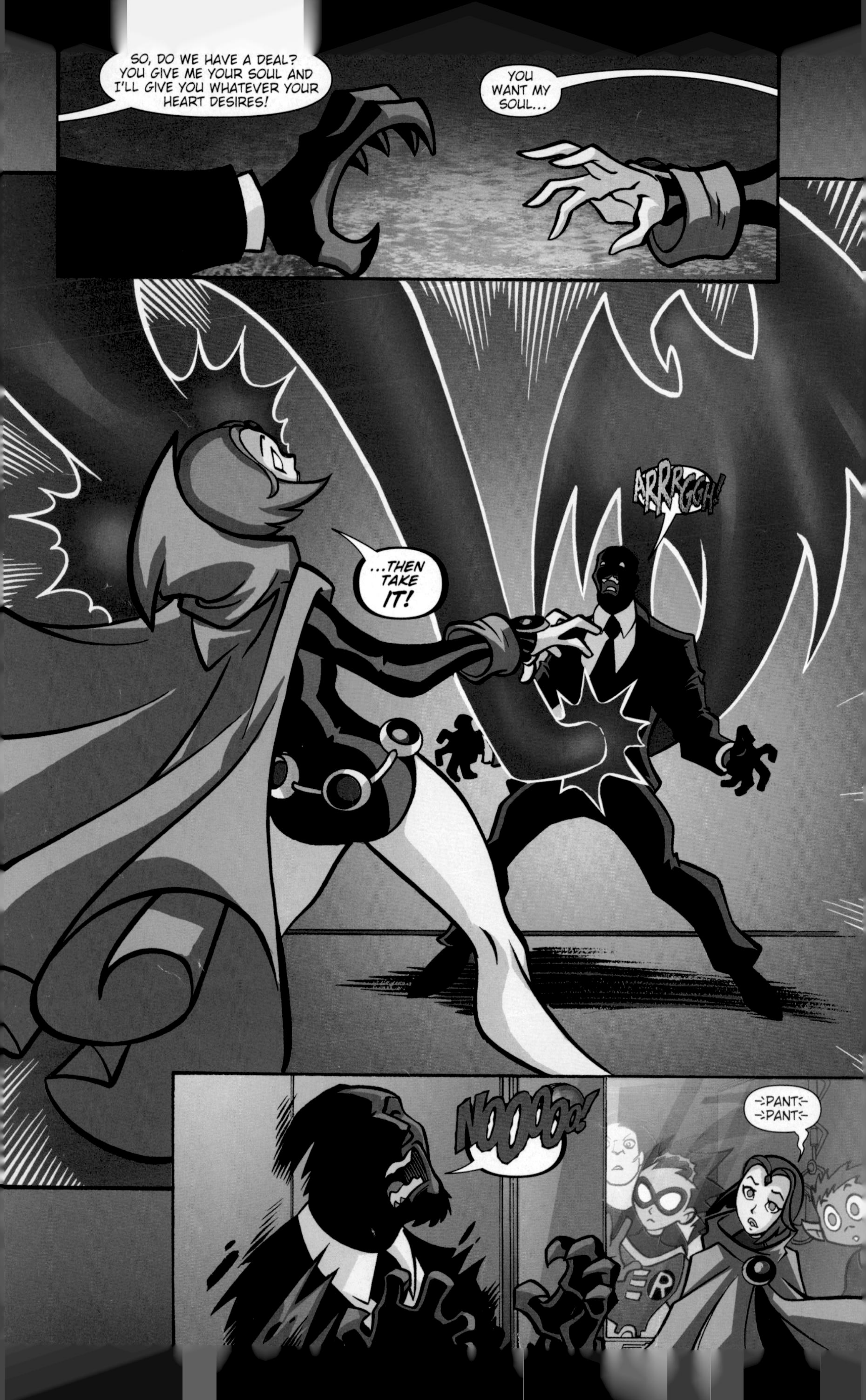
SO, DO WE HAVE A DEAL? YOU GIVE ME YOUR SOUL AND I'LL GIVE YOU WHATEVER YOUR HEART DESIRES!
YOU WANT MY SOUL...
...THEN TAKE IT!
ARRRGGH!
NOOOOO!
-PANT- -PANT-

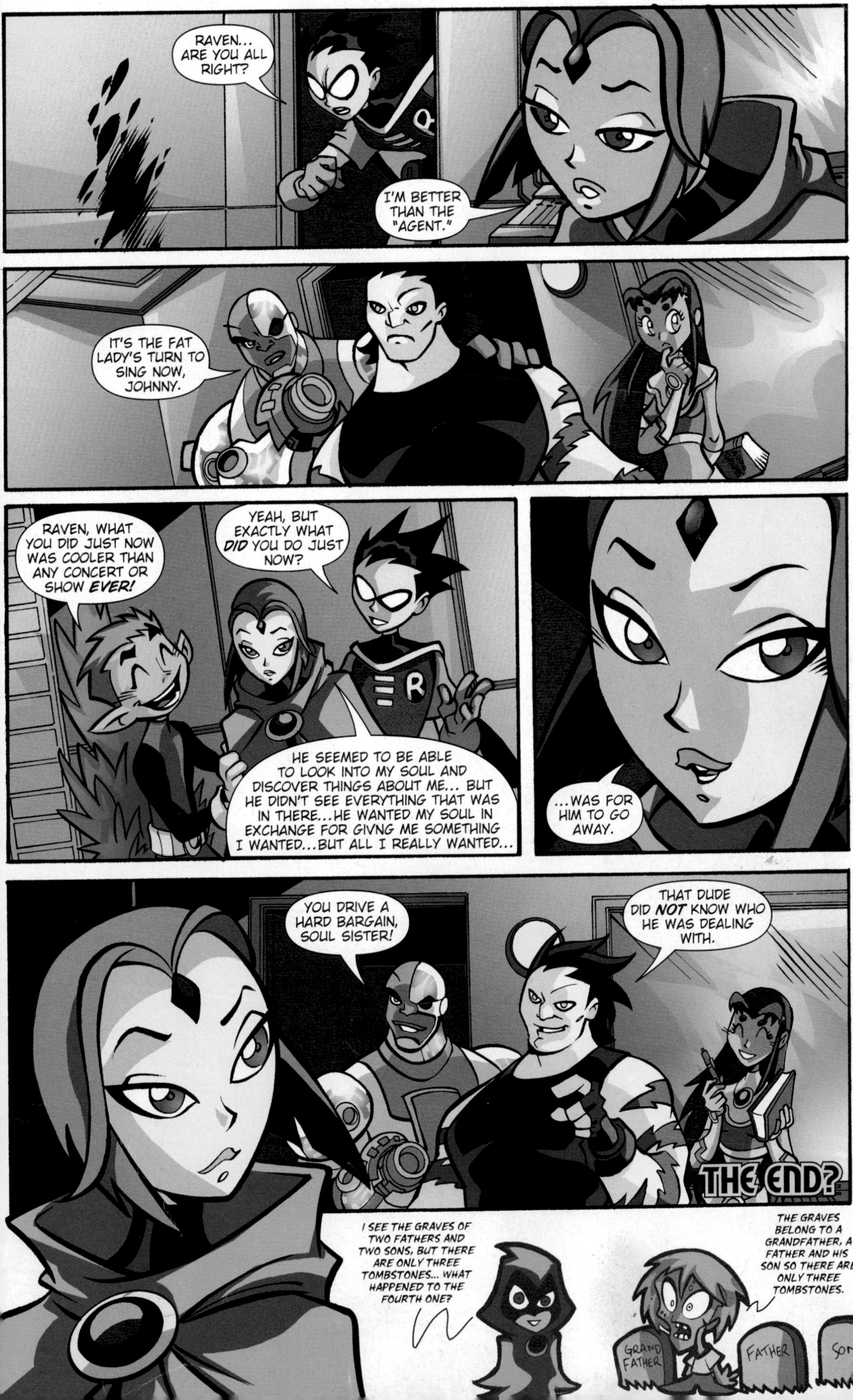
RAVEN... ARE YOU ALL RIGHT?
I'M BETTER THAN THE "AGENT."
IT'S THE FAT LADY'S TURN TO SING NOW, JOHNNY.
RAVEN, WHAT YOU DID JUST NOW WAS COOLER THAN ANY CONCERT OR SHOW EVER!
YEAH, BUT EXACTLY WHAT DID YOU DO JUST NOW?
HE SEEMED TO BE ABLE TO LOOK INTO MY SOUL AND DISCOVER THINGS ABOUT ME... BUT HE DIDN'T SEE EVERYTHING THAT WAS IN THERE...HE WANTED MY SOUL IN EXCHANGE FOR GIVNG ME SOMETHING I WANTED...BUT ALL I REALLY WANTED...
...WAS FOR HIM TO GO AWAY.
YOU DRIVE A HARD BARGAIN, SOUL SISTER!
THAT DUDE DID NOT KNOW WHO HE WAS DEALING WITH.
THE END?
I SEE THE GRAVES OF TWO FATHERS AND TWO SONS, BUT THERE ARE ONLY THREE TOMBSTONES... WHAT HAPPENED TO THE FOURTH ONE?
THE GRAVES BELONG TO A GRANDFATHER, A FATHER AND HIS SON SO THERE ARE ONLY THREE TOMBSTONES.
GRAND FATHER
FATHER
SON

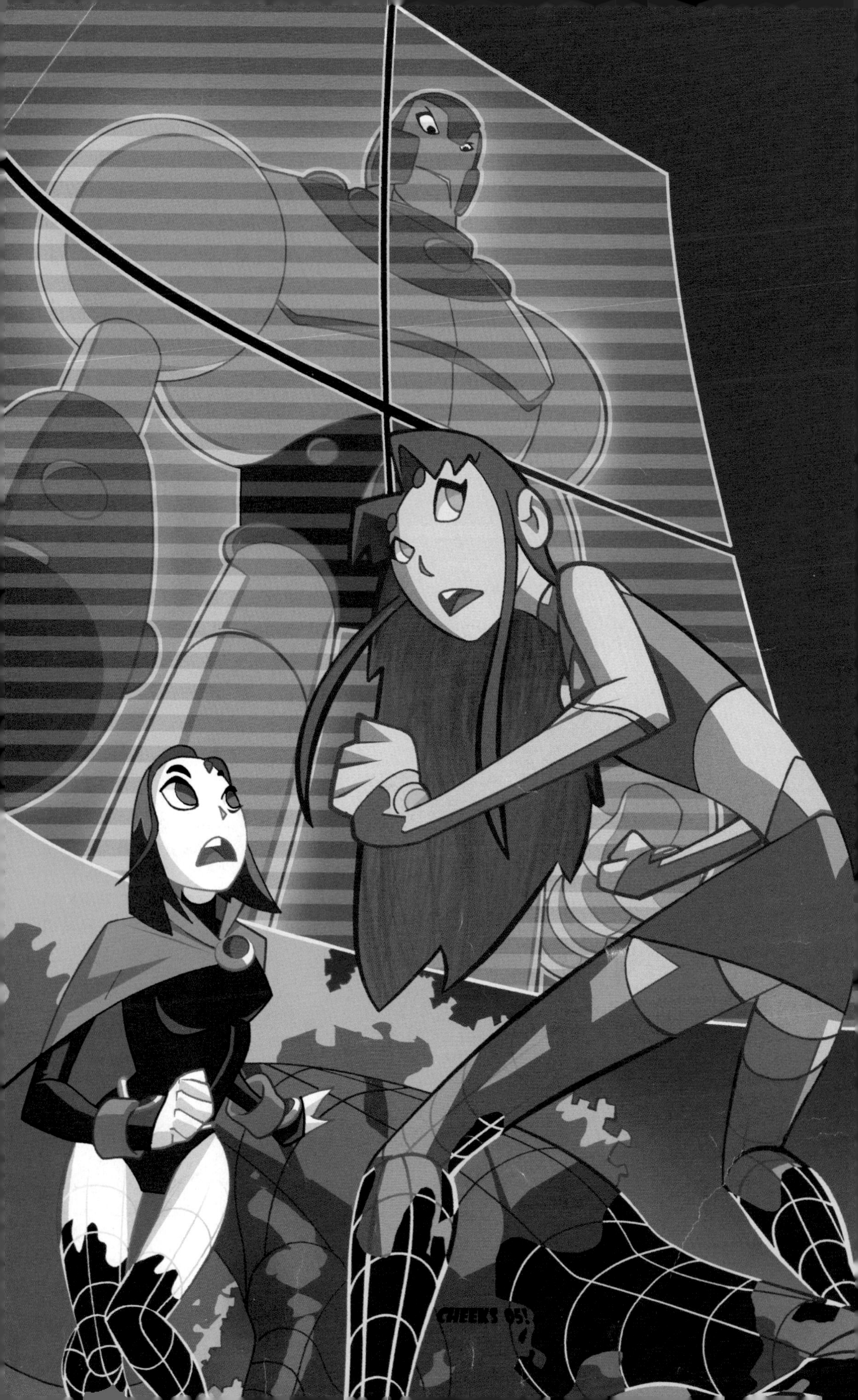
CHEEKS 05!

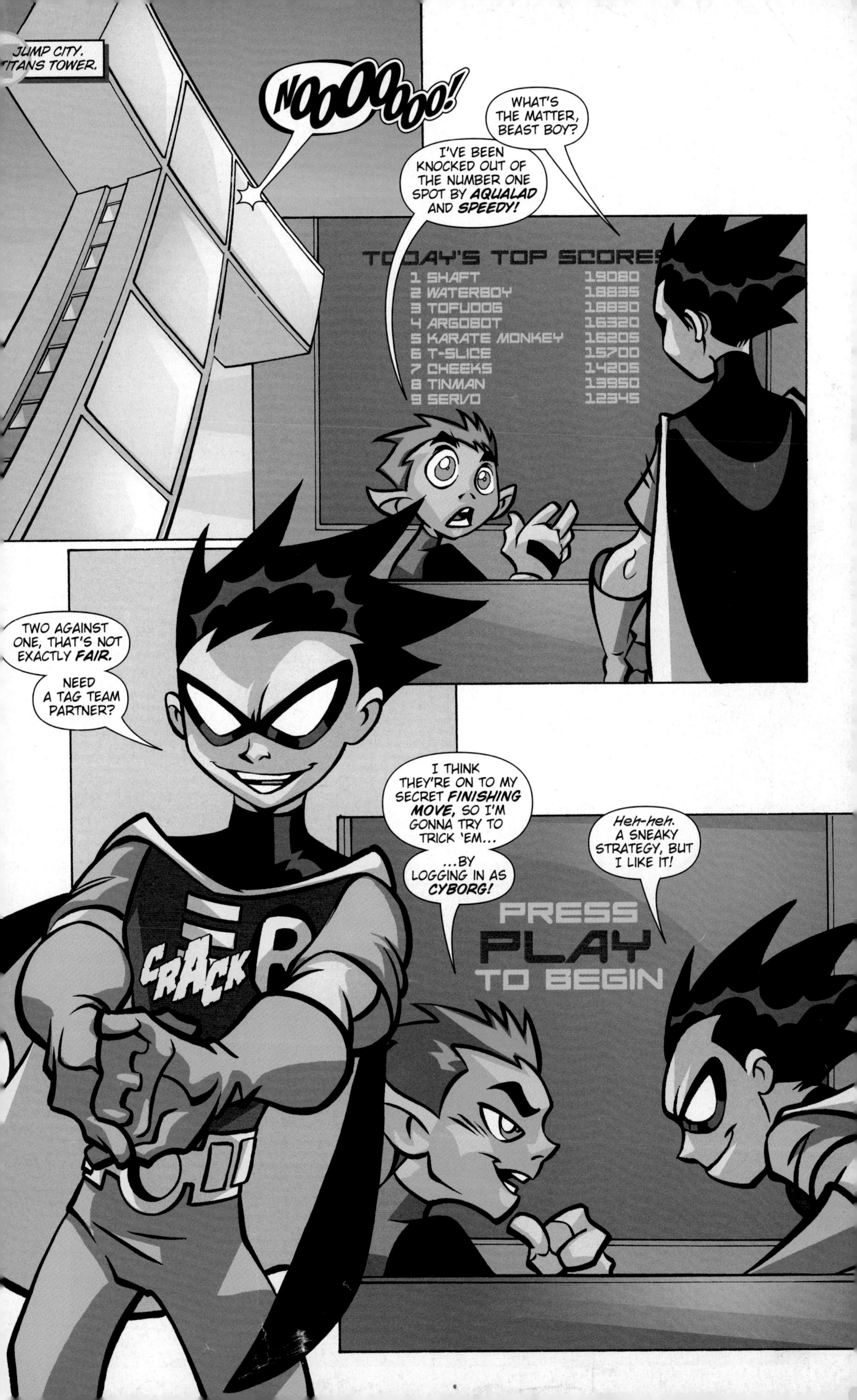
JUMP CITY. TITANS TOWER.
NOOOOOOO!
WHAT'S THE MATTER, BEAST BOY?
I'VE BEEN KNOCKED OUT OF THE NUMBER ONE SPOT BY AQUALAD AND SPEEDY!
TODAY'S TOP SCORES
1 SHAFT 19080
2 WATERBOY 18835
3 TOFUDOG 18830
4 ARGOBOT 16320
5 KARATE MONKEY 16205
6 T-SLICE 15700
7 CHEEKS 14205
8 TINMAN 13950
9 SERVO 12345
TWO AGAINST ONE, THAT'S NOT EXACTLY FAIR.
NEED A TAG TEAM PARTNER?
CRACK
I THINK THEY'RE ON TO MY SECRET FINISHING MOVE, SO I'M GONNA TRY TO TRICK 'EM...
...BY LOGGING IN AS CYBORG!
Heh-heh. A SNEAKY STRATEGY, BUT I LIKE IT!
PRESS PLAY TO BEGIN

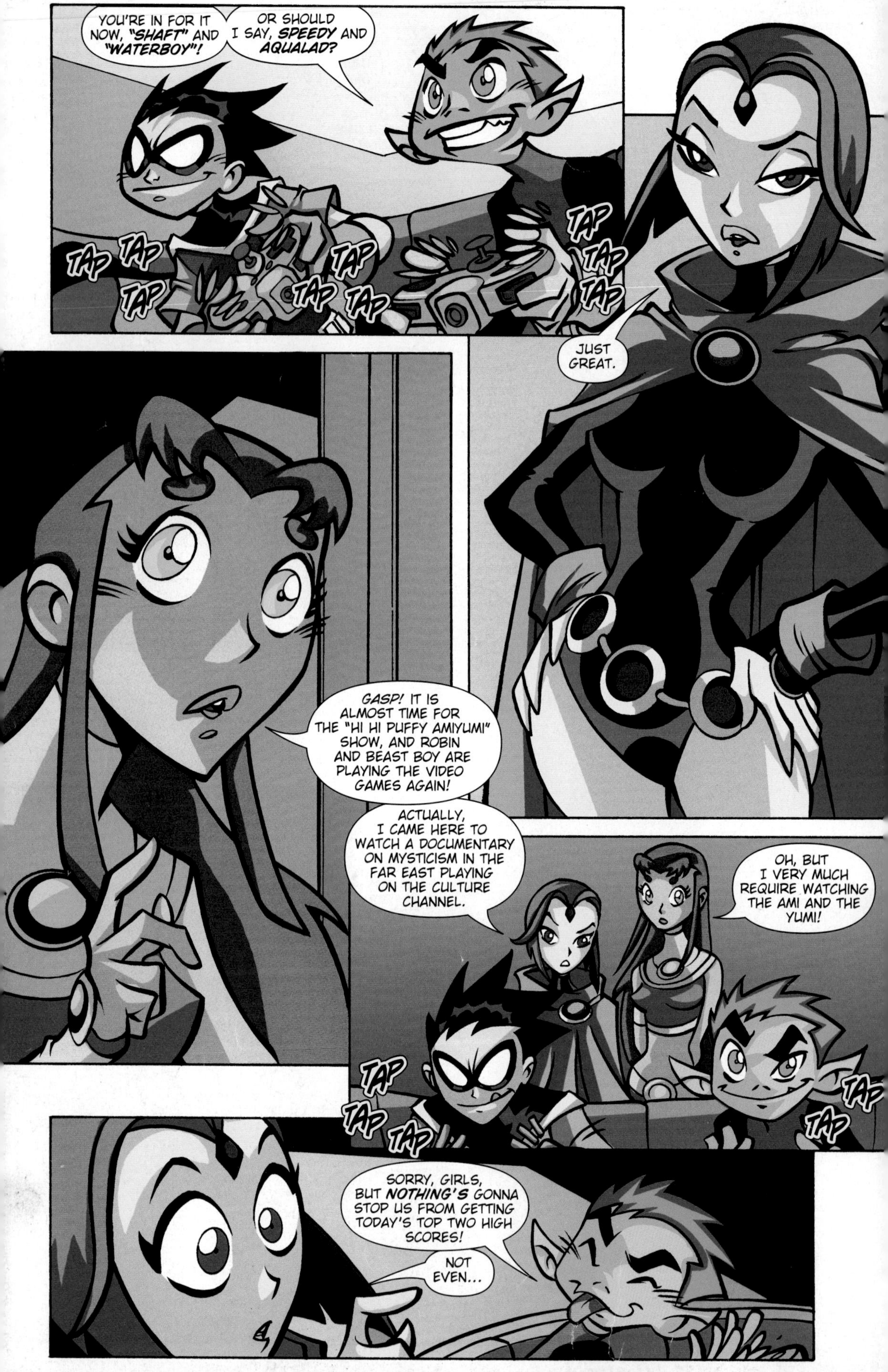
YOU'RE IN FOR IT NOW, "SHAFT" AND "WATERBOY"!
OR SHOULD I SAY, SPEEDY AND AQUALAD?
TAP TAP TAP TAP TAP TAP TAP TAP TAP
JUST GREAT.
GASP! IT IS ALMOST TIME FOR THE "HI HI PUFFY AMIYUMI" SHOW, AND ROBIN AND BEAST BOY ARE PLAYING THE VIDEO GAMES AGAIN!
ACTUALLY, I CAME HERE TO WATCH A DOCUMENTARY ON MYSTICISM IN THE FAR EAST PLAYING ON THE CULTURE CHANNEL.
OH, BUT I VERY MUCH REQUIRE WATCHING THE AMI AND THE YUMI!
TAP TAP TAP TAP TAP
SORRY, GIRLS, BUT NOTHING'S GONNA STOP US FROM GETTING TODAY'S TOP TWO HIGH SCORES!
NOT EVEN...

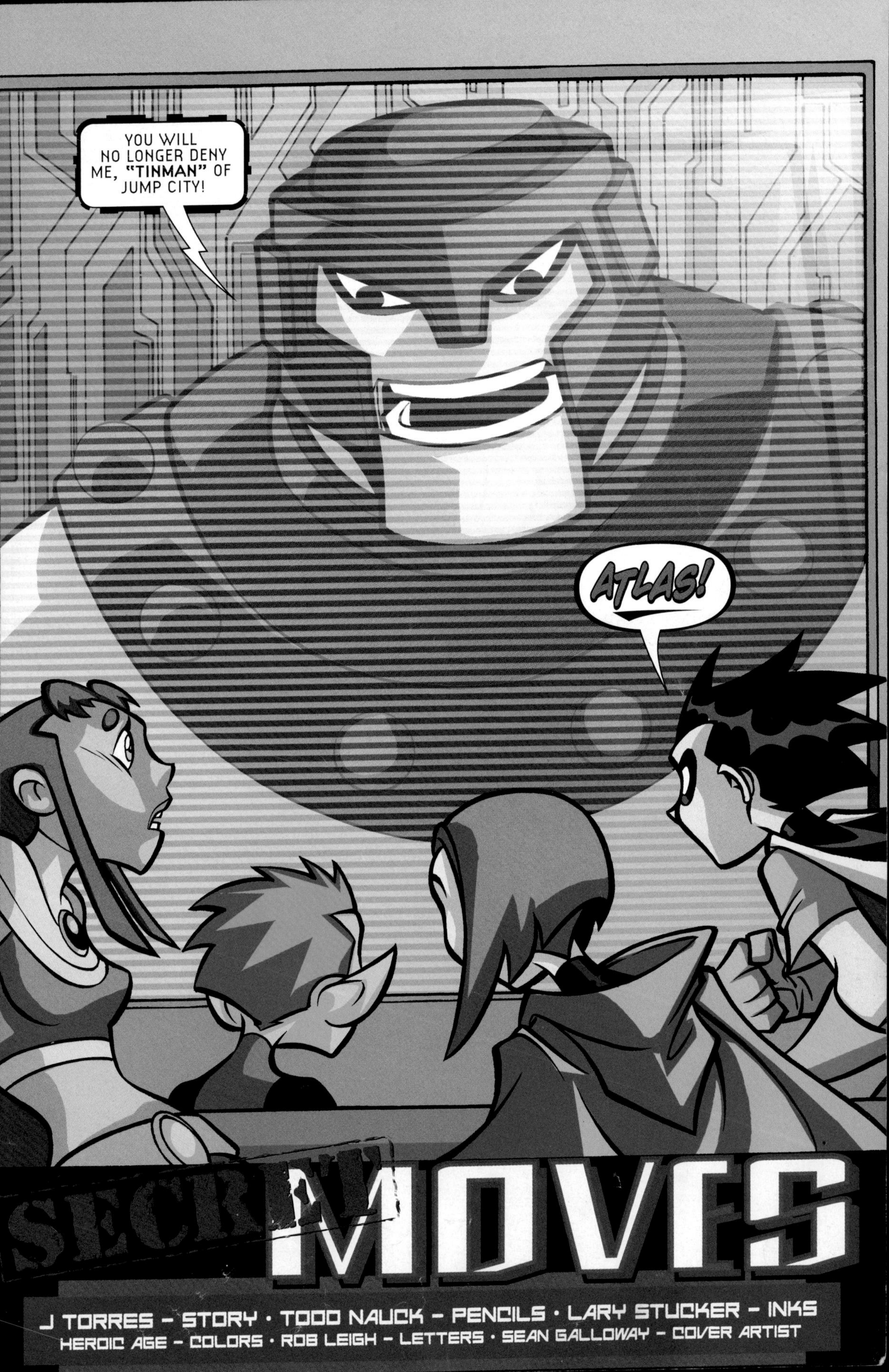
YOU WILL NO LONGER DENY ME, "TINMAN" OF JUMP CITY!
ATLAS!
MOVES
J TORRES - STORY · TODD NAUCK - PENCILS · LARY STUCKER - INKS
HEROIC AGE - COLORS · ROB LEIGH - LETTERS · SEAN GALLOWAY - COVER ARTIST

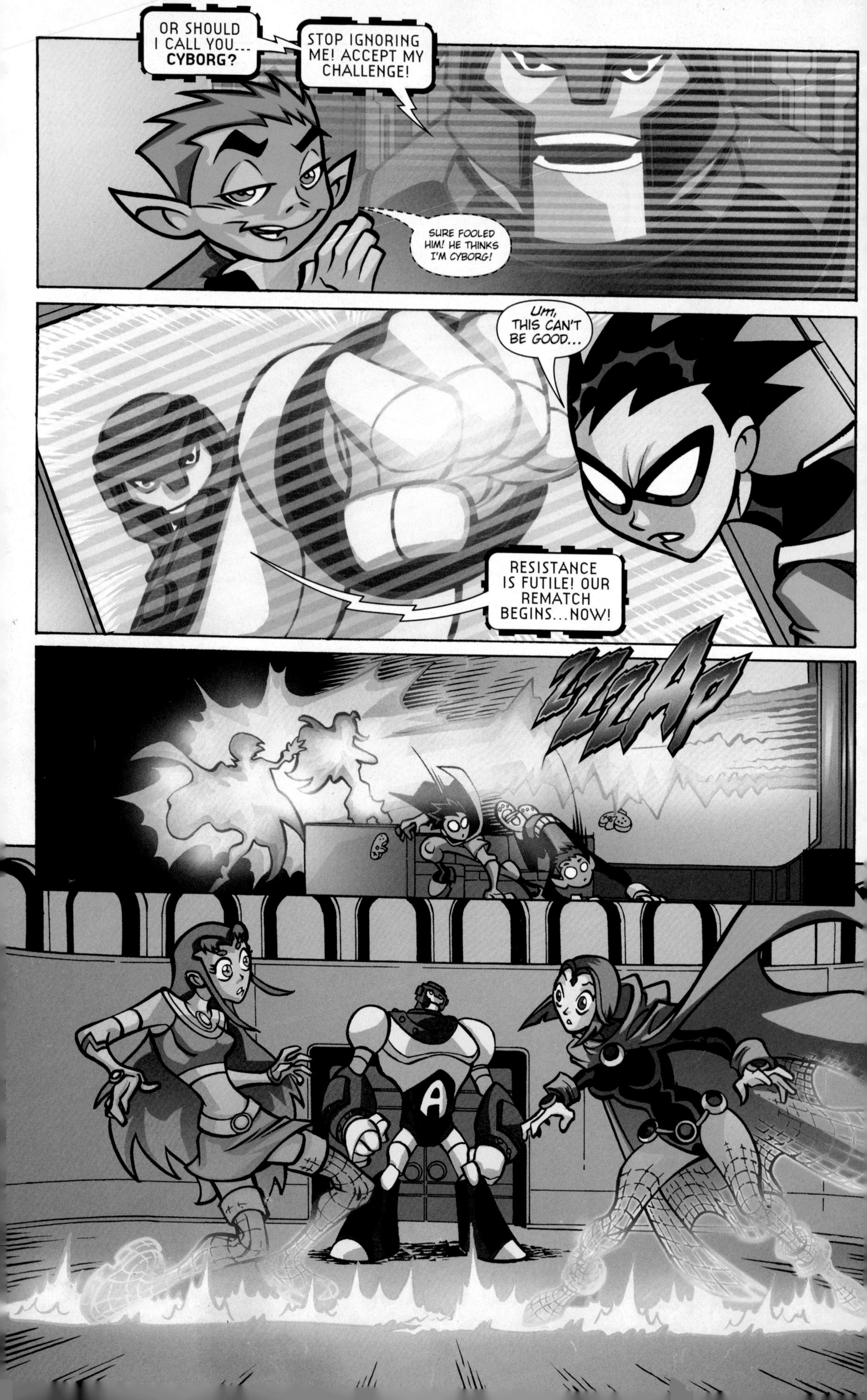
OR SHOULD I CALL YOU... CYBORG?
STOP IGNORING ME! ACCEPT MY CHALLENGE!
SURE FOOLED HIM! HE THINKS I'M CYBORG!
Um, THIS CAN'T BE GOOD...
RESISTANCE IS FUTILE! OUR REMATCH BEGINS...NOW!
ZZZAP

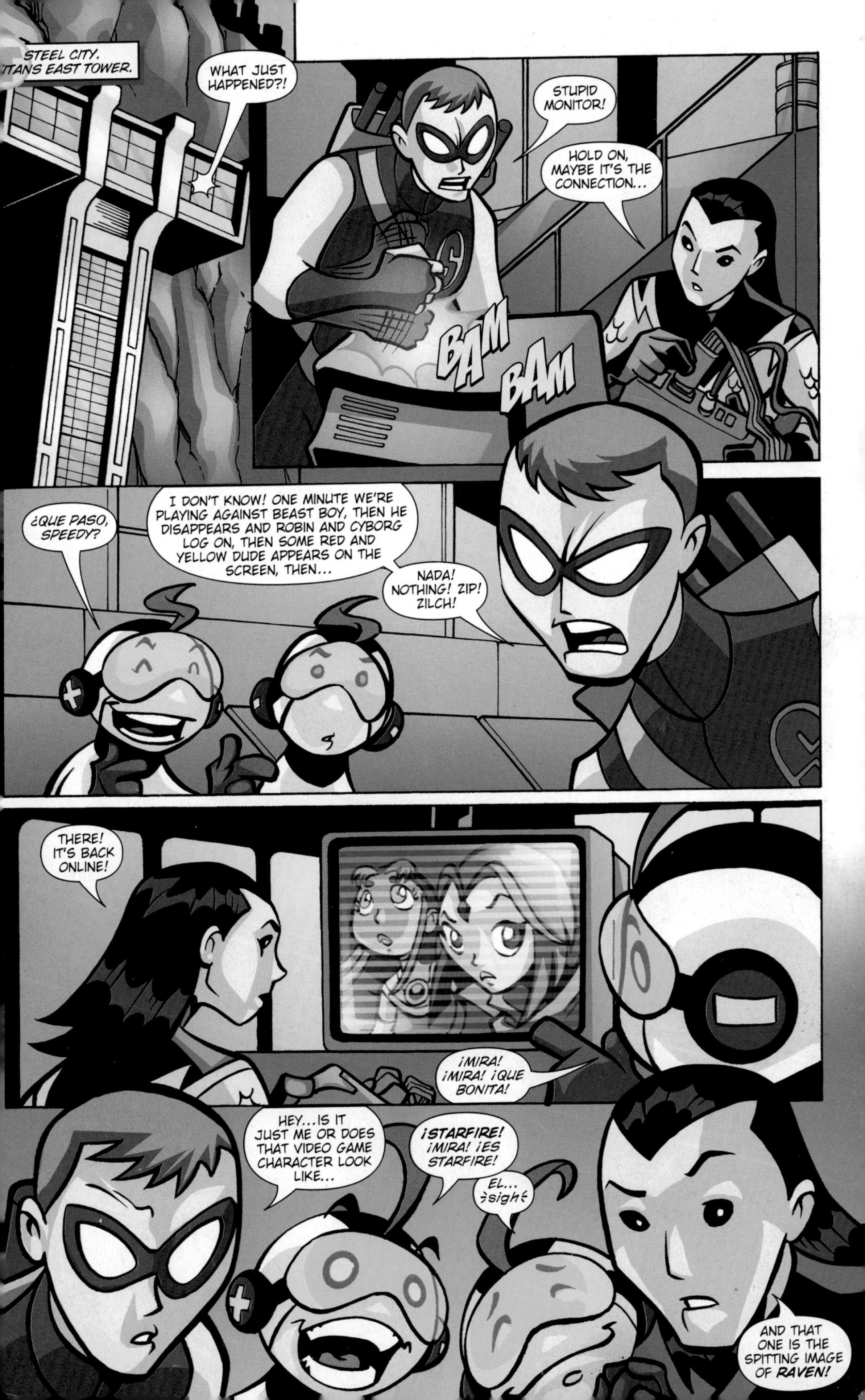

STEEL CITY. TITANS EAST TOWER.
WHAT JUST HAPPENED?!
STUPID MONITOR!
HOLD ON, MAYBE IT'S THE CONNECTION...
BAM
BAM
¿QUE PASO, SPEEDY?
I DON'T KNOW! ONE MINUTE WE'RE PLAYING AGAINST BEAST BOY, THEN HE DISAPPEARS AND ROBIN AND CYBORG LOG ON, THEN SOME RED AND YELLOW DUDE APPEARS ON THE SCREEN, THEN...
NADA! NOTHING! ZIP! ZILCH!
THERE! IT'S BACK ONLINE!
¡MIRA! ¡MIRA! ¡QUE BONITA!
HEY...IS IT JUST ME OR DOES THAT VIDEO GAME CHARACTER LOOK LIKE...
¡STARFIRE! ¡MIRA! ¡ES STARFIRE!
EL... ≻sigh≺
AND THAT ONE IS THE SPITTING IMAGE OF RAVEN!

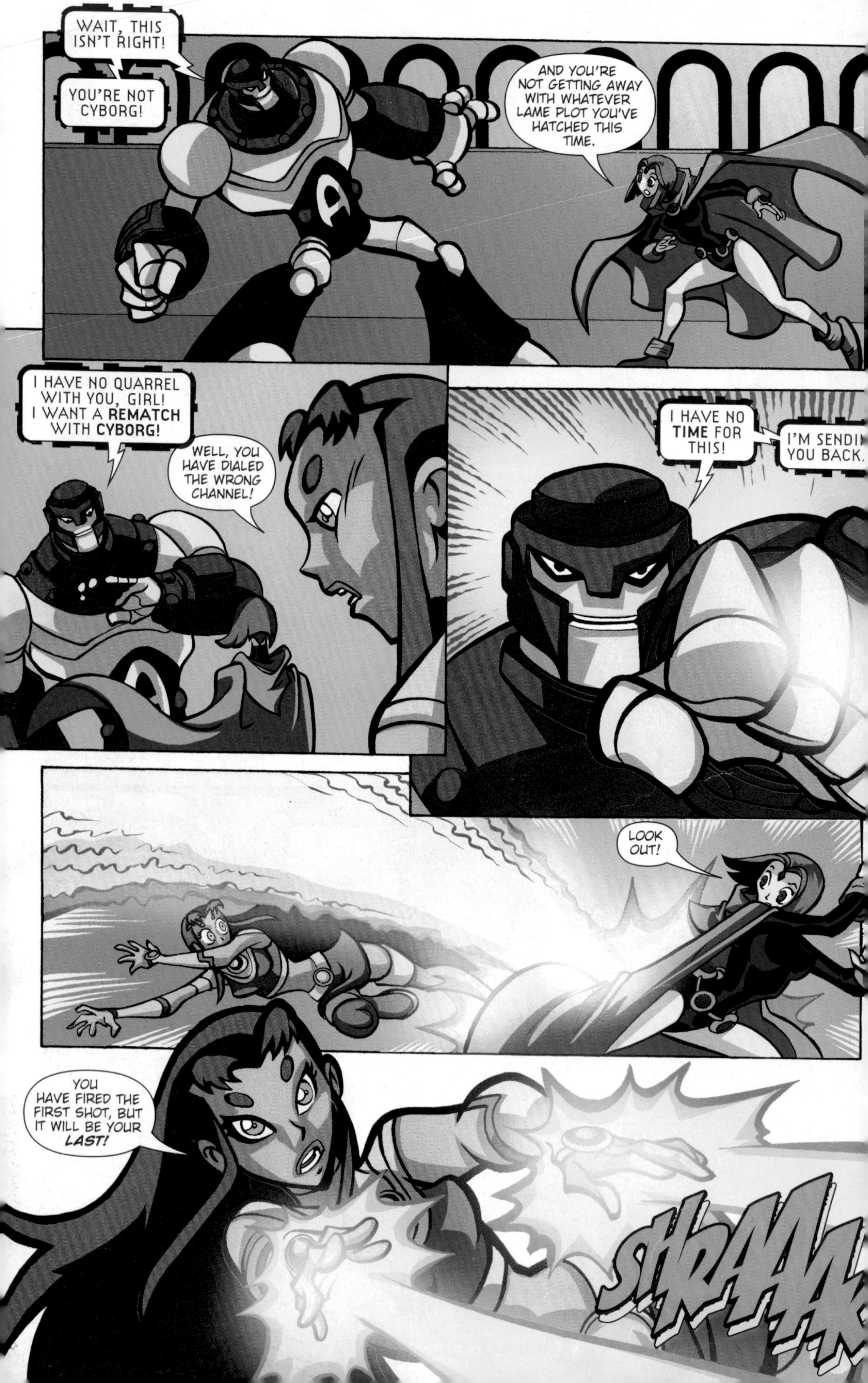
WAIT, THIS ISN'T RIGHT!
YOU'RE NOT CYBORG!
AND YOU'RE NOT GETTING AWAY WITH WHATEVER LAME PLOT YOU'VE HATCHED THIS TIME.
I HAVE NO QUARREL WITH YOU, GIRL! I WANT A **REMATCH** WITH **CYBORG!**
WELL, YOU HAVE DIALED THE WRONG CHANNEL!
I HAVE NO **TIME** FOR THIS!
LOOK OUT!
YOU HAVE FIRED THE FIRST SHOT, BUT IT WILL BE YOUR ***LAST!***

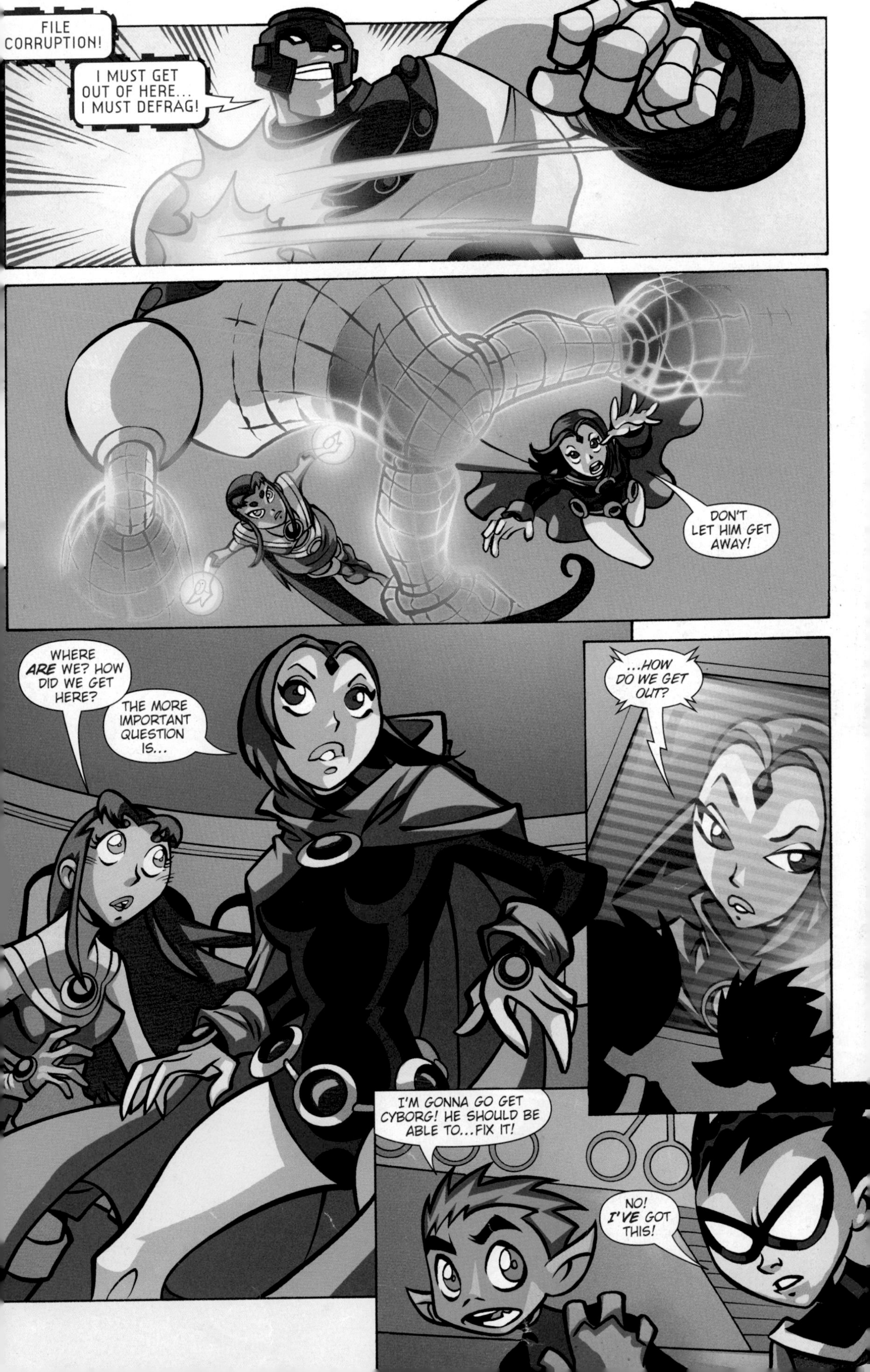
FILE CORRUPTION!
I MUST GET OUT OF HERE... I MUST DEFRAG!
DON'T LET HIM GET AWAY!
WHERE ARE WE? HOW DID WE GET HERE?
THE MORE IMPORTANT QUESTION IS...
...HOW DO WE GET OUT?
I'M GONNA GO GET CYBORG! HE SHOULD BE ABLE TO...FIX IT!
NO! I'VE GOT THIS!

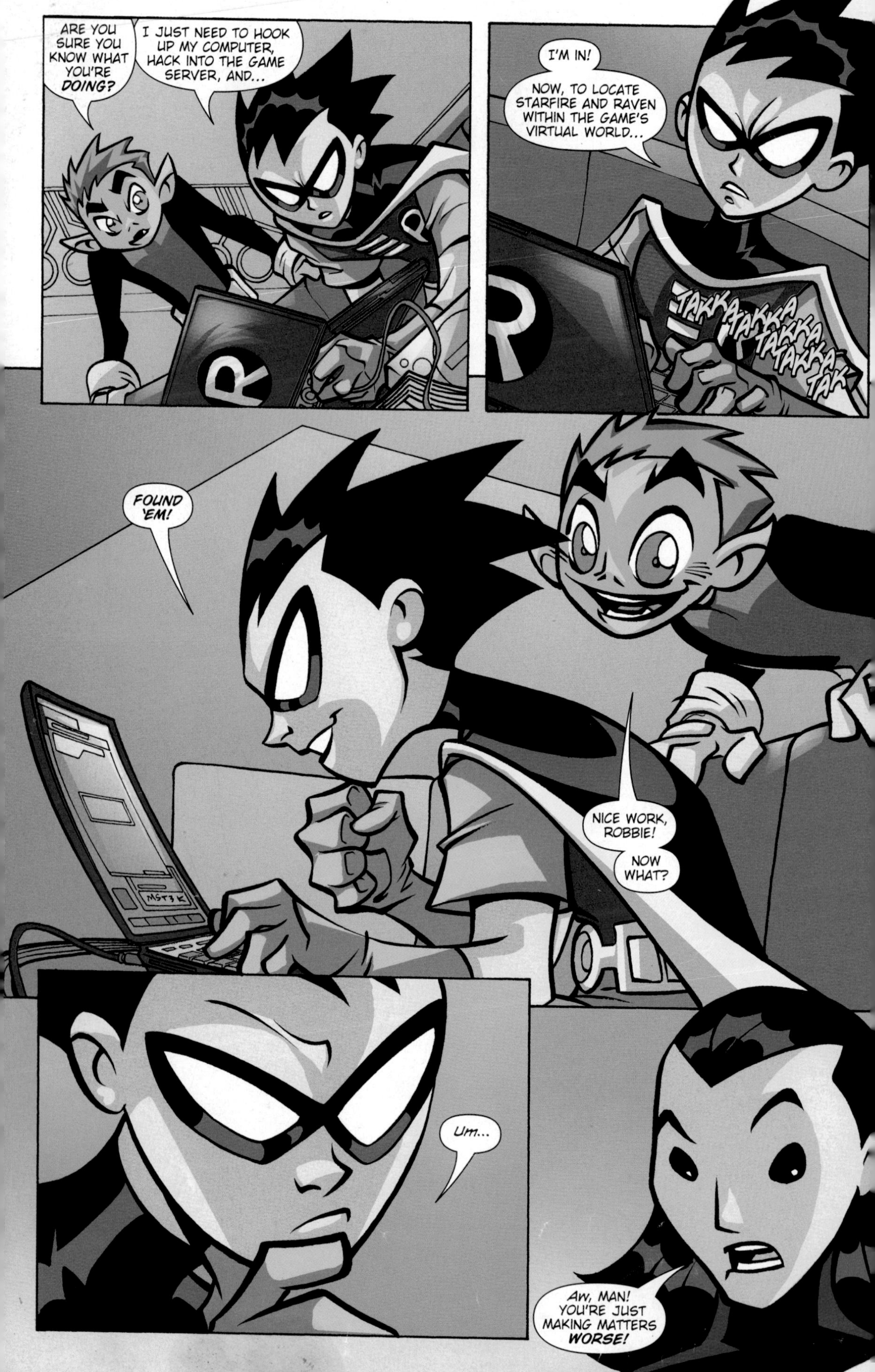
ARE YOU SURE YOU KNOW WHAT YOU'RE *DOING?*
I JUST NEED TO HOOK UP MY COMPUTER, HACK INTO THE GAME SERVER, AND...
I'M IN!
NOW, TO LOCATE STARFIRE AND RAVEN WITHIN THE GAME'S VIRTUAL WORLD...
TAKKA TAKKA TAKKA TAKKA TAKKA TAK
FOUND 'EM!
NICE WORK, ROBBIE!
NOW WHAT?
MST3K
Um...
AW, MAN! YOU'RE JUST MAKING MATTERS ***WORSE!***

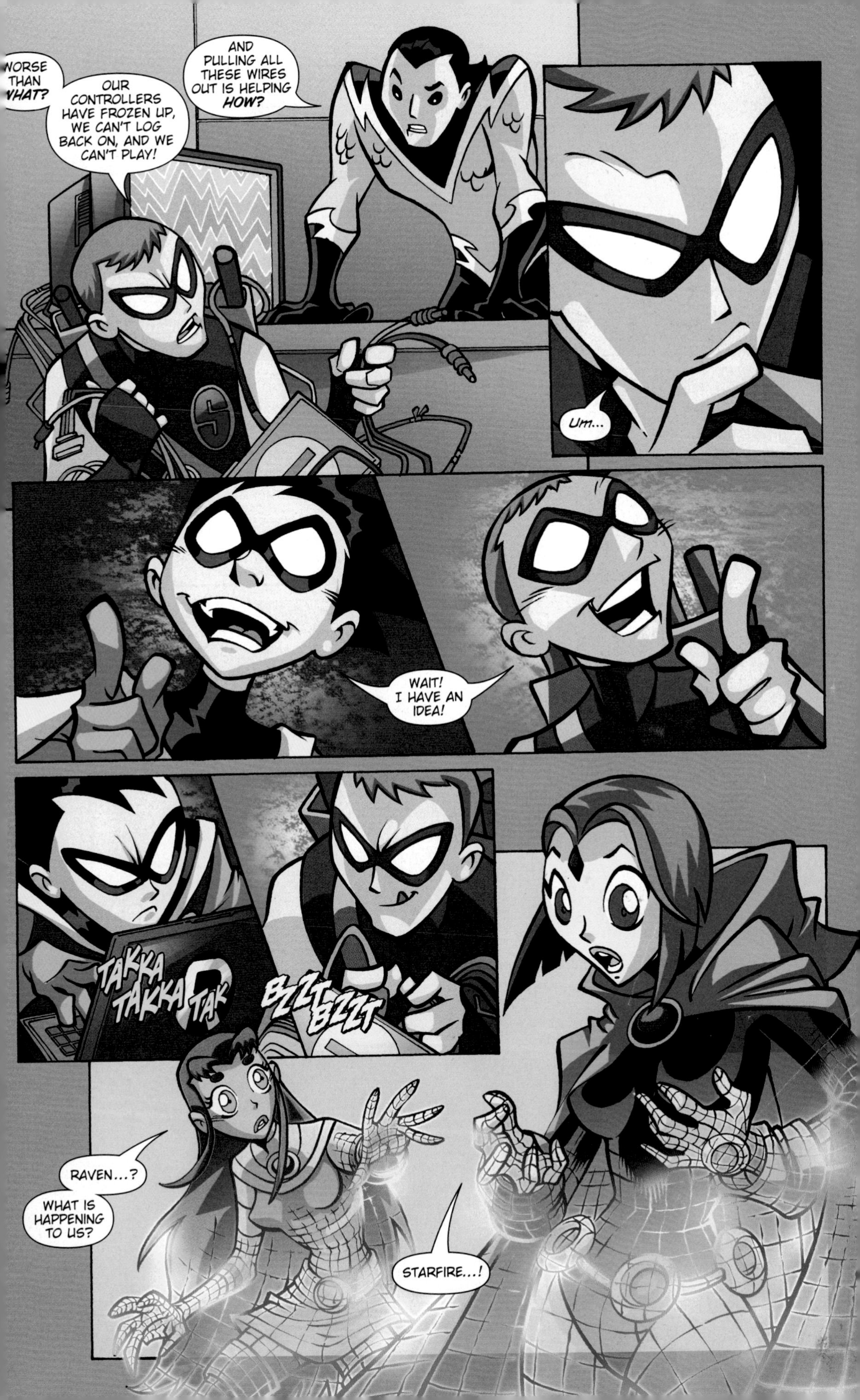
WORSE THAN WHAT?
OUR CONTROLLERS HAVE FROZEN UP, WE CAN'T LOG BACK ON, AND WE CAN'T PLAY!
AND PULLING ALL THESE WIRES OUT IS HELPING HOW?
Um...
WAIT! I HAVE AN IDEA!
TAKKA TAKKA TAK
BZZT-BZZT
RAVEN...?
WHAT IS HAPPENING TO US?
STARFIRE...!

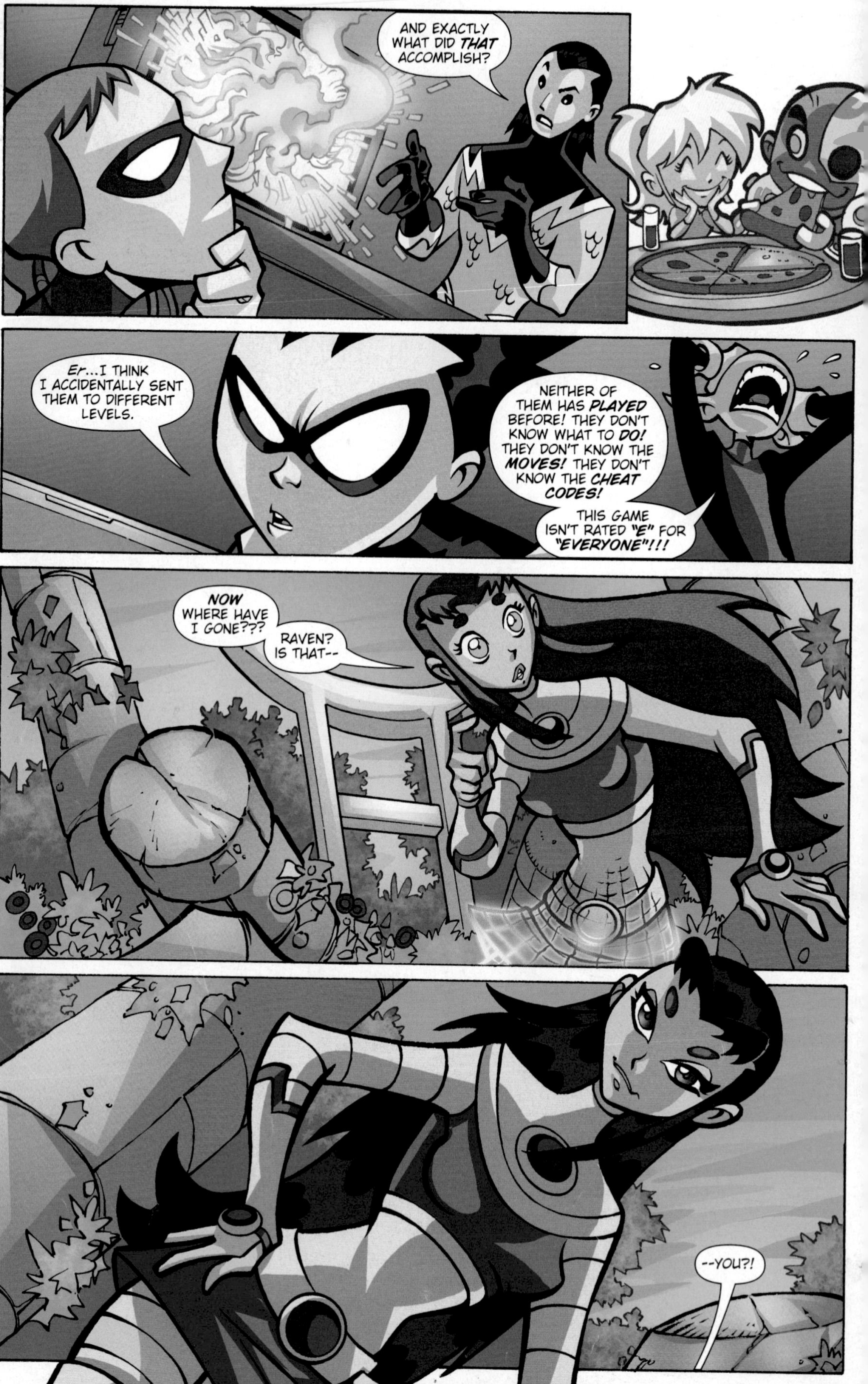
AND EXACTLY WHAT DID THAT ACCOMPLISH?
Er...I THINK I ACCIDENTALLY SENT THEM TO DIFFERENT LEVELS.
NEITHER OF THEM HAS PLAYED BEFORE! THEY DON'T KNOW WHAT TO DO! THEY DON'T KNOW THE MOVES! THEY DON'T KNOW THE CHEAT CODES!
THIS GAME ISN'T RATED "E" FOR "EVERYONE"!!!
NOW WHERE HAVE I GONE???
RAVEN? IS THAT--
--YOU?!

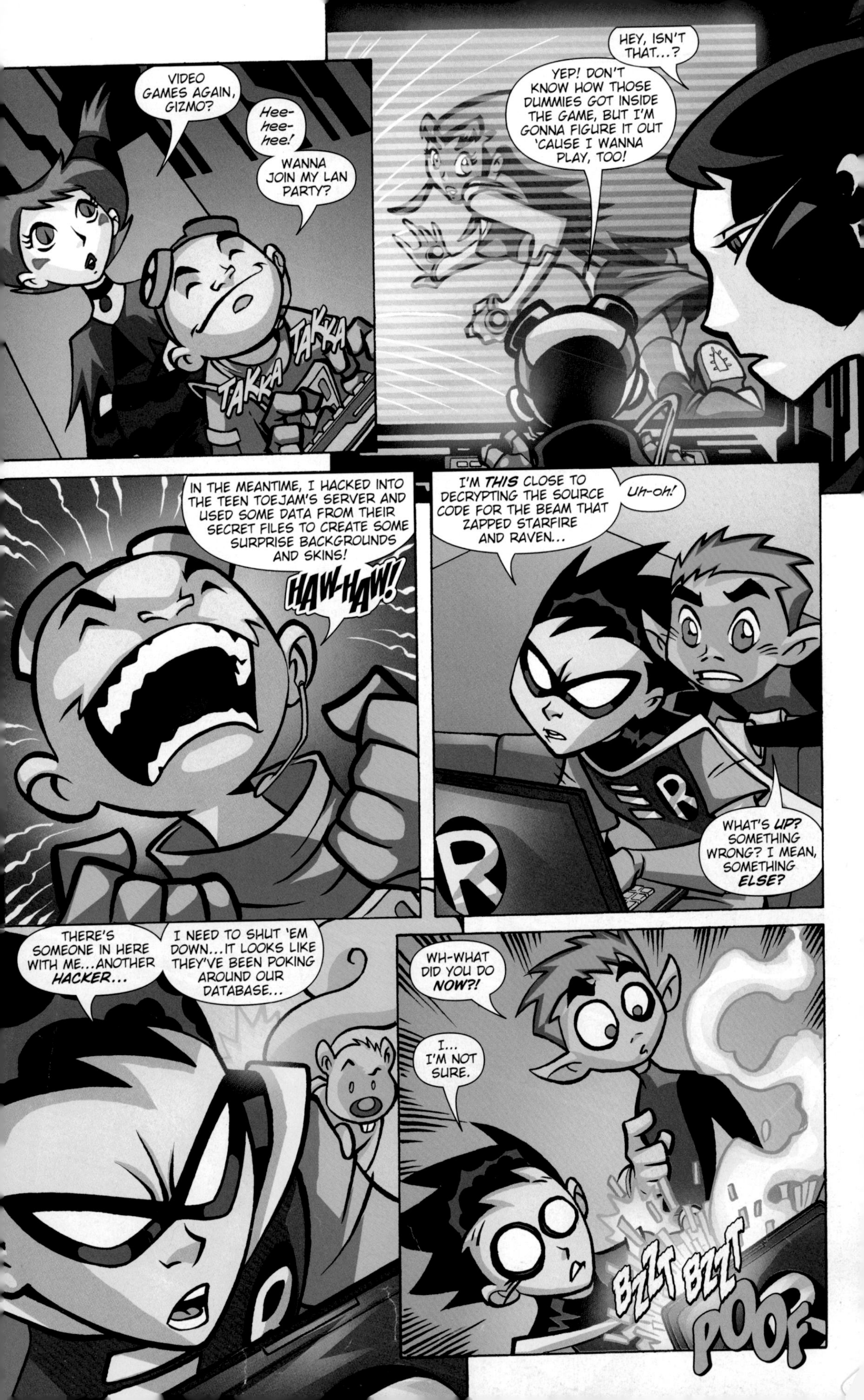

VIDEO GAMES AGAIN, GIZMO?
Hee-hee-hee!
WANNA JOIN MY LAN PARTY?
TAKKA TAKKA TAKKA
HEY, ISN'T THAT...?
YEP! DON'T KNOW HOW THOSE DUMMIES GOT INSIDE THE GAME, BUT I'M GONNA FIGURE IT OUT 'CAUSE I WANNA PLAY, TOO!
IN THE MEANTIME, I HACKED INTO THE TEEN TOEJAM'S SERVER AND USED SOME DATA FROM THEIR SECRET FILES TO CREATE SOME SURPRISE BACKGROUNDS AND SKINS!
HAW-HAW!
I'M THIS CLOSE TO DECRYPTING THE SOURCE CODE FOR THE BEAM THAT ZAPPED STARFIRE AND RAVEN...
Uh-oh!
WHAT'S UP? SOMETHING WRONG? I MEAN, SOMETHING ELSE?
THERE'S SOMEONE IN HERE WITH ME...ANOTHER HACKER...
I NEED TO SHUT 'EM DOWN...IT LOOKS LIKE THEY'VE BEEN POKING AROUND OUR DATABASE...
WH-WHAT DID YOU DO NOW?!
I... I'M NOT SURE.
BZZT BZZT
POOF

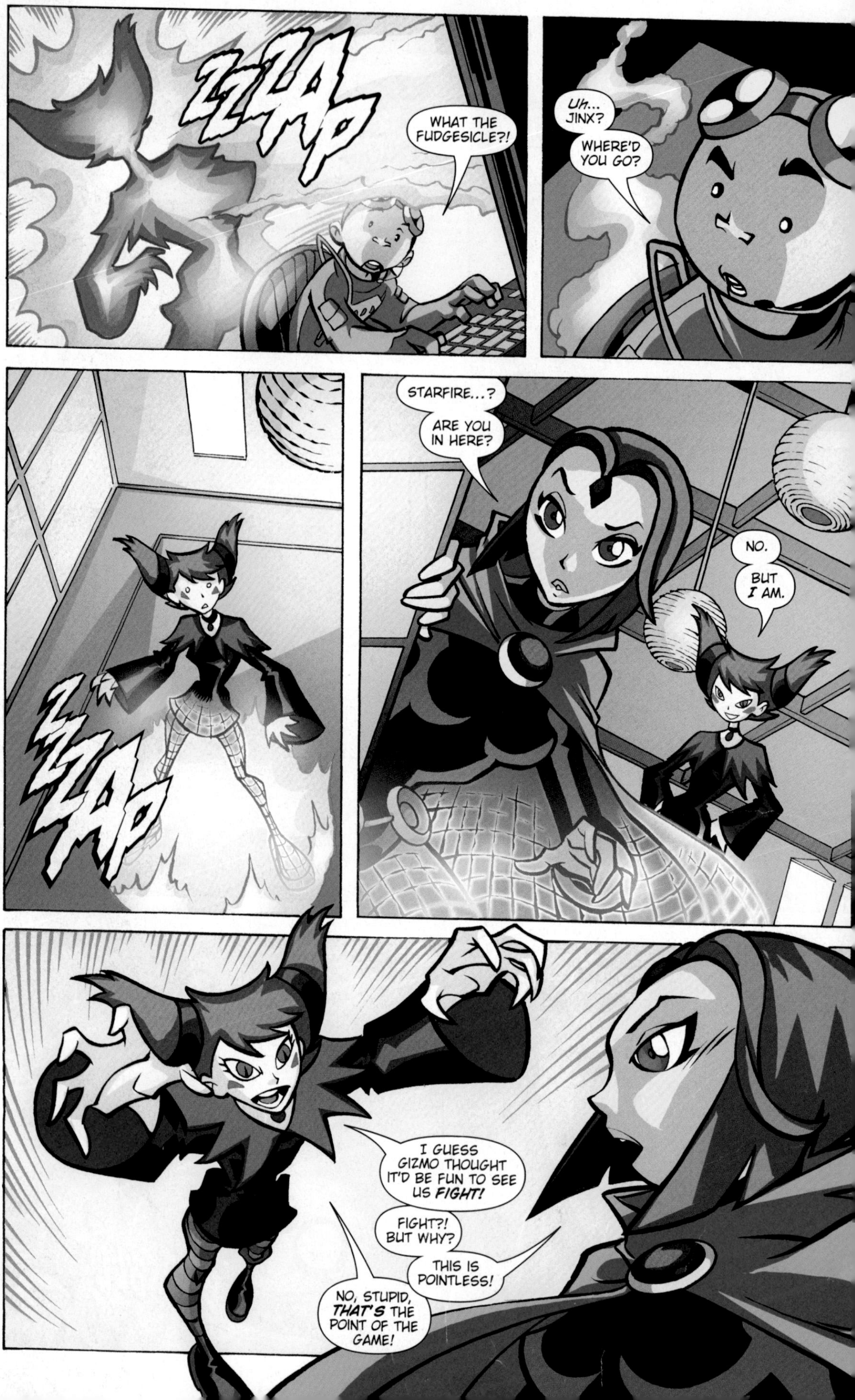
ZZZAP
WHAT THE FUDGESICLE?!
Uh... JINX?
WHERE'D YOU GO?
ZZZAP
STARFIRE...?
ARE YOU IN HERE?
NO.
BUT I AM.
I GUESS GIZMO THOUGHT IT'D BE FUN TO SEE US FIGHT!
FIGHT?! BUT WHY?
THIS IS POINTLESS!
NO, STUPID, THAT'S THE POINT OF THE GAME!

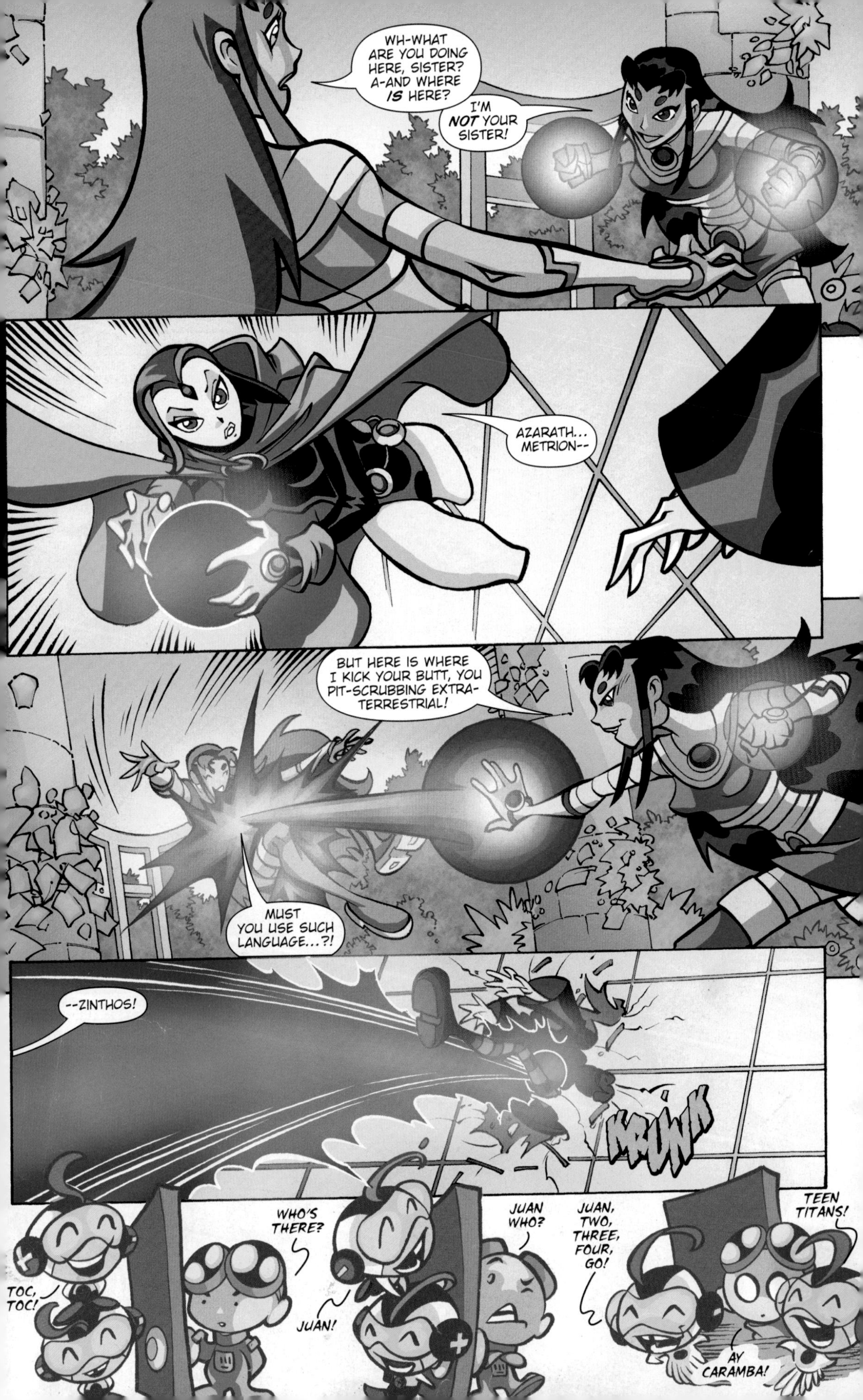
WH-WHAT ARE YOU DOING HERE, SISTER? A-AND WHERE *IS* HERE?
I'M *NOT* YOUR SISTER!
AZARATH... METRION--
BUT HERE IS WHERE I KICK YOUR BUTT, YOU PIT-SCRUBBING EXTRA-TERRESTRIAL!
MUST YOU USE SUCH LANGUAGE...?!
--ZINTHOS!
KRUNK
TOC, TOC!
WHO'S THERE?
JUAN!
JUAN WHO?
JUAN, TWO, THREE, FOUR, GO!
TEEN TITANS!
AY CARAMBA!

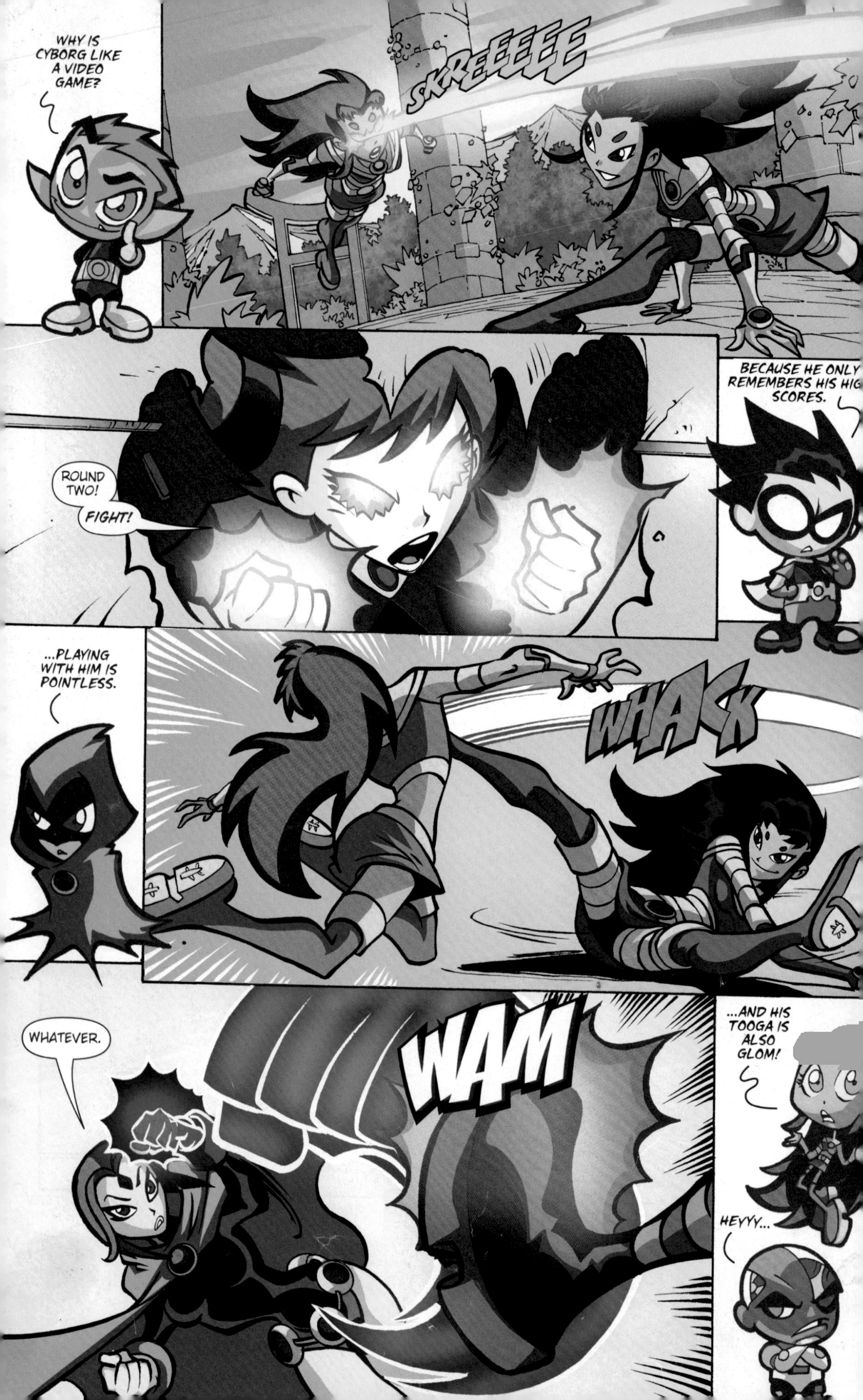
WHY IS CYBORG LIKE A VIDEO GAME?
SKREEEEE
BECAUSE HE ONLY REMEMBERS HIS HIGH SCORES.
ROUND TWO!
FIGHT!
...PLAYING WITH HIM IS POINTLESS.
WHACK
WHATEVER.
WAM
...AND HIS TOOGA IS ALSO GLOM!
HEYYY...

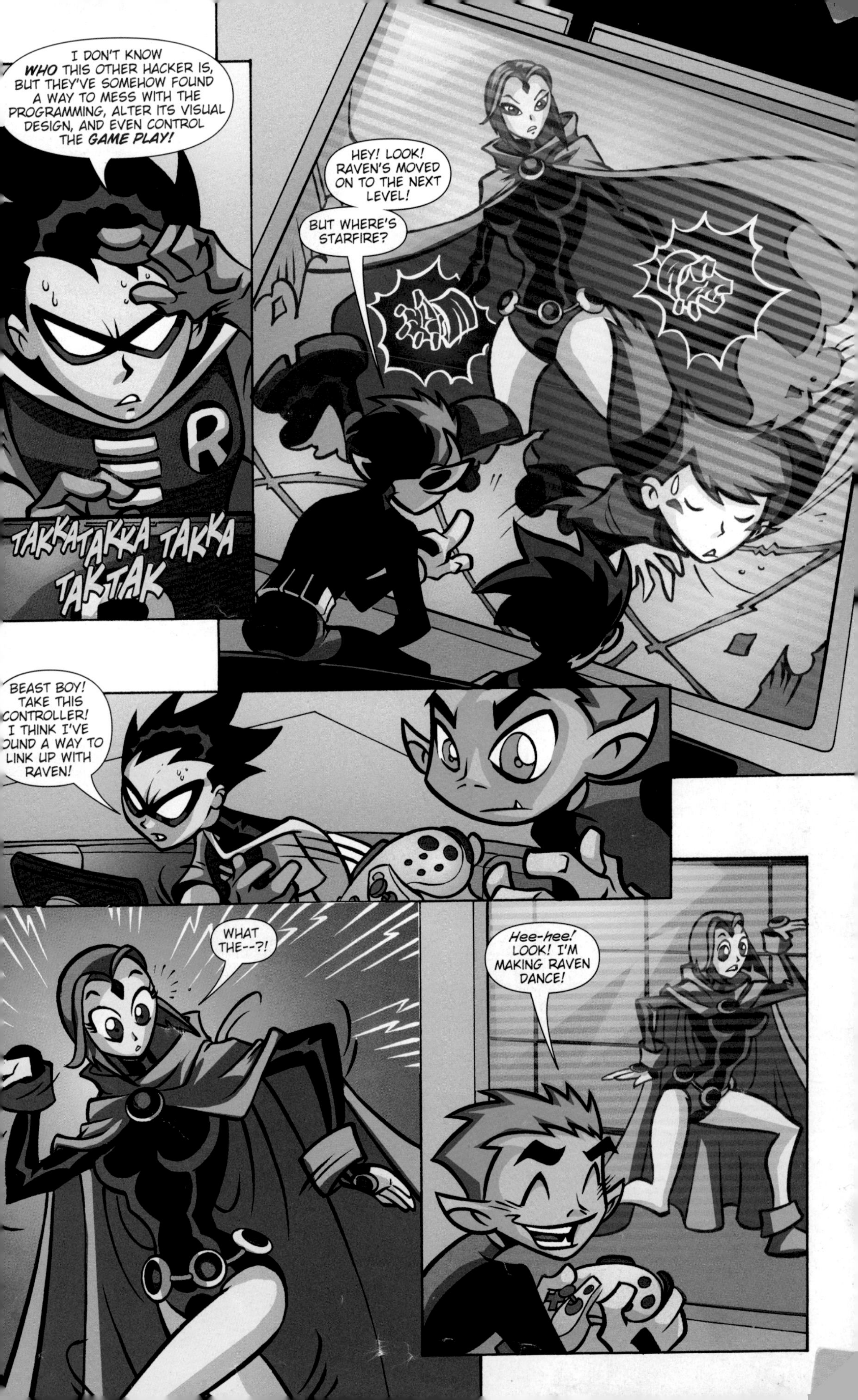

I DON'T KNOW WHO THIS OTHER HACKER IS, BUT THEY'VE SOMEHOW FOUND A WAY TO MESS WITH THE PROGRAMMING, ALTER ITS VISUAL DESIGN, AND EVEN CONTROL THE GAME PLAY!
TAKKATAKKA TAKKA TAKTAK
HEY! LOOK! RAVEN'S MOVED ON TO THE NEXT LEVEL!
BUT WHERE'S STARFIRE?
BEAST BOY! TAKE THIS CONTROLLER! I THINK I'VE FOUND A WAY TO LINK UP WITH RAVEN!
WHAT THE--?!
Hee-hee! LOOK! I'M MAKING RAVEN DANCE!

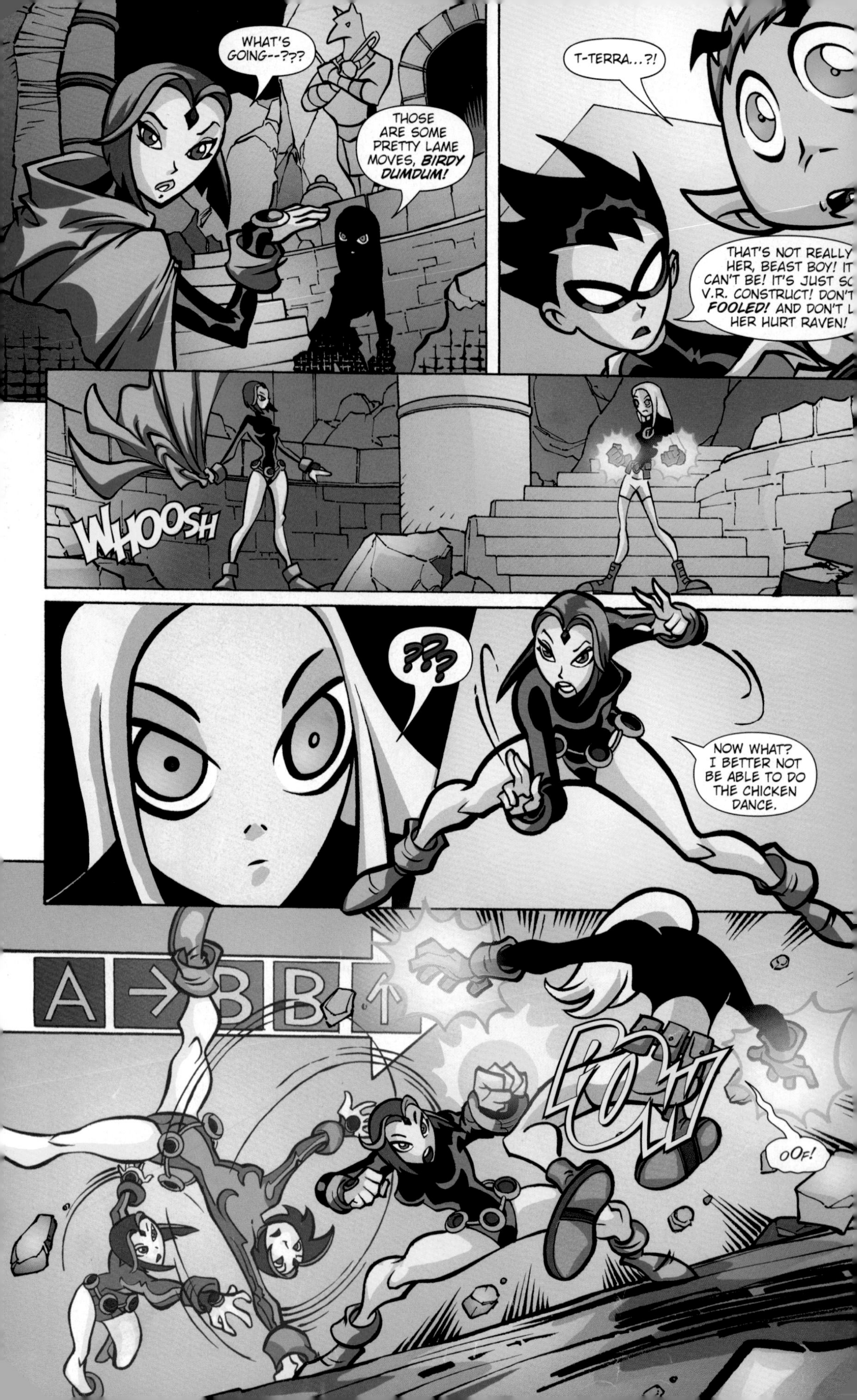
WHAT'S GOING--???
THOSE ARE SOME PRETTY LAME MOVES, BIRDY DUMDUM!
T-TERRA...?!
THAT'S NOT REALLY HER, BEAST BOY! IT CAN'T BE! IT'S JUST SO V.R. CONSTRUCT! DON'T FOOLED! AND DON'T L HER HURT RAVEN!
WHOOSH
???
NOW WHAT? I BETTER NOT BE ABLE TO DO THE CHICKEN DANCE.
A → B B ↑
POW
OOF!

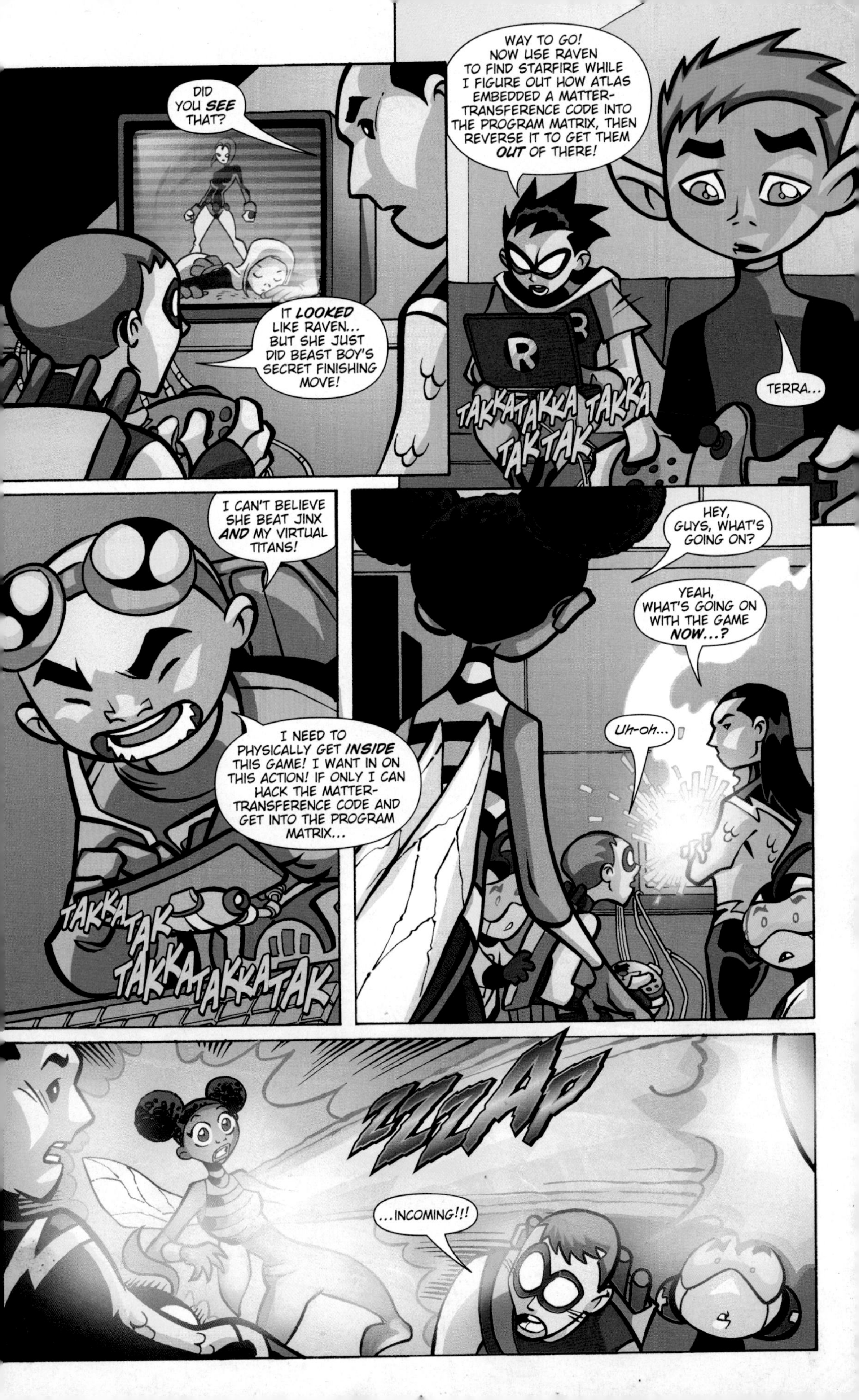
DID YOU SEE THAT?
IT LOOKED LIKE RAVEN... BUT SHE JUST DID BEAST BOY'S SECRET FINISHING MOVE!
WAY TO GO! NOW USE RAVEN TO FIND STARFIRE WHILE I FIGURE OUT HOW ATLAS EMBEDDED A MATTER-TRANSFERENCE CODE INTO THE PROGRAM MATRIX, THEN REVERSE IT TO GET THEM OUT OF THERE!
TAKKATAKKA TAKKA TAKTAK
TERRA...
I CAN'T BELIEVE SHE BEAT JINX AND MY VIRTUAL TITANS!
I NEED TO PHYSICALLY GET INSIDE THIS GAME! I WANT IN ON THIS ACTION! IF ONLY I CAN HACK THE MATTER-TRANSFERENCE CODE AND GET INTO THE PROGRAM MATRIX...
TAKKATAK TAKKATAKKATAK
HEY, GUYS, WHAT'S GOING ON?
YEAH, WHAT'S GOING ON WITH THE GAME NOW...?
Uh-oh...
ZZZAP
...INCOMING!!!

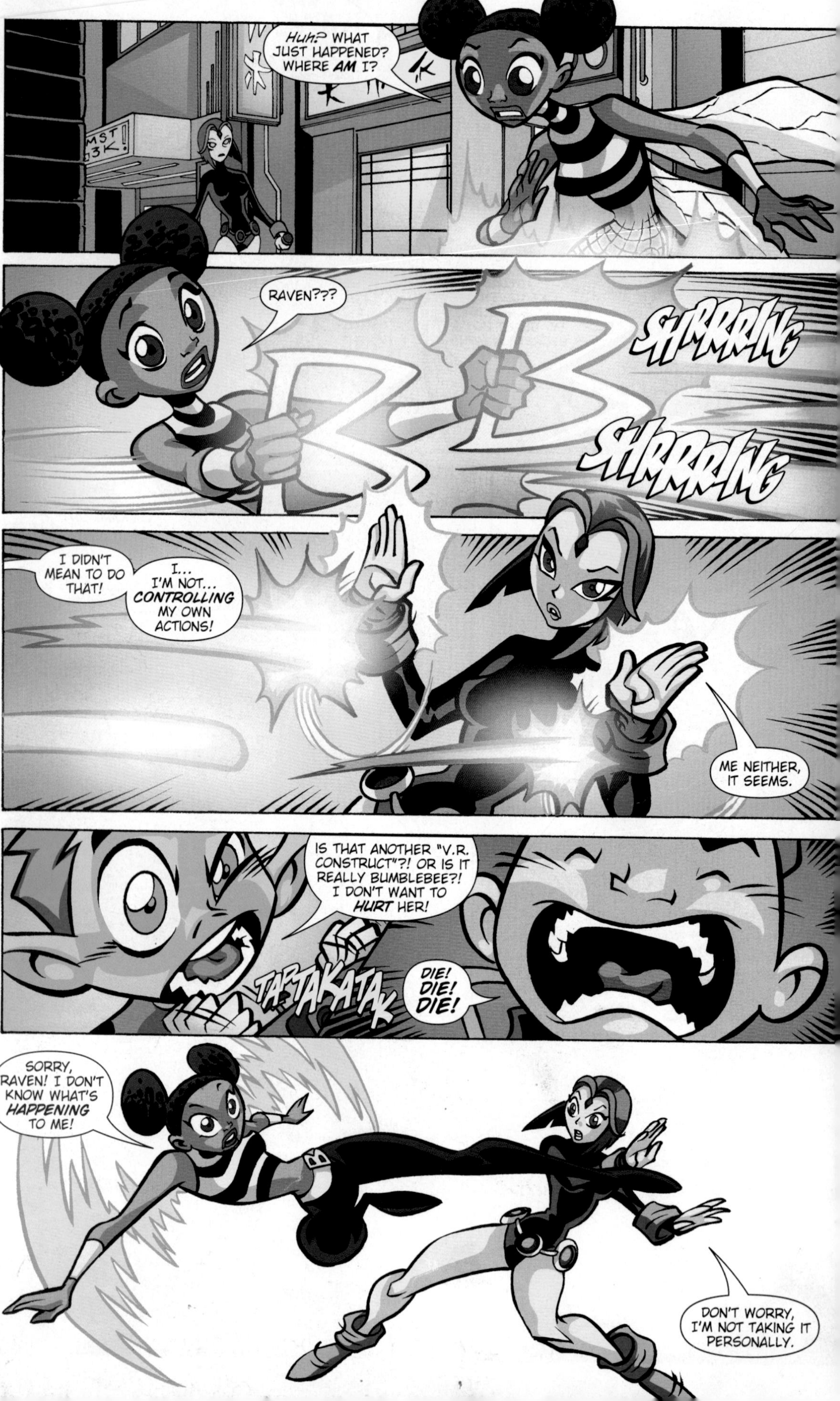
HUH? WHAT JUST HAPPENED? WHERE AM I?
MST 3K!
RAVEN???
SHRRRING
SHRRRING
I DIDN'T MEAN TO DO THAT!
I... I'M NOT... CONTROLLING MY OWN ACTIONS!
ME NEITHER, IT SEEMS.
IS THAT ANOTHER "V.R. CONSTRUCT"?! OR IS IT REALLY BUMBLEBEE?! I DON'T WANT TO HURT HER!
TAKATAKATAK
DIE! DIE! DIE!
SORRY, RAVEN! I DON'T KNOW WHAT'S HAPPENING TO ME!
DON'T WORRY, I'M NOT TAKING IT PERSONALLY.

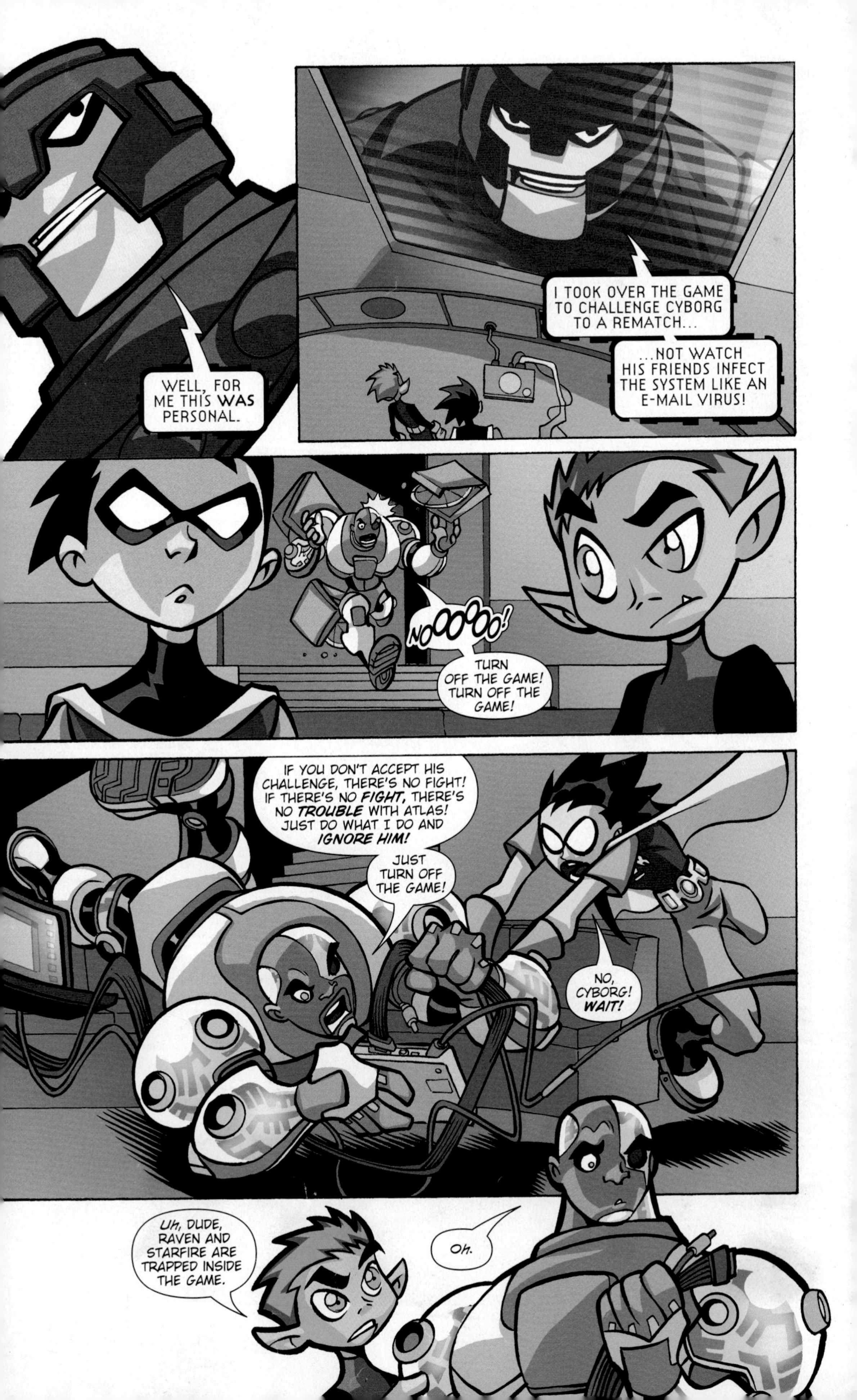
WELL, FOR ME THIS WAS PERSONAL.
I TOOK OVER THE GAME TO CHALLENGE CYBORG TO A REMATCH...
...NOT WATCH HIS FRIENDS INFECT THE SYSTEM LIKE AN E-MAIL VIRUS!
NOOOOOO!
TURN OFF THE GAME! TURN OFF THE GAME!
IF YOU DON'T ACCEPT HIS CHALLENGE, THERE'S NO FIGHT! IF THERE'S NO FIGHT, THERE'S NO TROUBLE WITH ATLAS! JUST DO WHAT I DO AND IGNORE HIM!
JUST TURN OFF THE GAME!
NO, CYBORG! WAIT!
Uh, DUDE, RAVEN AND STARFIRE ARE TRAPPED INSIDE THE GAME.
Oh.

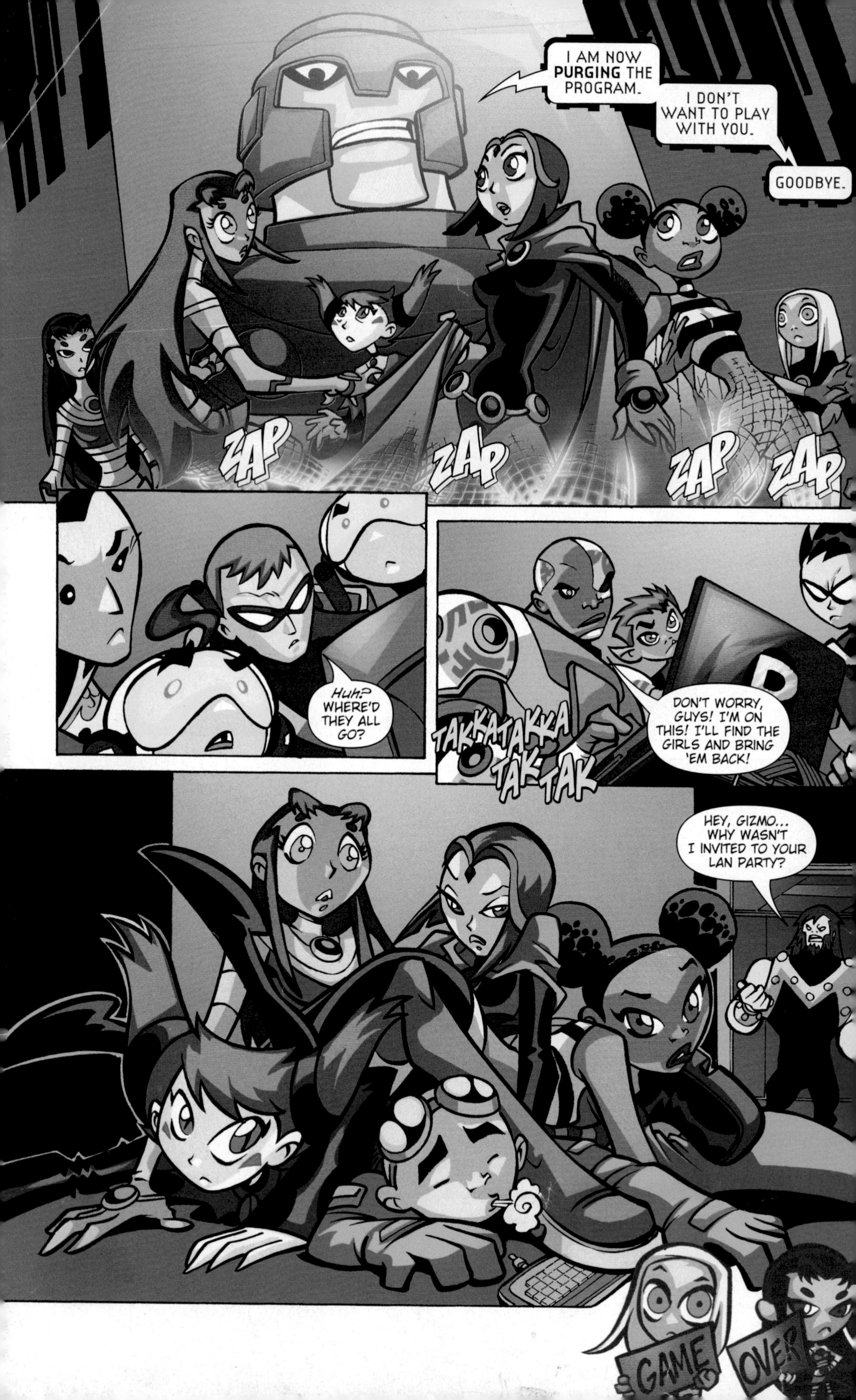
I AM NOW PURGING THE PROGRAM.
I DON'T WANT TO PLAY WITH YOU.
GOODBYE.
ZAP
ZAP
ZAP
ZAP
Huh? WHERE'D THEY ALL GO?
TAKKATAKKA TAK TAK
DON'T WORRY, GUYS! I'M ON THIS! I'LL FIND THE GIRLS AND BRING 'EM BACK!
HEY, GIZMO... WHY WASN'T I INVITED TO YOUR LAN PARTY?
GAME
OVER

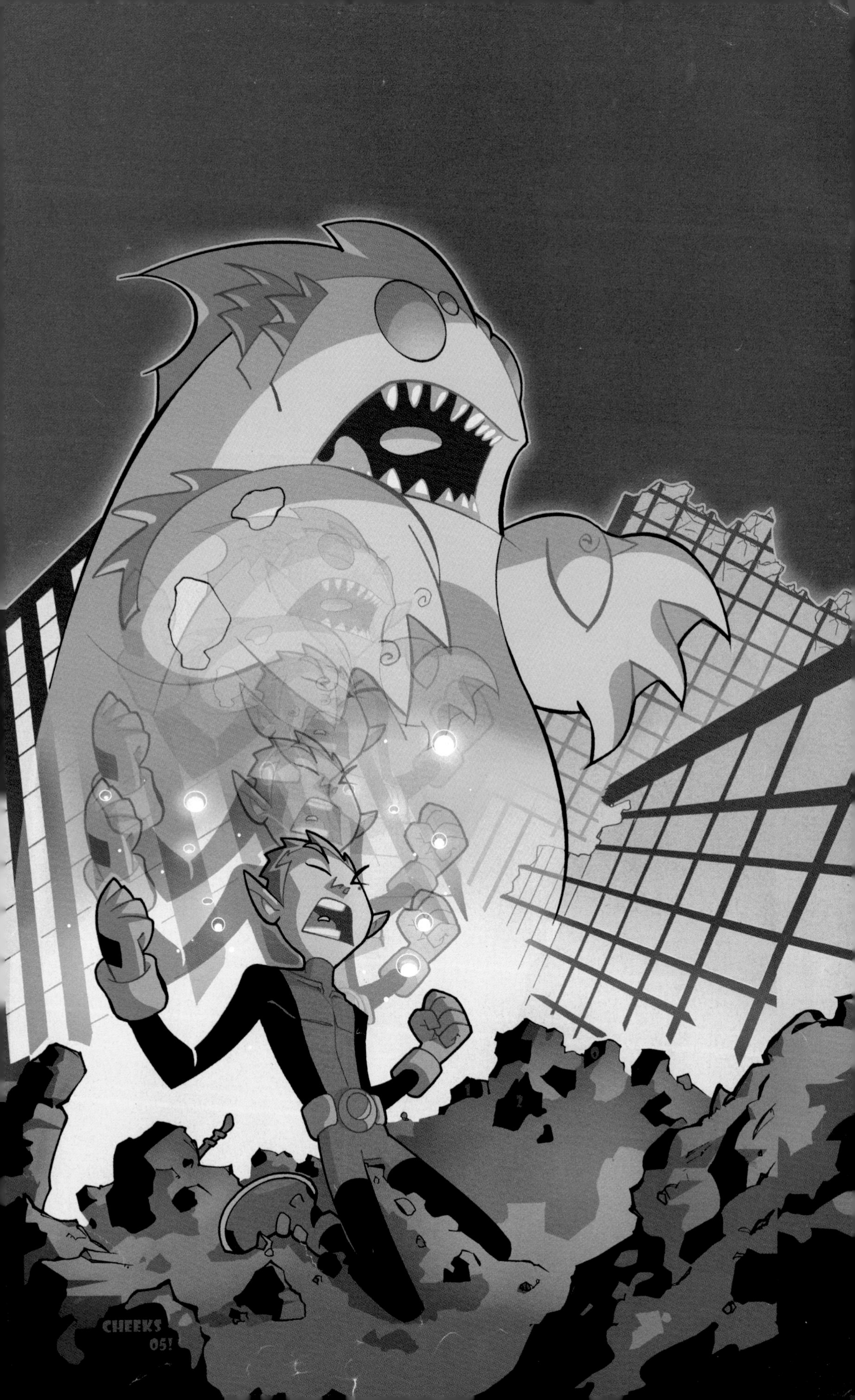
CHEEKS
05!

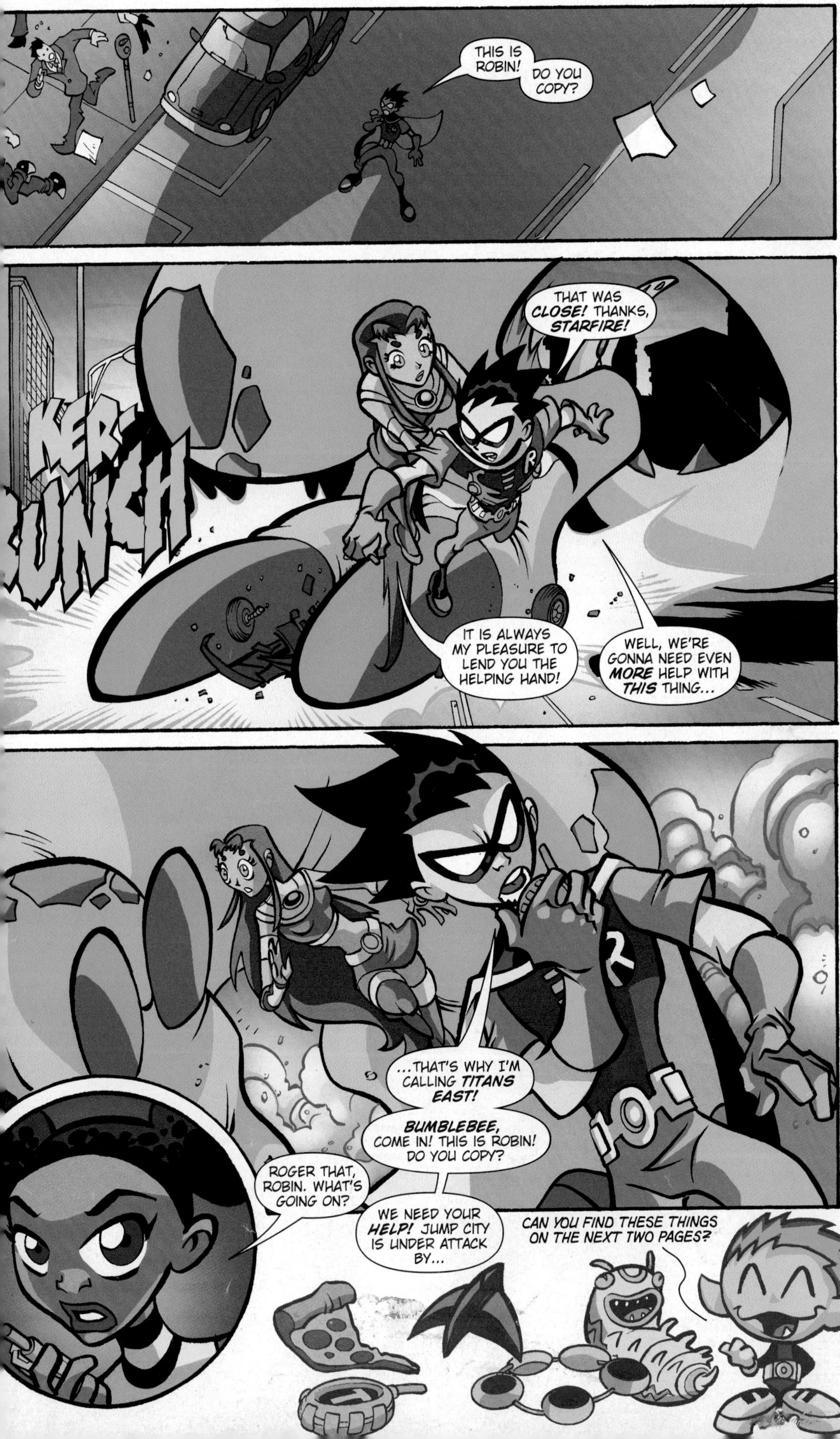

THIS IS ROBIN!
DO YOU COPY?
KER-RUNCH
THAT WAS CLOSE! THANKS, STARFIRE!
IT IS ALWAYS MY PLEASURE TO LEND YOU THE HELPING HAND!
WELL, WE'RE GONNA NEED EVEN MORE HELP WITH THIS THING...
...THAT'S WHY I'M CALLING TITANS EAST!
BUMBLEBEE, COME IN! THIS IS ROBIN! DO YOU COPY?
ROGER THAT, ROBIN. WHAT'S GOING ON?
WE NEED YOUR HELP! JUMP CITY IS UNDER ATTACK BY...
CAN YOU FIND THESE THINGS ON THE NEXT TWO PAGES?

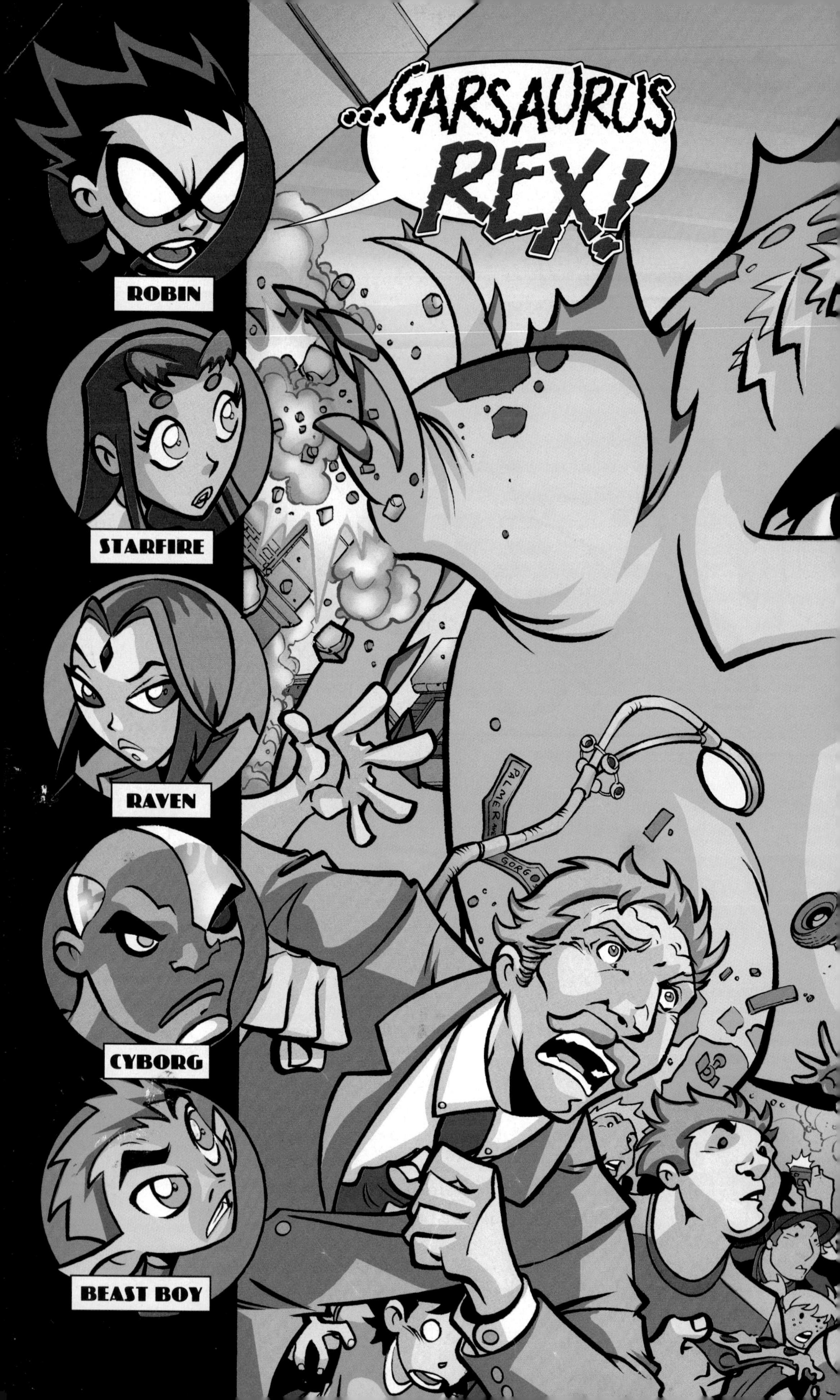

ROBIN
STARFIRE
RAVEN
CYBORG
BEAST BOY
...GARSAURUS REX!
PALMER AVE
GORG

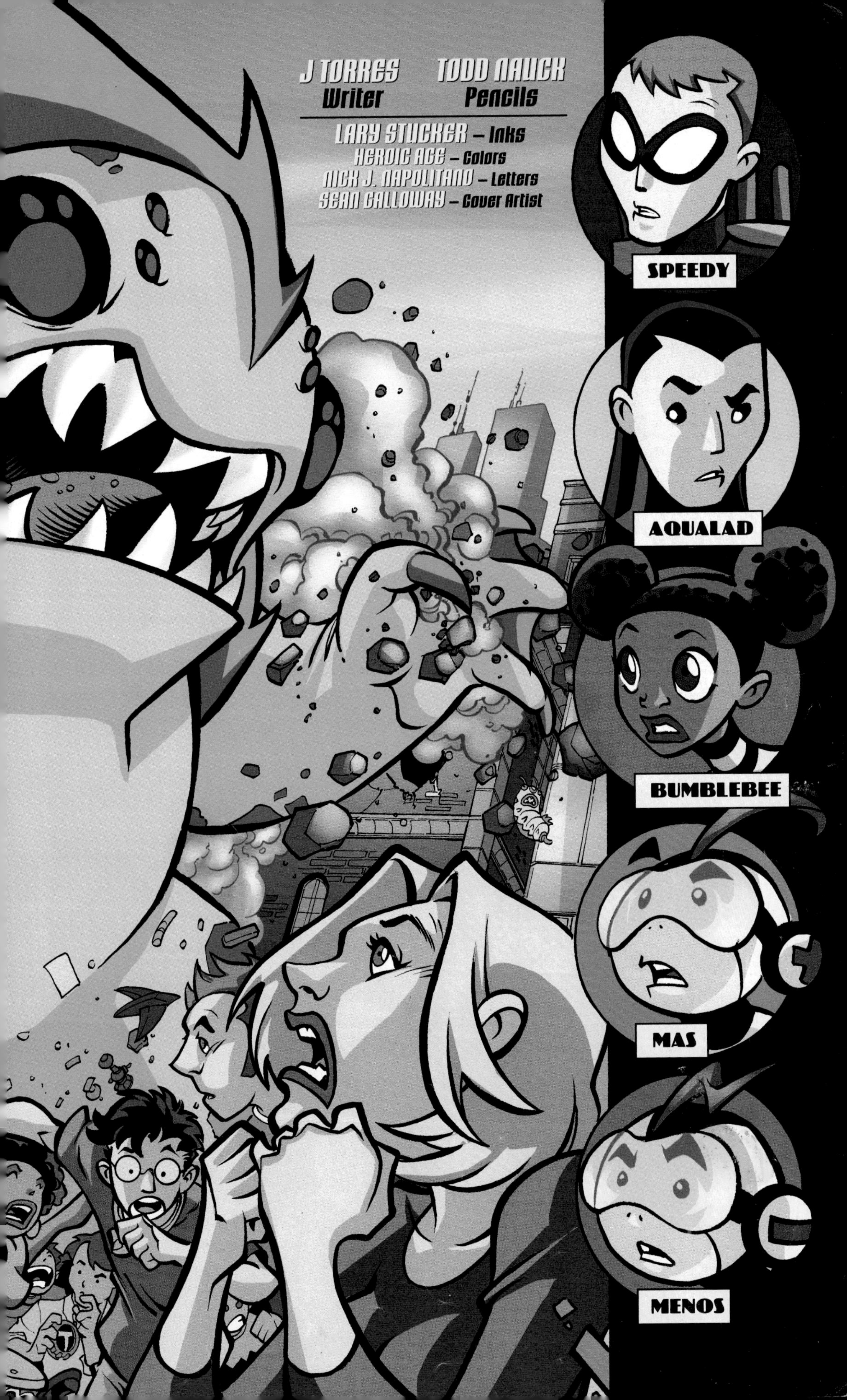

J TORRES Writer
TODD NAUCK Pencils
LARY STUCKER – Inks
HEROIC AGE – Colors
NICK J. NAPOLITANO – Letters
SEAN GALLOWAY – Cover Artist
SPEEDY
AQUALAD
BUMBLEBEE
MAS
MENOS

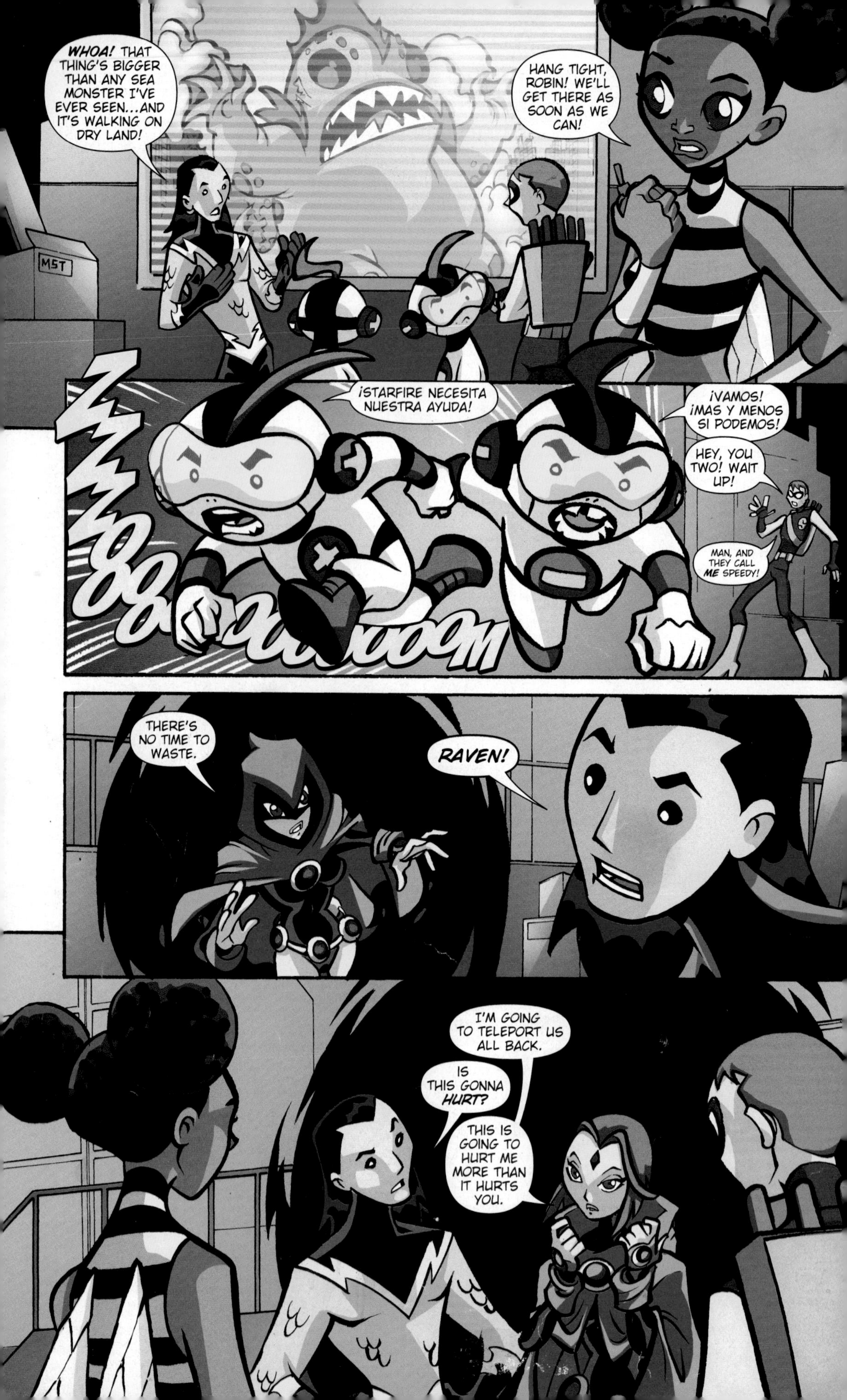
WHOA! THAT THING'S BIGGER THAN ANY SEA MONSTER I'VE EVER SEEN...AND IT'S WALKING ON DRY LAND!
HANG TIGHT, ROBIN! WE'LL GET THERE AS SOON AS WE CAN!
MST
ZMMOOOOOOOOOOM
¡STARFIRE NECESITA NUESTRA AYUDA!
¡VAMOS! ¡MAS Y MENOS SI PODEMOS!
HEY, YOU TWO! WAIT UP!
MAN, AND THEY CALL ME SPEEDY!
THERE'S NO TIME TO WASTE.
RAVEN!
I'M GOING TO TELEPORT US ALL BACK.
IS THIS GONNA HURT?
THIS IS GOING TO HURT ME MORE THAN IT HURTS YOU.

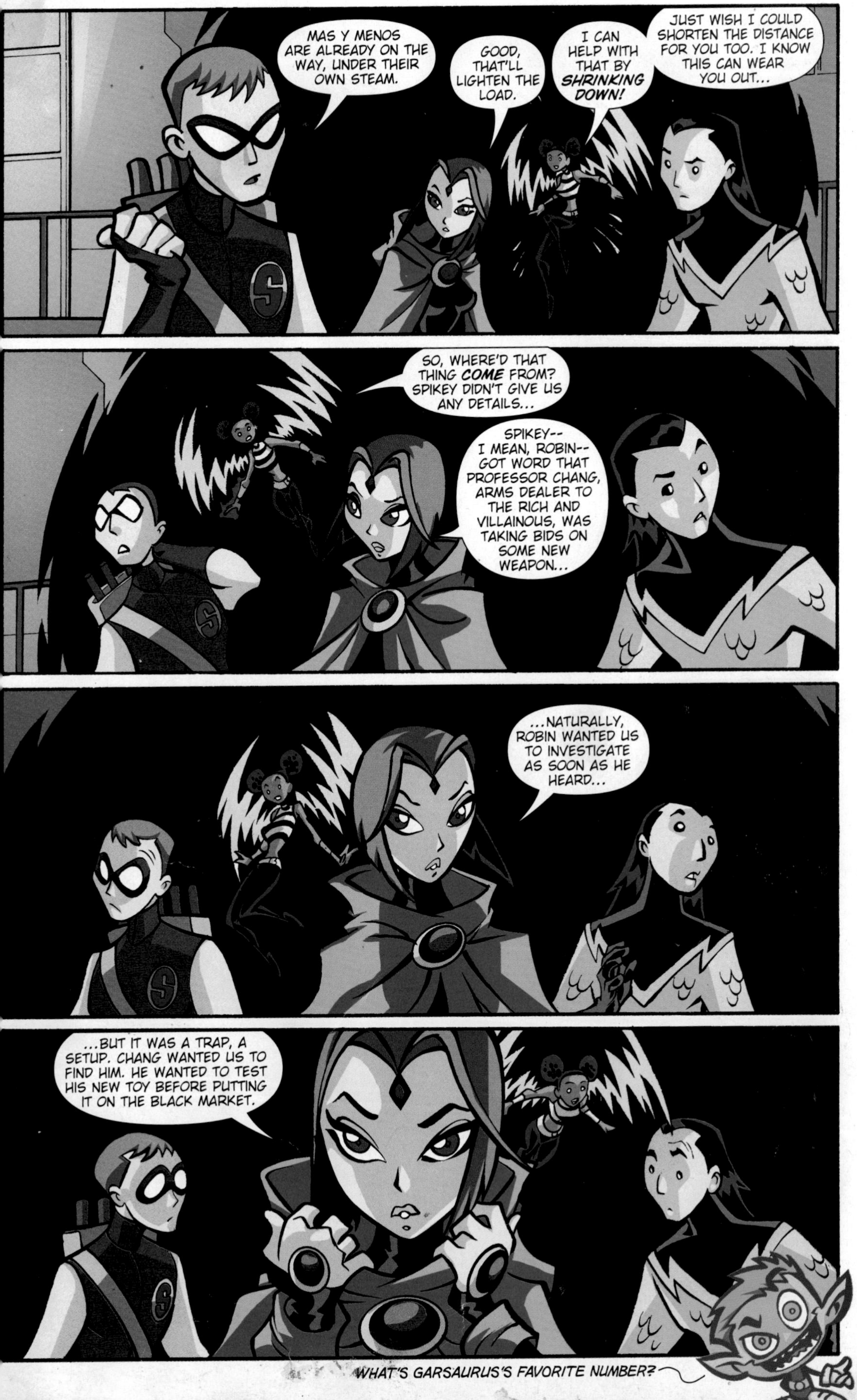
MAS Y MENOS ARE ALREADY ON THE WAY, UNDER THEIR OWN STEAM.
GOOD, THAT'LL LIGHTEN THE LOAD.
I CAN HELP WITH THAT BY SHRINKING DOWN!
JUST WISH I COULD SHORTEN THE DISTANCE FOR YOU TOO. I KNOW THIS CAN WEAR YOU OUT...
SO, WHERE'D THAT THING COME FROM? SPIKEY DIDN'T GIVE US ANY DETAILS...
SPIKEY-- I MEAN, ROBIN-- GOT WORD THAT PROFESSOR CHANG, ARMS DEALER TO THE RICH AND VILLAINOUS, WAS TAKING BIDS ON SOME NEW WEAPON...
...NATURALLY, ROBIN WANTED US TO INVESTIGATE AS SOON AS HE HEARD...
...BUT IT WAS A TRAP, A SETUP. CHANG WANTED US TO FIND HIM. HE WANTED TO TEST HIS NEW TOY BEFORE PUTTING IT ON THE BLACK MARKET.
WHAT'S GARSAURUS'S FAVORITE NUMBER?

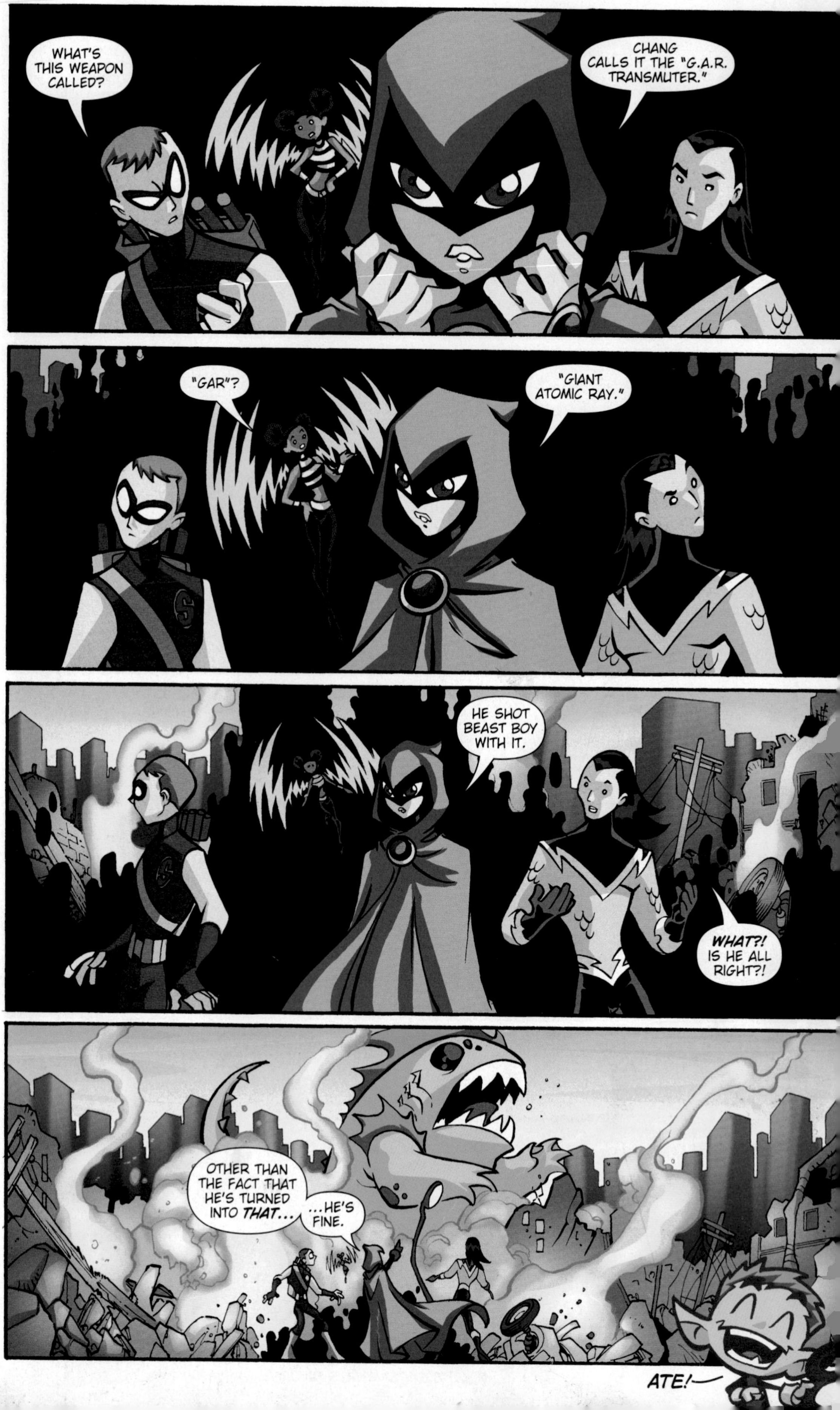
WHAT'S THIS WEAPON CALLED?
CHANG CALLS IT THE "G.A.R. TRANSMUTER."
"GAR"?
"GIANT ATOMIC RAY."
HE SHOT BEAST BOY WITH IT.
WHAT?! IS HE ALL RIGHT?!
OTHER THAN THE FACT THAT HE'S TURNED INTO THAT...
...HE'S FINE.
ATE!

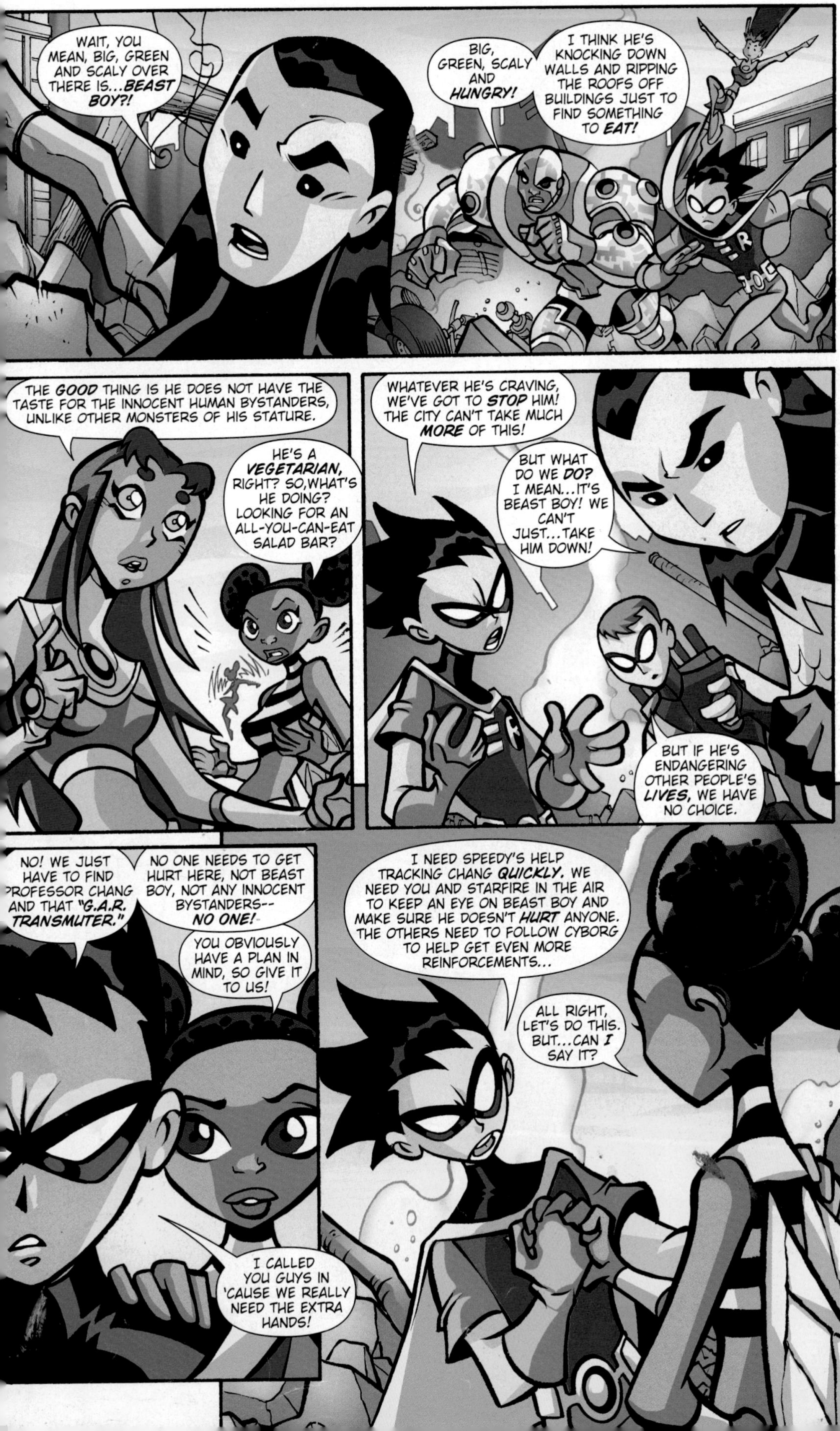
WAIT, YOU MEAN, BIG, GREEN AND SCALY OVER THERE IS...BEAST BOY?!
BIG, GREEN, SCALY AND HUNGRY!
I THINK HE'S KNOCKING DOWN WALLS AND RIPPING THE ROOFS OFF BUILDINGS JUST TO FIND SOMETHING TO EAT!
THE GOOD THING IS HE DOES NOT HAVE THE TASTE FOR THE INNOCENT HUMAN BYSTANDERS, UNLIKE OTHER MONSTERS OF HIS STATURE.
HE'S A VEGETARIAN, RIGHT? SO,WHAT'S HE DOING? LOOKING FOR AN ALL-YOU-CAN-EAT SALAD BAR?
WHATEVER HE'S CRAVING, WE'VE GOT TO STOP HIM! THE CITY CAN'T TAKE MUCH MORE OF THIS!
BUT WHAT DO WE DO? I MEAN...IT'S BEAST BOY! WE CAN'T JUST...TAKE HIM DOWN!
BUT IF HE'S ENDANGERING OTHER PEOPLE'S LIVES, WE HAVE NO CHOICE.
NO! WE JUST HAVE TO FIND PROFESSOR CHANG AND THAT "G.A.R. TRANSMUTER."
NO ONE NEEDS TO GET HURT HERE, NOT BEAST BOY, NOT ANY INNOCENT BYSTANDERS-- NO ONE!
YOU OBVIOUSLY HAVE A PLAN IN MIND, SO GIVE IT TO US!
I CALLED YOU GUYS IN 'CAUSE WE REALLY NEED THE EXTRA HANDS!
I NEED SPEEDY'S HELP TRACKING CHANG QUICKLY. WE NEED YOU AND STARFIRE IN THE AIR TO KEEP AN EYE ON BEAST BOY AND MAKE SURE HE DOESN'T HURT ANYONE. THE OTHERS NEED TO FOLLOW CYBORG TO HELP GET EVEN MORE REINFORCEMENTS...
ALL RIGHT, LET'S DO THIS. BUT...CAN I SAY IT?

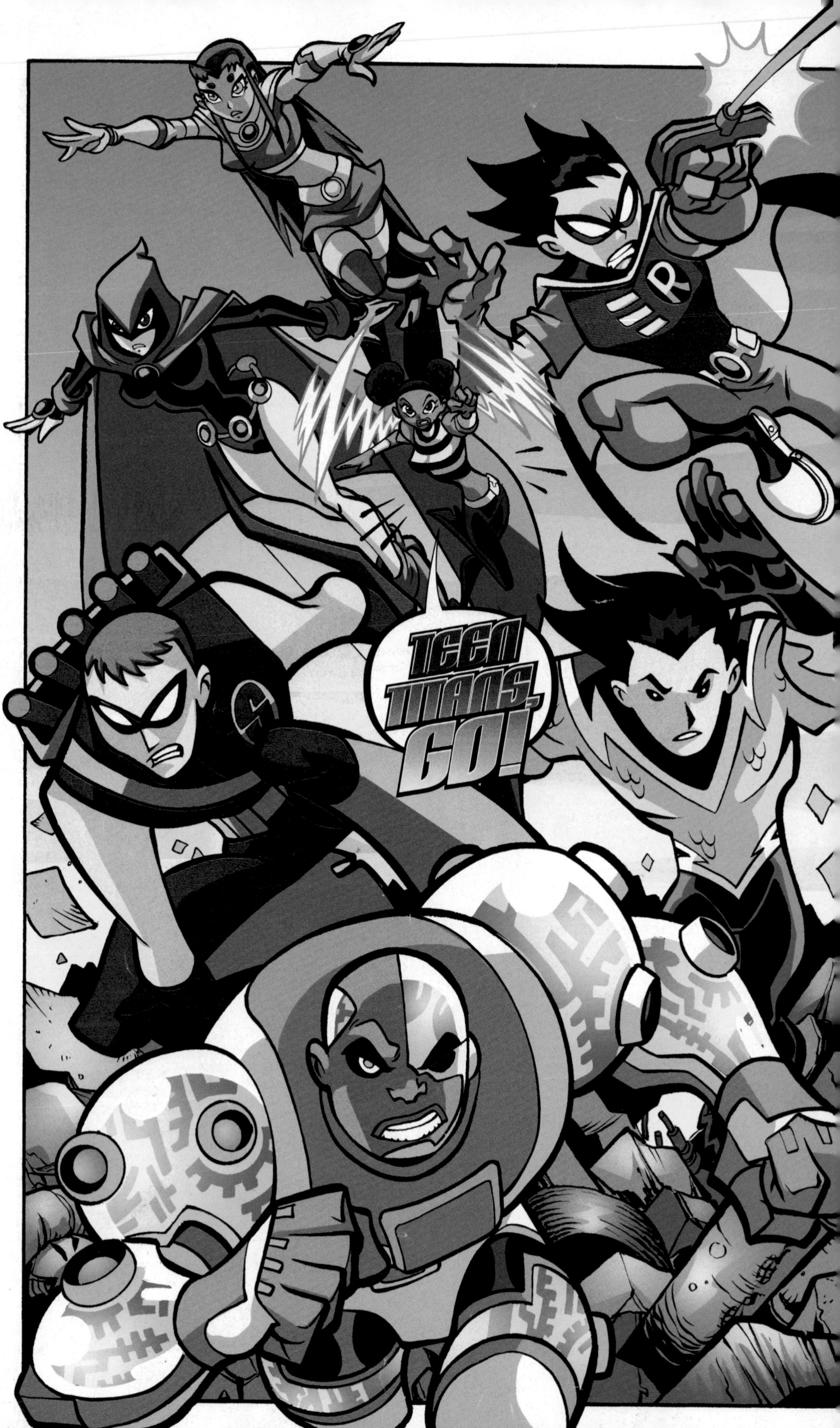
TEEN TITANS, GO!

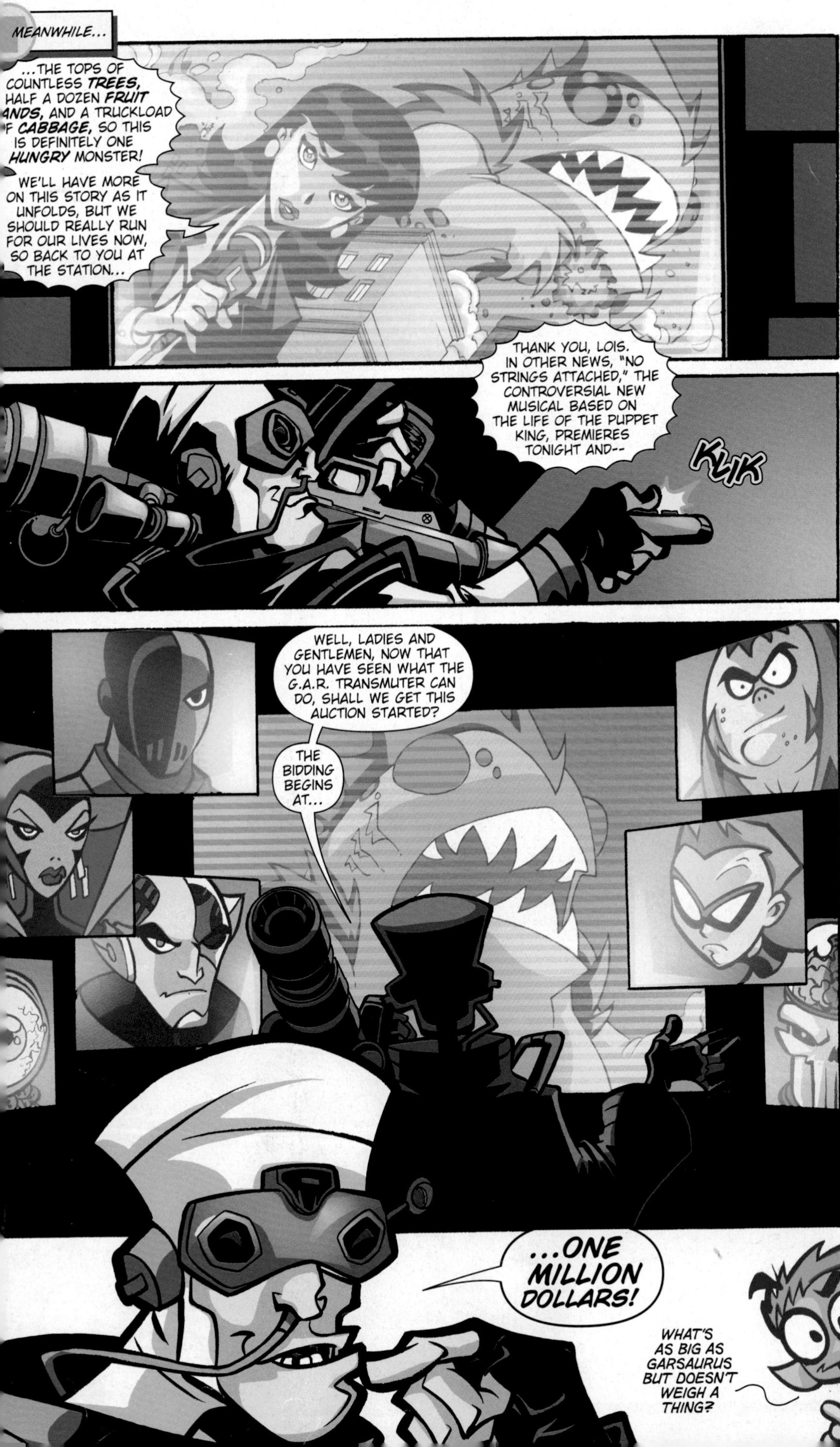
MEANWHILE...
...THE TOPS OF COUNTLESS TREES, HALF A DOZEN FRUIT ANDS, AND A TRUCKLOAD F CABBAGE, SO THIS IS DEFINITELY ONE HUNGRY MONSTER!
WE'LL HAVE MORE ON THIS STORY AS IT UNFOLDS, BUT WE SHOULD REALLY RUN FOR OUR LIVES NOW, SO BACK TO YOU AT THE STATION...
THANK YOU, LOIS. IN OTHER NEWS, "NO STRINGS ATTACHED," THE CONTROVERSIAL NEW MUSICAL BASED ON THE LIFE OF THE PUPPET KING, PREMIERES TONIGHT AND--
KLIK
WELL, LADIES AND GENTLEMEN, NOW THAT YOU HAVE SEEN WHAT THE G.A.R. TRANSMUTER CAN DO, SHALL WE GET THIS AUCTION STARTED?
THE BIDDING BEGINS AT...
...ONE MILLION DOLLARS!
WHAT'S AS BIG AS GARSAURUS BUT DOESN'T WEIGH A THING?

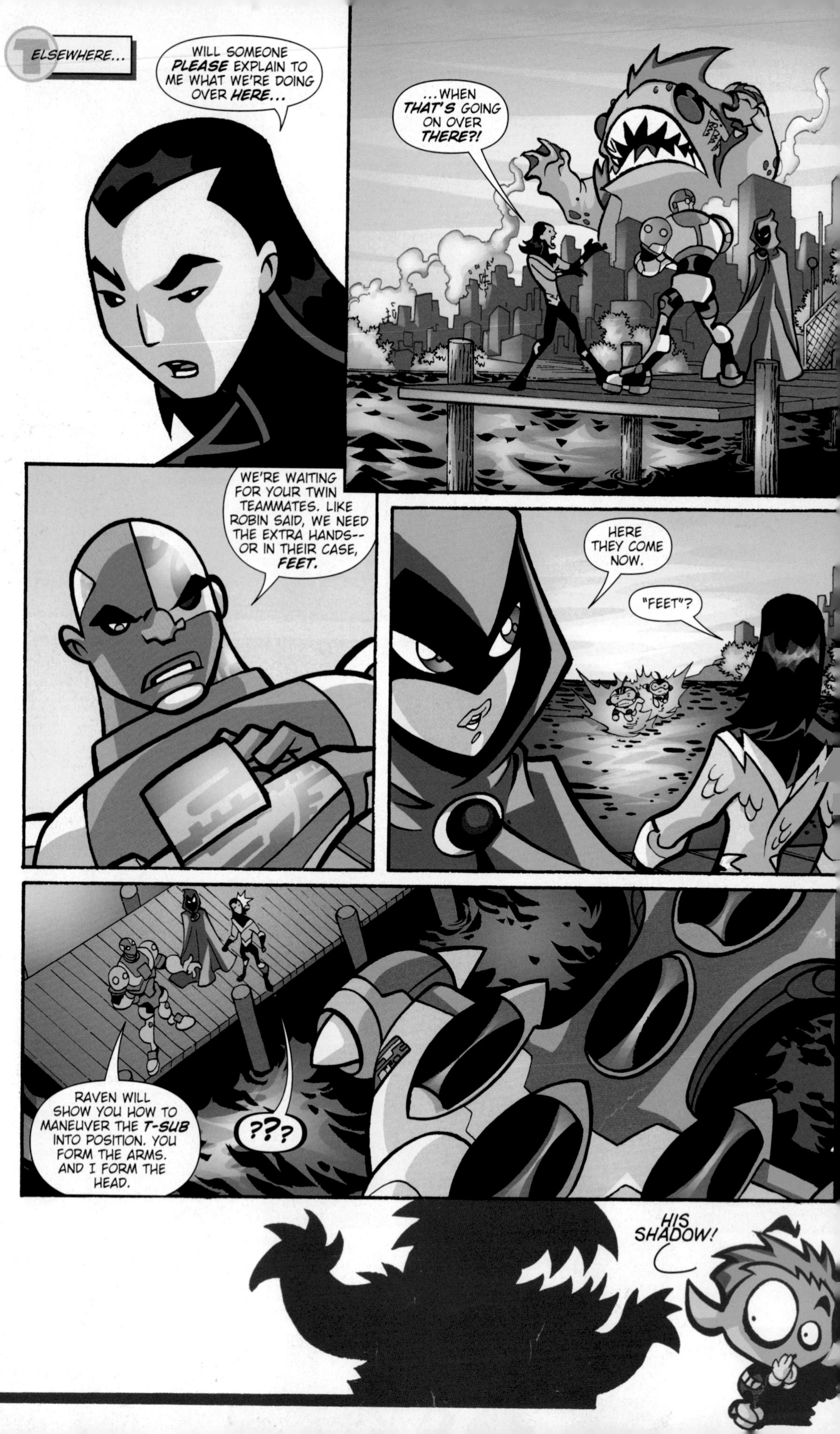
ELSEWHERE...
WILL SOMEONE PLEASE EXPLAIN TO ME WHAT WE'RE DOING OVER HERE...
...WHEN THAT'S GOING ON OVER THERE?!
WE'RE WAITING FOR YOUR TWIN TEAMMATES. LIKE ROBIN SAID, WE NEED THE EXTRA HANDS--OR IN THEIR CASE, FEET.
HERE THEY COME NOW.
"FEET"?
RAVEN WILL SHOW YOU HOW TO MANEUVER THE T-SUB INTO POSITION. YOU FORM THE ARMS. AND I FORM THE HEAD.
???
HIS SHADOW!

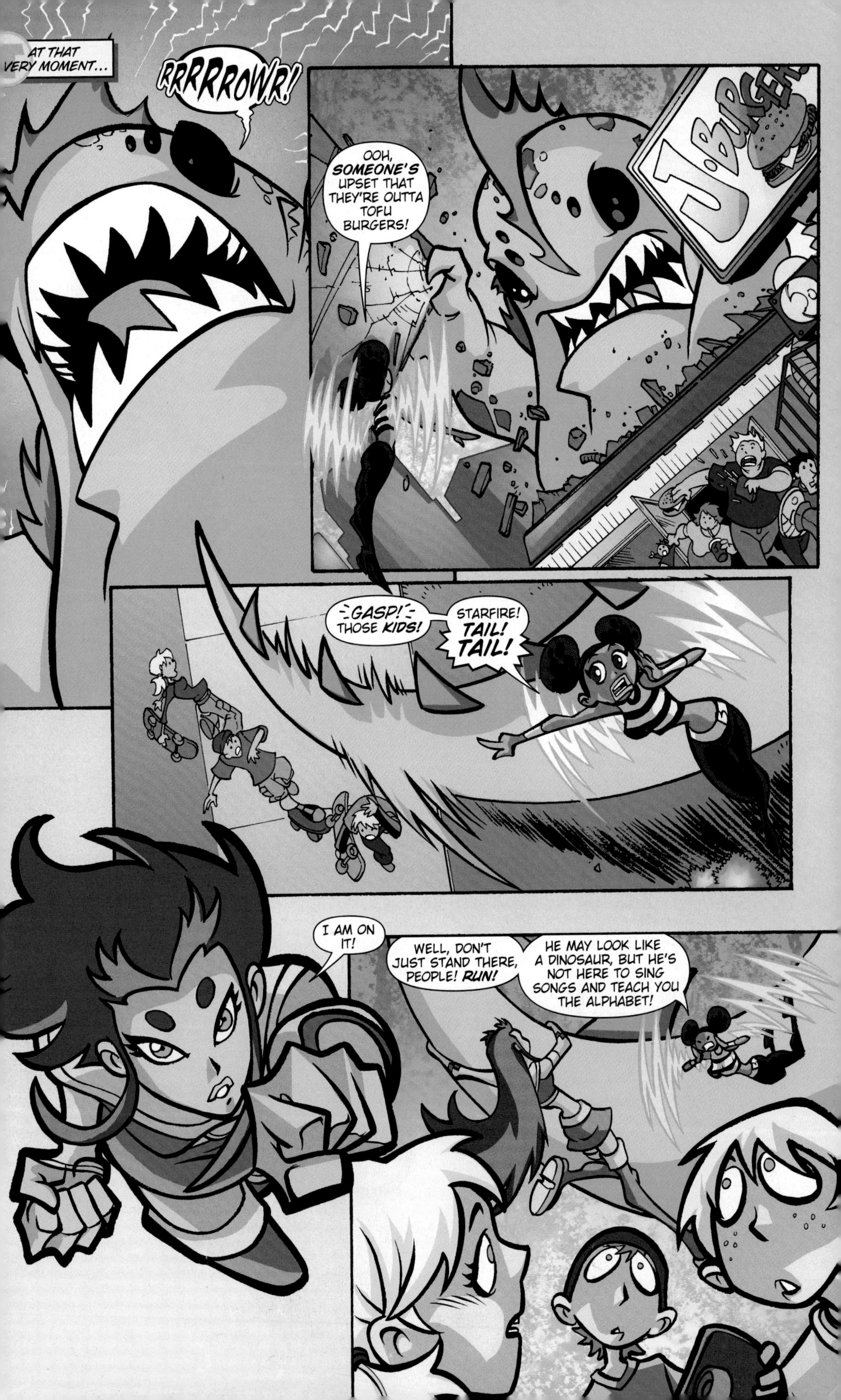
AT THAT VERY MOMENT...
RRRRROWR!
OOH, SOMEONE'S UPSET THAT THEY'RE OUTTA TOFU BURGERS!
J. BURGER
-GASP!- THOSE KIDS!
STARFIRE! TAIL! TAIL!
I AM ON IT!
WELL, DON'T JUST STAND THERE, PEOPLE! RUN!
HE MAY LOOK LIKE A DINOSAUR, BUT HE'S NOT HERE TO SING SONGS AND TEACH YOU THE ALPHABET!

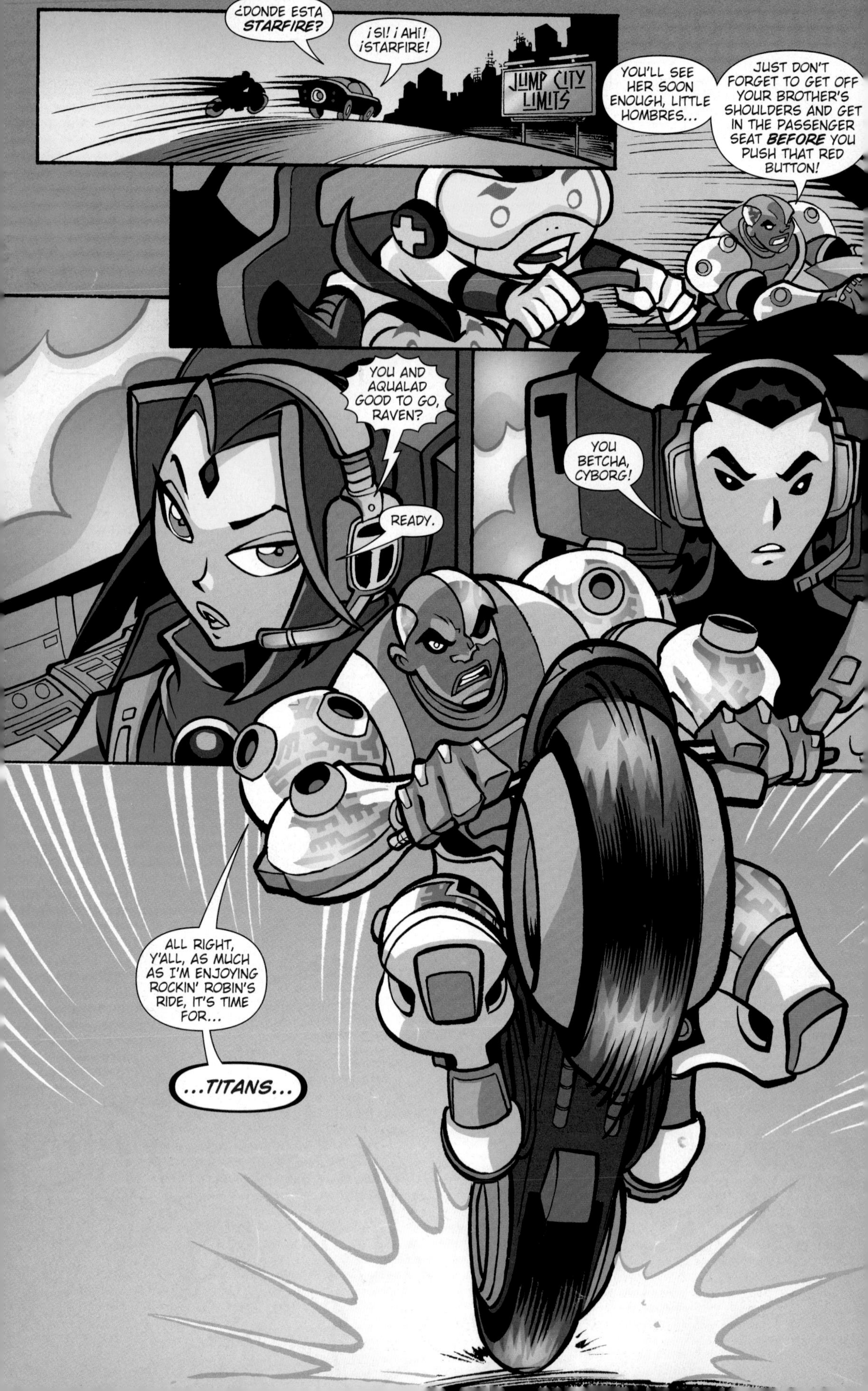
¿DONDE ESTA STARFIRE?
¡SI! ¡AHI! ¡STARFIRE!
JUMP CITY LIMITS
YOU'LL SEE HER SOON ENOUGH, LITTLE HOMBRES...
JUST DON'T FORGET TO GET OFF YOUR BROTHER'S SHOULDERS AND GET IN THE PASSENGER SEAT BEFORE YOU PUSH THAT RED BUTTON!
YOU AND AQUALAD GOOD TO GO, RAVEN?
READY.
YOU BETCHA, CYBORG!
ALL RIGHT, Y'ALL, AS MUCH AS I'M ENJOYING ROCKIN' ROBIN'S RIDE, IT'S TIME FOR...
...TITANS...

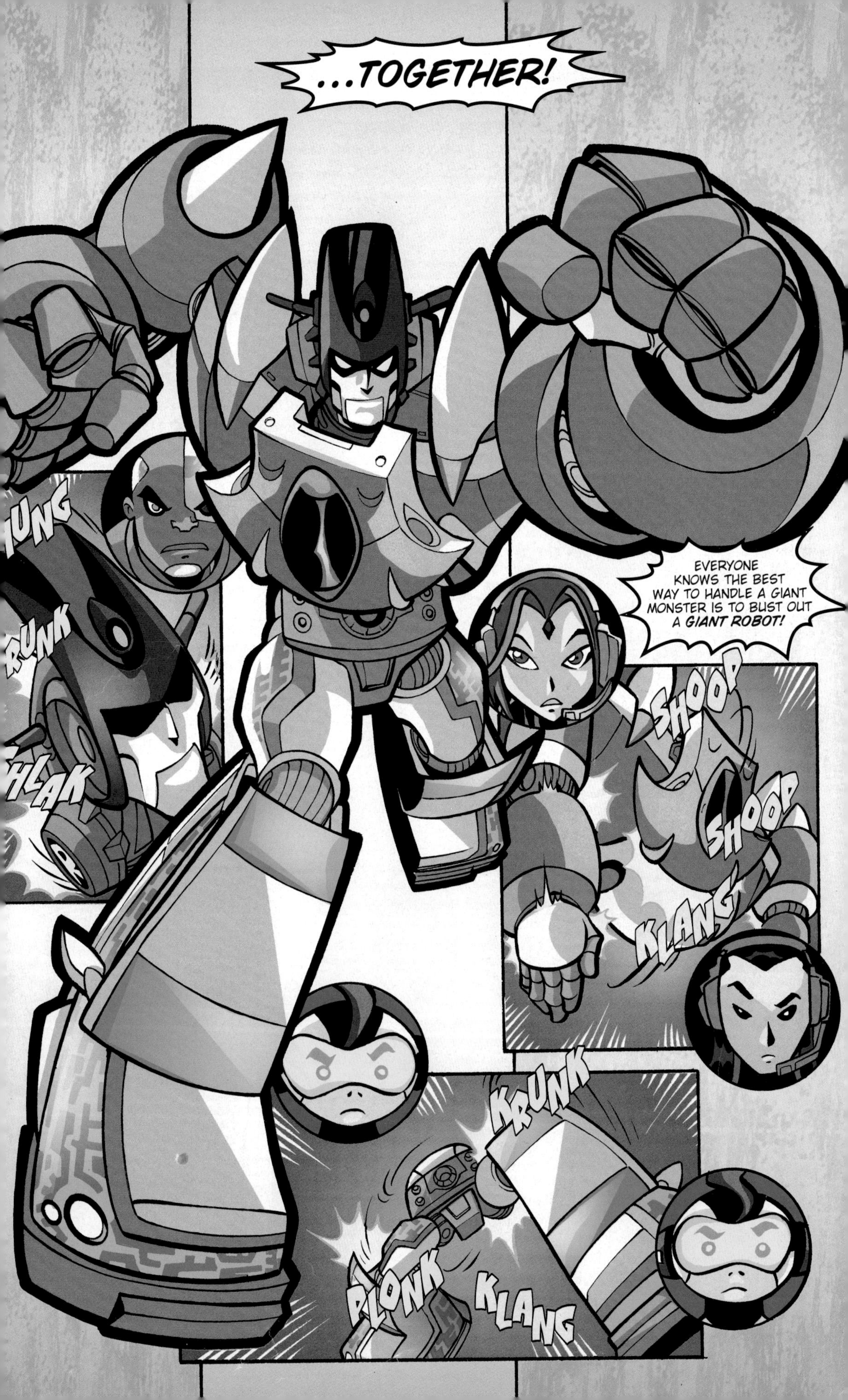
...TOGETHER!
EVERYONE KNOWS THE BEST WAY TO HANDLE A GIANT MONSTER IS TO BUST OUT A *GIANT ROBOT!*
SHOOP
SHOOP
KLANG
KRUNK
PLONK
KLANG

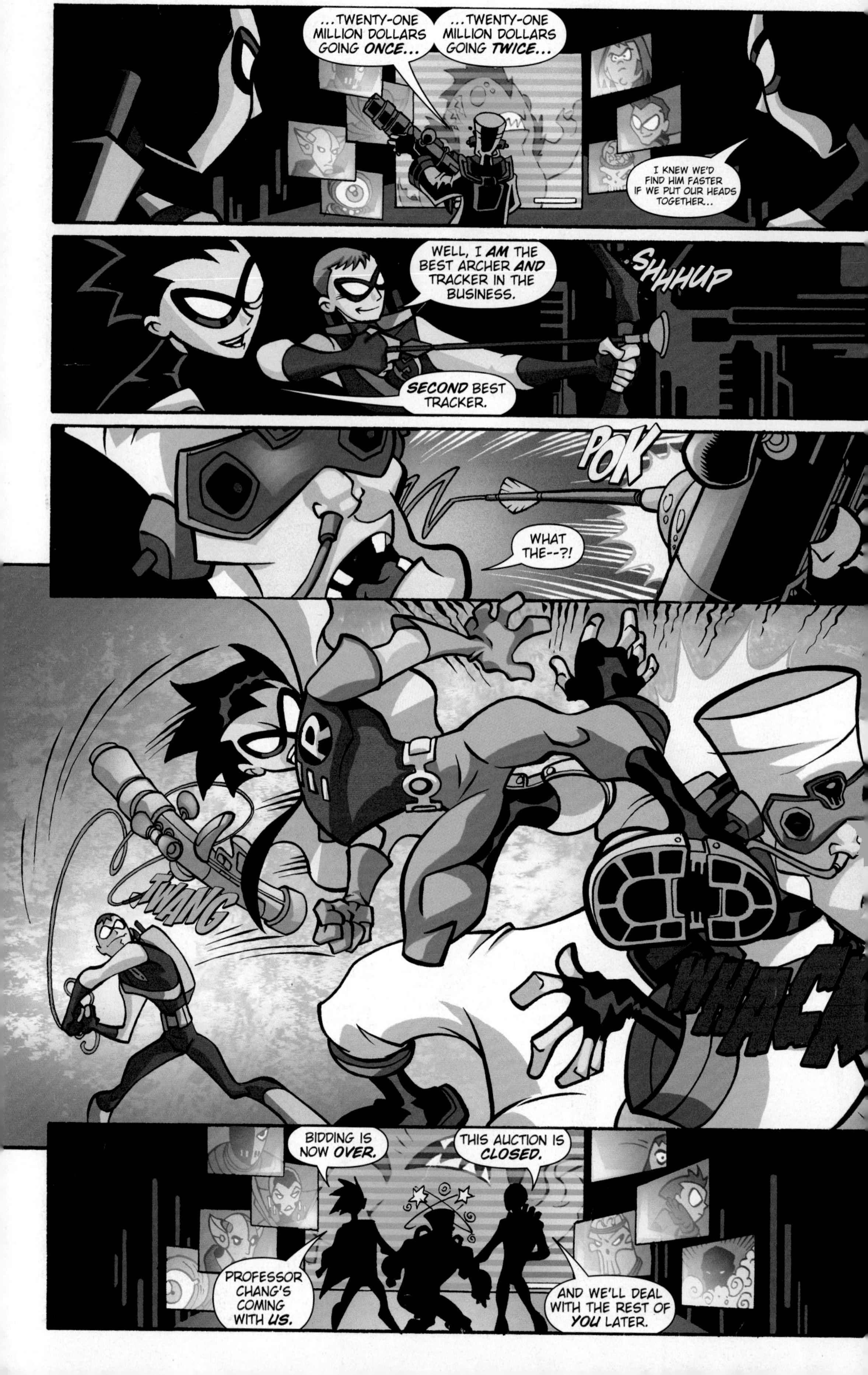
...TWENTY-ONE MILLION DOLLARS GOING ONCE...
...TWENTY-ONE MILLION DOLLARS GOING TWICE...
I KNEW WE'D FIND HIM FASTER IF WE PUT OUR HEADS TOGETHER...
WELL, I AM THE BEST ARCHER AND TRACKER IN THE BUSINESS.
SHHHUP
SECOND BEST TRACKER.
POK
WHAT THE--?!
TWANG
WHACK
BIDDING IS NOW OVER.
THIS AUCTION IS CLOSED.
PROFESSOR CHANG'S COMING WITH US.
AND WE'LL DEAL WITH THE REST OF YOU LATER.

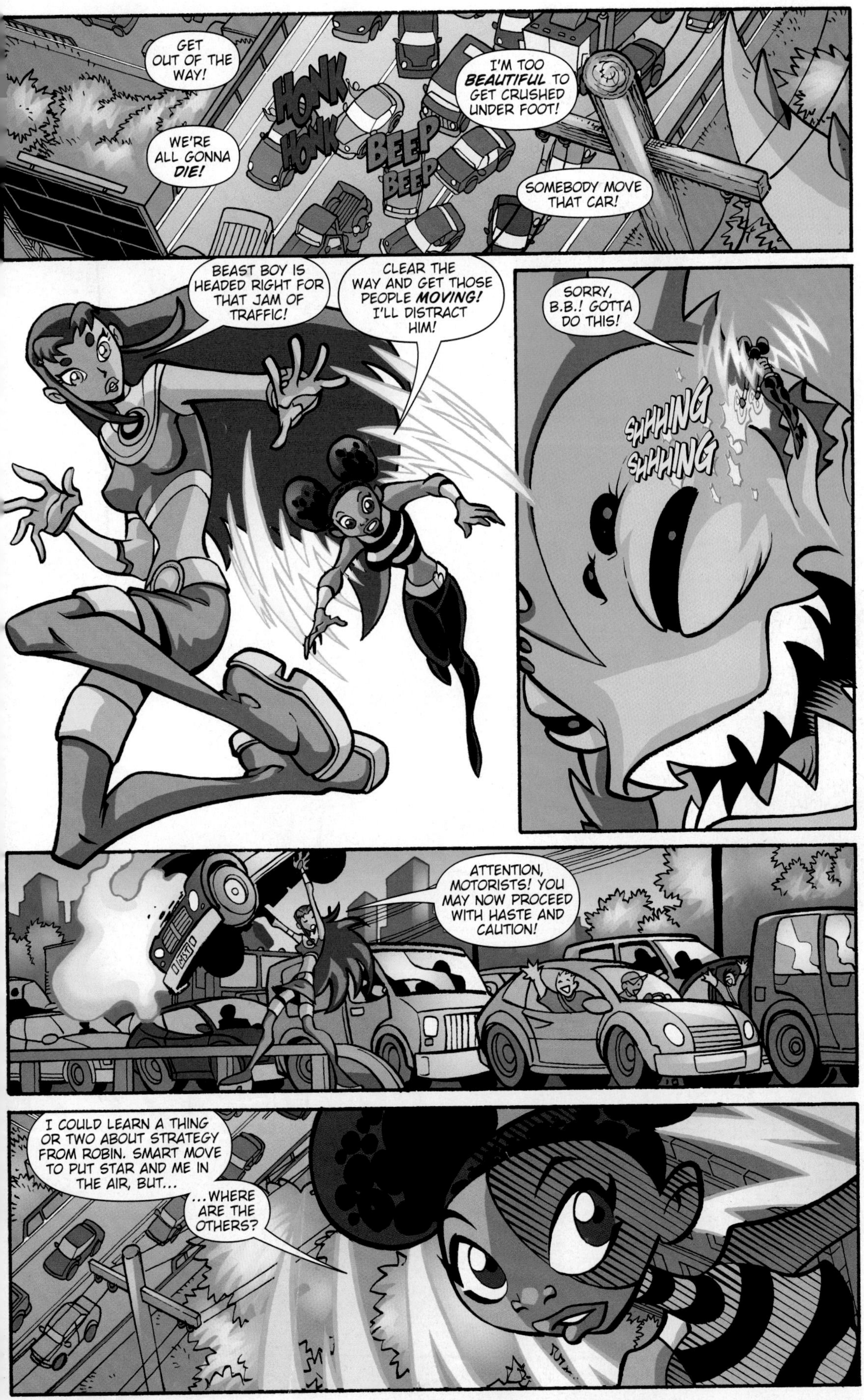
GET OUT OF THE WAY!
HONK HONK
WE'RE ALL GONNA DIE!
BEEP BEEP
I'M TOO BEAUTIFUL TO GET CRUSHED UNDER FOOT!
SOMEBODY MOVE THAT CAR!
BEAST BOY IS HEADED RIGHT FOR THAT JAM OF TRAFFIC!
CLEAR THE WAY AND GET THOSE PEOPLE MOVING! I'LL DISTRACT HIM!
SORRY, B.B.! GOTTA DO THIS!
SHHHING SHHHING
ATTENTION, MOTORISTS! YOU MAY NOW PROCEED WITH HASTE AND CAUTION!
I COULD LEARN A THING OR TWO ABOUT STRATEGY FROM ROBIN. SMART MOVE TO PUT STAR AND ME IN THE AIR, BUT...
...WHERE ARE THE OTHERS?

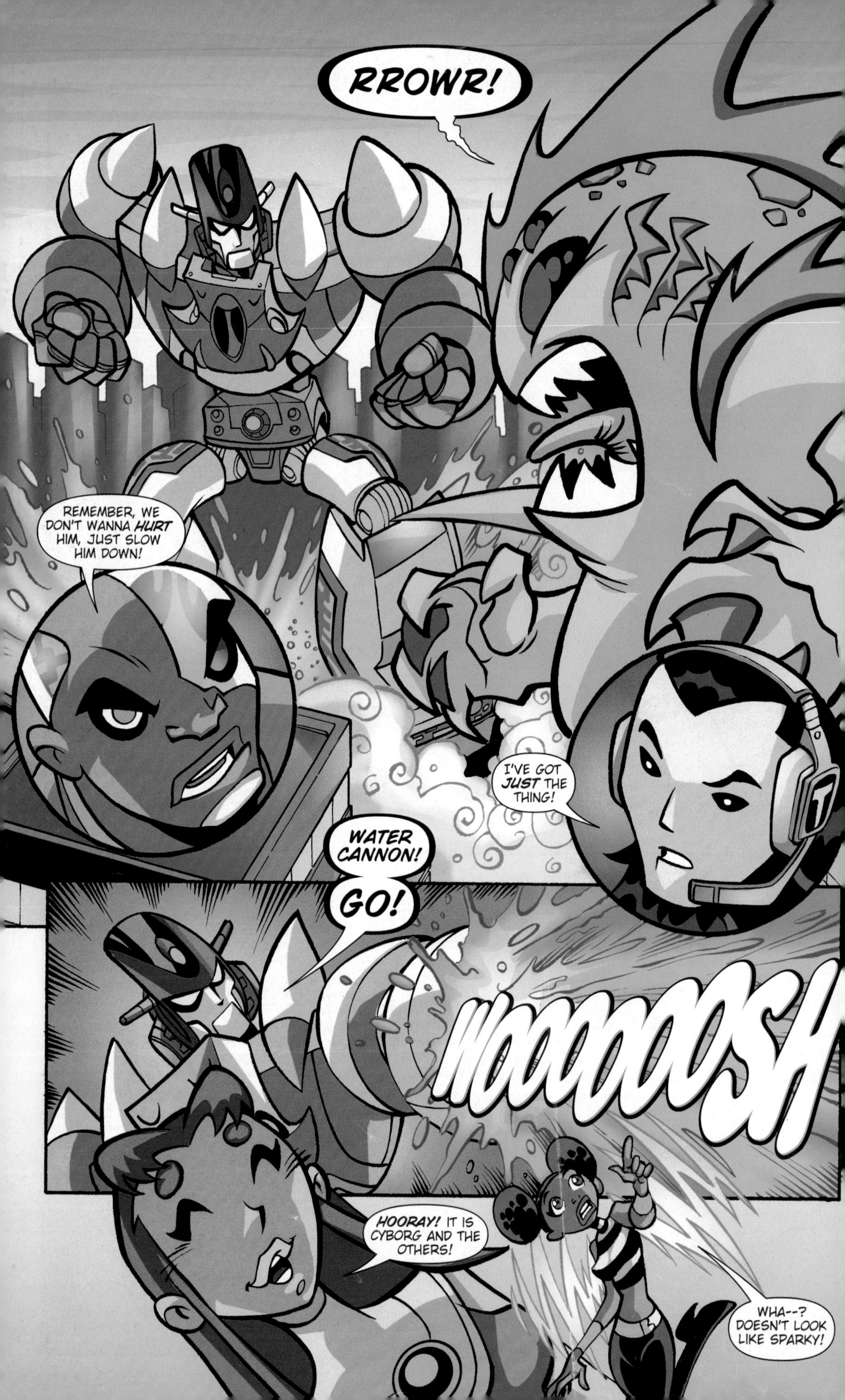

RROWR!
REMEMBER, WE DON'T WANNA HURT HIM, JUST SLOW HIM DOWN!
I'VE GOT JUST THE THING!
WATER CANNON!
GO!
WOOOOOOSH
HOORAY! IT IS CYBORG AND THE OTHERS!
WHA--? DOESN'T LOOK LIKE SPARKY!

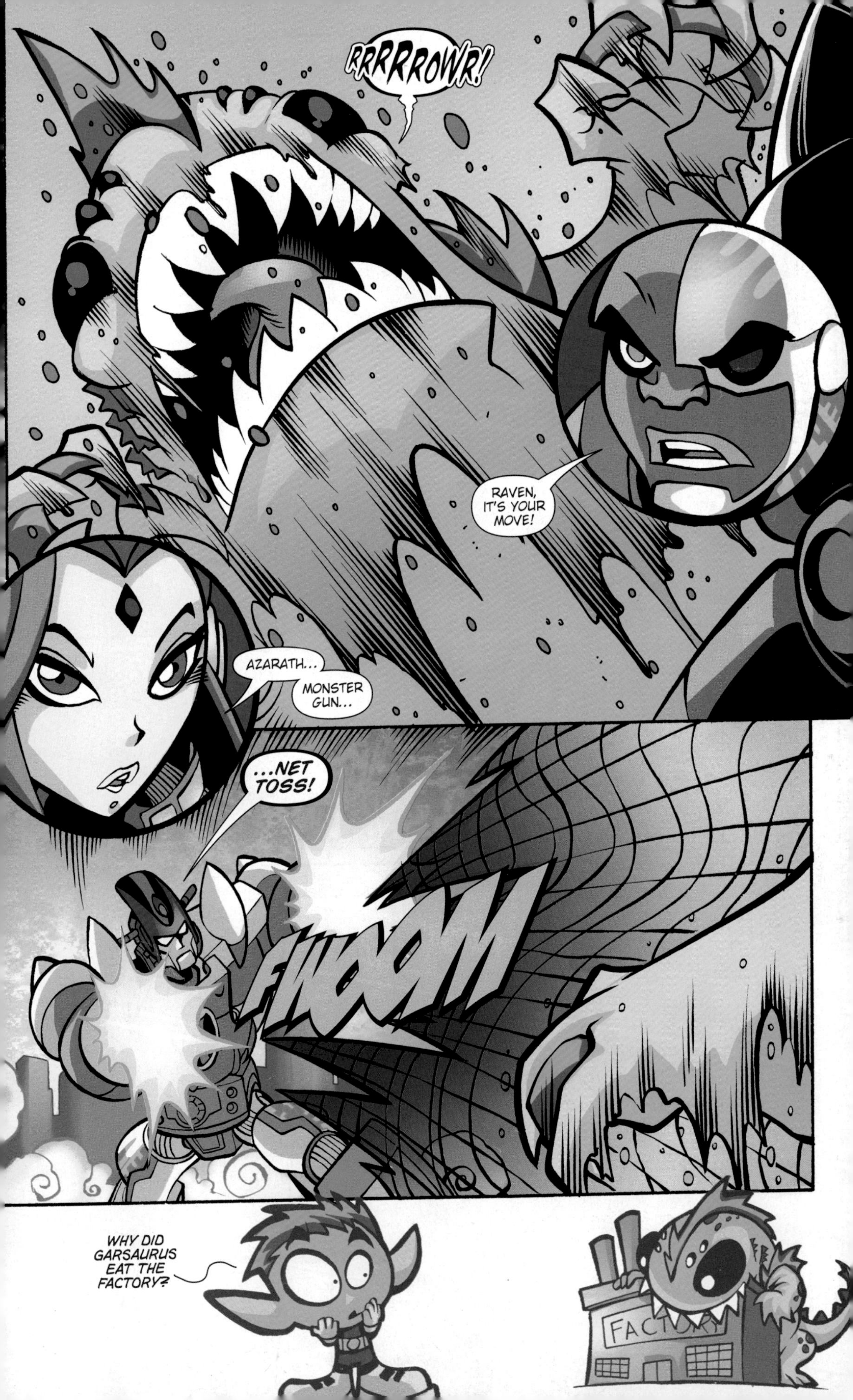
RRRRROWR!
RAVEN, IT'S YOUR MOVE!
AZARATH...
MONSTER GUN...
...NET TOSS!
FWOOM
WHY DID GARSAURUS EAT THE FACTORY?
FACTORY

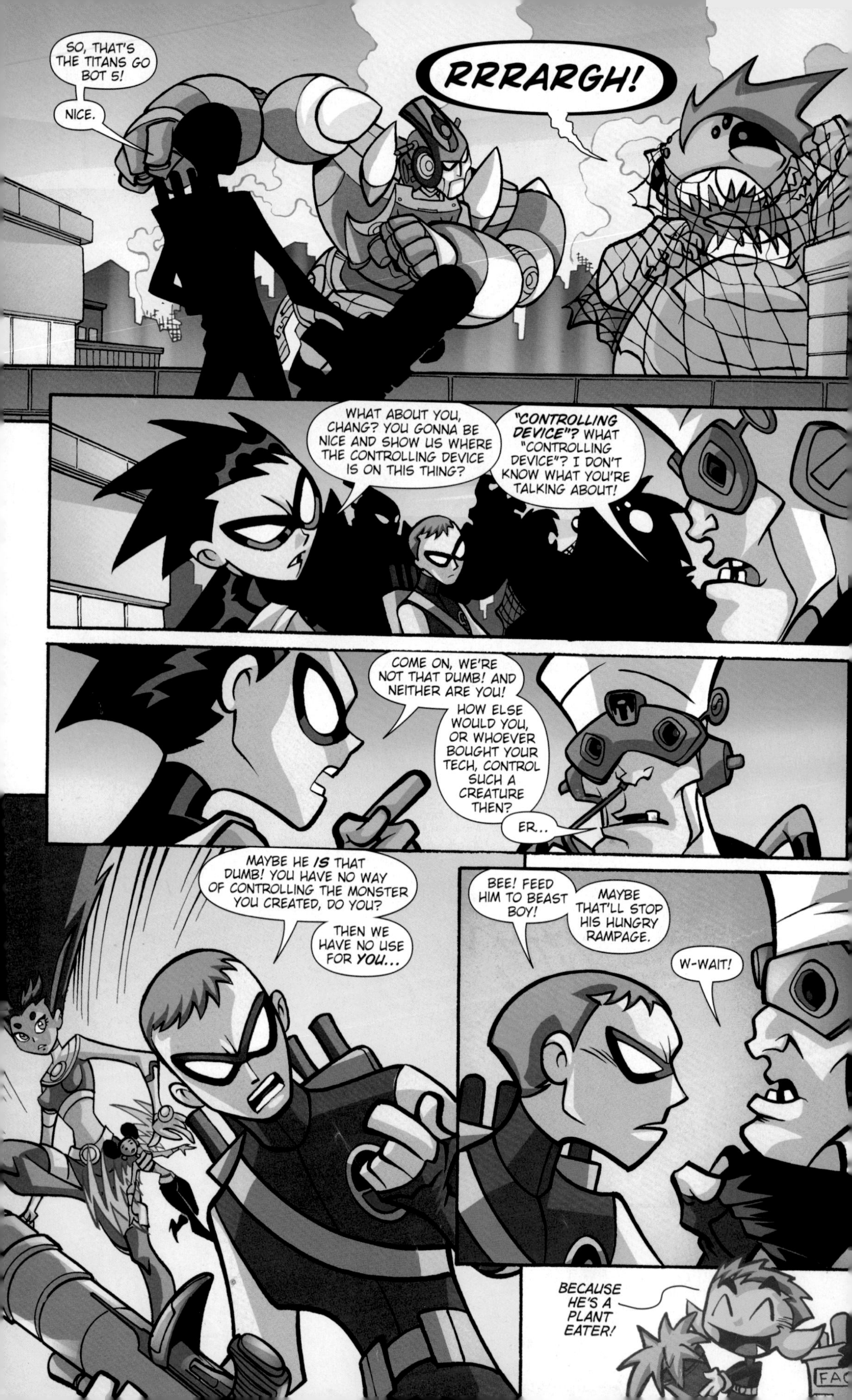

SO, THAT'S THE TITANS GO BOT 5!
NICE.
RRRARGH!
WHAT ABOUT YOU, CHANG? YOU GONNA BE NICE AND SHOW US WHERE THE CONTROLLING DEVICE IS ON THIS THING?
"CONTROLLING DEVICE"? WHAT "CONTROLLING DEVICE"? I DON'T KNOW WHAT YOU'RE TALKING ABOUT!
COME ON, WE'RE NOT THAT DUMB! AND NEITHER ARE YOU!
HOW ELSE WOULD YOU, OR WHOEVER BOUGHT YOUR TECH, CONTROL SUCH A CREATURE THEN?
ER...
MAYBE HE IS THAT DUMB! YOU HAVE NO WAY OF CONTROLLING THE MONSTER YOU CREATED, DO YOU?
THEN WE HAVE NO USE FOR YOU...
BEE! FEED HIM TO BEAST BOY!
MAYBE THAT'LL STOP HIS HUNGRY RAMPAGE.
W-WAIT!
BECAUSE HE'S A PLANT EATER!

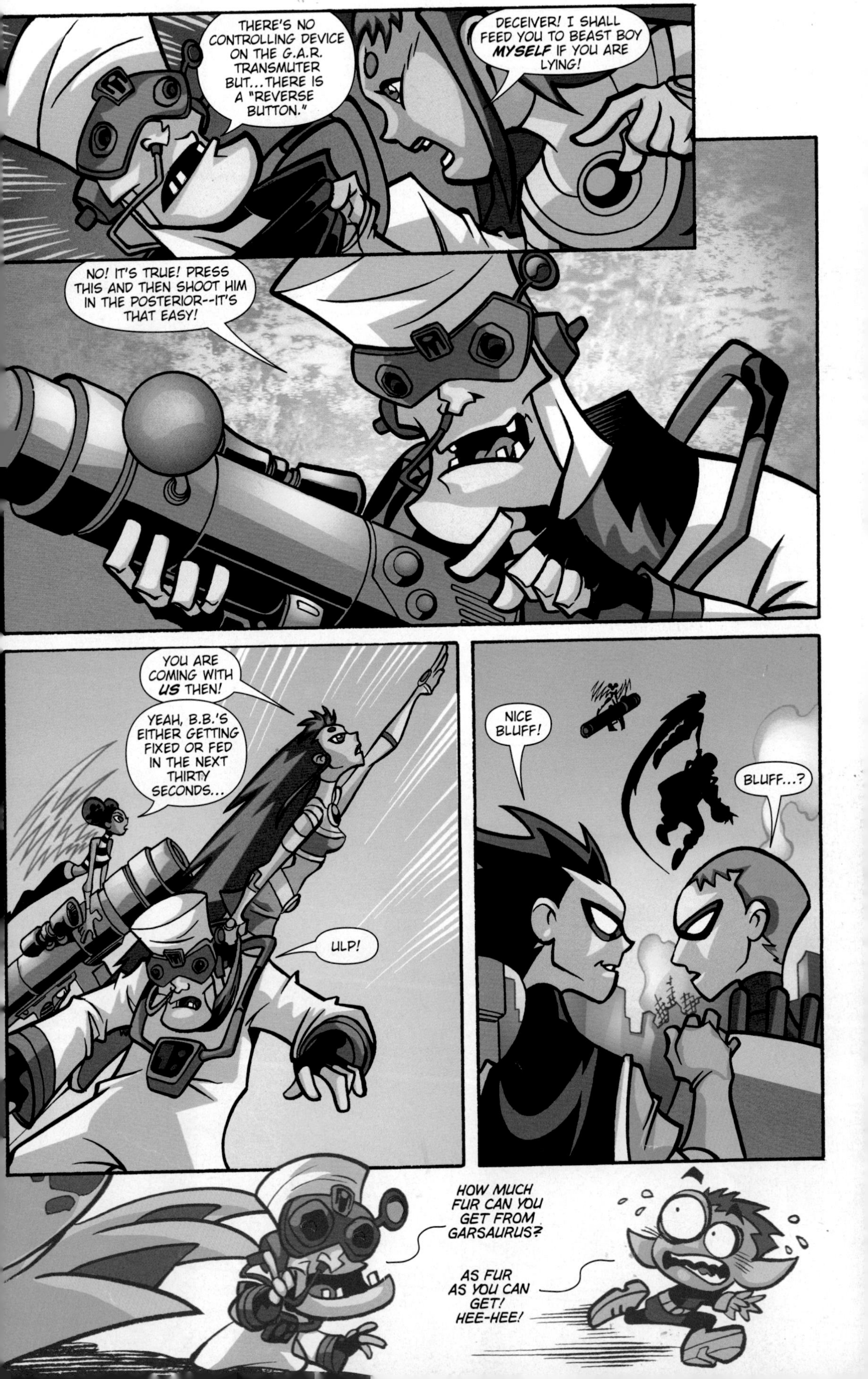
THERE'S NO CONTROLLING DEVICE ON THE G.A.R. TRANSMUTER BUT...THERE IS A "REVERSE BUTTON."
DECEIVER! I SHALL FEED YOU TO BEAST BOY MYSELF IF YOU ARE LYING!
NO! IT'S TRUE! PRESS THIS AND THEN SHOOT HIM IN THE POSTERIOR--IT'S THAT EASY!
YOU ARE COMING WITH US THEN!
YEAH, B.B.'S EITHER GETTING FIXED OR FED IN THE NEXT THIRTY SECONDS...
ULP!
NICE BLUFF!
BLUFF...?
HOW MUCH FUR CAN YOU GET FROM GARSAURUS?
AS FUR AS YOU CAN GET! HEE-HEE!

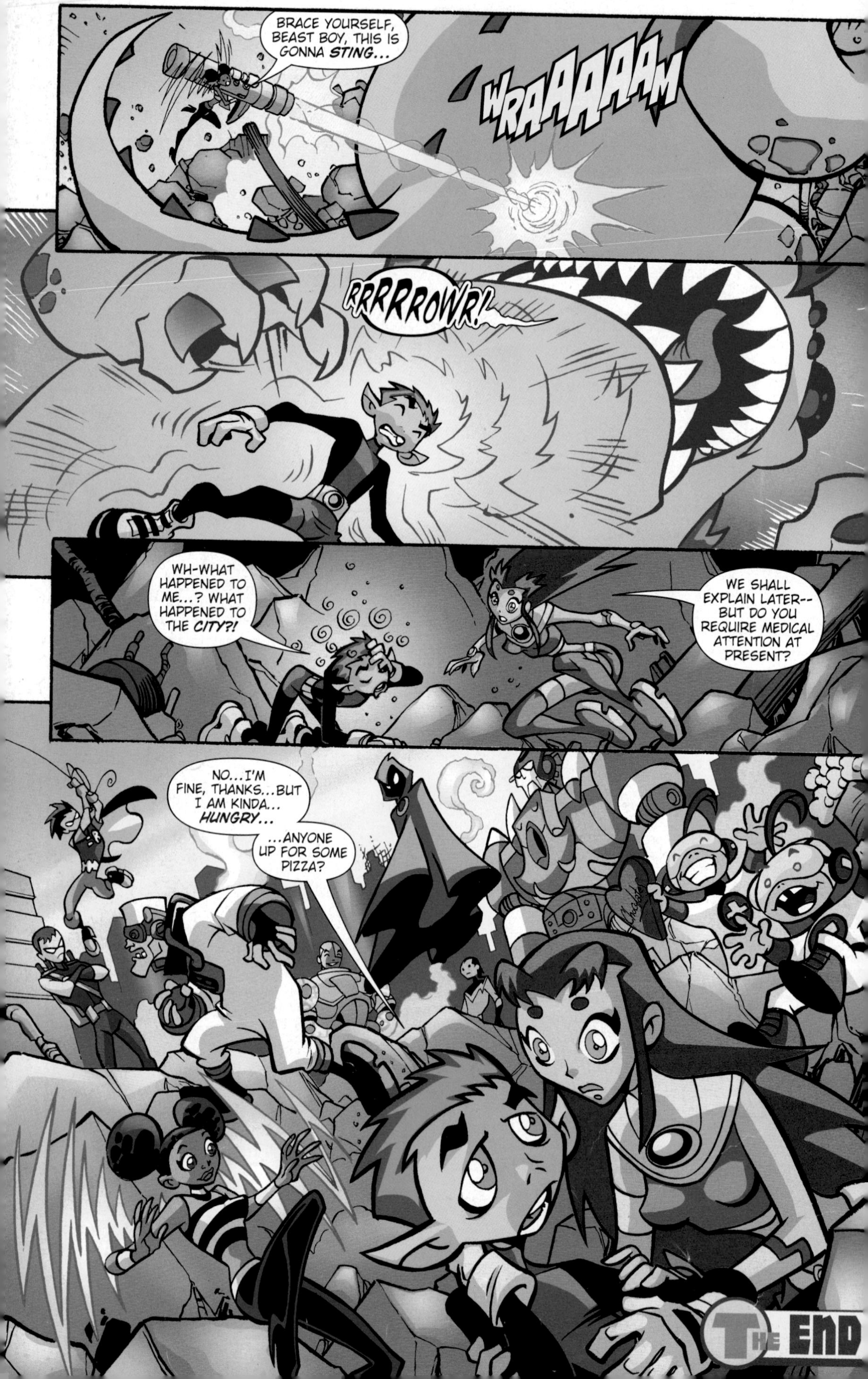
BRACE YOURSELF, BEAST BOY, THIS IS GONNA STING...
WRAAAAAM
RRRRROWR!
WH-WHAT HAPPENED TO ME...? WHAT HAPPENED TO THE CITY?!
WE SHALL EXPLAIN LATER-- BUT DO YOU REQUIRE MEDICAL ATTENTION AT PRESENT?
NO...I'M FINE, THANKS...BUT I AM KINDA... HUNGRY...
...ANYONE UP FOR SOME PIZZA?
THE END

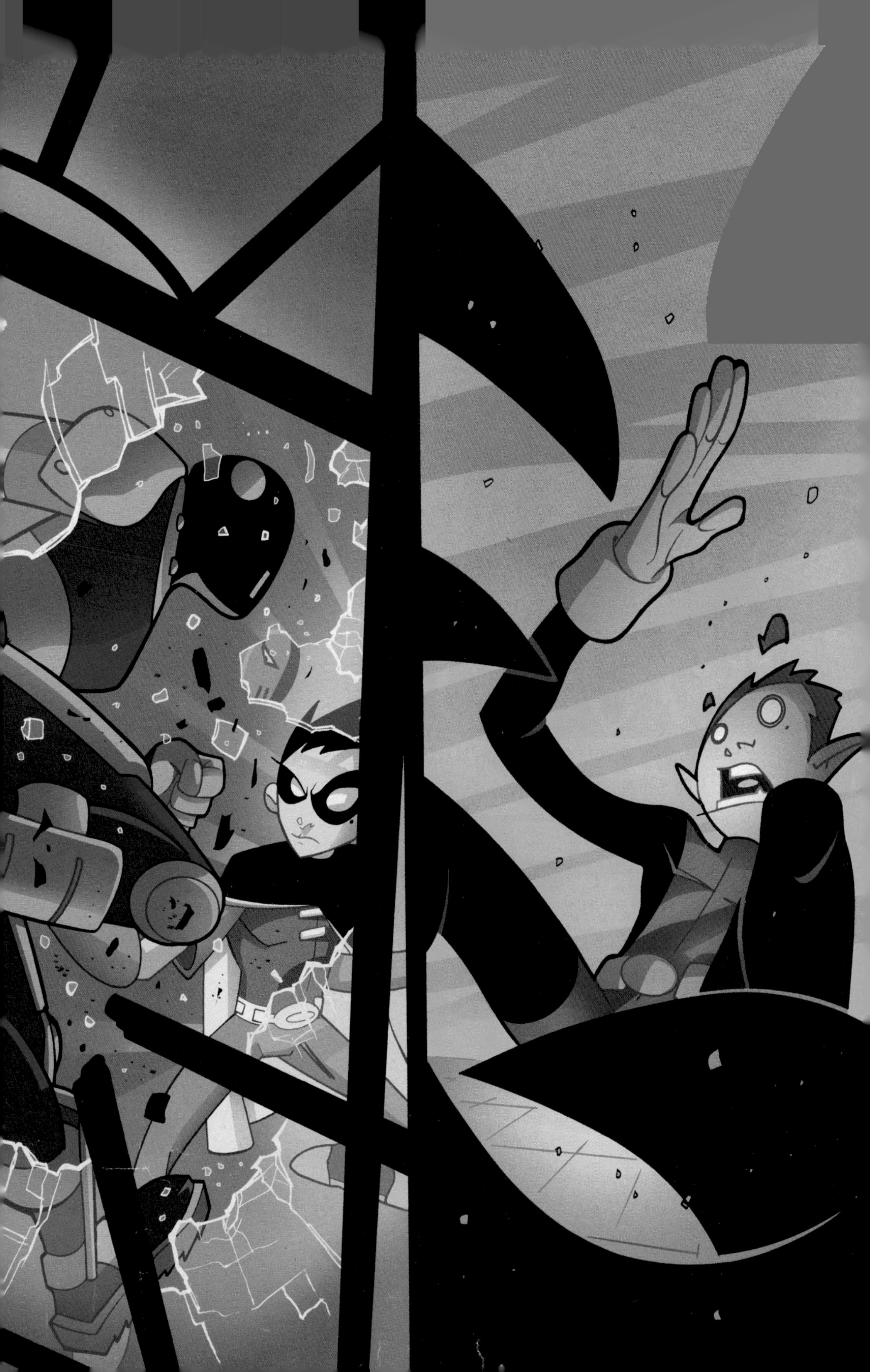

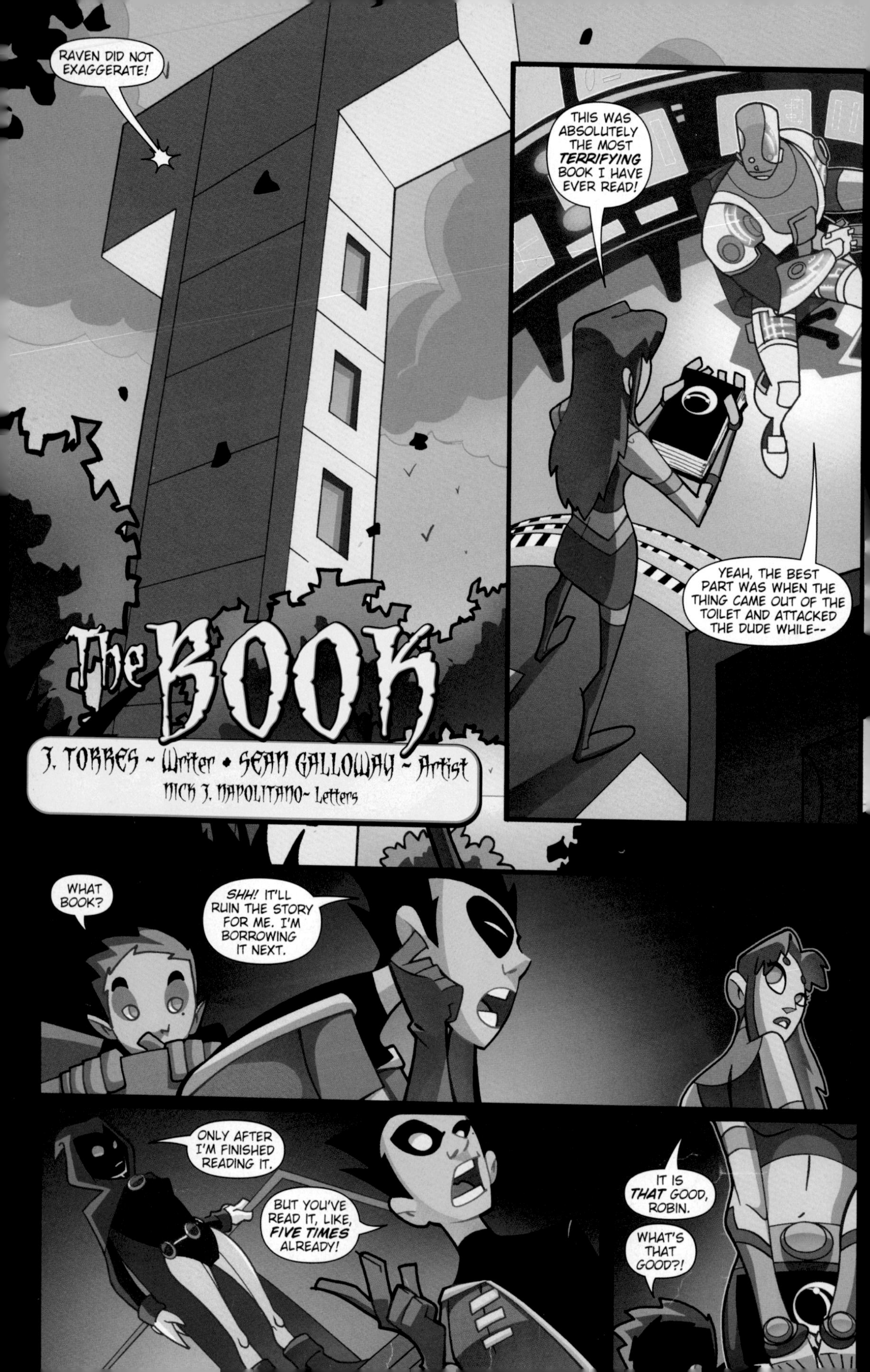

RAVEN DID NOT EXAGGERATE!
THIS WAS ABSOLUTELY THE MOST TERRIFYING BOOK I HAVE EVER READ!
YEAH, THE BEST PART WAS WHEN THE THING CAME OUT OF THE TOILET AND ATTACKED THE DUDE WHILE--
The BOOK
J. TORRES ~ Writer • SEAN GALLOWAY ~ Artist
NICK J. NAPOLITANO~ Letters
WHAT BOOK?
SHH! IT'LL RUIN THE STORY FOR ME. I'M BORROWING IT NEXT.
ONLY AFTER I'M FINISHED READING IT.
BUT YOU'VE READ IT, LIKE, FIVE TIMES ALREADY!
IT IS THAT GOOD, ROBIN.
WHAT'S THAT GOOD?!

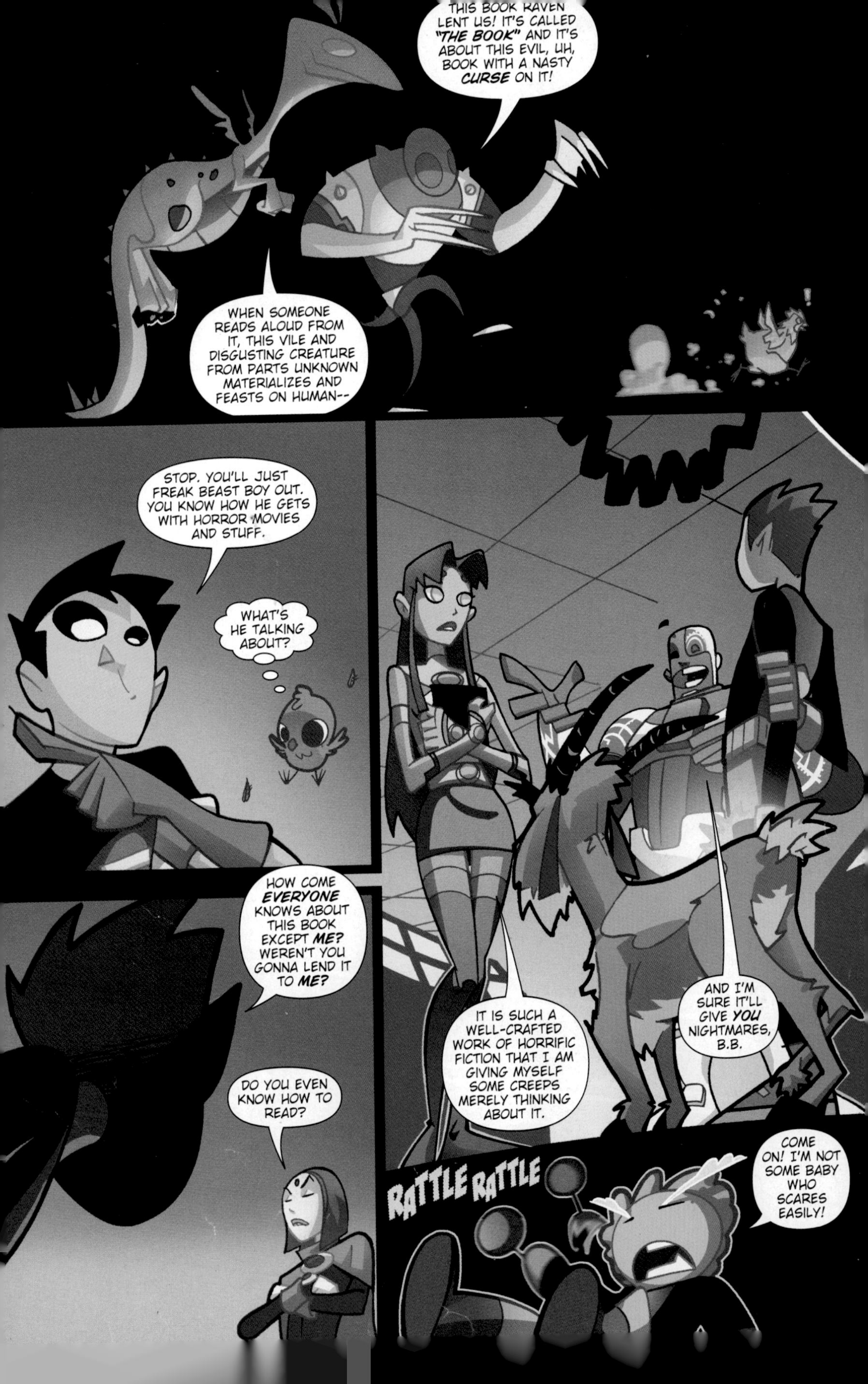
THIS BOOK RAVEN LENT US! IT'S CALLED "THE BOOK" AND IT'S ABOUT THIS EVIL, UH, BOOK WITH A NASTY CURSE ON IT!
WHEN SOMEONE READS ALOUD FROM IT, THIS VILE AND DISGUSTING CREATURE FROM PARTS UNKNOWN MATERIALIZES AND FEASTS ON HUMAN--
STOP. YOU'LL JUST FREAK BEAST BOY OUT. YOU KNOW HOW HE GETS WITH HORROR MOVIES AND STUFF.
WHAT'S HE TALKING ABOUT?
HOW COME EVERYONE KNOWS ABOUT THIS BOOK EXCEPT ME? WEREN'T YOU GONNA LEND IT TO ME?
DO YOU EVEN KNOW HOW TO READ?
IT IS SUCH A WELL-CRAFTED WORK OF HORRIFIC FICTION THAT I AM GIVING MYSELF SOME CREEPS MERELY THINKING ABOUT IT.
AND I'M SURE IT'LL GIVE YOU NIGHTMARES, B.B.
RATTLE RATTLE
COME ON! I'M NOT SOME BABY WHO SCARES EASILY!

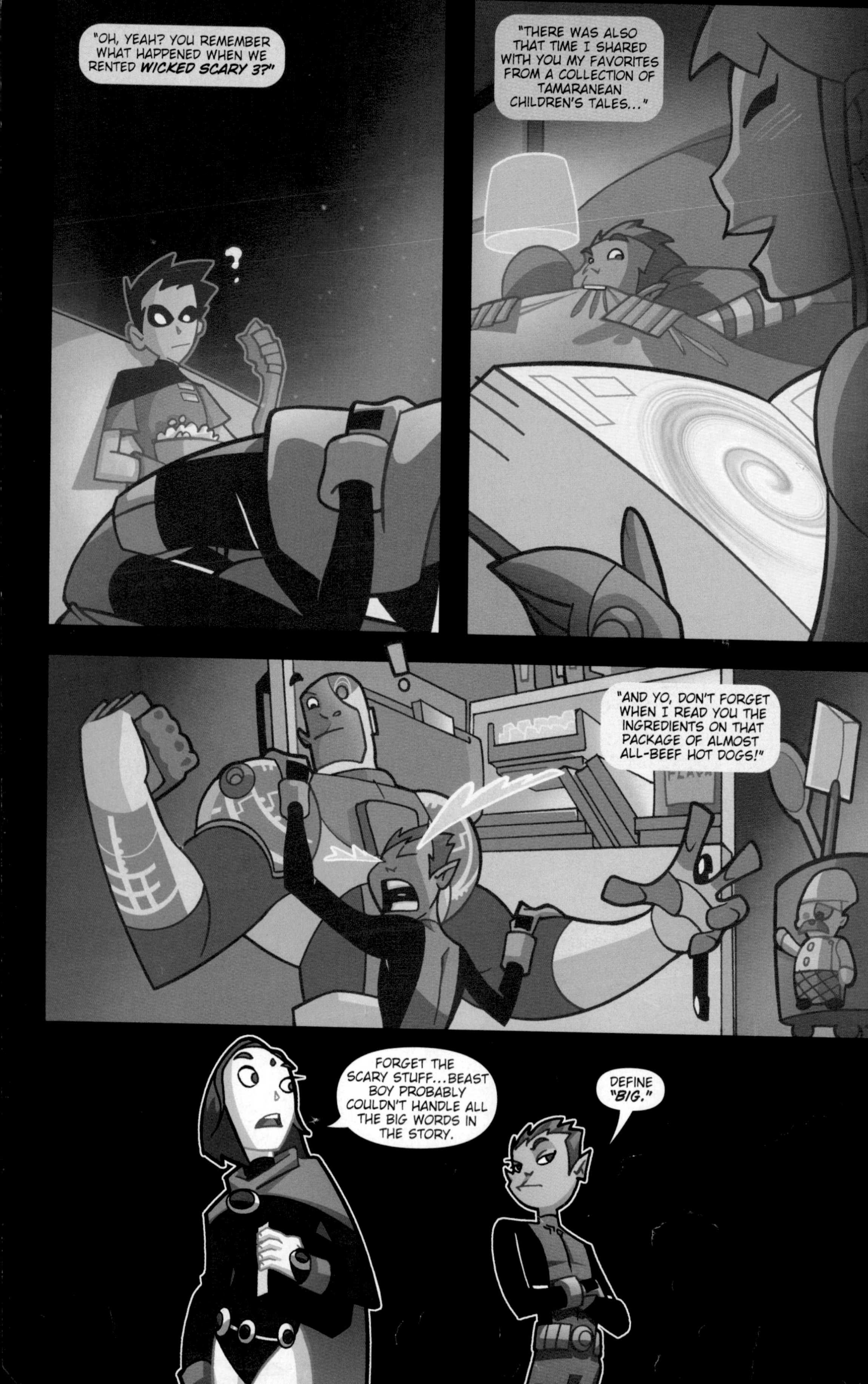
"OH, YEAH? YOU REMEMBER WHAT HAPPENED WHEN WE RENTED WICKED SCARY 3?"
?
"THERE WAS ALSO THAT TIME I SHARED WITH YOU MY FAVORITES FROM A COLLECTION OF TAMARANEAN CHILDREN'S TALES..."
!
"AND YO, DON'T FORGET WHEN I READ YOU THE INGREDIENTS ON THAT PACKAGE OF ALMOST ALL-BEEF HOT DOGS!"
FORGET THE SCARY STUFF...BEAST BOY PROBABLY COULDN'T HANDLE ALL THE BIG WORDS IN THE STORY.
DEFINE "BIG."

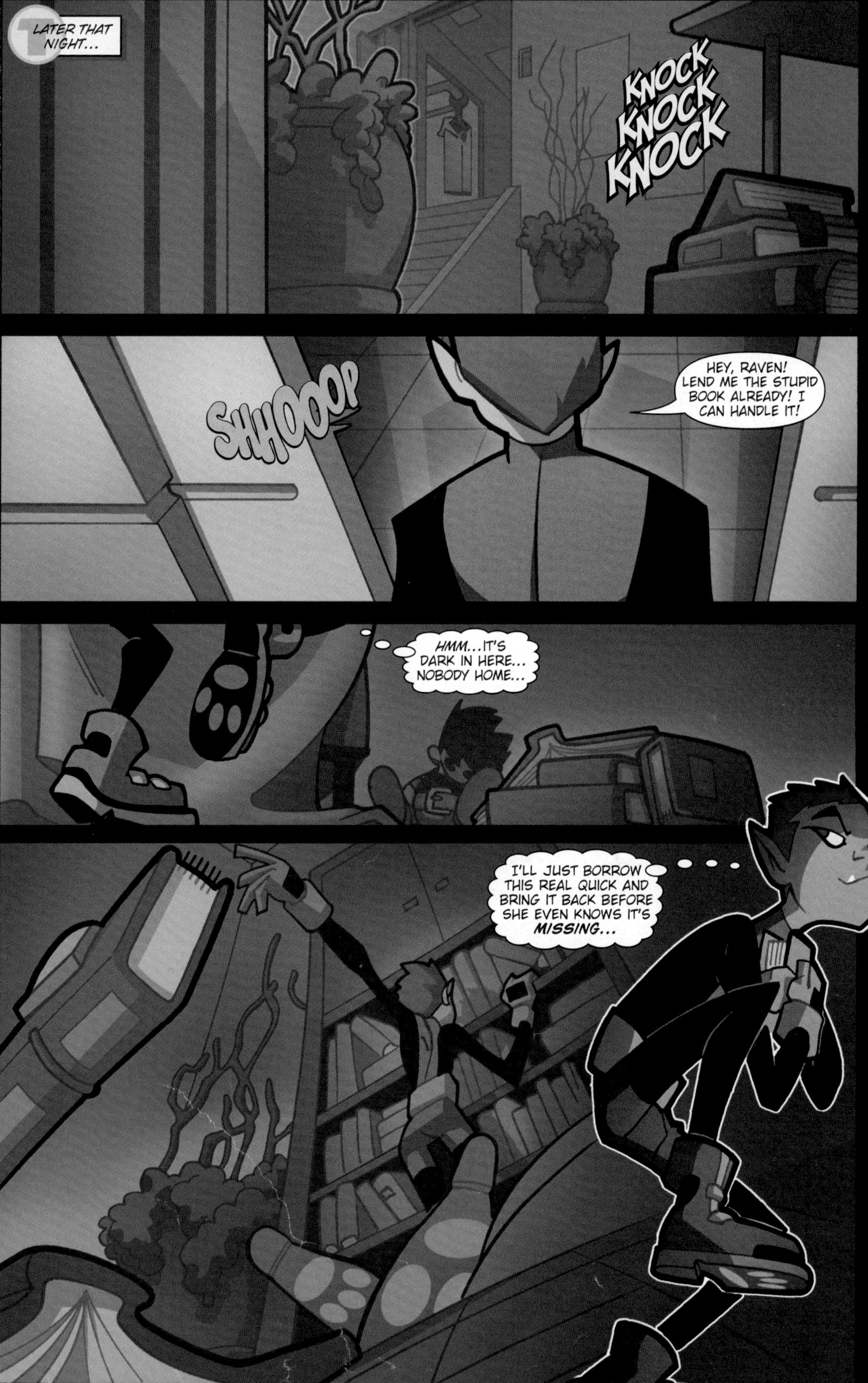
LATER THAT NIGHT...
KNOCK KNOCK KNOCK
SHHOOOP
HEY, RAVEN! LEND ME THE STUPID BOOK ALREADY! I CAN HANDLE IT!
HMM...IT'S DARK IN HERE... NOBODY HOME...
I'LL JUST BORROW THIS REAL QUICK AND BRING IT BACK BEFORE SHE EVEN KNOWS IT'S MISSING...

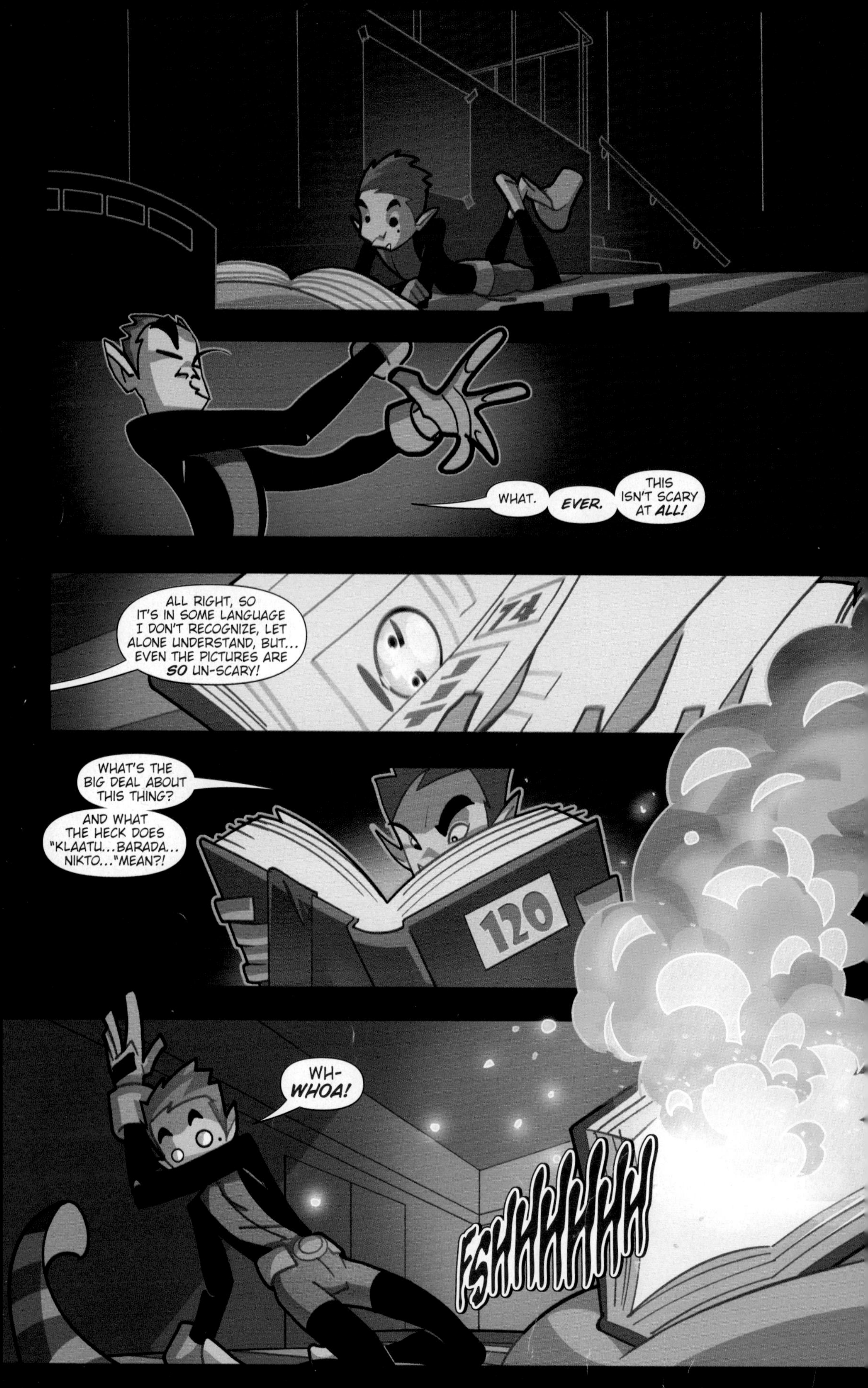
WHAT.
EVER.
THIS ISN'T SCARY AT ALL!
ALL RIGHT, SO IT'S IN SOME LANGUAGE I DON'T RECOGNIZE, LET ALONE UNDERSTAND, BUT... EVEN THE PICTURES ARE SO UN-SCARY!
74
WHAT'S THE BIG DEAL ABOUT THIS THING?
AND WHAT THE HECK DOES "KLAATU...BARADA... NIKTO..."MEAN?!
120
WH- WHOA!
FSHHHHHHH

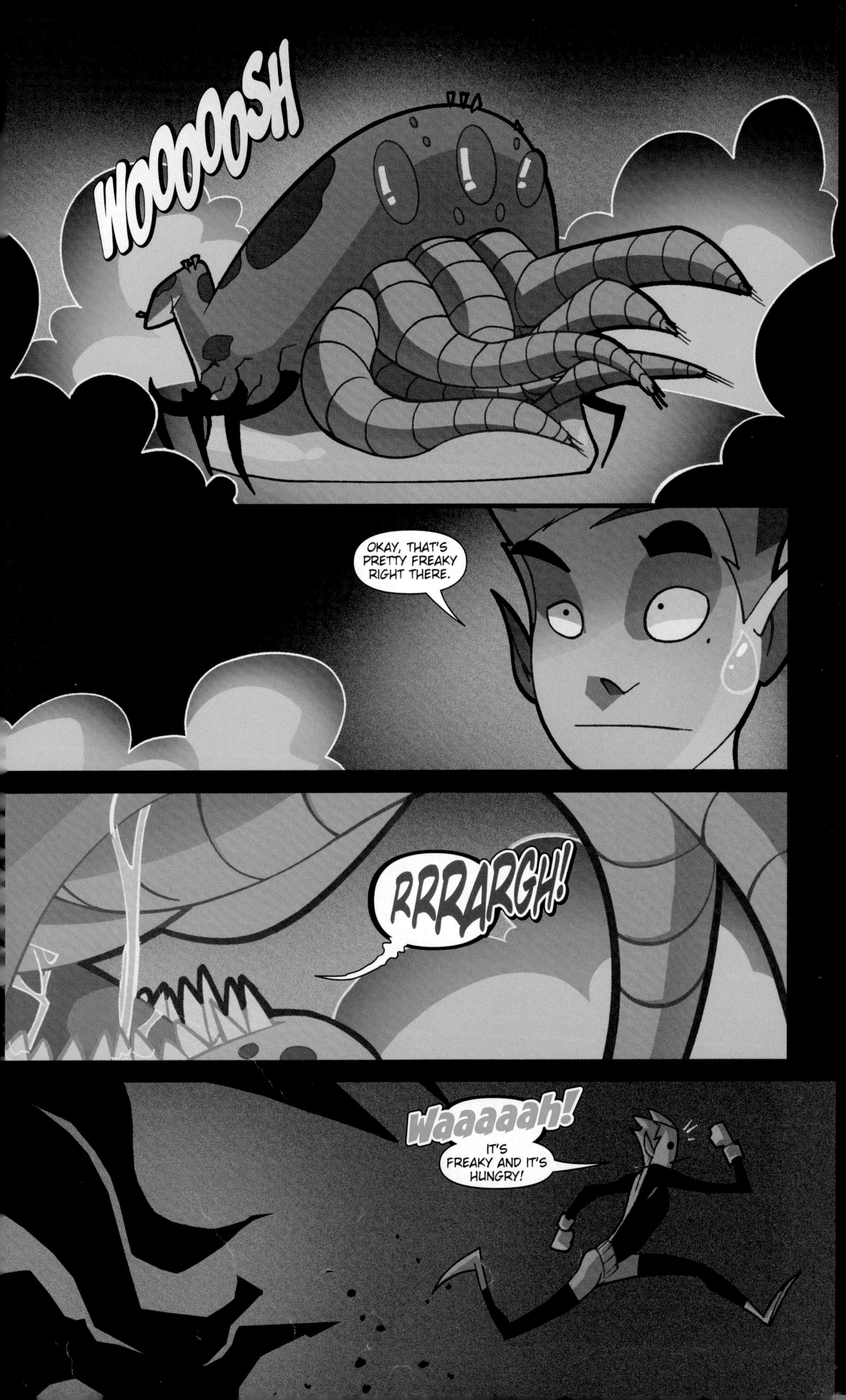
WOOOOOSH
OKAY, THAT'S PRETTY FREAKY RIGHT THERE.
RRRARGH!
Waaaaah!
IT'S FREAKY AND IT'S HUNGRY!

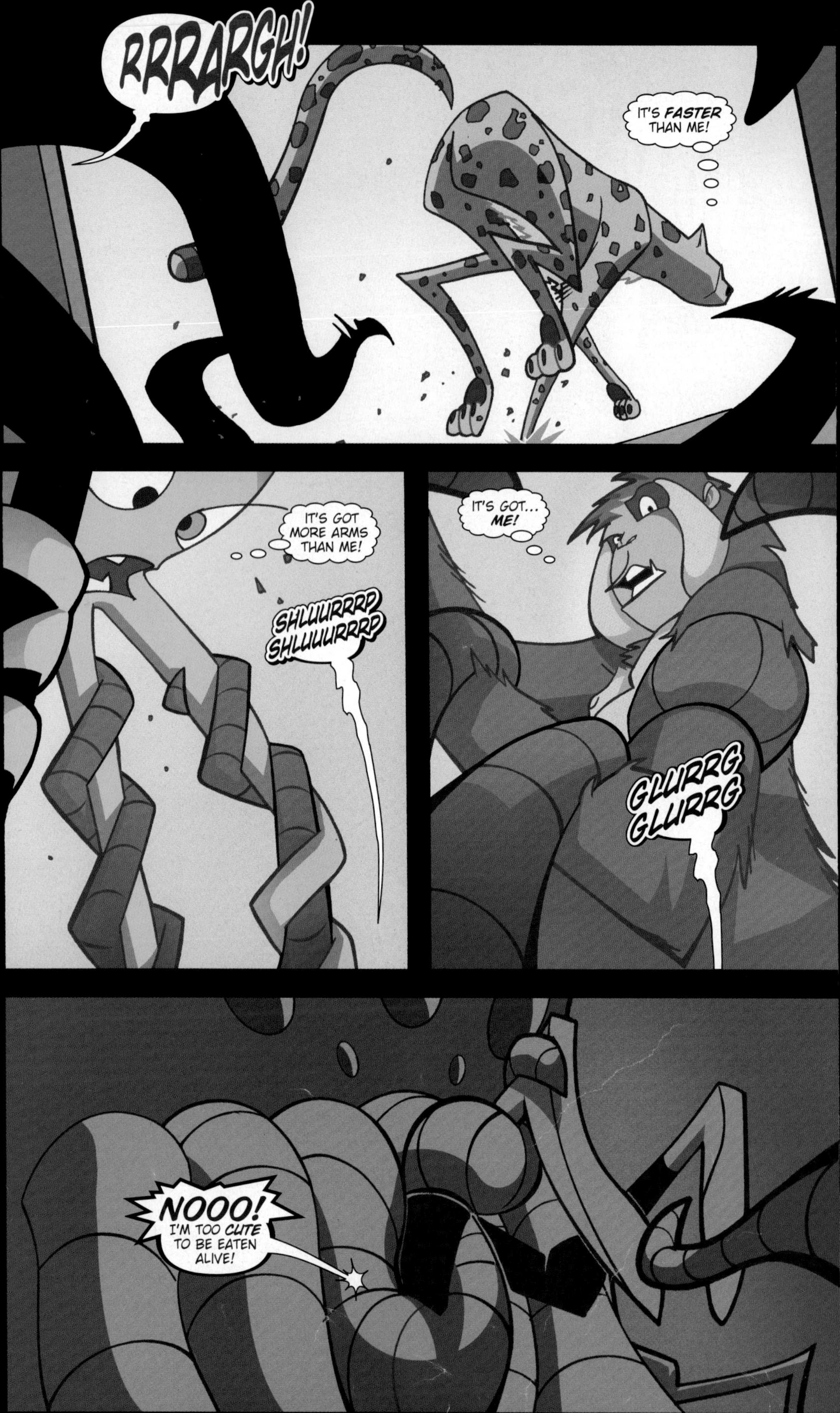
RRRARGH!
IT'S FASTER THAN ME!
IT'S GOT MORE ARMS THAN ME!
SHLUURRRP SHLUUURRRP
IT'S GOT... ME!
GLURRG GLURRG
NOOO! I'M TOO CUTE TO BE EATEN ALIVE!

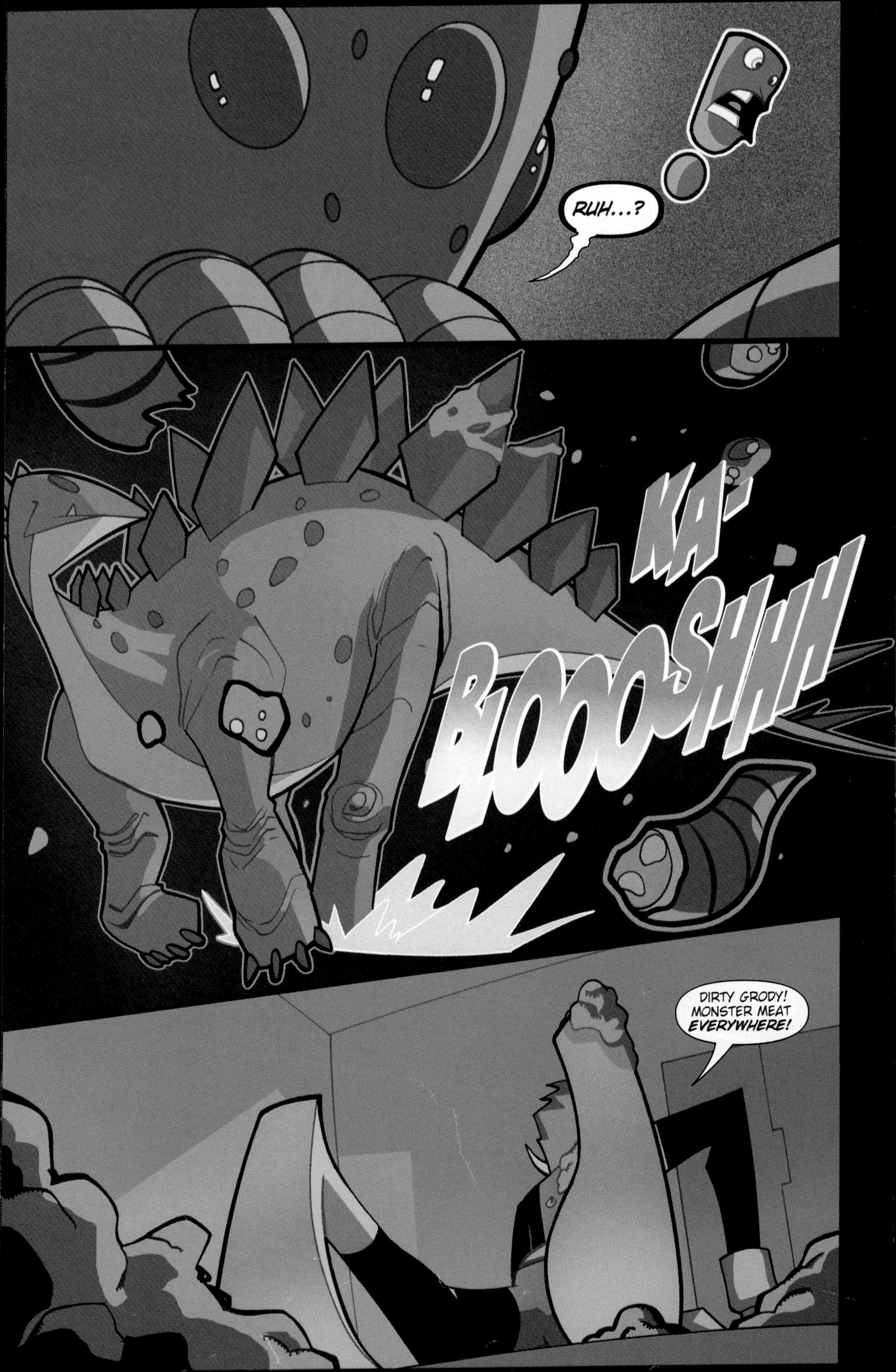
RUH...?
KA-BLOOOSHHH
DIRTY GRODY! MONSTER MEAT EVERYWHERE!

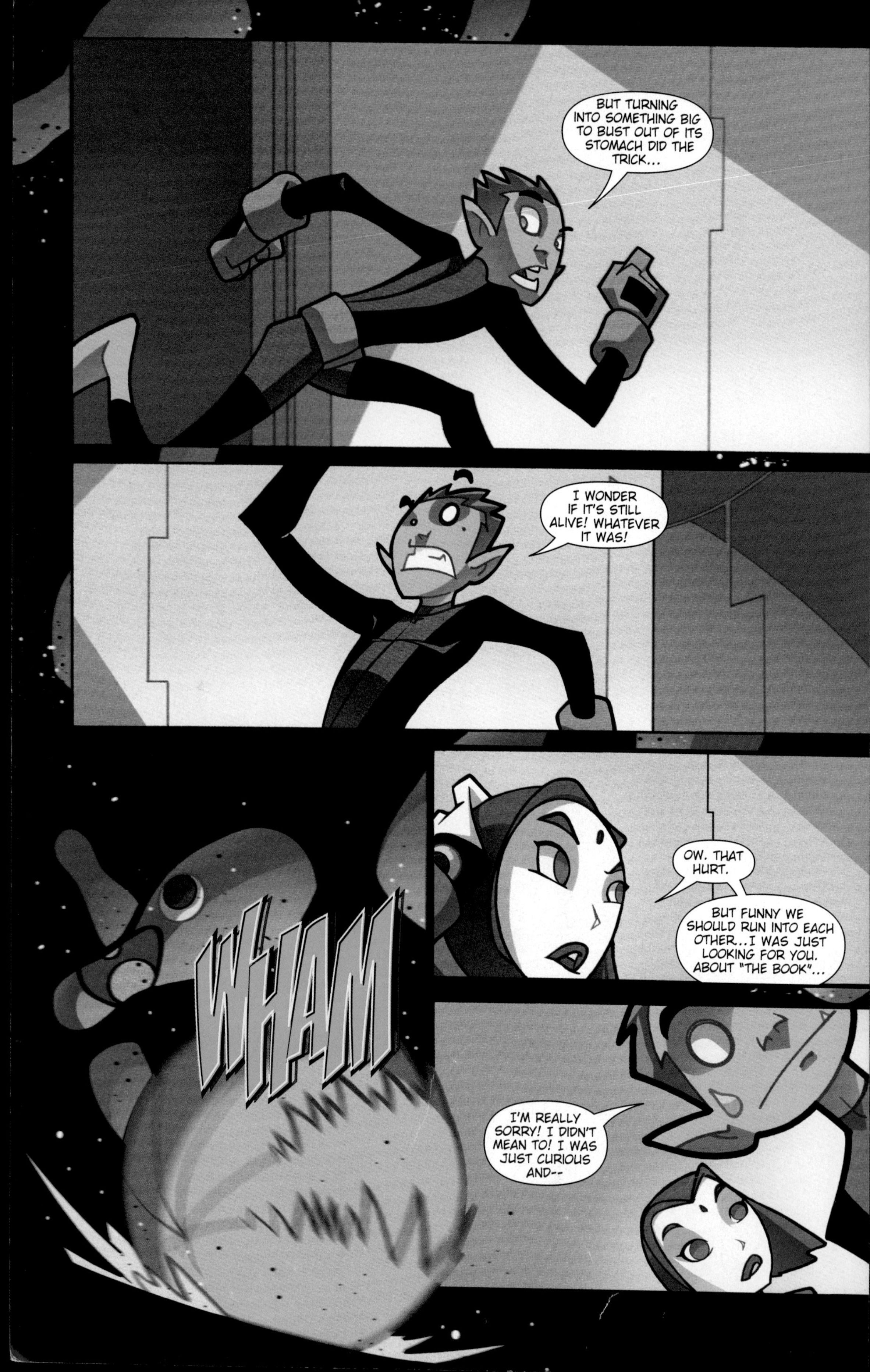
BUT TURNING INTO SOMETHING BIG TO BUST OUT OF ITS STOMACH DID THE TRICK...
I WONDER IF IT'S STILL ALIVE! WHATEVER IT WAS!
WHAM
OW. THAT HURT.
BUT FUNNY WE SHOULD RUN INTO EACH OTHER...I WAS JUST LOOKING FOR YOU. ABOUT "THE BOOK"...
I'M REALLY SORRY! I DIDN'T MEAN TO! I WAS JUST CURIOUS AND--

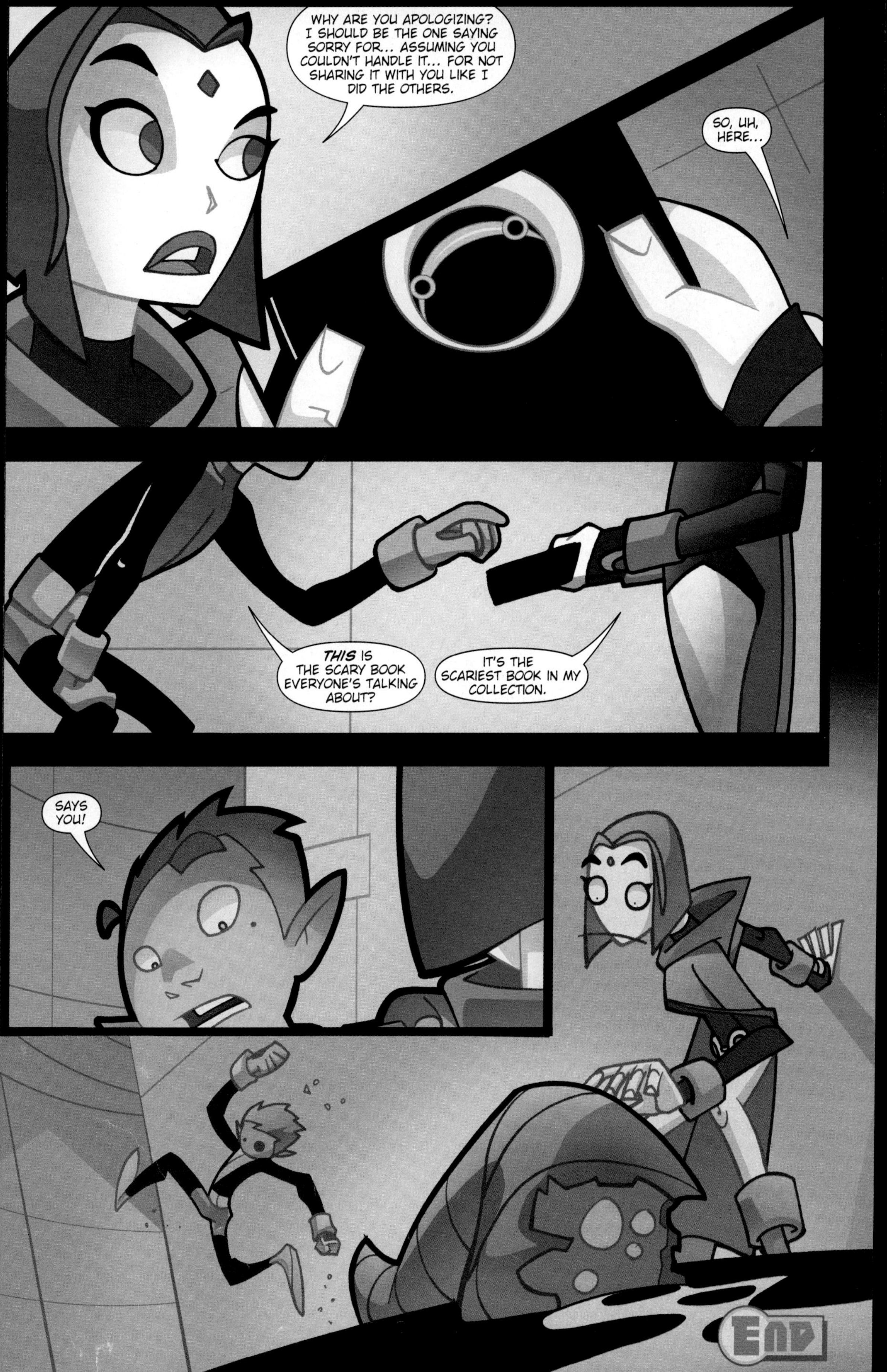

WHY ARE YOU APOLOGIZING? I SHOULD BE THE ONE SAYING SORRY FOR... ASSUMING YOU COULDN'T HANDLE IT... FOR NOT SHARING IT WITH YOU LIKE I DID THE OTHERS.
SO, UH, HERE...
THIS IS THE SCARY BOOK EVERYONE'S TALKING ABOUT?
IT'S THE SCARIEST BOOK IN MY COLLECTION.
SAYS YOU!
END

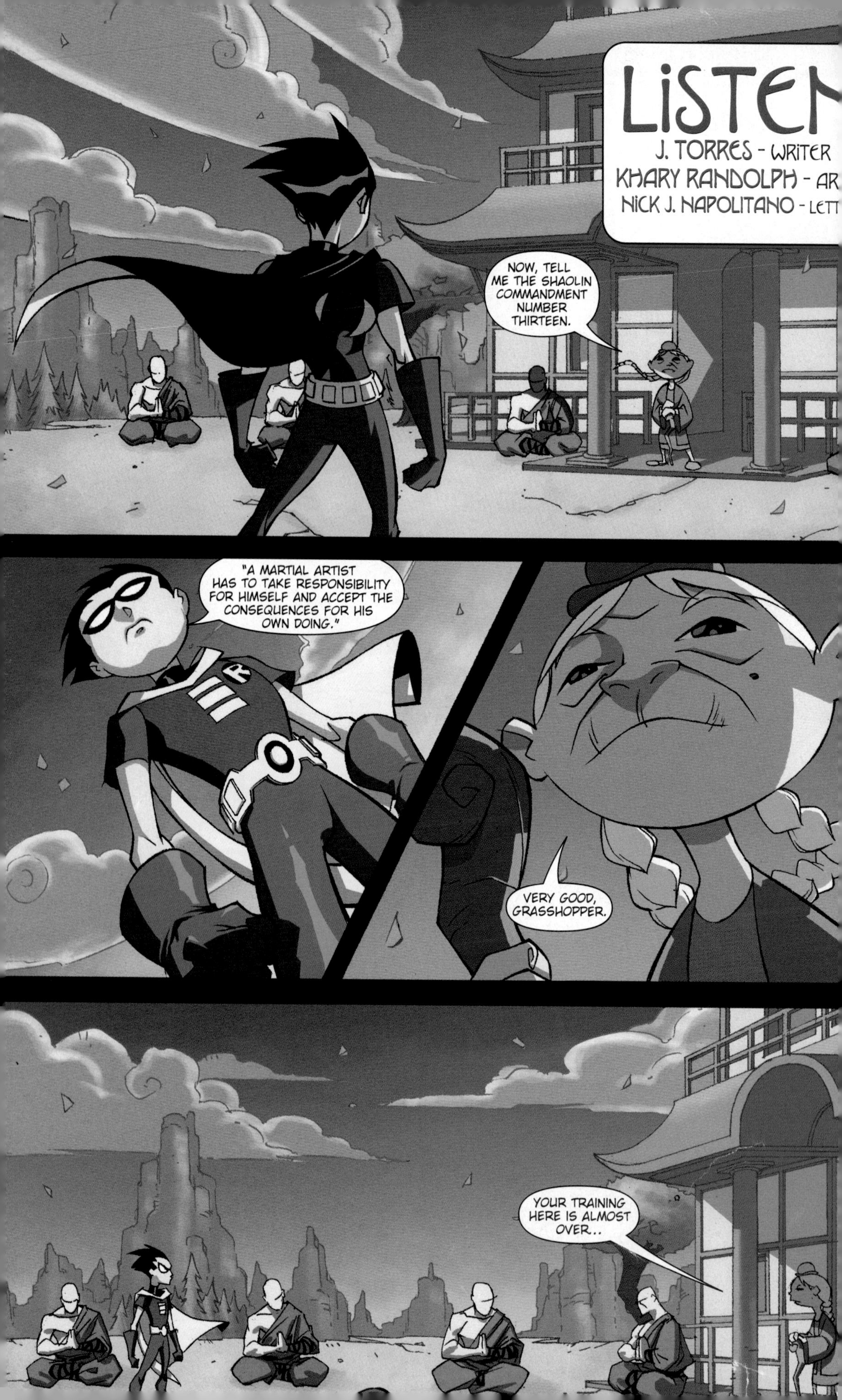

LiSTEN
J. TORRES - WRiTER
KHARY RANDOLPH - AR
NiCK J. NAPOLITANO - LETT
NOW, TELL ME THE SHAOLIN COMMANDMENT NUMBER THIRTEEN.
"A MARTIAL ARTIST HAS TO TAKE RESPONSIBILITY FOR HIMSELF AND ACCEPT THE CONSEQUENCES FOR HIS OWN DOING."
VERY GOOD, GRASSHOPPER.
YOUR TRAINING HERE IS ALMOST OVER...

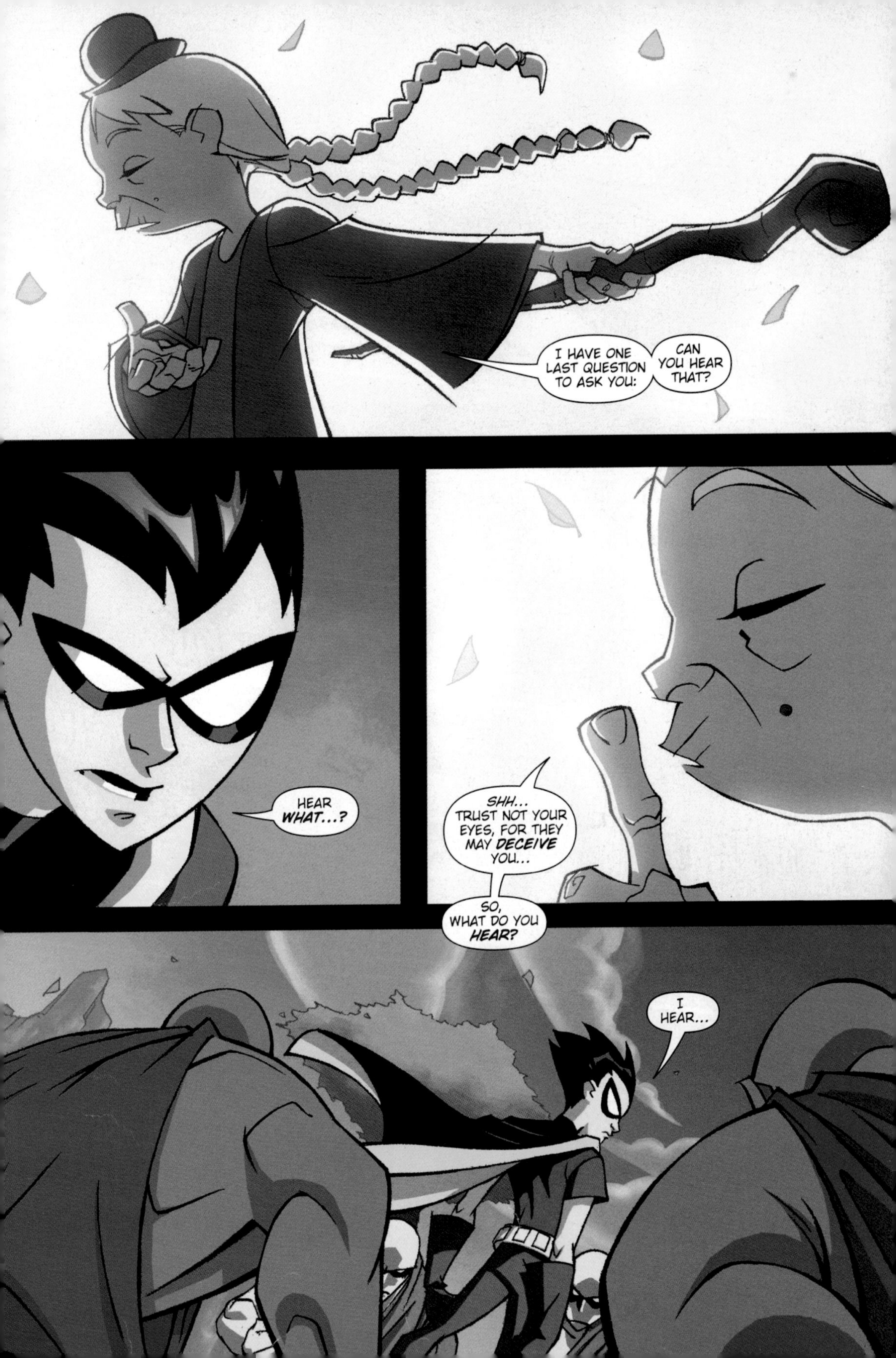
I HAVE ONE LAST QUESTION TO ASK YOU:
CAN YOU HEAR THAT?
HEAR WHAT...?
SHH... TRUST NOT YOUR EYES, FOR THEY MAY DECEIVE YOU...
SO, WHAT DO YOU HEAR?
I HEAR...

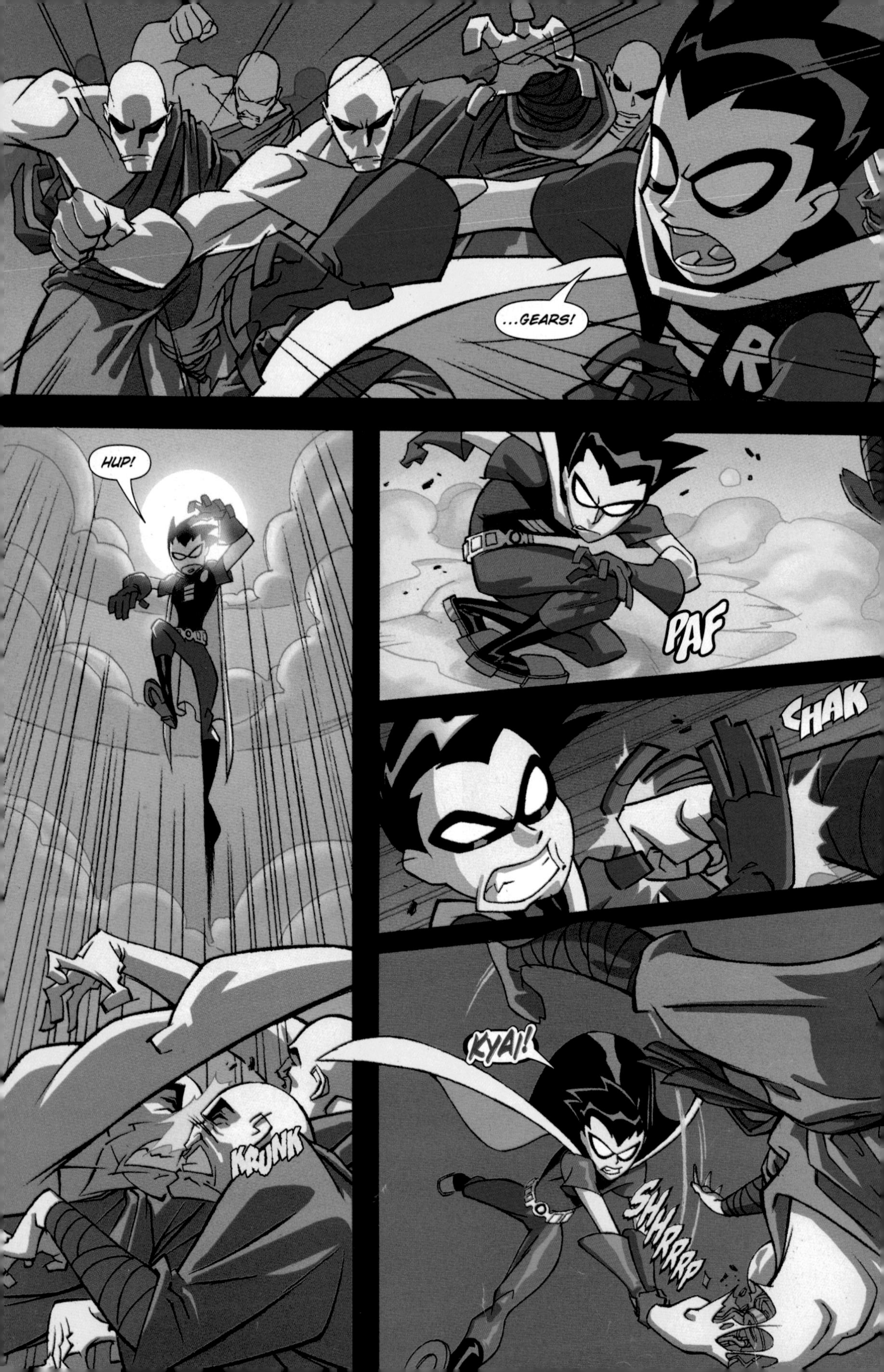
...GEARS!
HUP!
PAF
CHAK
KYAI!
KRUNK
SHHRRRP

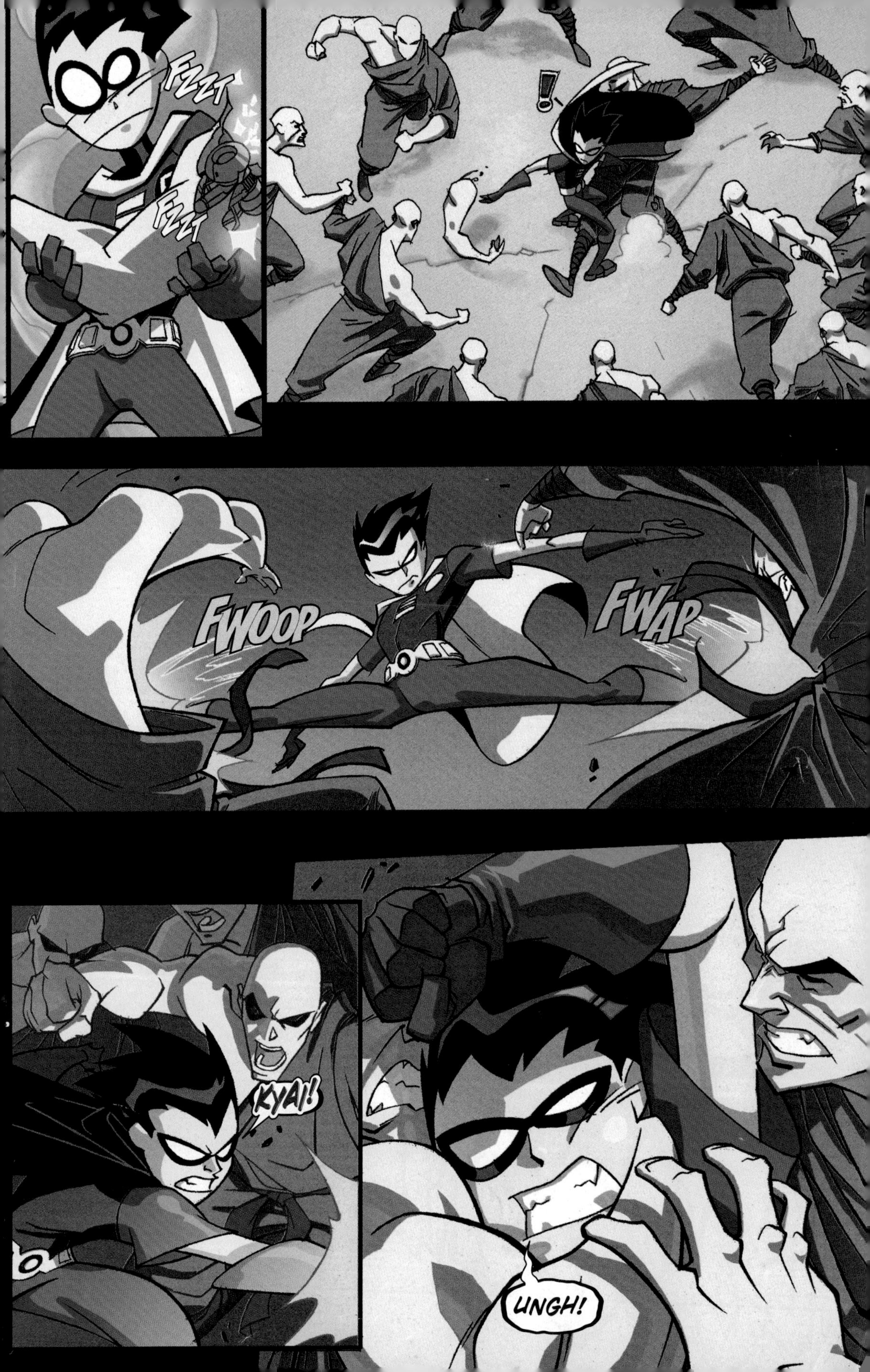

FZZZT
FZZZT
!
FWOOP
FWAP
KYAI!
UNGH!

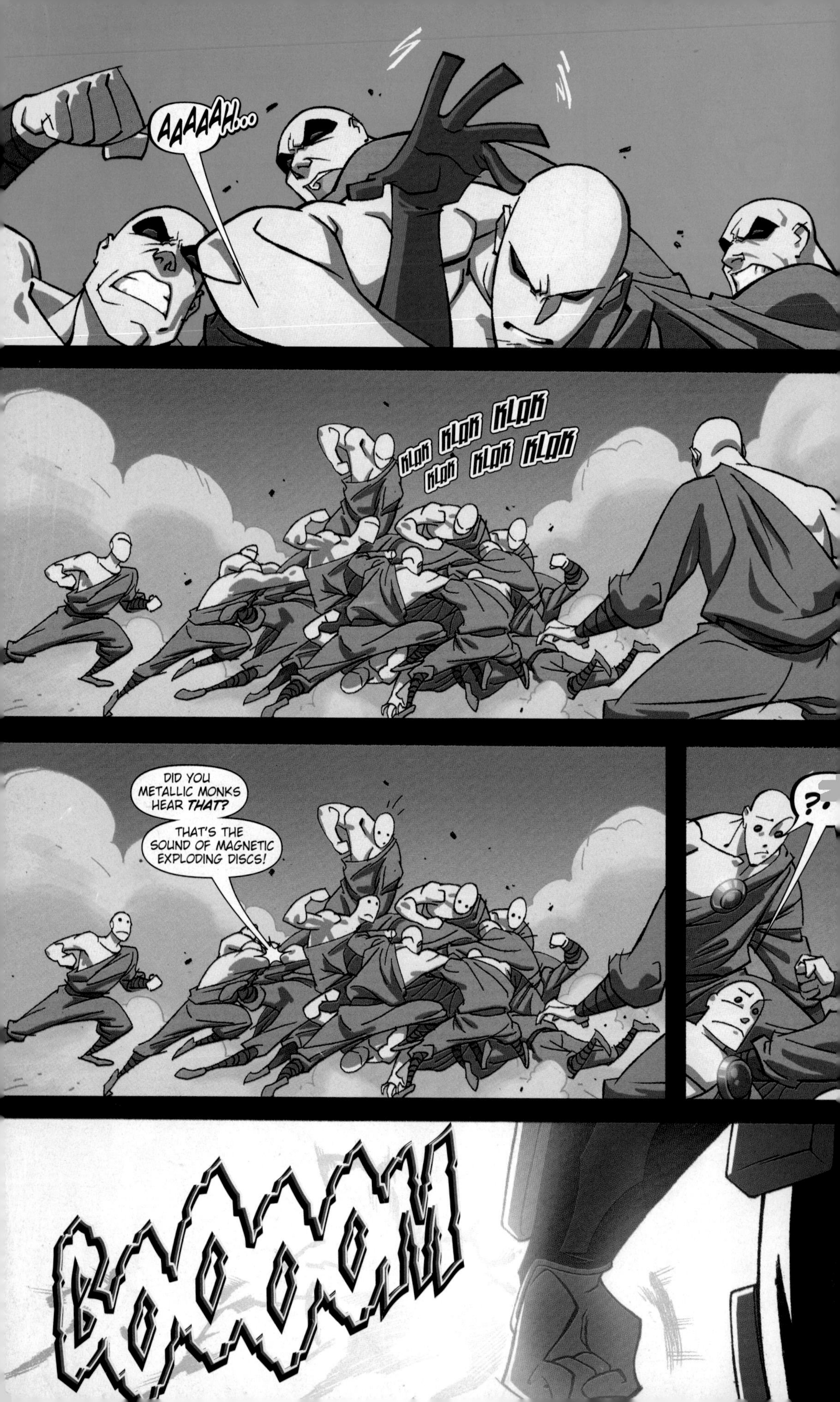

AAAAAH...
KLAK KLAK KLAK
KLAK KLAK KLAK
DID YOU METALLIC MONKS HEAR *THAT?*
THAT'S THE SOUND OF MAGNETIC EXPLODING DISCS!
?
BOOOOOM

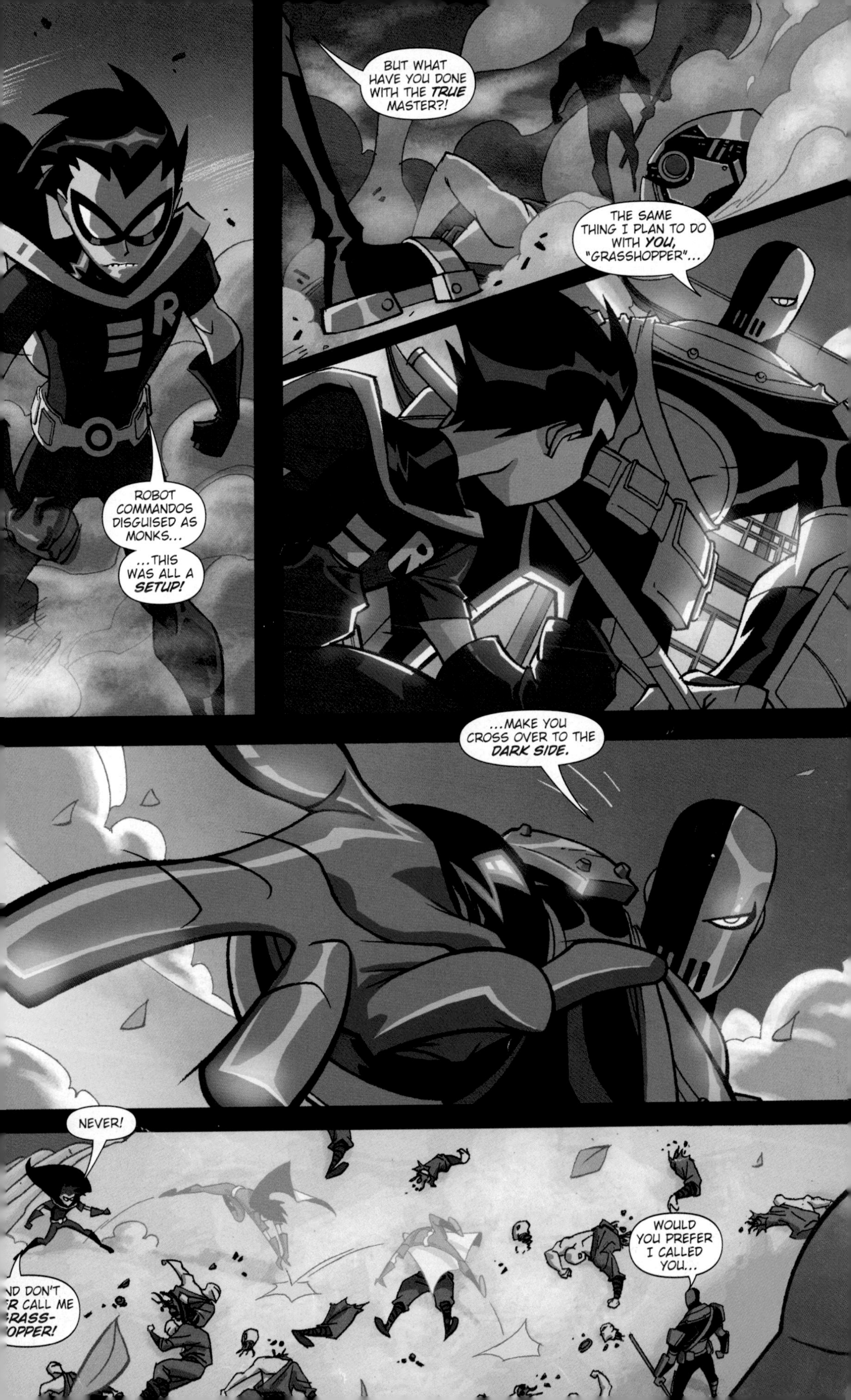
ROBOT COMMANDOS DISGUISED AS MONKS...
...THIS WAS ALL A SETUP!
BUT WHAT HAVE YOU DONE WITH THE TRUE MASTER?!
THE SAME THING I PLAN TO DO WITH YOU, "GRASSHOPPER"...
...MAKE YOU CROSS OVER TO THE DARK SIDE.
NEVER!
ND DON'T CALL ME RASS-OPPER!
WOULD YOU PREFER I CALLED YOU...

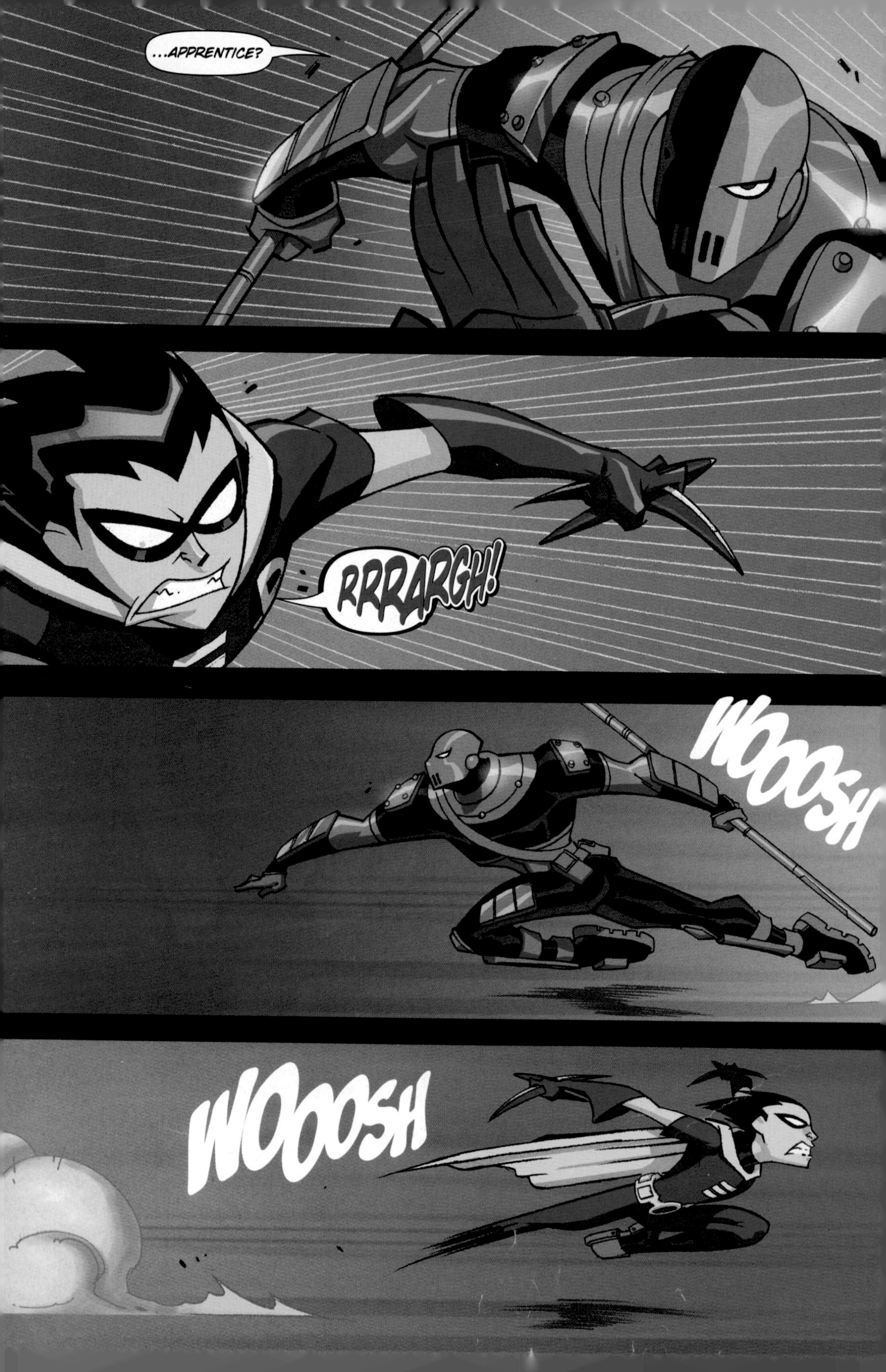
...APPRENTICE?
RRRARGH!
WOOOSH
WOOOSH

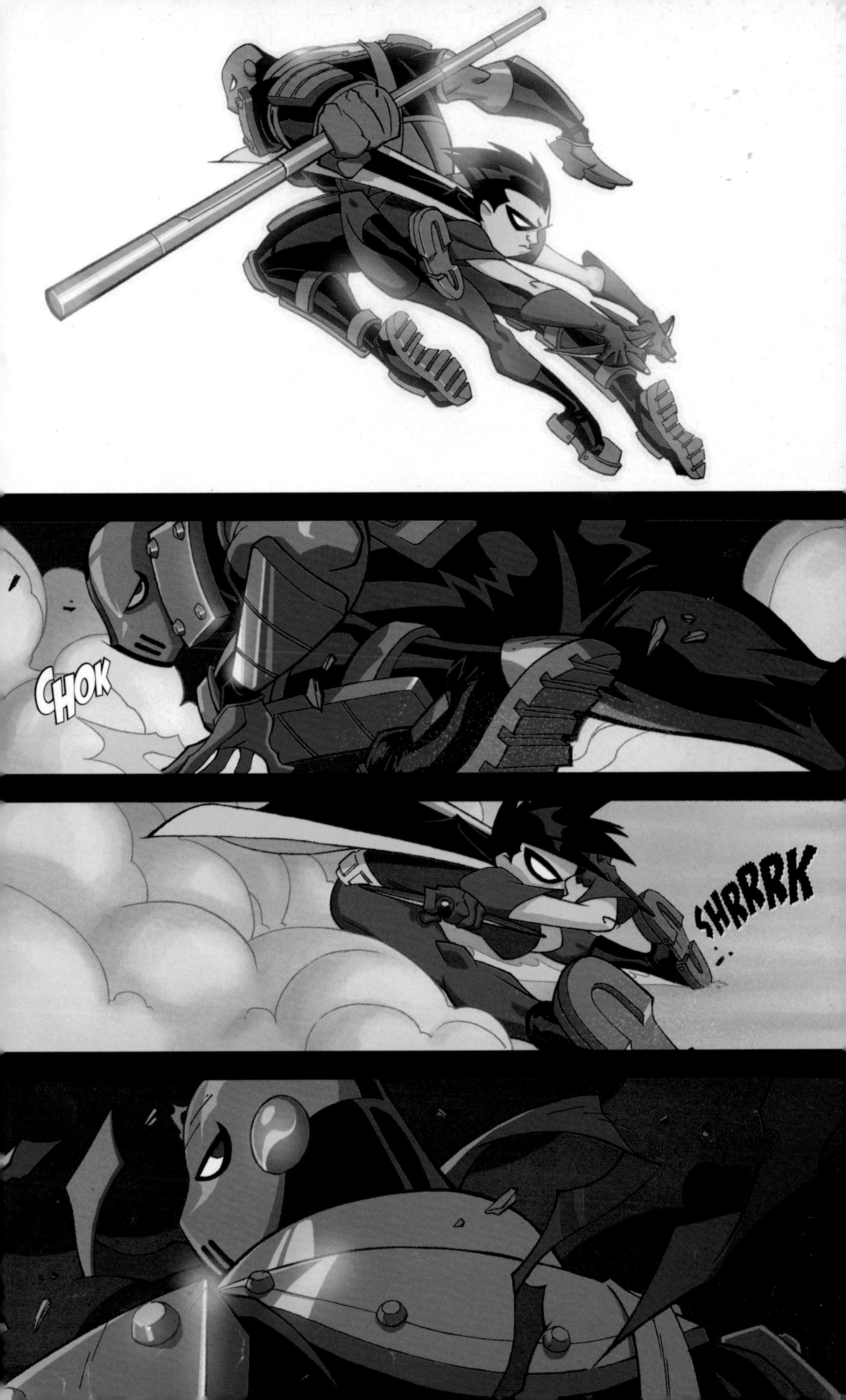
CHOK
SHRRRK

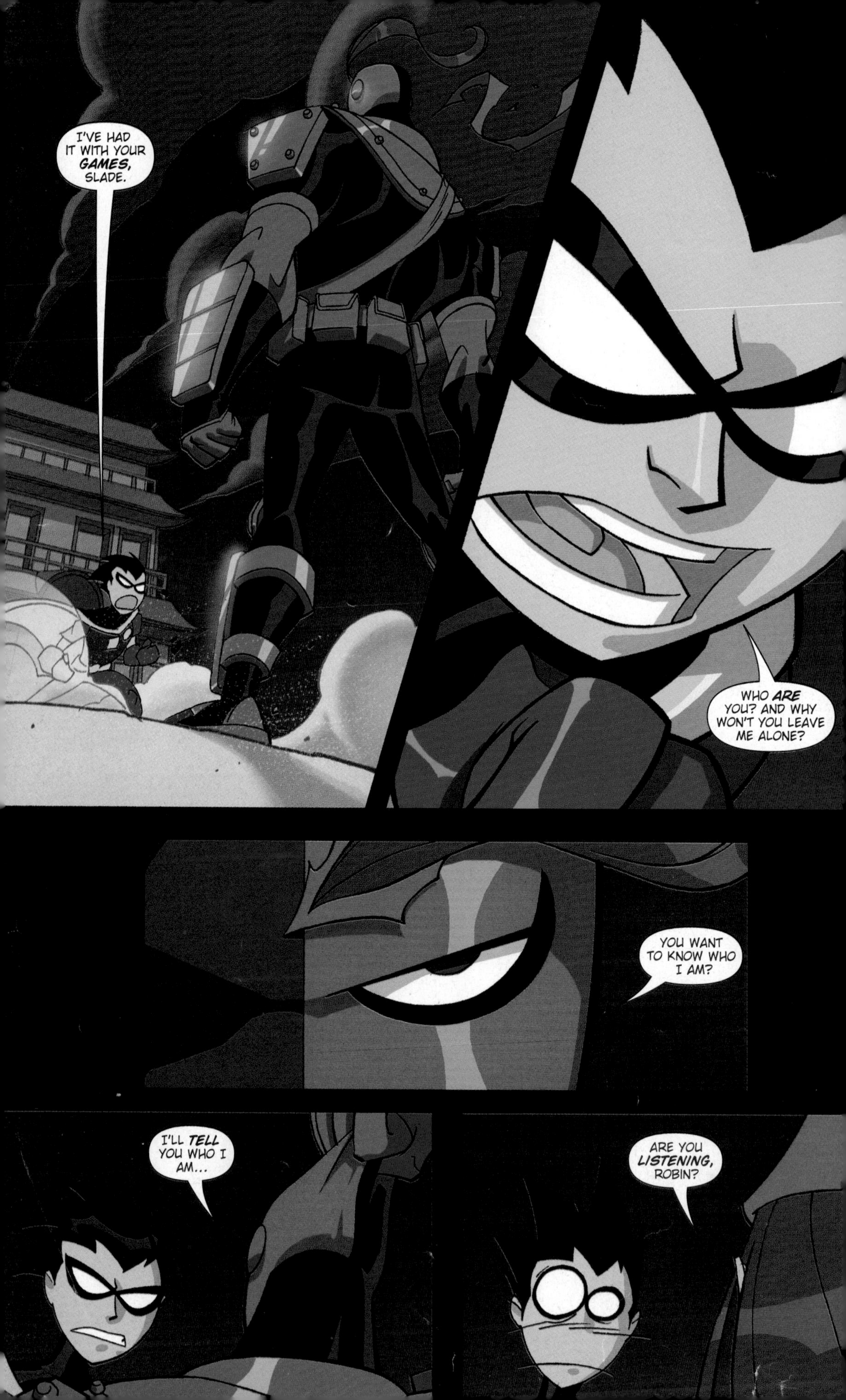
I'VE HAD IT WITH YOUR GAMES, SLADE.
WHO ARE YOU? AND WHY WON'T YOU LEAVE ME ALONE?
YOU WANT TO KNOW WHO I AM?
I'LL TELL YOU WHO I AM...
ARE YOU LISTENING, ROBIN?

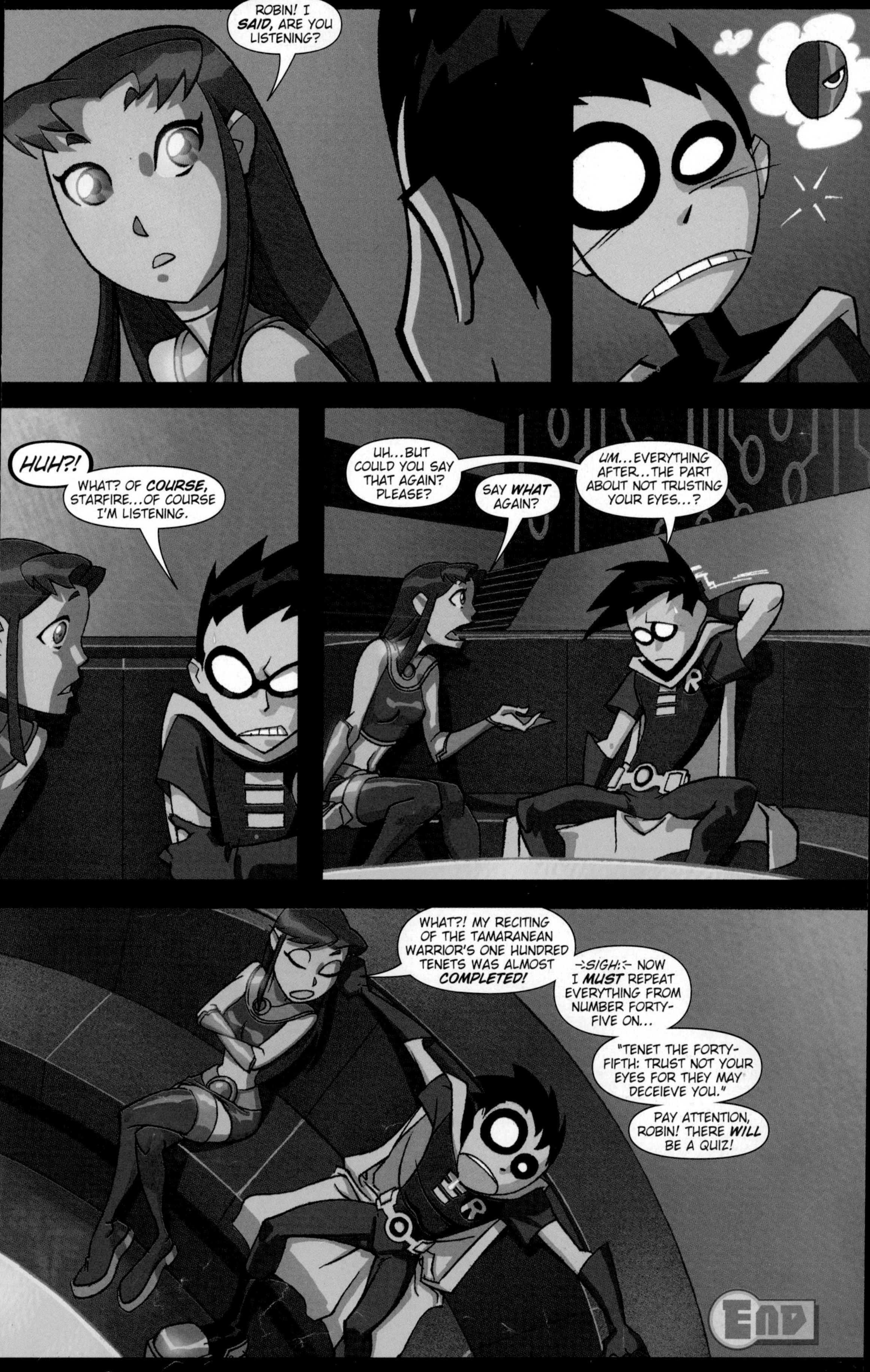

ROBIN! I SAID, ARE YOU LISTENING?
HUH?!
WHAT? OF COURSE, STARFIRE...OF COURSE I'M LISTENING.
UH...BUT COULD YOU SAY THAT AGAIN? PLEASE?
SAY WHAT AGAIN?
UM...EVERYTHING AFTER...THE PART ABOUT NOT TRUSTING YOUR EYES...?
WHAT?! MY RECITING OF THE TAMARANEAN WARRIOR'S ONE HUNDRED TENETS WAS ALMOST COMPLETED!
-SIGH- NOW I MUST REPEAT EVERYTHING FROM NUMBER FORTY-FIVE ON...
"TENET THE FORTY-FIFTH: TRUST NOT YOUR EYES FOR THEY MAY DECEIVE YOU."
PAY ATTENTION, ROBIN! THERE WILL BE A QUIZ!
END

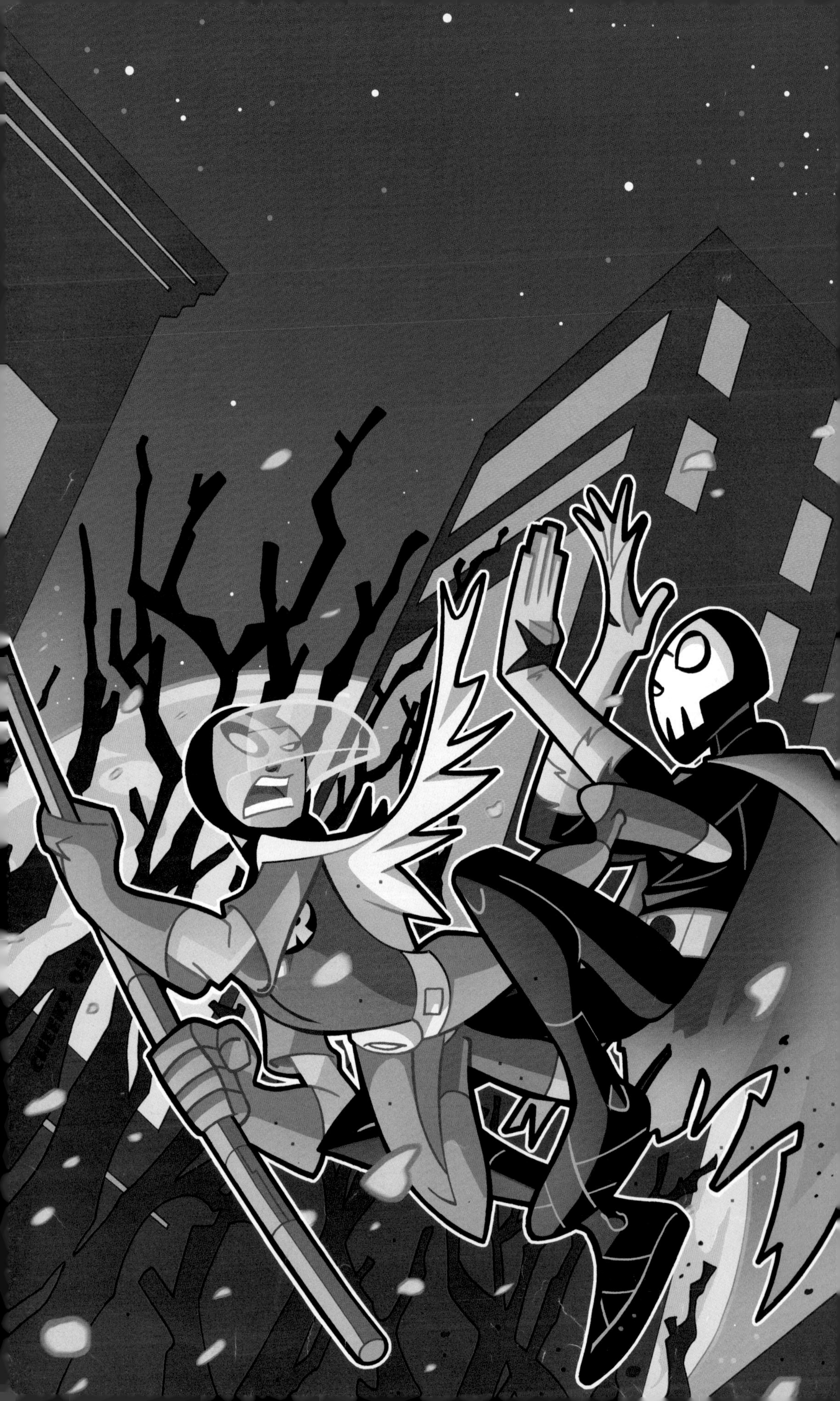

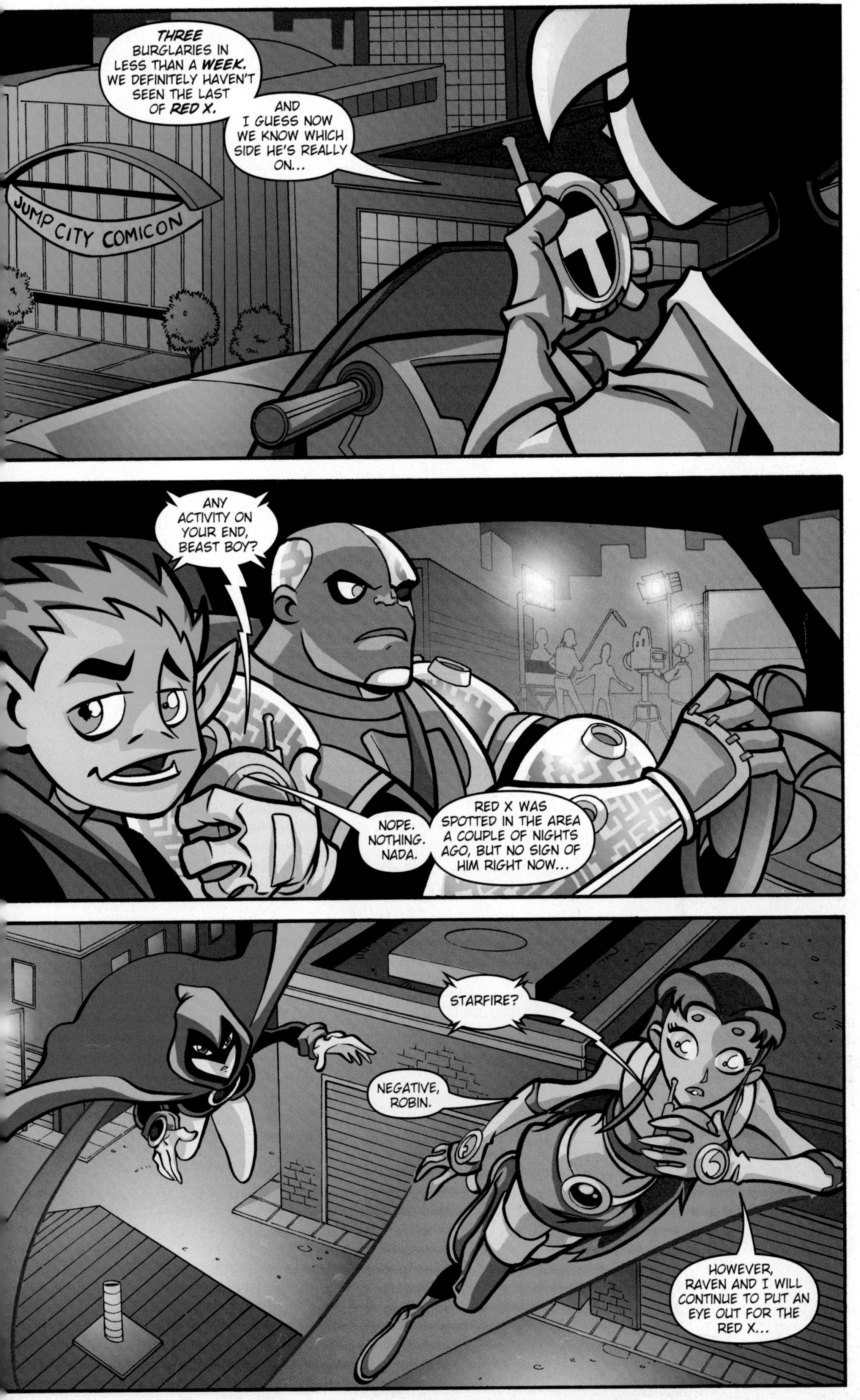

THREE BURGLARIES IN LESS THAN A WEEK. WE DEFINITELY HAVEN'T SEEN THE LAST OF RED X.
AND I GUESS NOW WE KNOW WHICH SIDE HE'S REALLY ON...
JUMP CITY COMICON
ANY ACTIVITY ON YOUR END, BEAST BOY?
NOPE. NOTHING. NADA.
RED X WAS SPOTTED IN THE AREA A COUPLE OF NIGHTS AGO, BUT NO SIGN OF HIM RIGHT NOW...
STARFIRE?
NEGATIVE, ROBIN.
HOWEVER, RAVEN AND I WILL CONTINUE TO PUT AN EYE OUT FOR THE RED X...

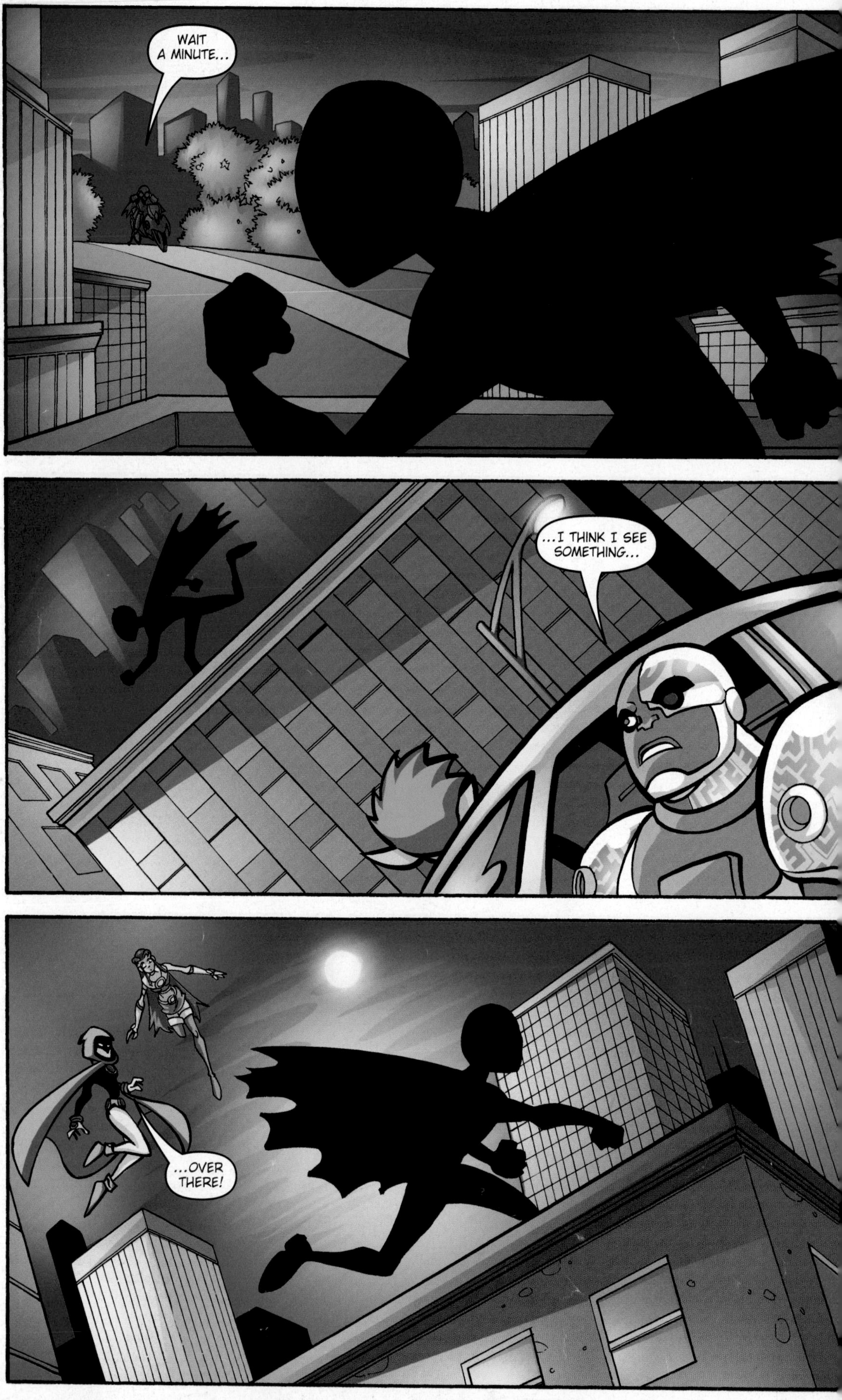
WAIT A MINUTE...
...I THINK I SEE SOMETHING...
...OVER THERE!

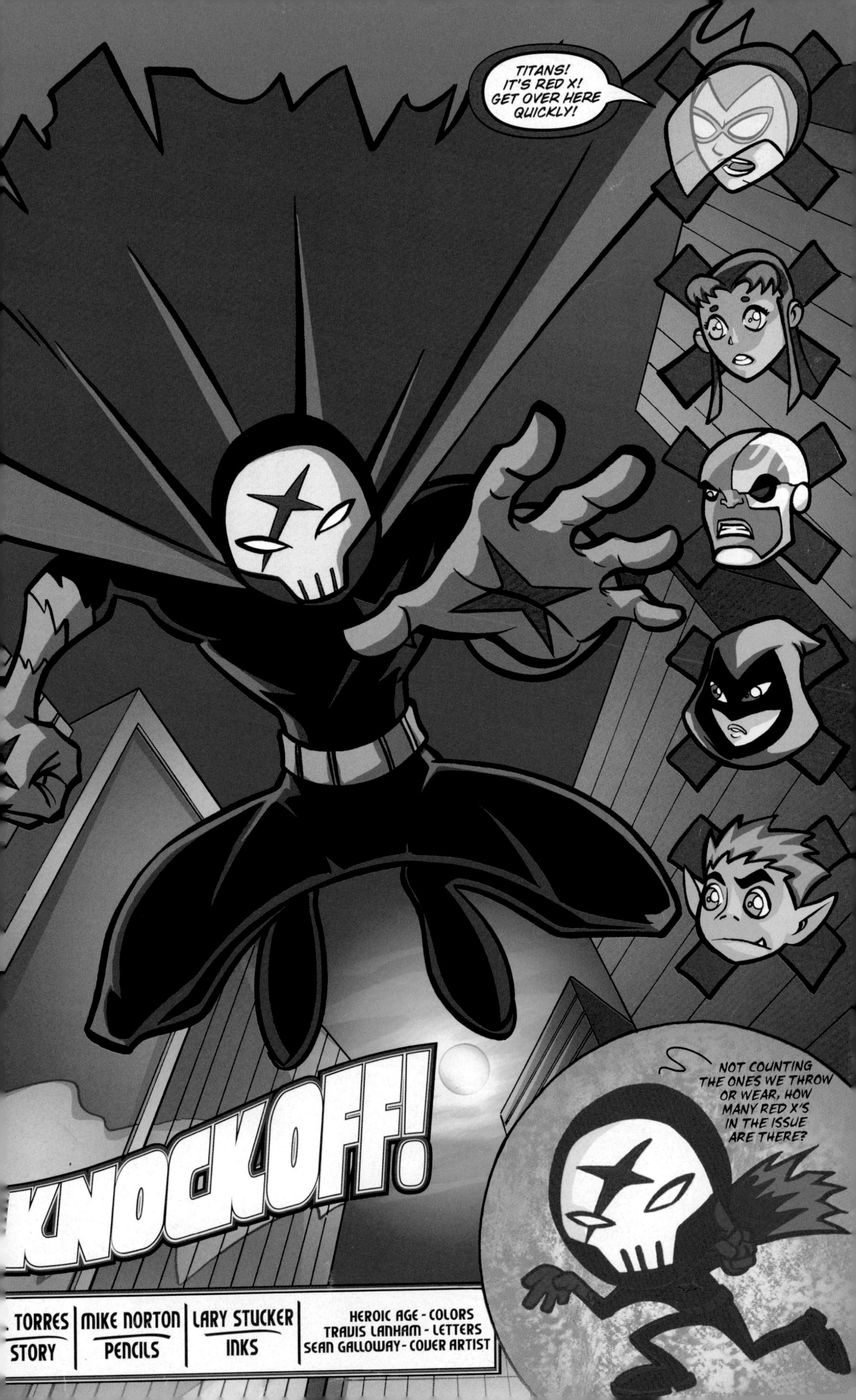
TITANS! IT'S RED X! GET OVER HERE QUICKLY!
KNOCKOFF!
NOT COUNTING THE ONES WE THROW OR WEAR, HOW MANY RED X'S IN THE ISSUE ARE THERE?
TORRES STORY
MIKE NORTON PENCILS
LARY STUCKER INKS
HEROIC AGE - COLORS
TRAVIS LANHAM - LETTERS
SEAN GALLOWAY - COVER ARTIST

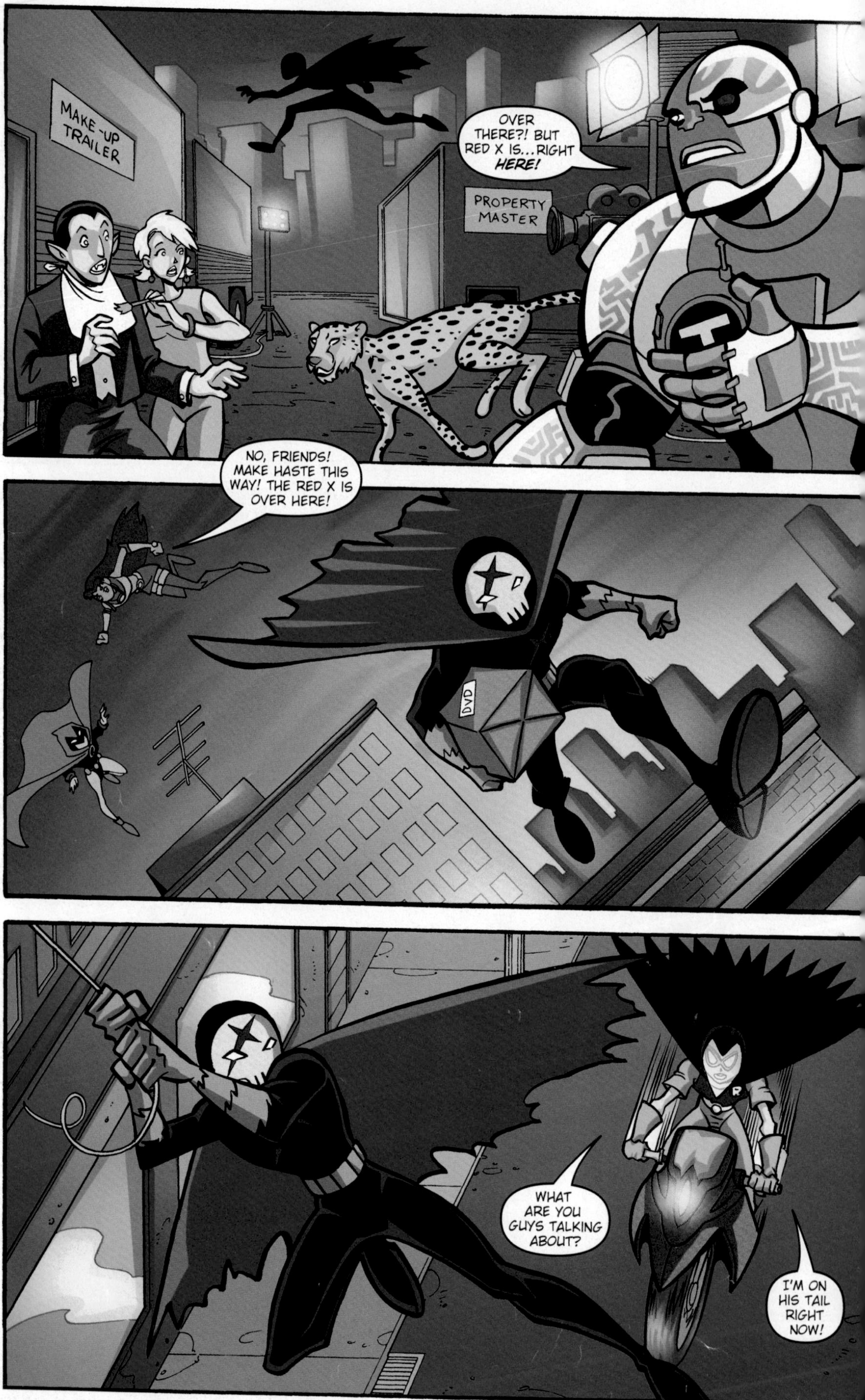
MAKE-UP TRAILER
PROPERTY MASTER
OVER THERE?! BUT RED X IS...RIGHT *HERE!*
NO, FRIENDS! MAKE HASTE THIS WAY! THE RED X IS OVER HERE!
DVD
WHAT ARE YOU GUYS TALKING ABOUT?
I'M ON HIS TAIL RIGHT NOW!

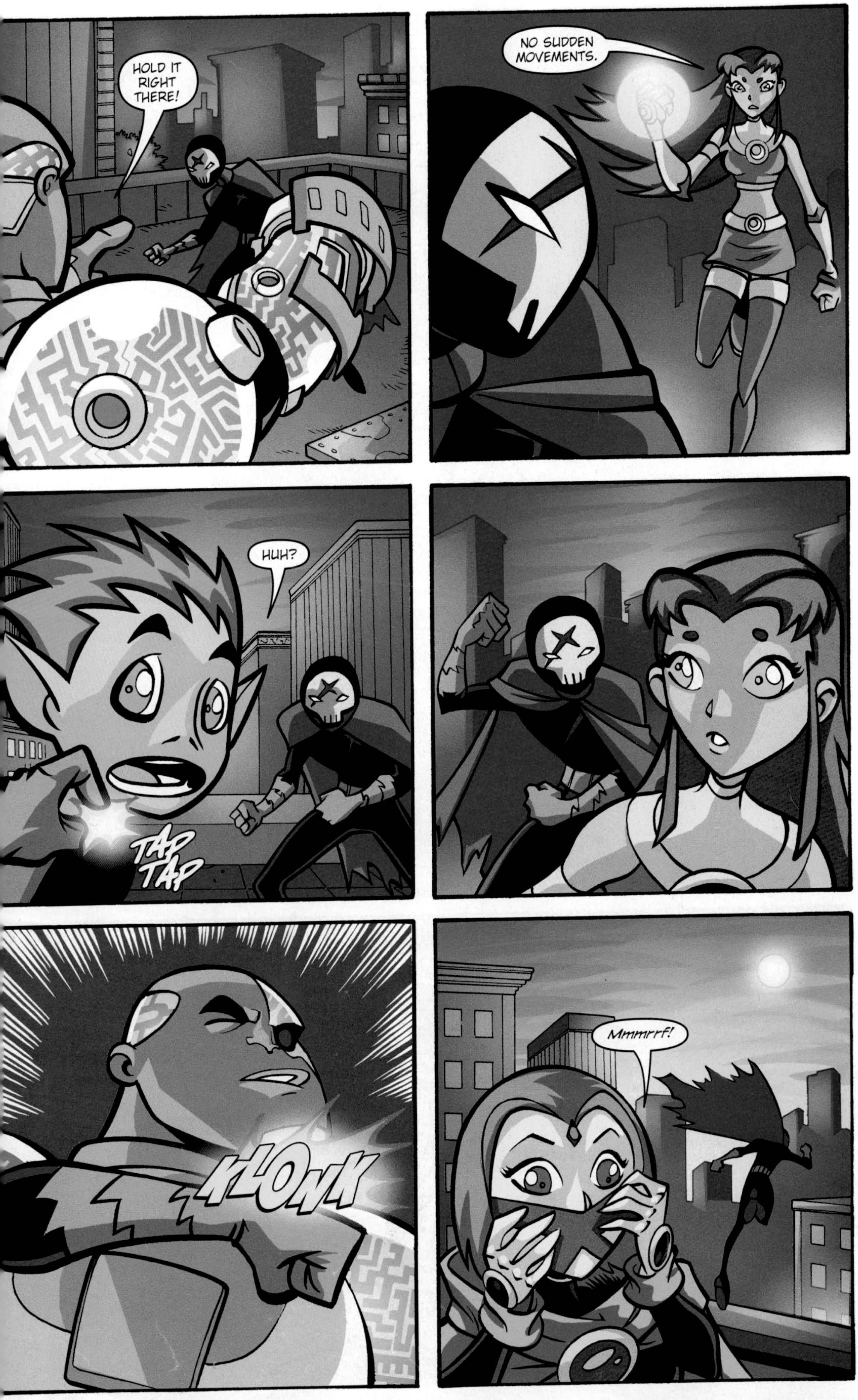
HOLD IT RIGHT THERE!
NO SUDDEN MOVEMENTS.
HUH?
TAP TAP
KLONK
Mmmrrf!

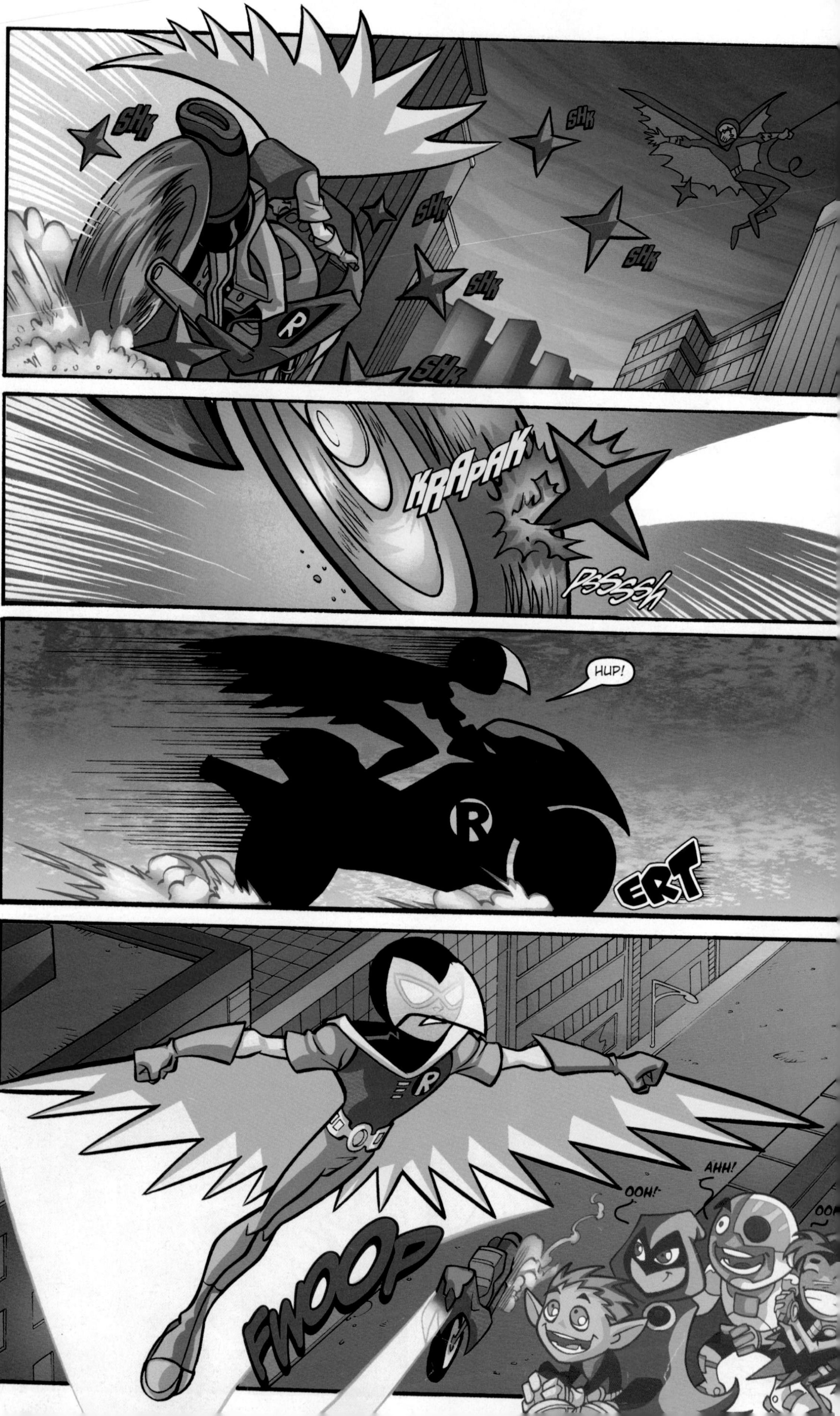
SHK
SHK
SHK
SHK
SHK
SHK
KRAPAK
PSSSSH
HUP!
ERT
FWOOP
OOH!
AHH!

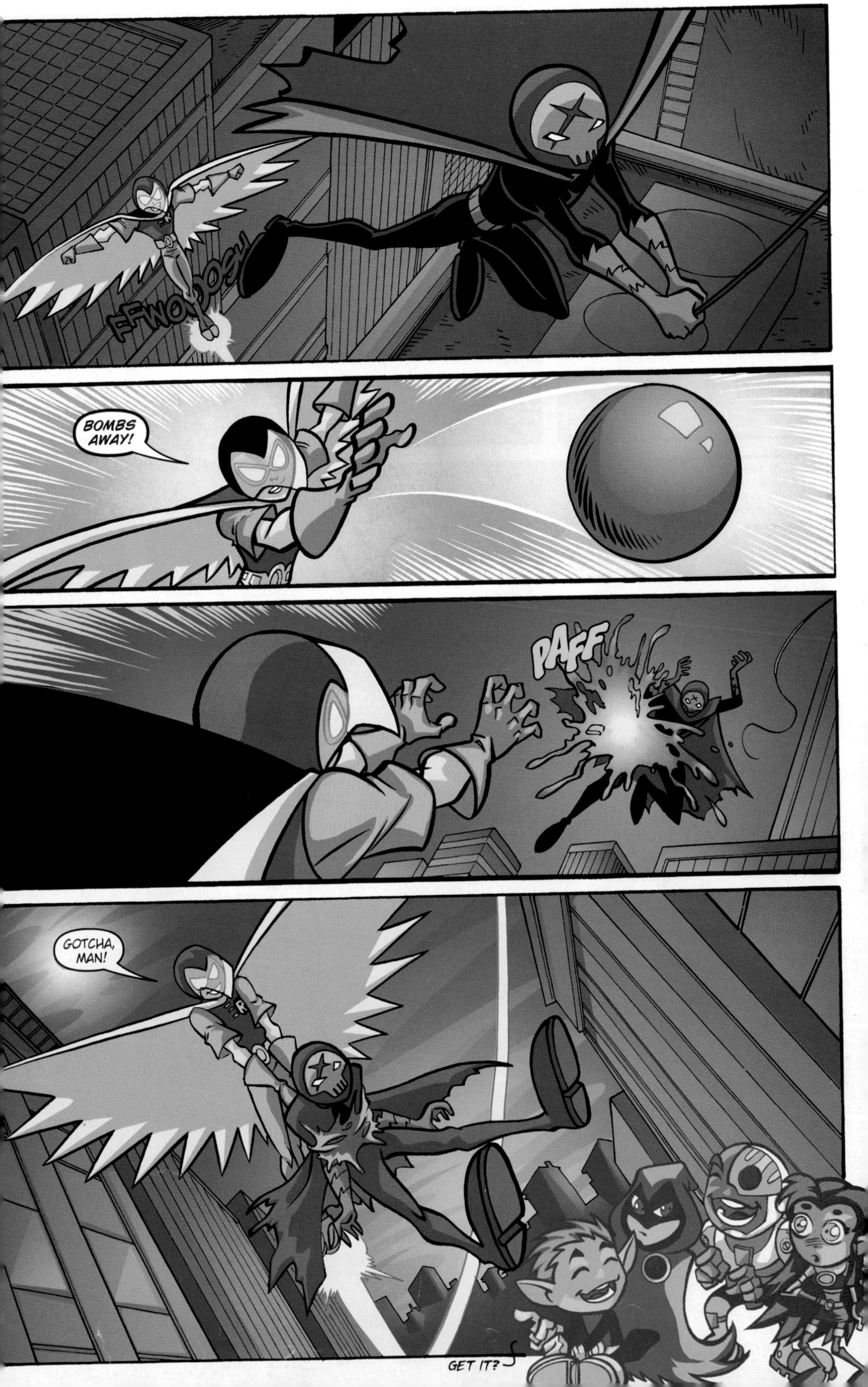
FFWOOOSH
BOMBS AWAY!
PAFF
GOTCHA, MAN!
GET IT?

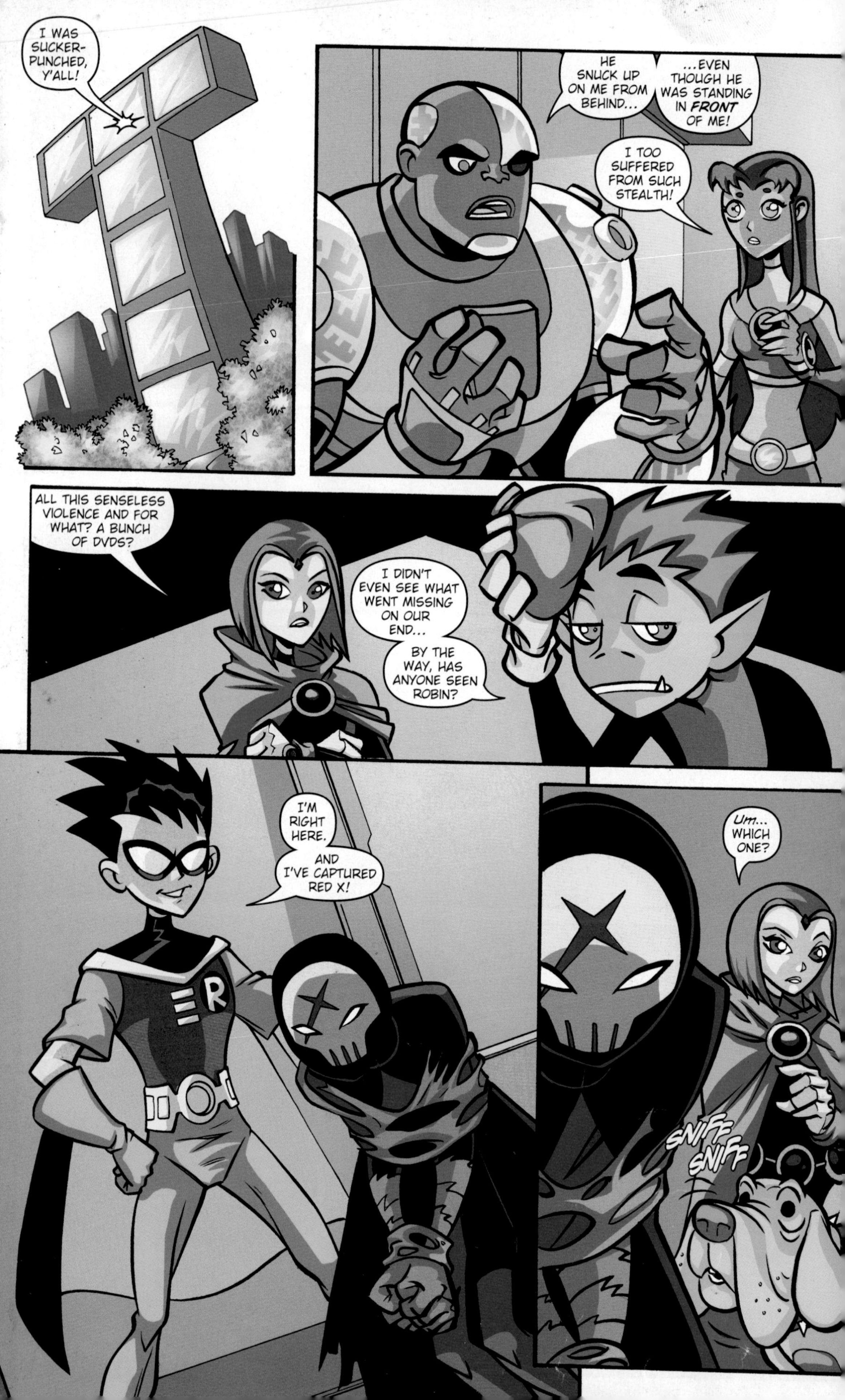

I WAS SUCKER-PUNCHED, Y'ALL!
HE SNUCK UP ON ME FROM BEHIND...
...EVEN THOUGH HE WAS STANDING IN *FRONT* OF ME!
I TOO SUFFERED FROM SUCH STEALTH!
ALL THIS SENSELESS VIOLENCE AND FOR WHAT? A BUNCH OF DVDS?
I DIDN'T EVEN SEE WHAT WENT MISSING ON OUR END...
BY THE WAY, HAS ANYONE SEEN ROBIN?
I'M RIGHT HERE.
AND I'VE CAPTURED RED X!
Um... WHICH ONE?
SNIFF SNIFF

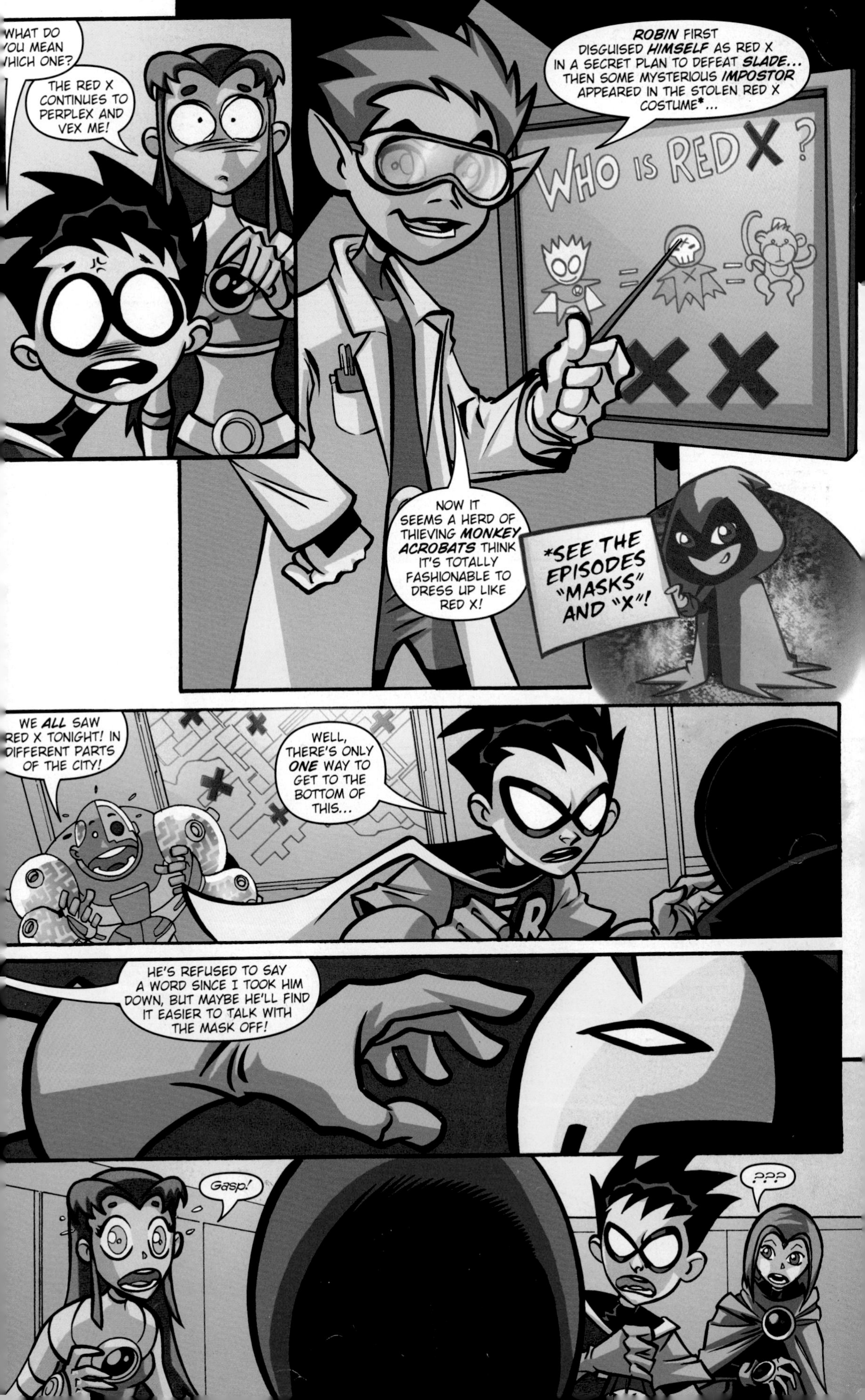
WHAT DO YOU MEAN WHICH ONE?
THE RED X CONTINUES TO PERPLEX AND VEX ME!
ROBIN FIRST DISGUISED HIMSELF AS RED X IN A SECRET PLAN TO DEFEAT SLADE... THEN SOME MYSTERIOUS IMPOSTOR APPEARED IN THE STOLEN RED X COSTUME*...
WHO IS RED X ?
NOW IT SEEMS A HERD OF THIEVING MONKEY ACROBATS THINK IT'S TOTALLY FASHIONABLE TO DRESS UP LIKE RED X!
*SEE THE EPISODES "MASKS" AND "X"!
WE ALL SAW RED X TONIGHT! IN DIFFERENT PARTS OF THE CITY!
WELL, THERE'S ONLY ONE WAY TO GET TO THE BOTTOM OF THIS...
HE'S REFUSED TO SAY A WORD SINCE I TOOK HIM DOWN, BUT MAYBE HE'LL FIND IT EASIER TO TALK WITH THE MASK OFF!
Gasp!
???

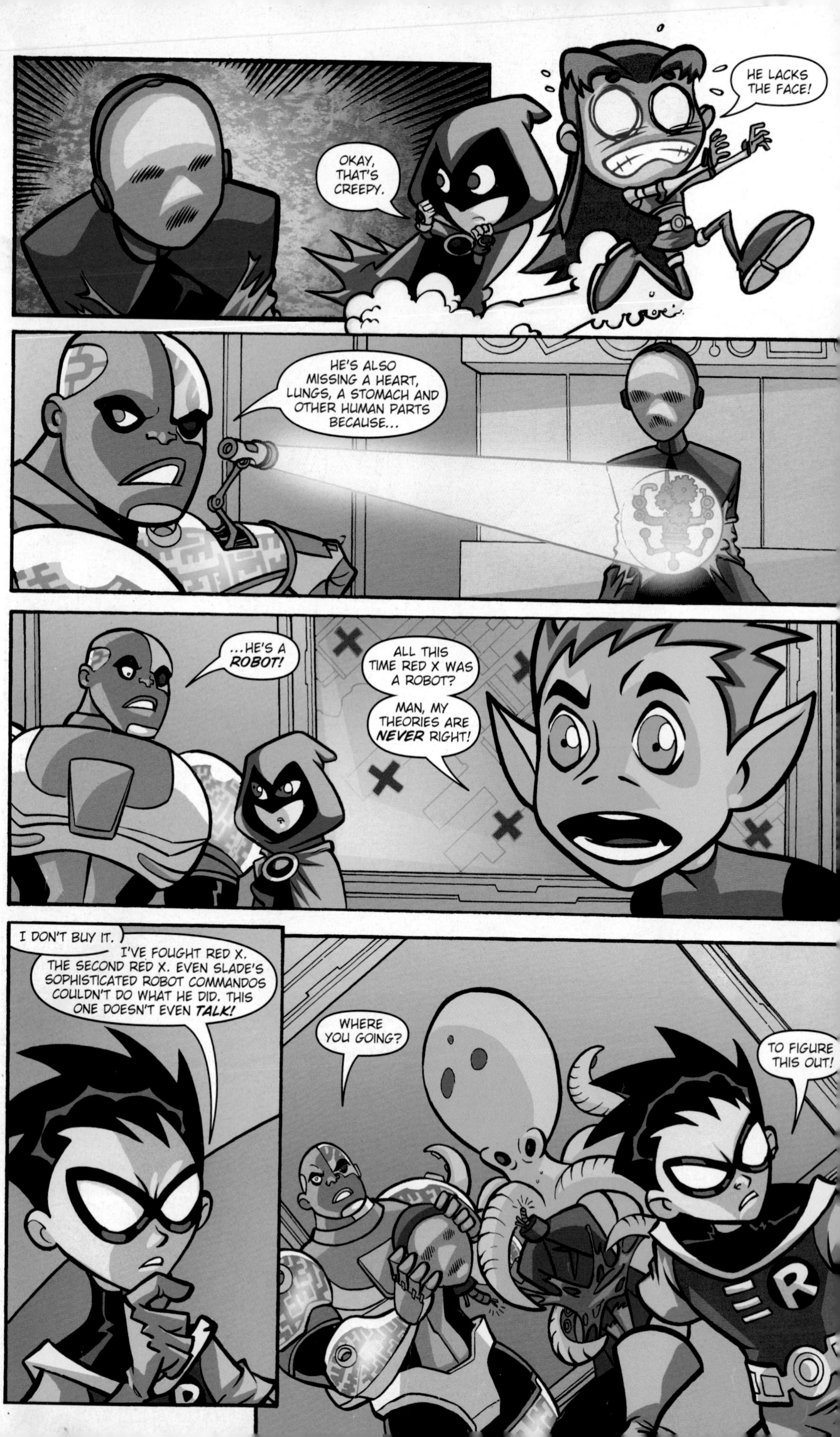
OKAY, THAT'S CREEPY.
HE LACKS THE FACE!
HE'S ALSO MISSING A HEART, LUNGS, A STOMACH AND OTHER HUMAN PARTS BECAUSE...
...HE'S A *ROBOT!*
ALL THIS TIME RED X WAS A ROBOT?
MAN, MY THEORIES ARE *NEVER* RIGHT!
I DON'T BUY IT.
I'VE FOUGHT RED X. THE SECOND RED X. EVEN SLADE'S SOPHISTICATED ROBOT COMMANDOS COULDN'T DO WHAT HE DID. THIS ONE DOESN'T EVEN *TALK!*
WHERE YOU GOING?
TO FIGURE THIS OUT!

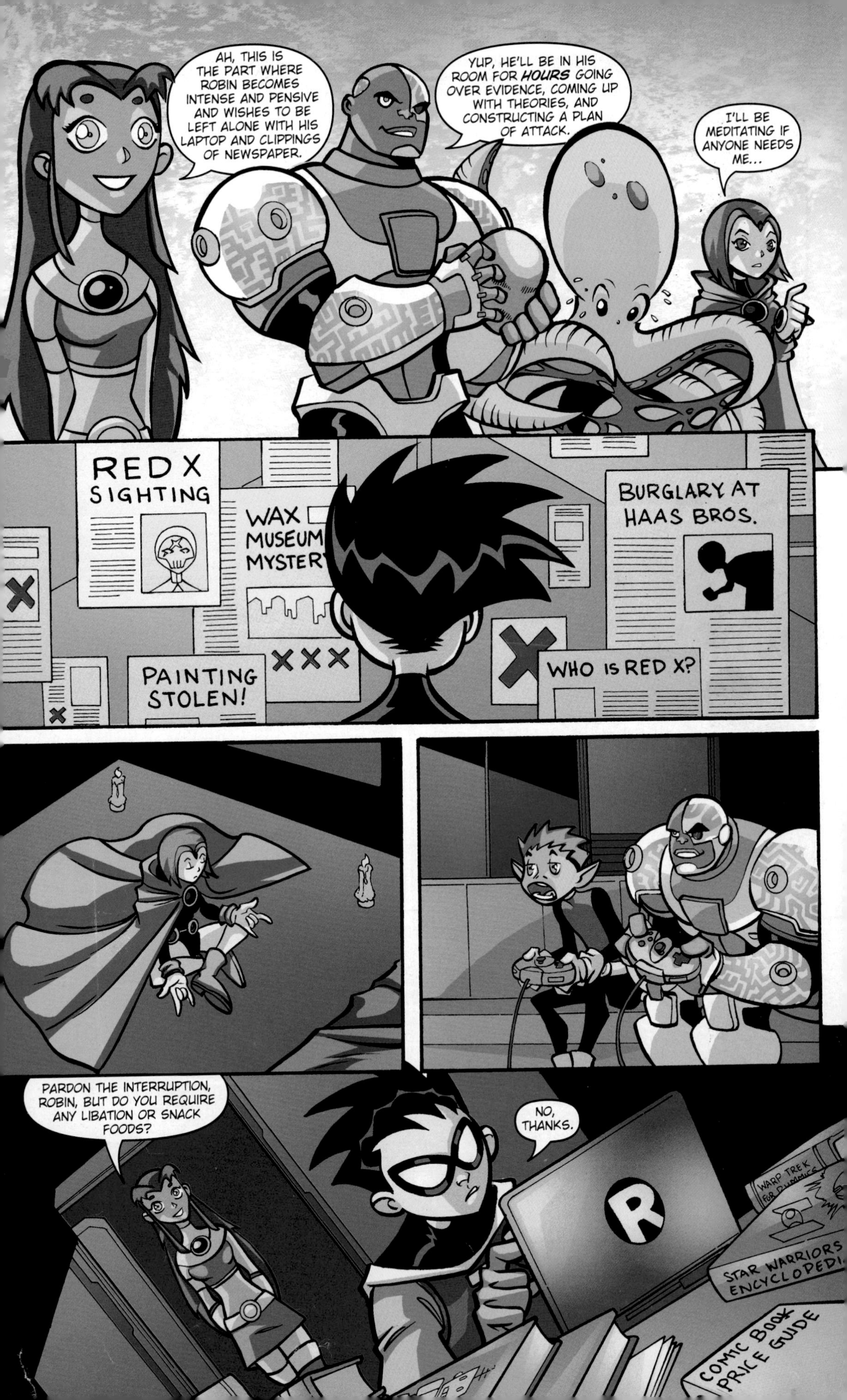
AH, THIS IS THE PART WHERE ROBIN BECOMES INTENSE AND PENSIVE AND WISHES TO BE LEFT ALONE WITH HIS LAPTOP AND CLIPPINGS OF NEWSPAPER.
YUP, HE'LL BE IN HIS ROOM FOR **HOURS** GOING OVER EVIDENCE, COMING UP WITH THEORIES, AND CONSTRUCTING A PLAN OF ATTACK.
I'LL BE MEDITATING IF ANYONE NEEDS ME...
RED X SIGHTING
WAX MUSEUM MYSTERY
BURGLARY AT HAAS BROS.
PAINTING STOLEN!
WHO IS RED X?
PARDON THE INTERRUPTION, ROBIN, BUT DO YOU REQUIRE ANY LIBATION OR SNACK FOODS?
NO, THANKS.
WARP TREK FOR DUMMIES
STAR WARRIORS ENCYCLOPEDI
COMIC BOOK PRICE GUIDE

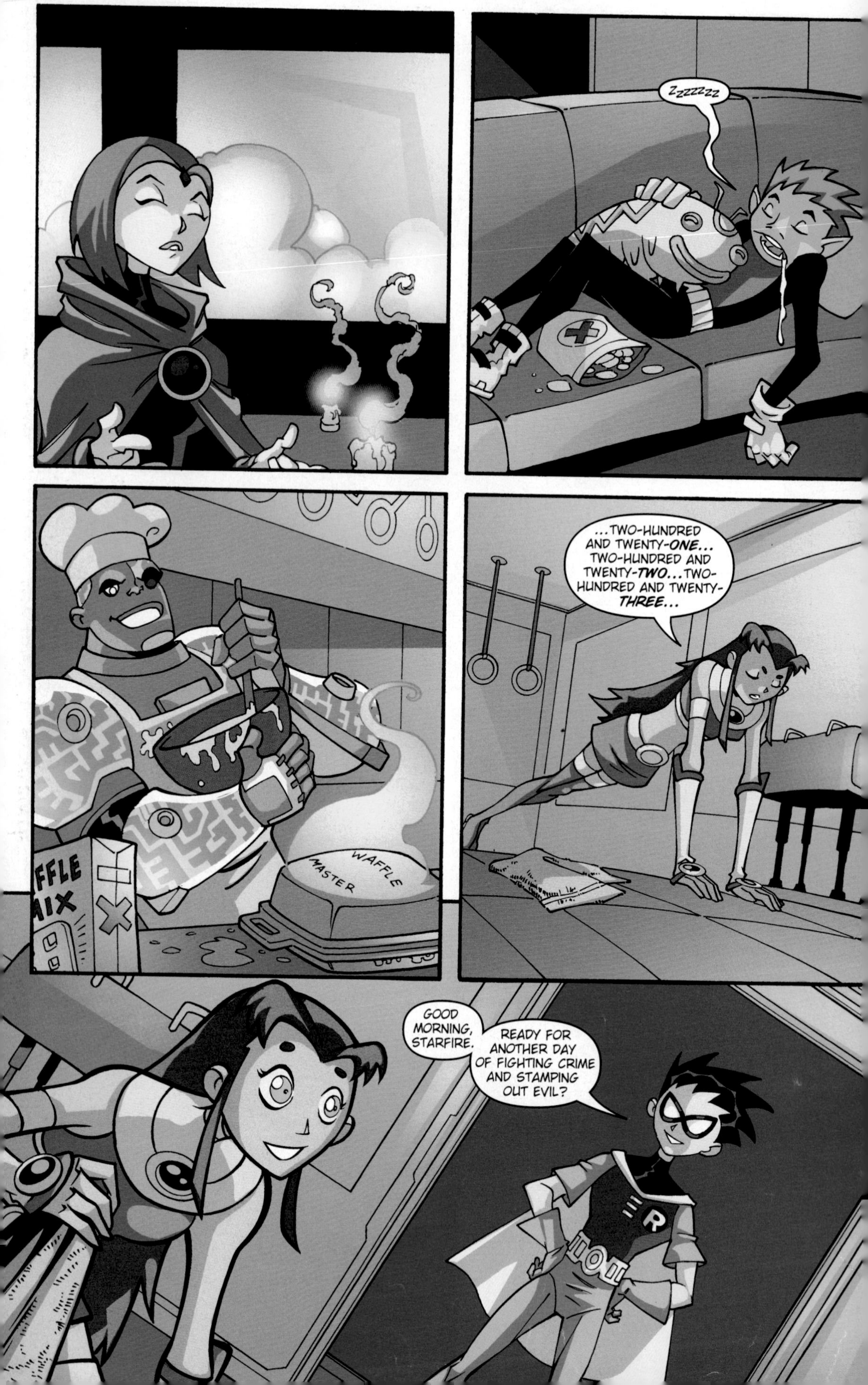
Zzzzzzz
WAFFLE MASTER
FFLE MIX
...TWO-HUNDRED AND TWENTY-ONE... TWO-HUNDRED AND TWENTY-TWO...TWO-HUNDRED AND TWENTY-THREE...
GOOD MORNING, STARFIRE.
READY FOR ANOTHER DAY OF FIGHTING CRIME AND STAMPING OUT EVIL?

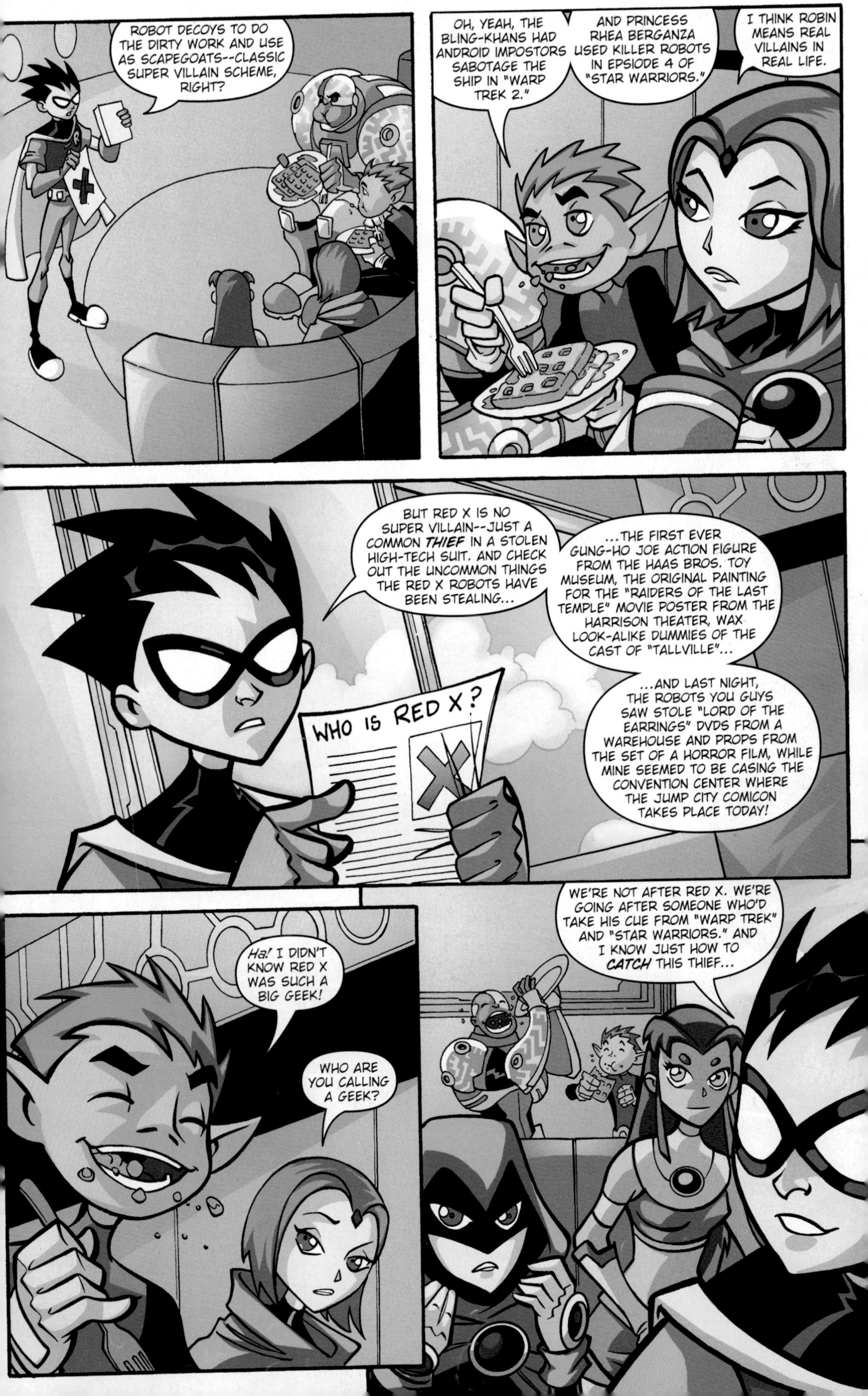
ROBOT DECOYS TO DO THE DIRTY WORK AND USE AS SCAPEGOATS--CLASSIC SUPER VILLAIN SCHEME, RIGHT?
OH, YEAH, THE BLING-KHANS HAD ANDROID IMPOSTORS SABOTAGE THE SHIP IN "WARP TREK 2."
AND PRINCESS RHEA BERGANZA USED KILLER ROBOTS IN EPSIODE 4 OF "STAR WARRIORS."
I THINK ROBIN MEANS REAL VILLAINS IN REAL LIFE.
BUT RED X IS NO SUPER VILLAIN--JUST A COMMON THIEF IN A STOLEN HIGH-TECH SUIT. AND CHECK OUT THE UNCOMMON THINGS THE RED X ROBOTS HAVE BEEN STEALING...
WHO IS RED X?
...THE FIRST EVER GUNG-HO JOE ACTION FIGURE FROM THE HAAS BROS. TOY MUSEUM, THE ORIGINAL PAINTING FOR THE "RAIDERS OF THE LAST TEMPLE" MOVIE POSTER FROM THE HARRISON THEATER, WAX LOOK-ALIKE DUMMIES OF THE CAST OF "TALLVILLE"...
...AND LAST NIGHT, THE ROBOTS YOU GUYS SAW STOLE "LORD OF THE EARRINGS" DVDS FROM A WAREHOUSE AND PROPS FROM THE SET OF A HORROR FILM, WHILE MINE SEEMED TO BE CASING THE CONVENTION CENTER WHERE THE JUMP CITY COMICON TAKES PLACE TODAY!
HA! I DIDN'T KNOW RED X WAS SUCH A BIG GEEK!
WHO ARE YOU CALLING A GEEK?
WE'RE NOT AFTER RED X. WE'RE GOING AFTER SOMEONE WHO'D TAKE HIS CUE FROM "WARP TREK" AND "STAR WARRIORS." AND I KNOW JUST HOW TO CATCH THIS THIEF...

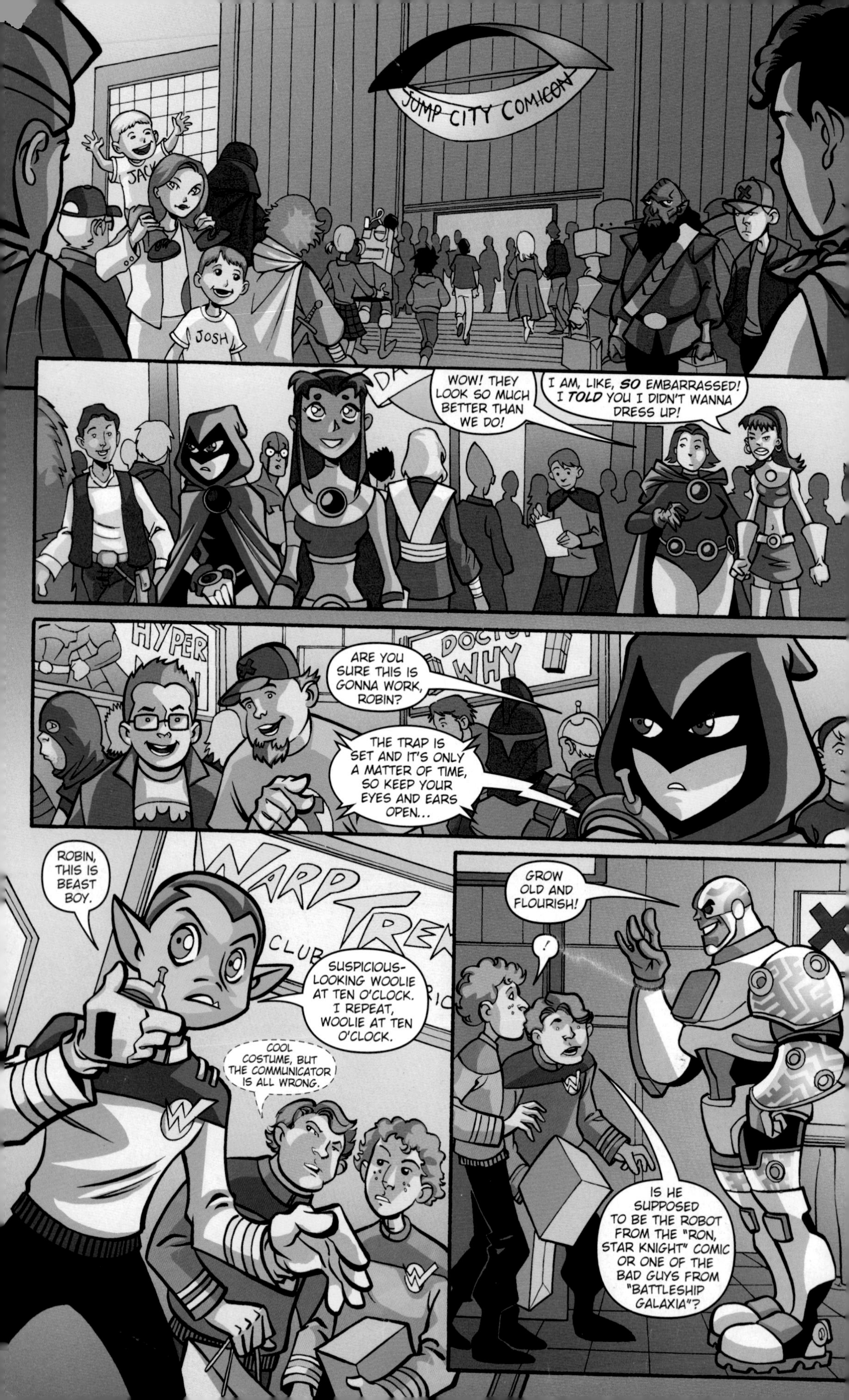
JUMP CITY COMICON
JACK
JOSH
WOW! THEY LOOK SO MUCH BETTER THAN WE DO!
I AM, LIKE, SO EMBARRASSED! I TOLD YOU I DIDN'T WANNA DRESS UP!
HYPER
DOCTOR WHY
ARE YOU SURE THIS IS GONNA WORK, ROBIN?
THE TRAP IS SET AND IT'S ONLY A MATTER OF TIME, SO KEEP YOUR EYES AND EARS OPEN...
ROBIN, THIS IS BEAST BOY.
WARP TREK
CLUB
SUSPICIOUS-LOOKING WOOLIE AT TEN O'CLOCK. I REPEAT, WOOLIE AT TEN O'CLOCK.
COOL COSTUME, BUT THE COMMUNICATOR IS ALL WRONG.
GROW OLD AND FLOURISH!
!
IS HE SUPPOSED TO BE THE ROBOT FROM THE "RON, STAR KNIGHT" COMIC OR ONE OF THE BAD GUYS FROM "BATTLESHIP GALAXIA"?

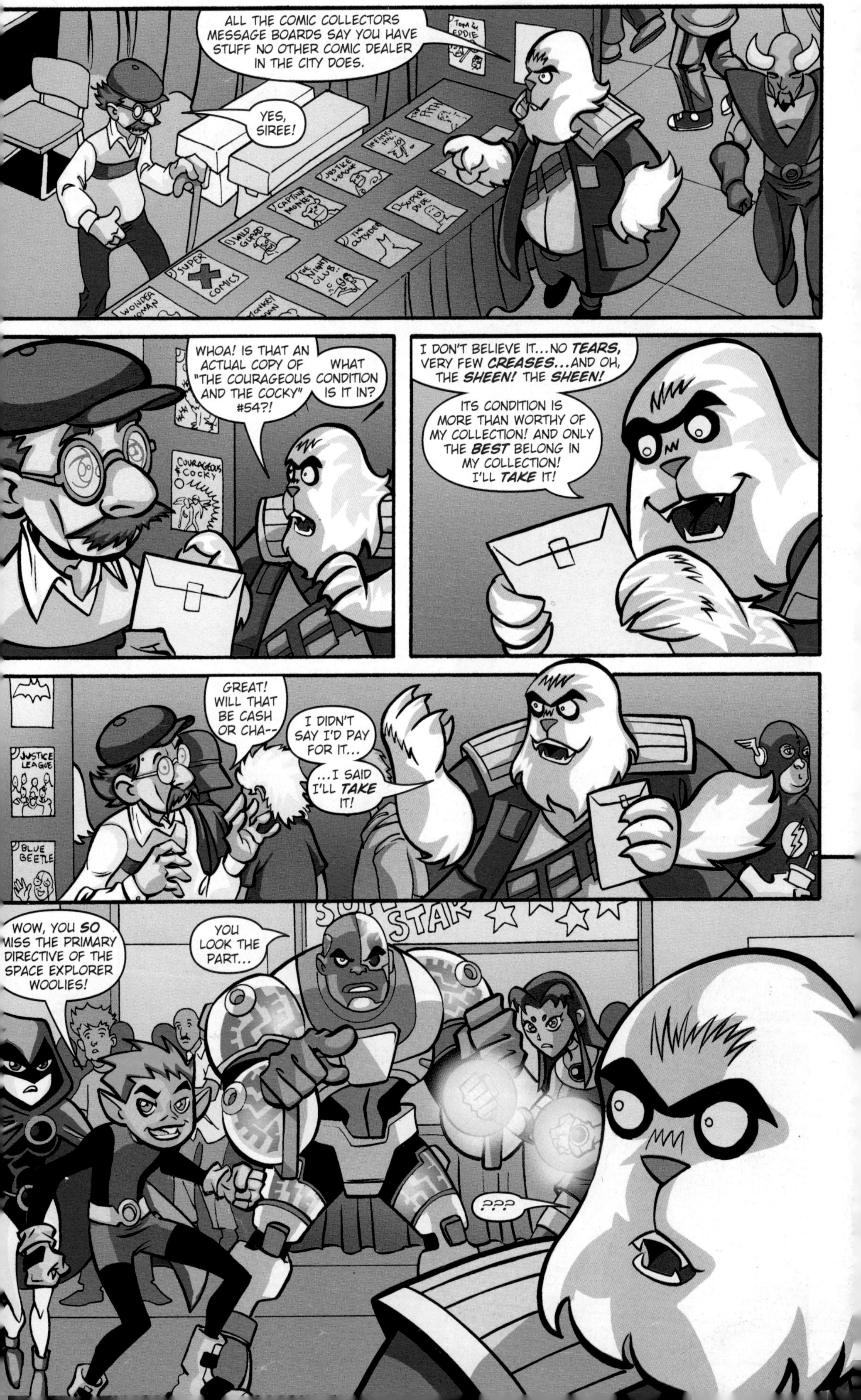

ALL THE COMIC COLLECTORS MESSAGE BOARDS SAY YOU HAVE STUFF NO OTHER COMIC DEALER IN THE CITY DOES.
YES, SIREE!
WHOA! IS THAT AN ACTUAL COPY OF "THE COURAGEOUS AND THE COCKY" #54?!
WHAT CONDITION IS IT IN?
I DON'T BELIEVE IT...NO TEARS, VERY FEW CREASES...AND OH, THE SHEEN! THE SHEEN!
ITS CONDITION IS MORE THAN WORTHY OF MY COLLECTION! AND ONLY THE BEST BELONG IN MY COLLECTION! I'LL TAKE IT!
GREAT! WILL THAT BE CASH OR CHA--
I DIDN'T SAY I'D PAY FOR IT...
...I SAID I'LL TAKE IT!
WOW, YOU SO MISS THE PRIMARY DIRECTIVE OF THE SPACE EXPLORER WOOLIES!
YOU LOOK THE PART...
???

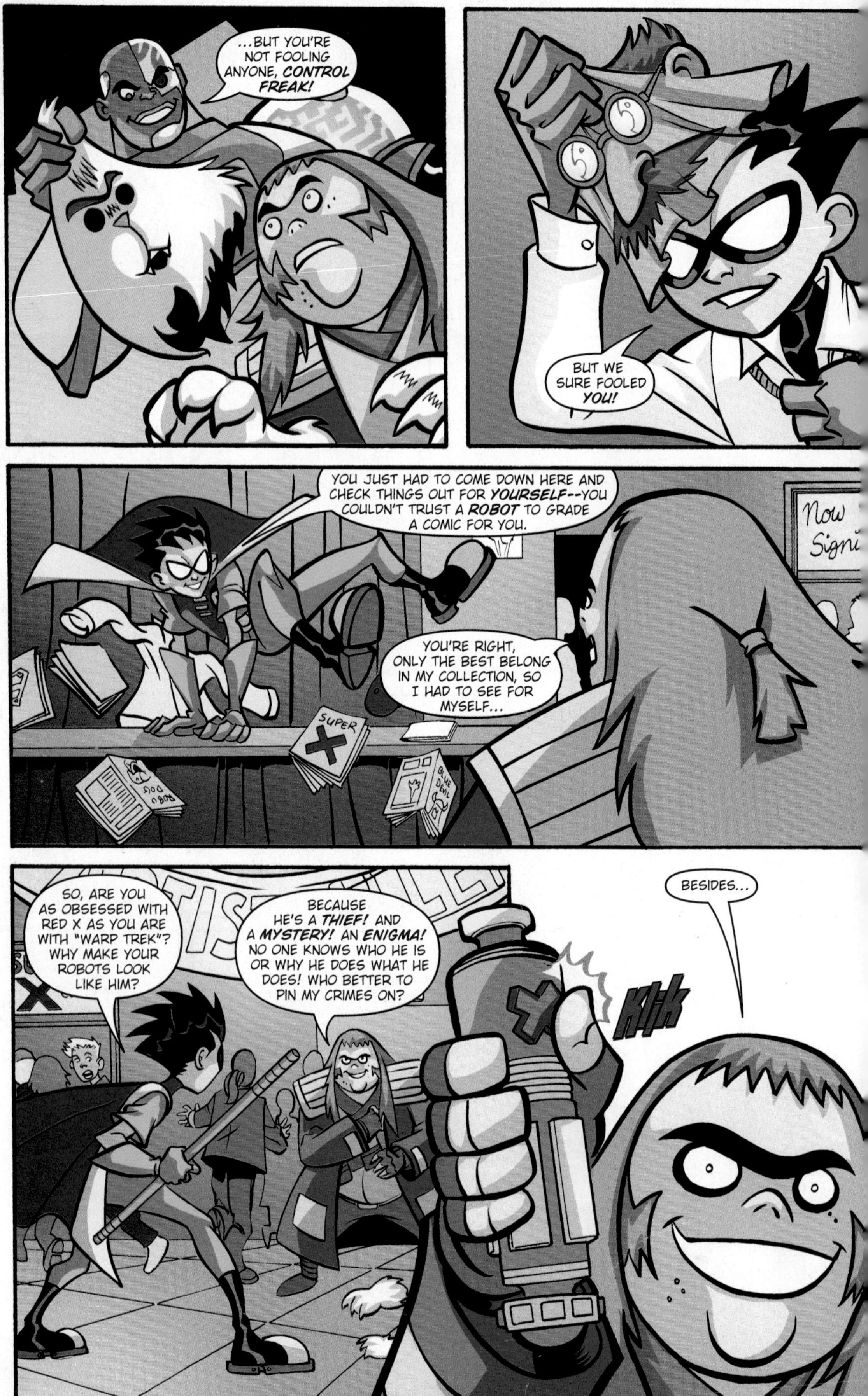

...BUT YOU'RE NOT FOOLING ANYONE, **CONTROL FREAK!**
BUT WE SURE FOOLED ***YOU!***
YOU JUST HAD TO COME DOWN HERE AND CHECK THINGS OUT FOR ***YOURSELF***--YOU COULDN'T TRUST A ***ROBOT*** TO GRADE A COMIC FOR YOU.
Now
YOU'RE RIGHT, ONLY THE BEST BELONG IN MY COLLECTION, SO I HAD TO SEE FOR MYSELF...
SUPER X
SO, ARE YOU AS OBSESSED WITH RED X AS YOU ARE WITH "WARP TREK"? WHY MAKE YOUR ROBOTS LOOK LIKE HIM?
BECAUSE HE'S A ***THIEF!*** AND A ***MYSTERY!*** AN ***ENIGMA!*** NO ONE KNOWS WHO HE IS OR WHY HE DOES WHAT HE DOES! WHO BETTER TO PIN MY CRIMES ON?
KLIK
BESIDES...

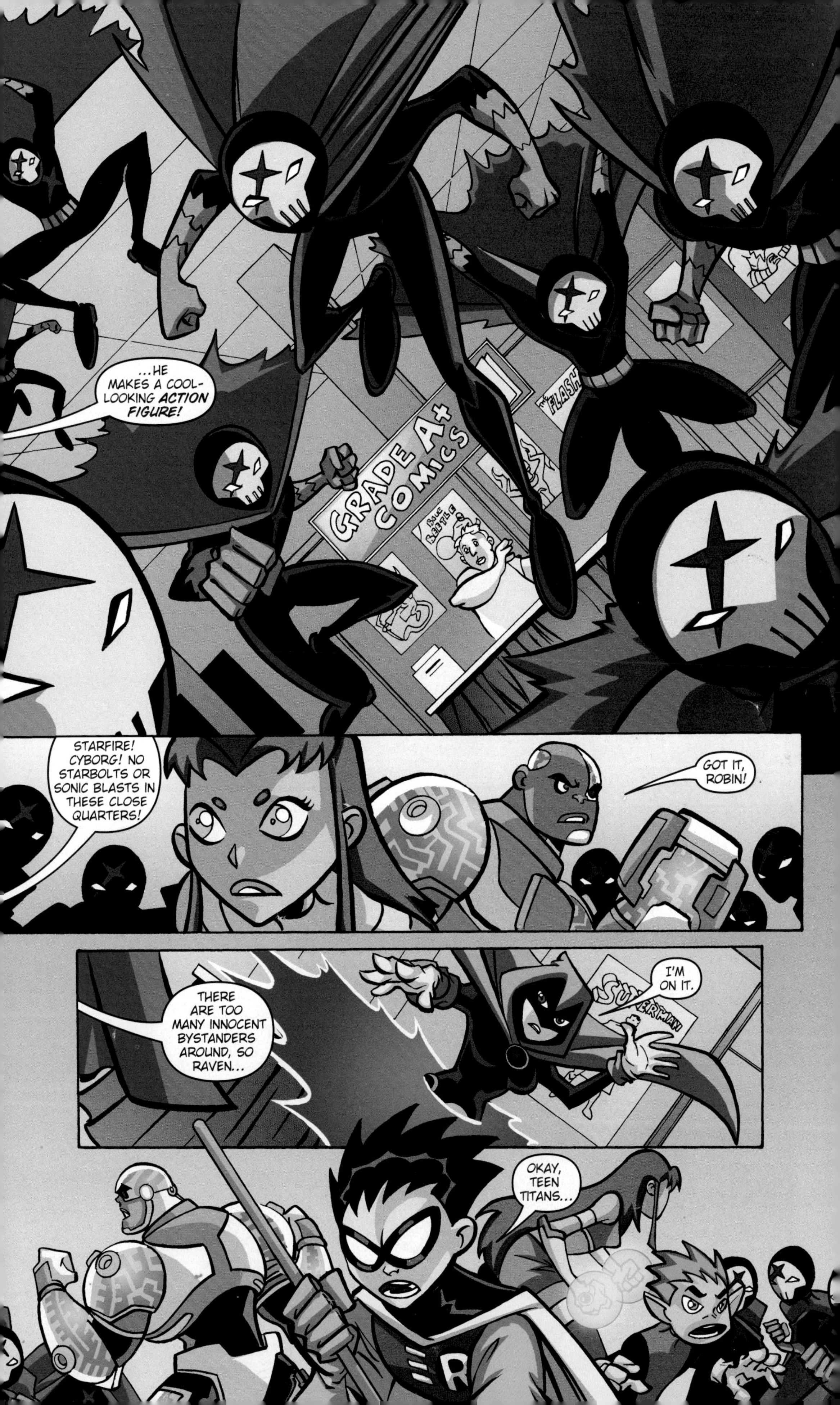

...HE MAKES A COOL-LOOKING ACTION FIGURE!
GRADE A+ COMICS
THE FLASH
BLUE BEETLE
STARFIRE! CYBORG! NO STARBOLTS OR SONIC BLASTS IN THESE CLOSE QUARTERS!
GOT IT, ROBIN!
THERE ARE TOO MANY INNOCENT BYSTANDERS AROUND, SO RAVEN...
I'M ON IT.
SUPERMAN
OKAY, TEEN TITANS...

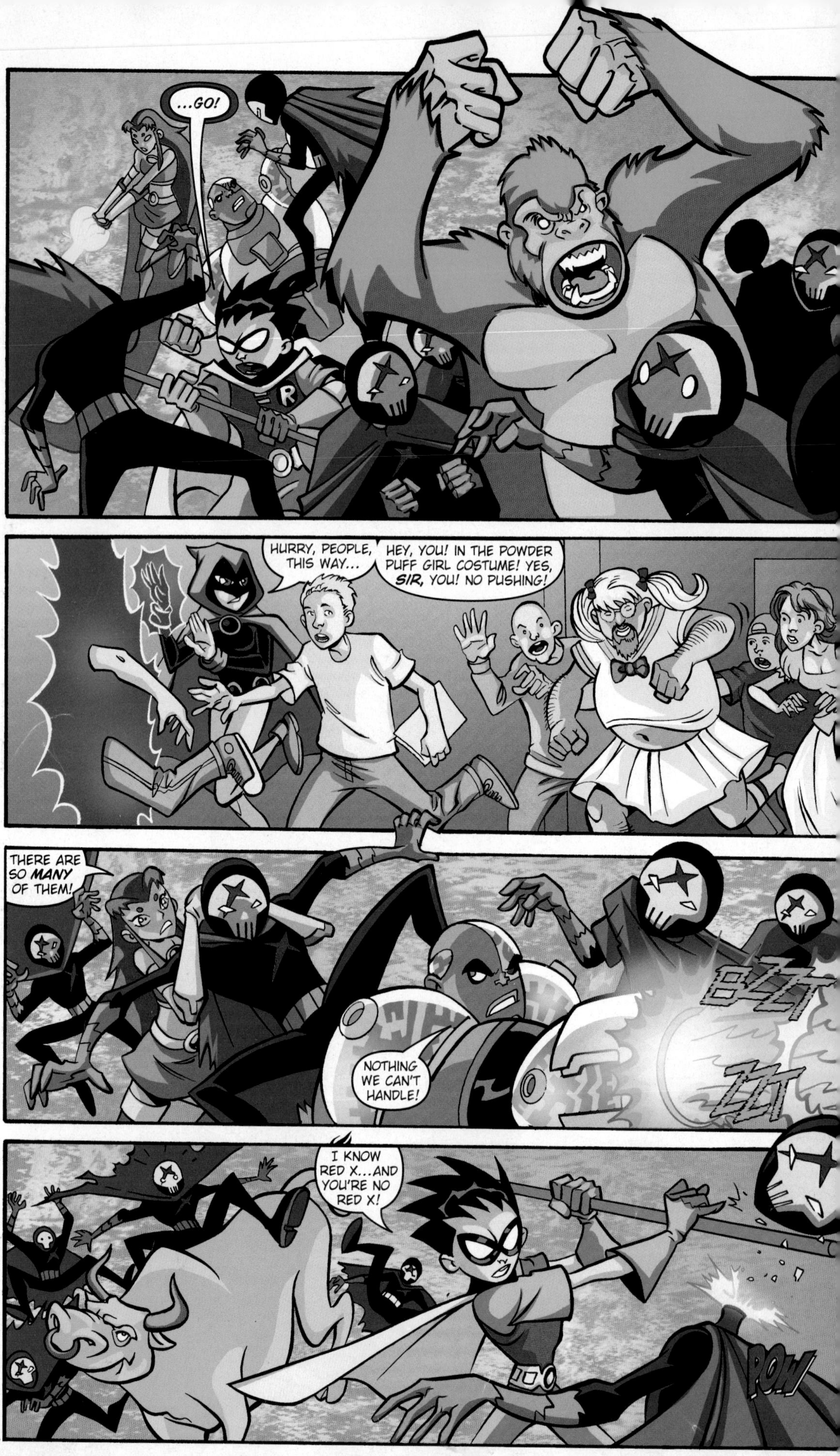
...GO!
HURRY, PEOPLE, THIS WAY...
HEY, YOU! IN THE POWDER PUFF GIRL COSTUME! YES, SIR, YOU! NO PUSHING!
THERE ARE SO MANY OF THEM!
NOTHING WE CAN'T HANDLE!
BZZT
ZZT
I KNOW RED X...AND YOU'RE NO RED X!
POW

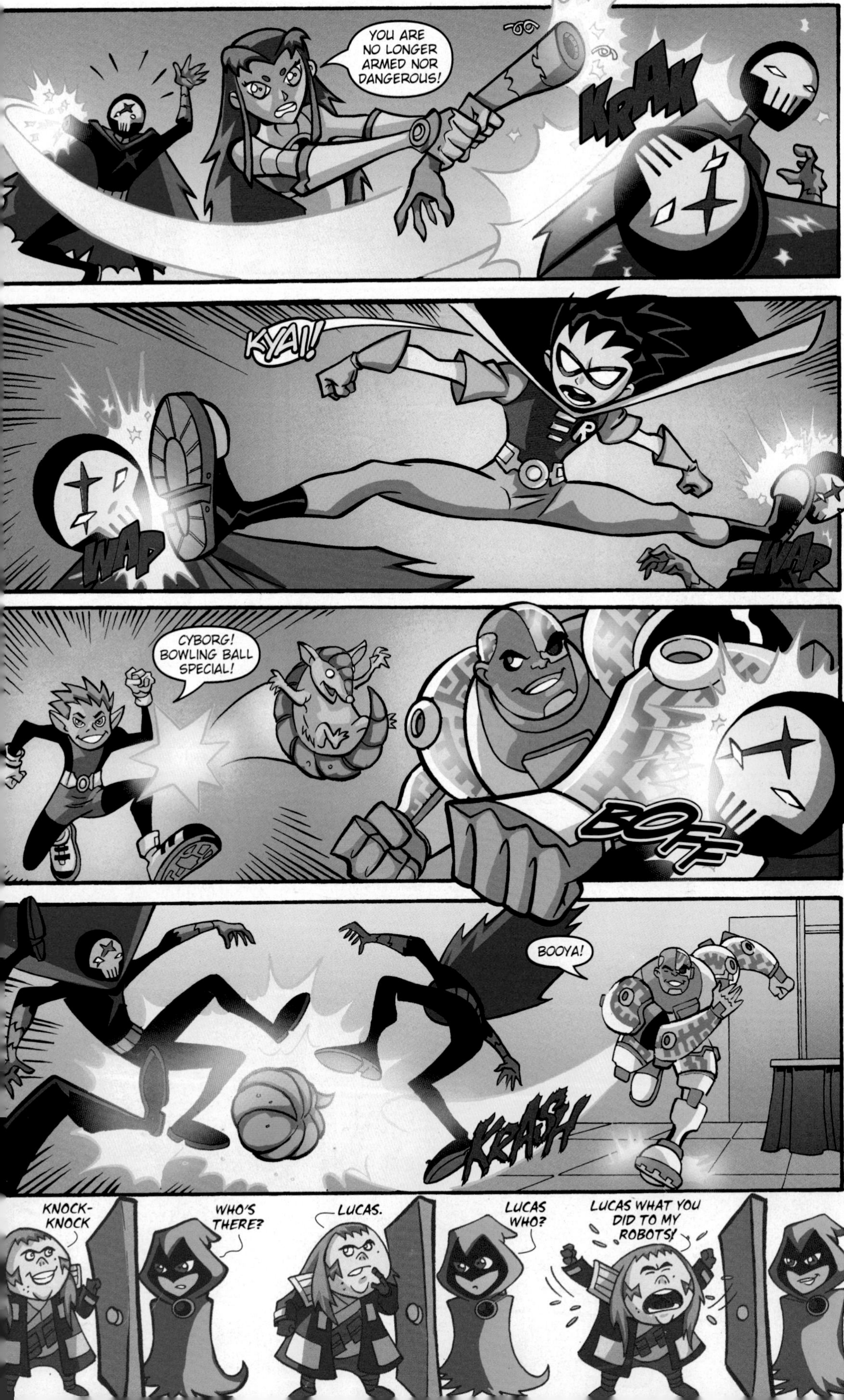

YOU ARE NO LONGER ARMED NOR DANGEROUS!
KRAAK
KYA!!
WAP
WAP
CYBORG! BOWLING BALL SPECIAL!
BOFF
BOOYA!
KRASH
KNOCK-KNOCK
WHO'S THERE?
LUCAS.
LUCAS WHO?
LUCAS WHAT YOU DID TO MY ROBOTS!

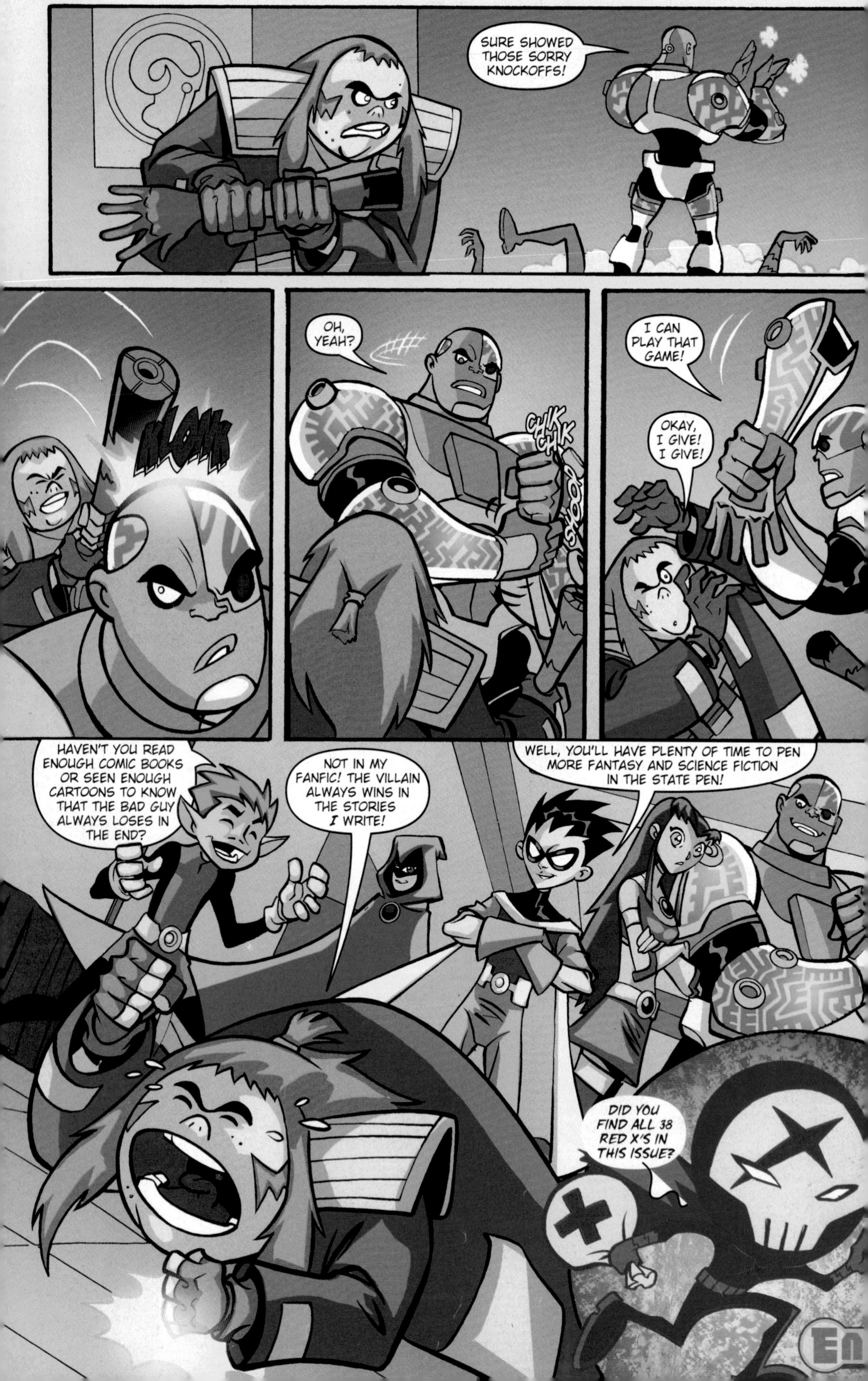
SURE SHOWED THOSE SORRY KNOCKOFFS!
KLONK
OH, YEAH?
CHIK CHIK
SHOOOP
I CAN PLAY THAT GAME!
OKAY, I GIVE! I GIVE!
HAVEN'T YOU READ ENOUGH COMIC BOOKS OR SEEN ENOUGH CARTOONS TO KNOW THAT THE BAD GUY ALWAYS LOSES IN THE END?
NOT IN MY FANFIC! THE VILLAIN ALWAYS WINS IN THE STORIES *I* WRITE!
WELL, YOU'LL HAVE PLENTY OF TIME TO PEN MORE FANTASY AND SCIENCE FICTION IN THE STATE PEN!
DID YOU FIND ALL 38 RED X'S IN THIS ISSUE?

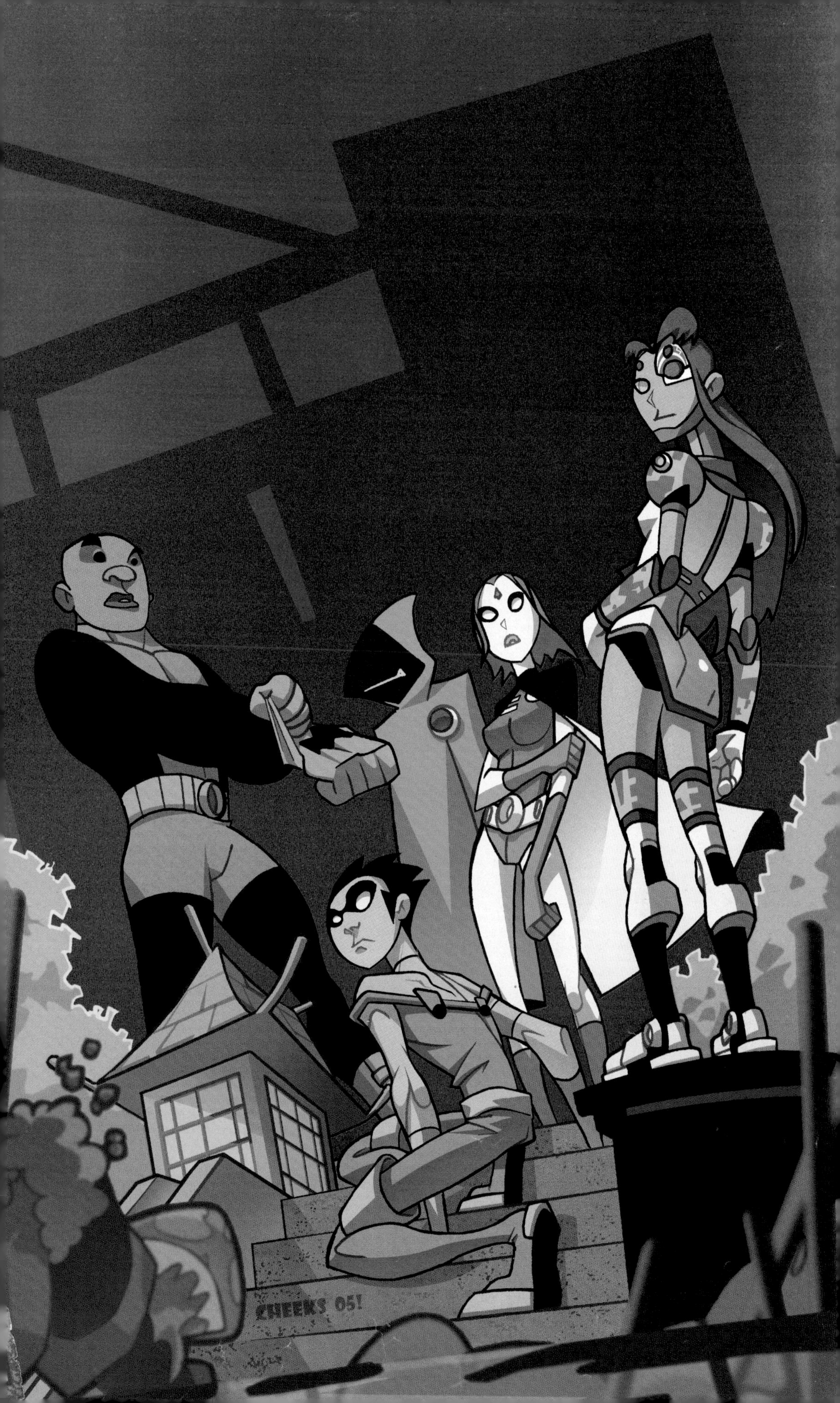
CHEEKS 05!

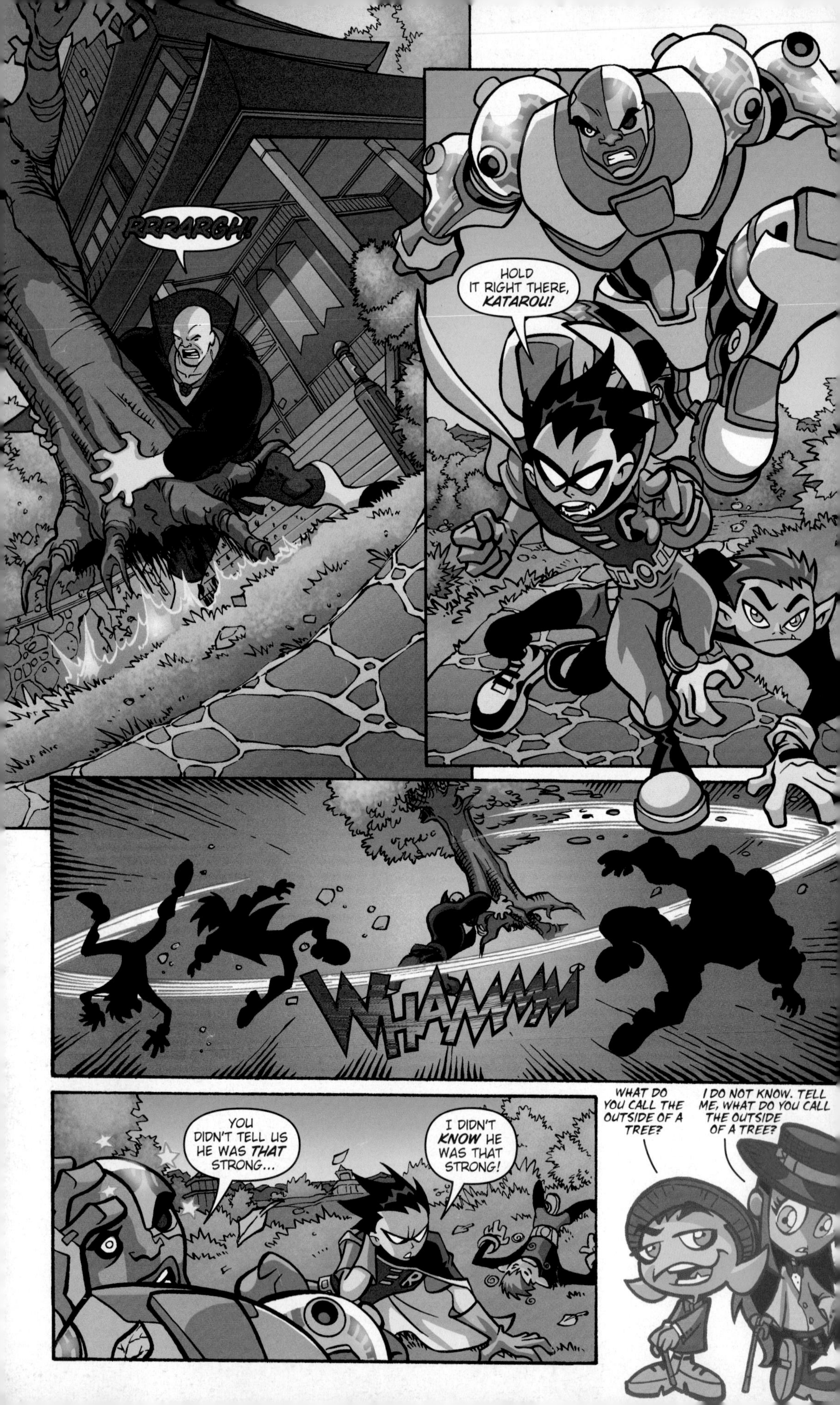
RRRARGH!
HOLD IT RIGHT THERE, KATAROU!
WHAMMM
YOU DIDN'T TELL US HE WAS THAT STRONG...
I DIDN'T KNOW HE WAS THAT STRONG!
WHAT DO YOU CALL THE OUTSIDE OF A TREE?
I DO NOT KNOW. TELL ME, WHAT DO YOU CALL THE OUTSIDE OF A TREE?

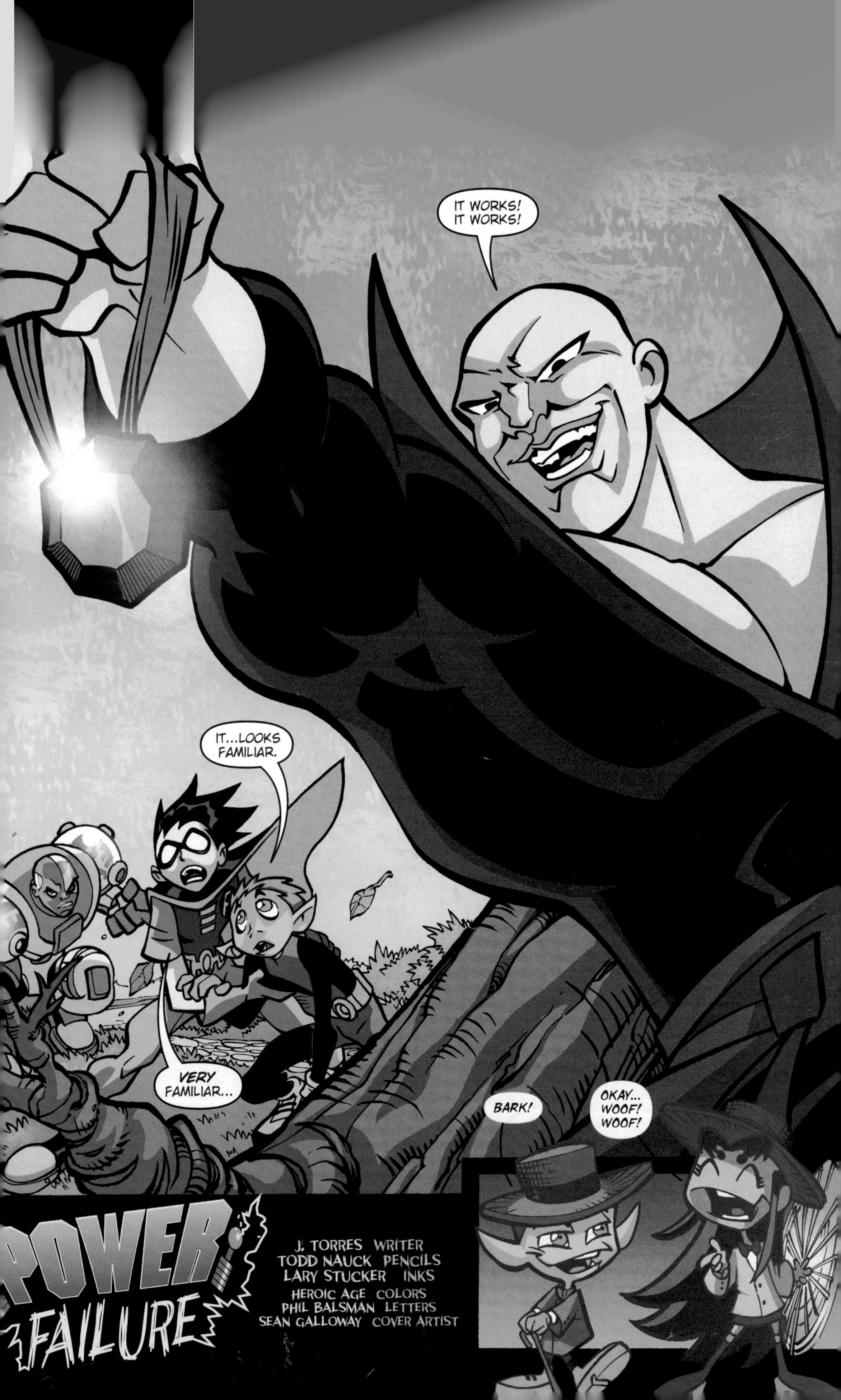
IT WORKS! IT WORKS!
IT...LOOKS FAMILIAR.
VERY FAMILIAR...
BARK!
OKAY... WOOF! WOOF!
POWER FAILURE
J. TORRES WRITER
TODD NAUCK PENCILS
LARY STUCKER INKS
HEROIC AGE COLORS
PHIL BALSMAN LETTERS
SEAN GALLOWAY COVER ARTIST

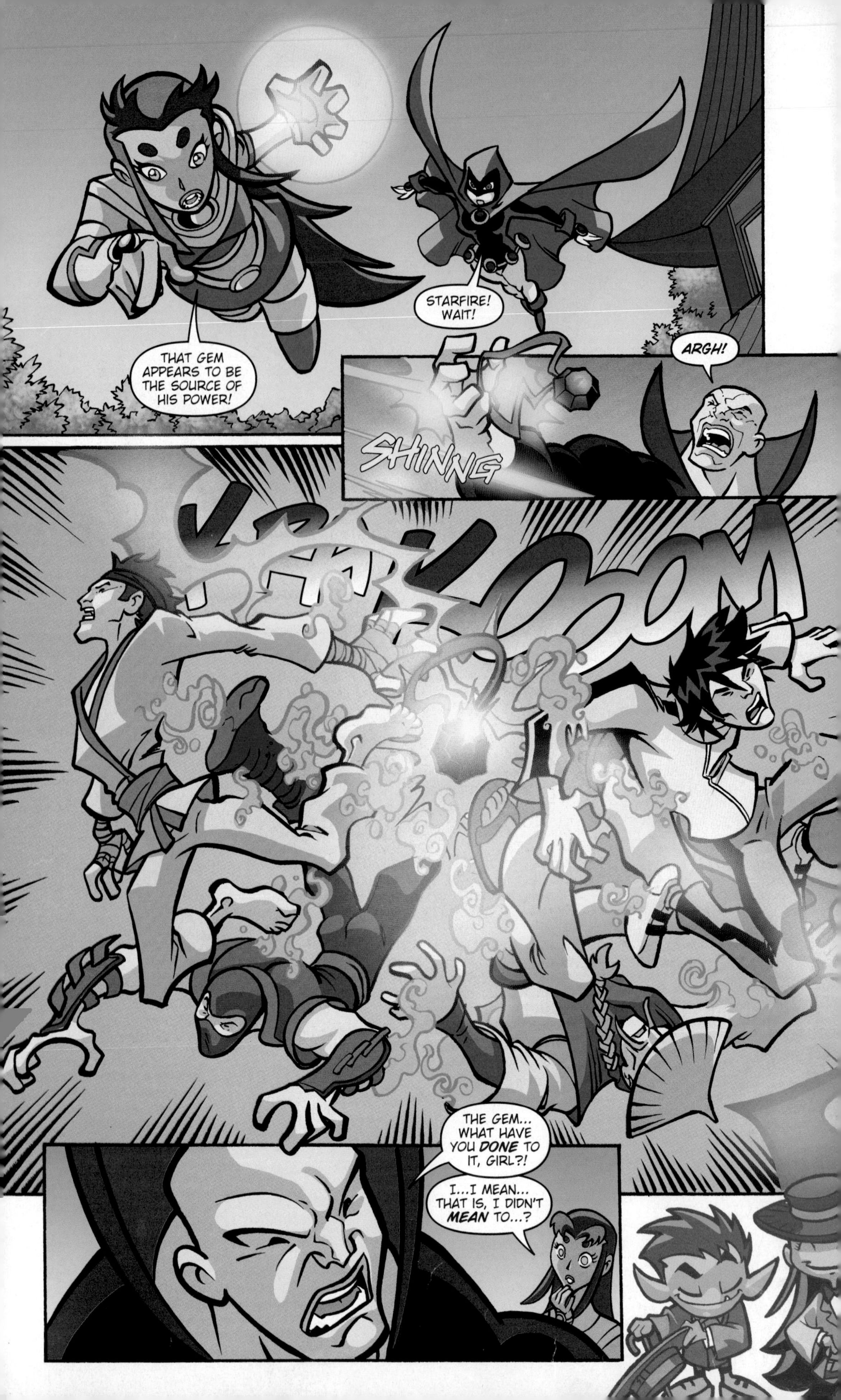

THAT GEM APPEARS TO BE THE SOURCE OF HIS POWER!
STARFIRE! WAIT!
ARGH!
SHINNG
THE GEM... WHAT HAVE YOU DONE TO IT, GIRL?!
I...I MEAN... THAT IS, I DIDN'T MEAN TO...?

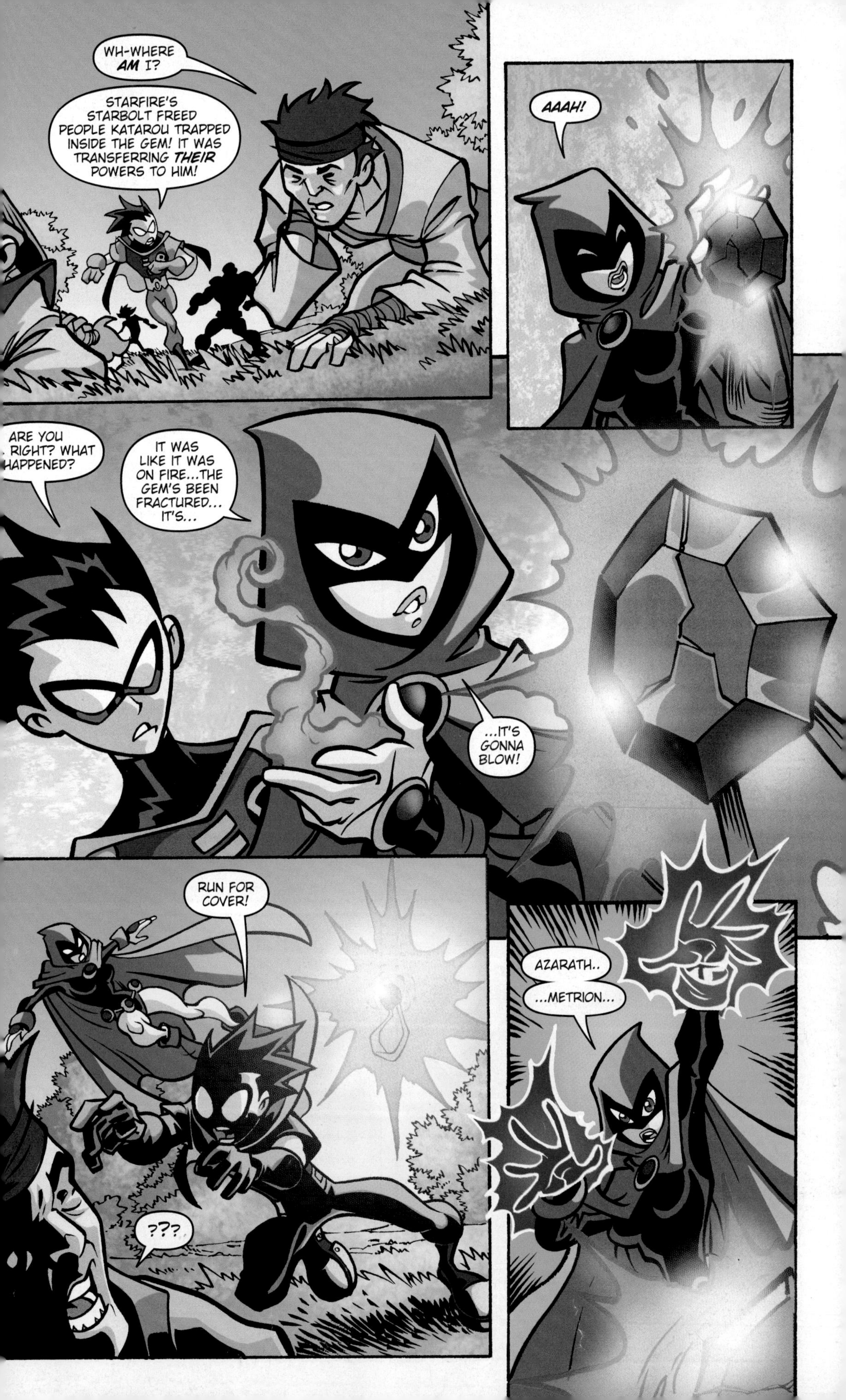
WH-WHERE AM I?
STARFIRE'S STARBOLT FREED PEOPLE KATAROU TRAPPED INSIDE THE GEM! IT WAS TRANSFERRING THEIR POWERS TO HIM!
AAAH!
ARE YOU RIGHT? WHAT HAPPENED?
IT WAS LIKE IT WAS ON FIRE...THE GEM'S BEEN FRACTURED... IT'S...
...IT'S GONNA BLOW!
RUN FOR COVER!
???
AZARATH..
...METRION...

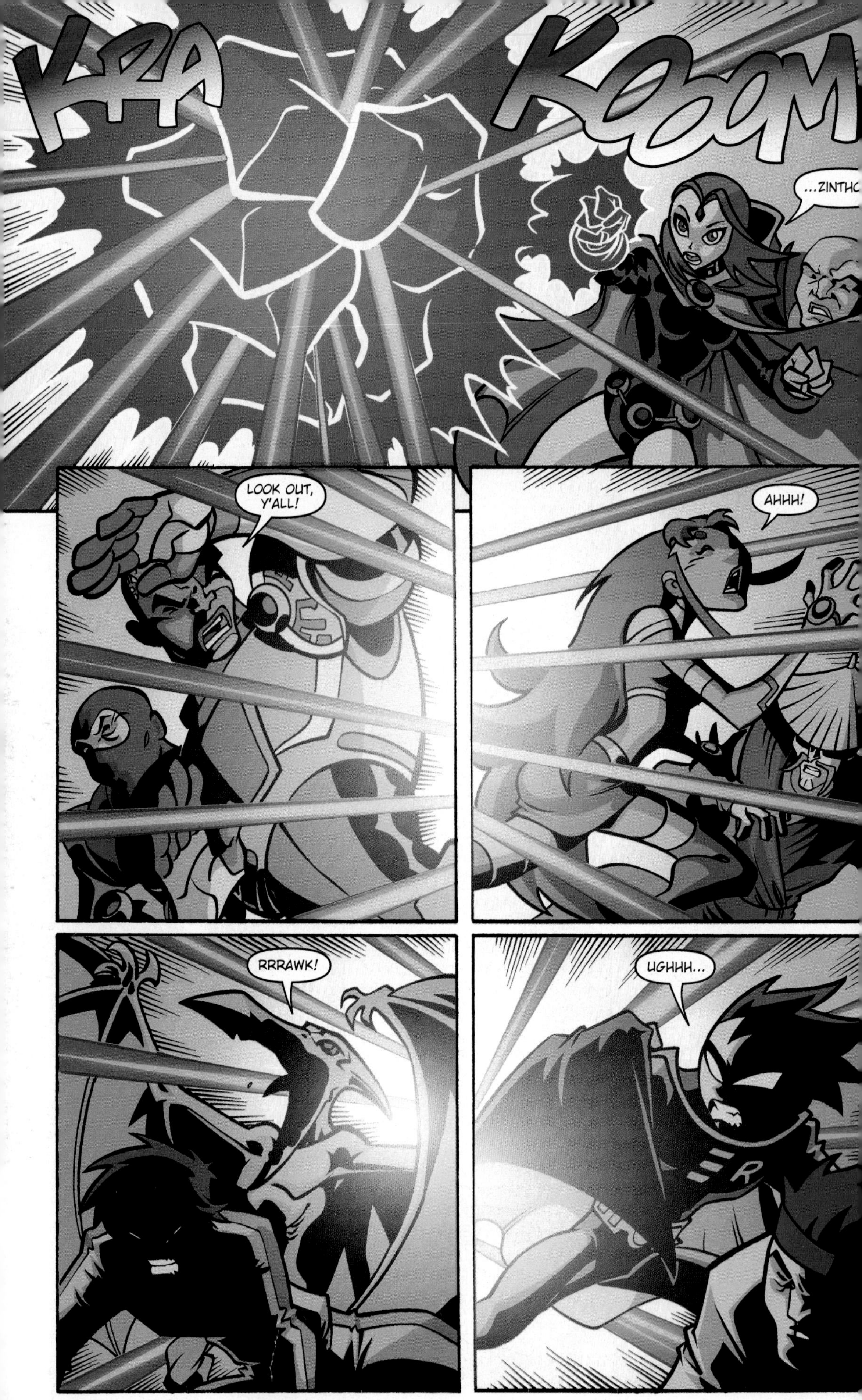
KRA
KOOOM
...ZINTHO
LOOK OUT, Y'ALL!
AHHH!
RRRAWK!
UGHHH...

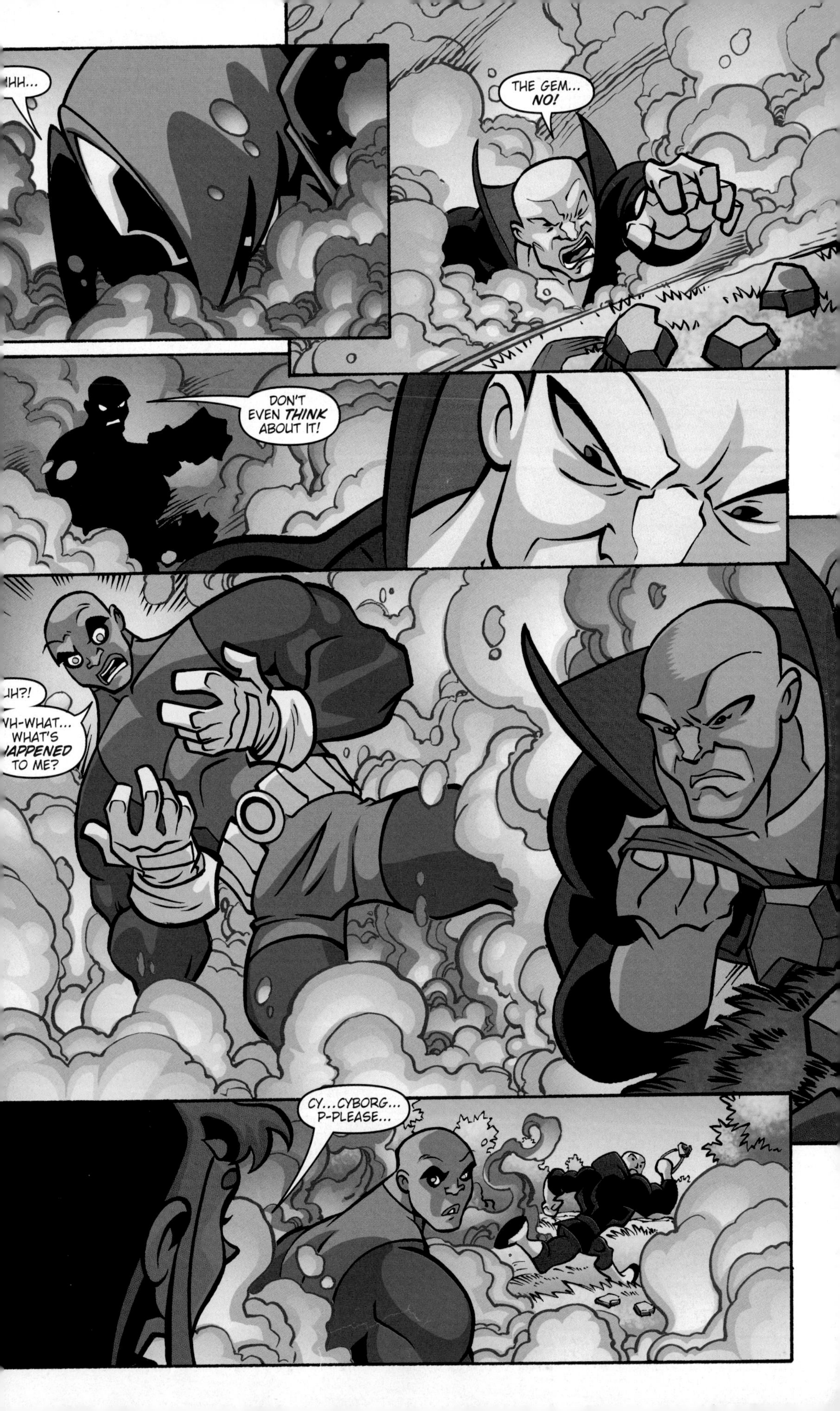
HH...
THE GEM... **NO!**
DON'T EVEN **THINK** ABOUT IT!
H?!
H-WHAT... WHAT'S **APPENED** TO ME?
CY...CYBORG... P-PLEASE...

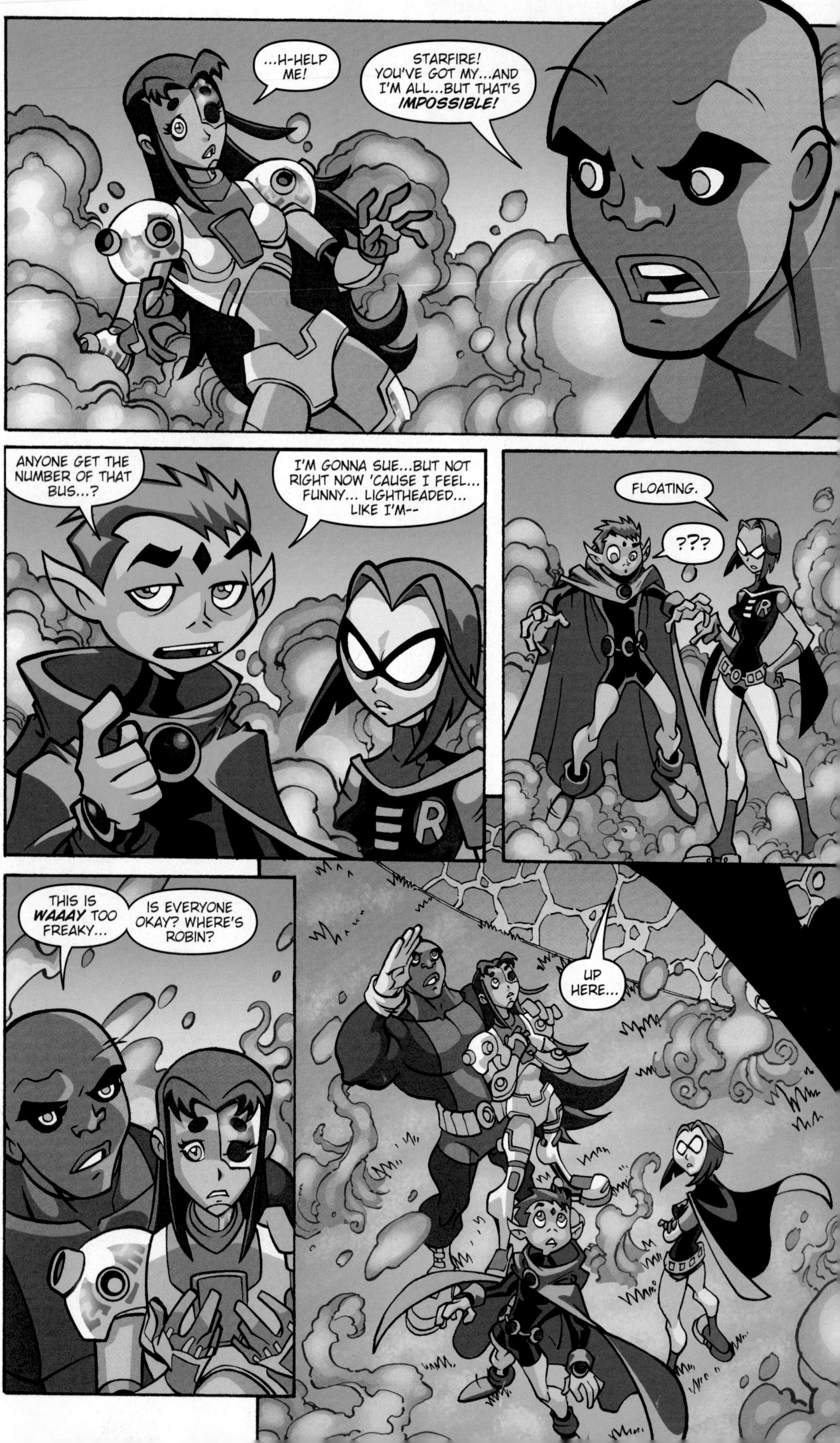
...H-HELP ME!
STARFIRE! YOU'VE GOT MY...AND I'M ALL...BUT THAT'S *IMPOSSIBLE!*
ANYONE GET THE NUMBER OF THAT BUS...?
I'M GONNA SUE...BUT NOT RIGHT NOW 'CAUSE I FEEL... FUNNY... LIGHTHEADED... LIKE I'M--
FLOATING.
???
THIS IS ***WAAAY*** TOO FREAKY...
IS EVERYONE OKAY? WHERE'S ROBIN?
UP HERE...

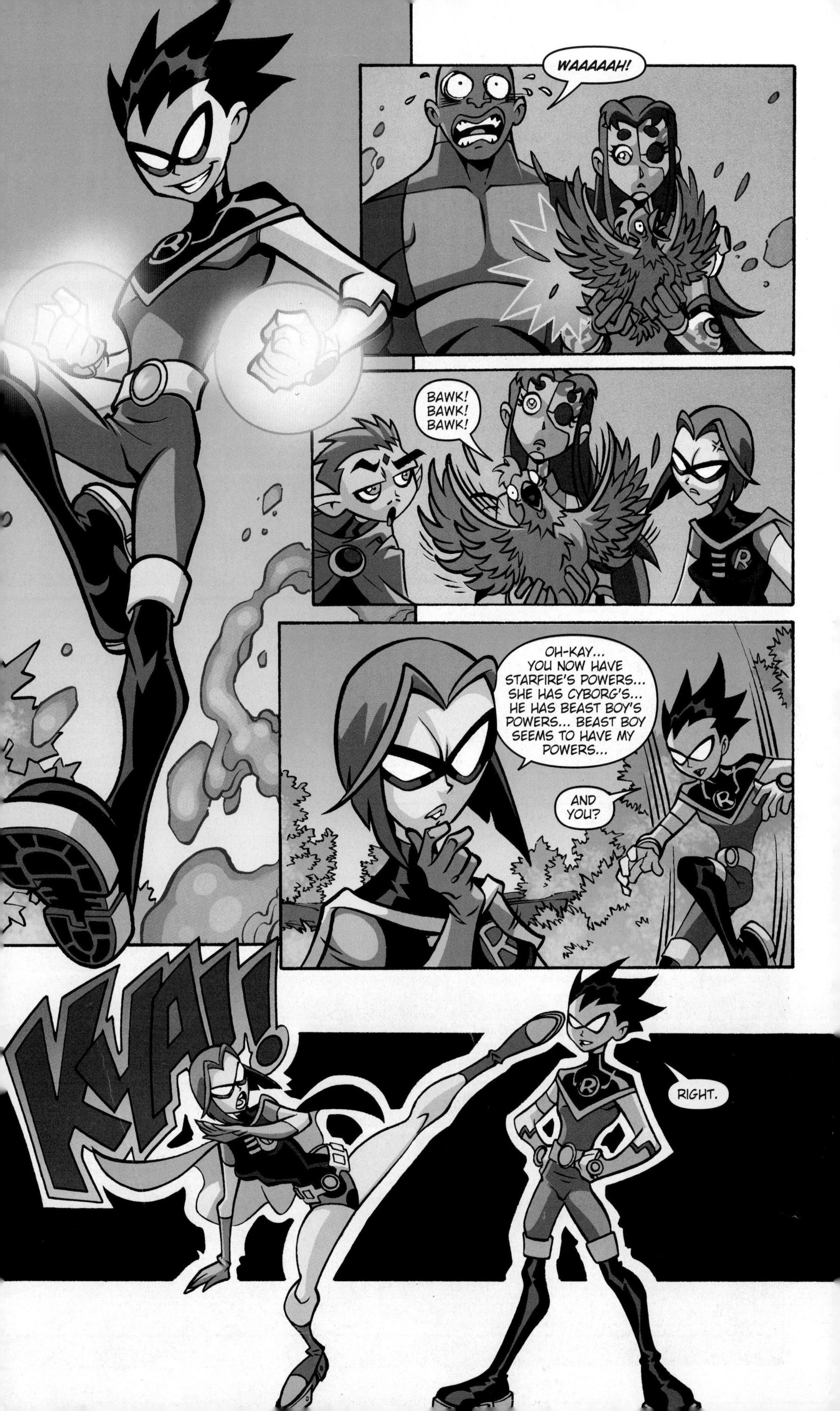
WAAAAAH!
BAWK! BAWK! BAWK!
OH-KAY... YOU NOW HAVE STARFIRE'S POWERS... SHE HAS CYBORG'S... HE HAS BEAST BOY'S POWERS... BEAST BOY SEEMS TO HAVE MY POWERS...
AND YOU?
KYAH!
RIGHT.

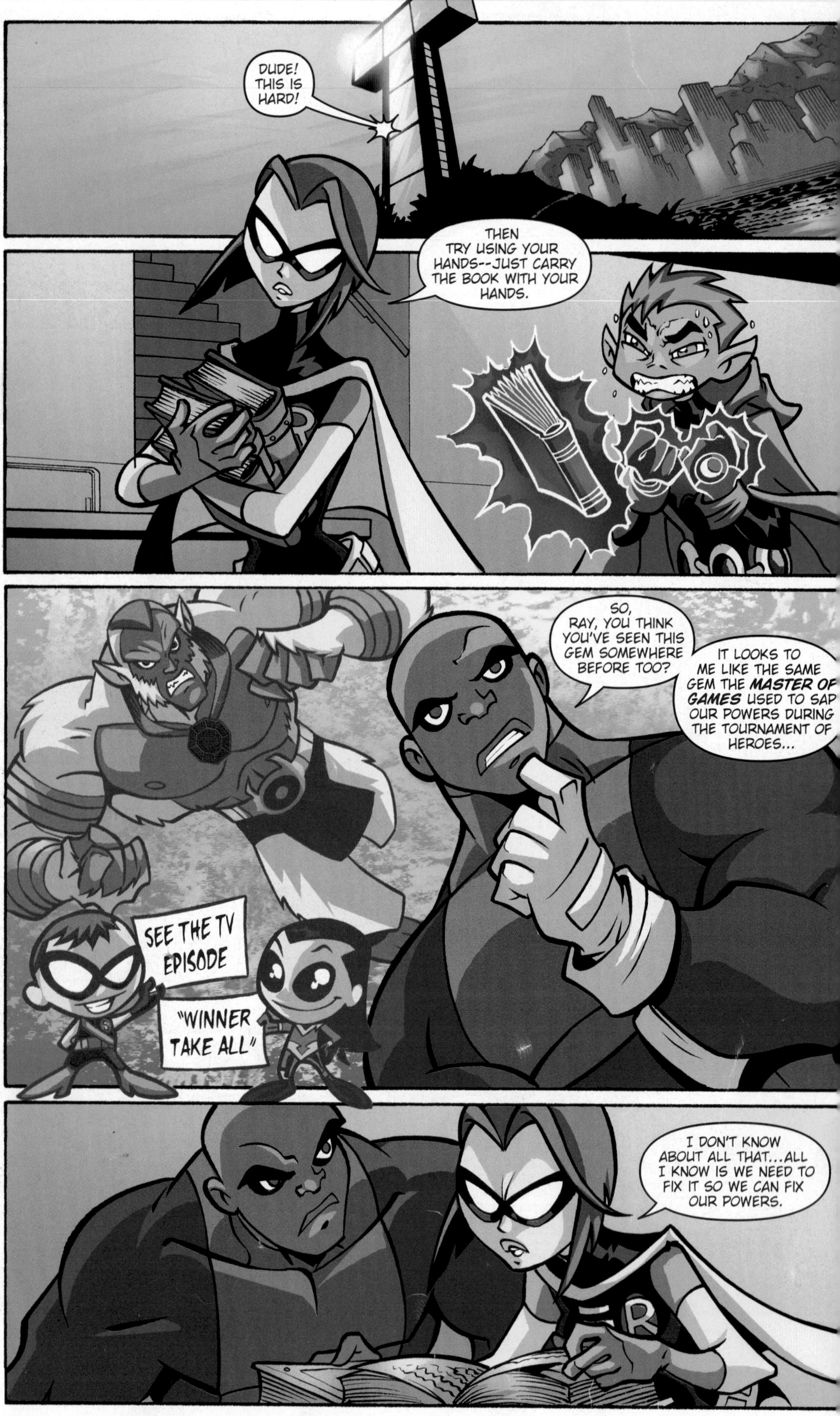
DUDE! THIS IS HARD!
THEN TRY USING YOUR HANDS--JUST CARRY THE BOOK WITH YOUR HANDS.
SO, RAY, YOU THINK YOU'VE SEEN THIS GEM SOMEWHERE BEFORE TOO?
IT LOOKS TO ME LIKE THE SAME GEM THE **MASTER OF GAMES** USED TO SAP OUR POWERS DURING THE TOURNAMENT OF HEROES...
SEE THE TV EPISODE
"WINNER TAKE ALL"
I DON'T KNOW ABOUT ALL THAT...ALL I KNOW IS WE NEED TO FIX IT SO WE CAN FIX OUR POWERS.

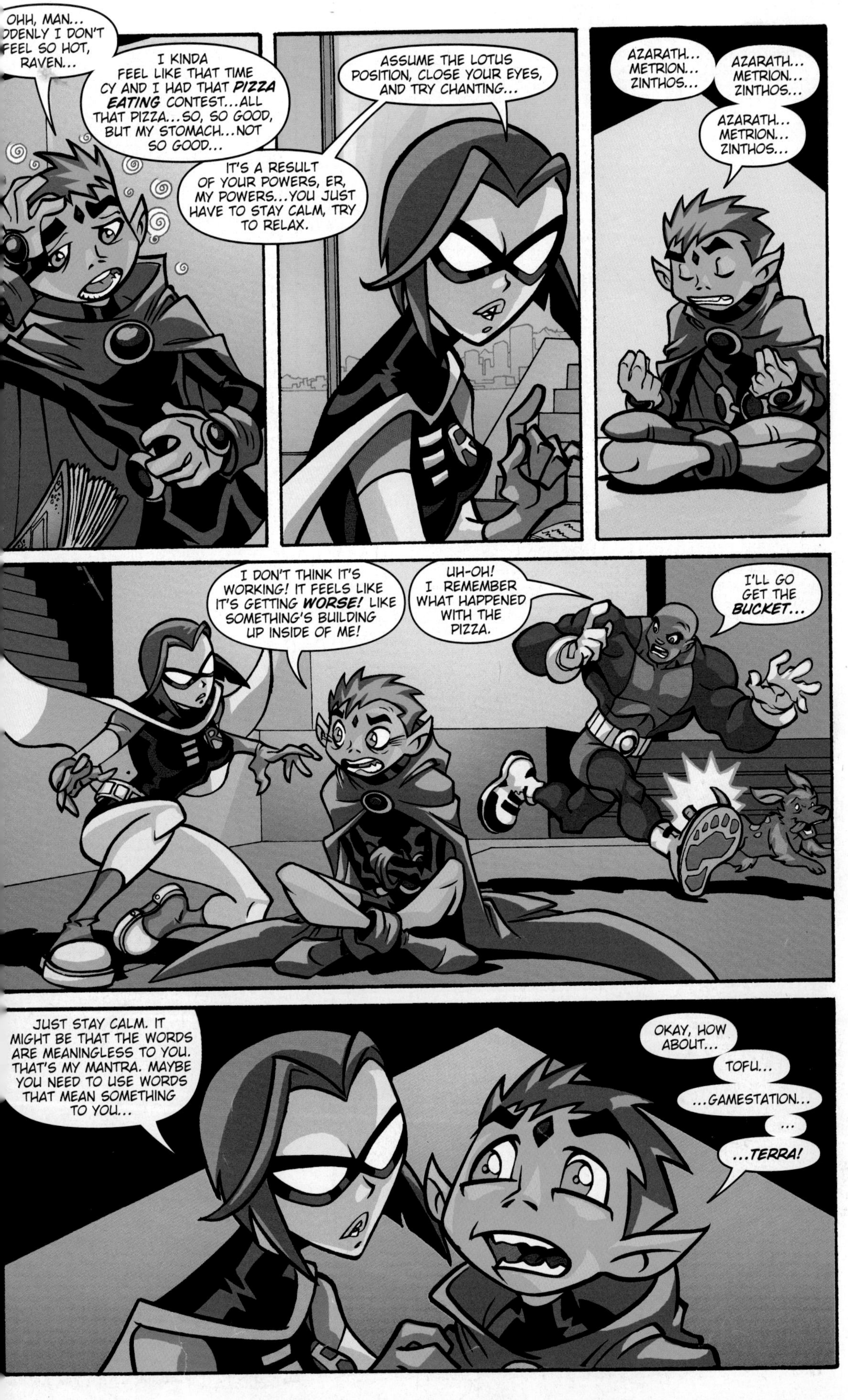
OHH, MAN... DDENLY I DON'T FEEL SO HOT, RAVEN...
I KINDA FEEL LIKE THAT TIME CY AND I HAD THAT PIZZA EATING CONTEST...ALL THAT PIZZA...SO, SO GOOD, BUT MY STOMACH...NOT SO GOOD...
IT'S A RESULT OF YOUR POWERS, ER, MY POWERS...YOU JUST HAVE TO STAY CALM, TRY TO RELAX.
ASSUME THE LOTUS POSITION, CLOSE YOUR EYES, AND TRY CHANTING...
AZARATH... METRION... ZINTHOS...
AZARATH... METRION... ZINTHOS...
AZARATH... METRION... ZINTHOS...
I DON'T THINK IT'S WORKING! IT FEELS LIKE IT'S GETTING WORSE! LIKE SOMETHING'S BUILDING UP INSIDE OF ME!
UH-OH! I REMEMBER WHAT HAPPENED WITH THE PIZZA.
I'LL GO GET THE BUCKET...
JUST STAY CALM. IT MIGHT BE THAT THE WORDS ARE MEANINGLESS TO YOU. THAT'S MY MANTRA. MAYBE YOU NEED TO USE WORDS THAT MEAN SOMETHING TO YOU...
OKAY, HOW ABOUT...
TOFU...
...GAMESTATION...
...
...TERRA!

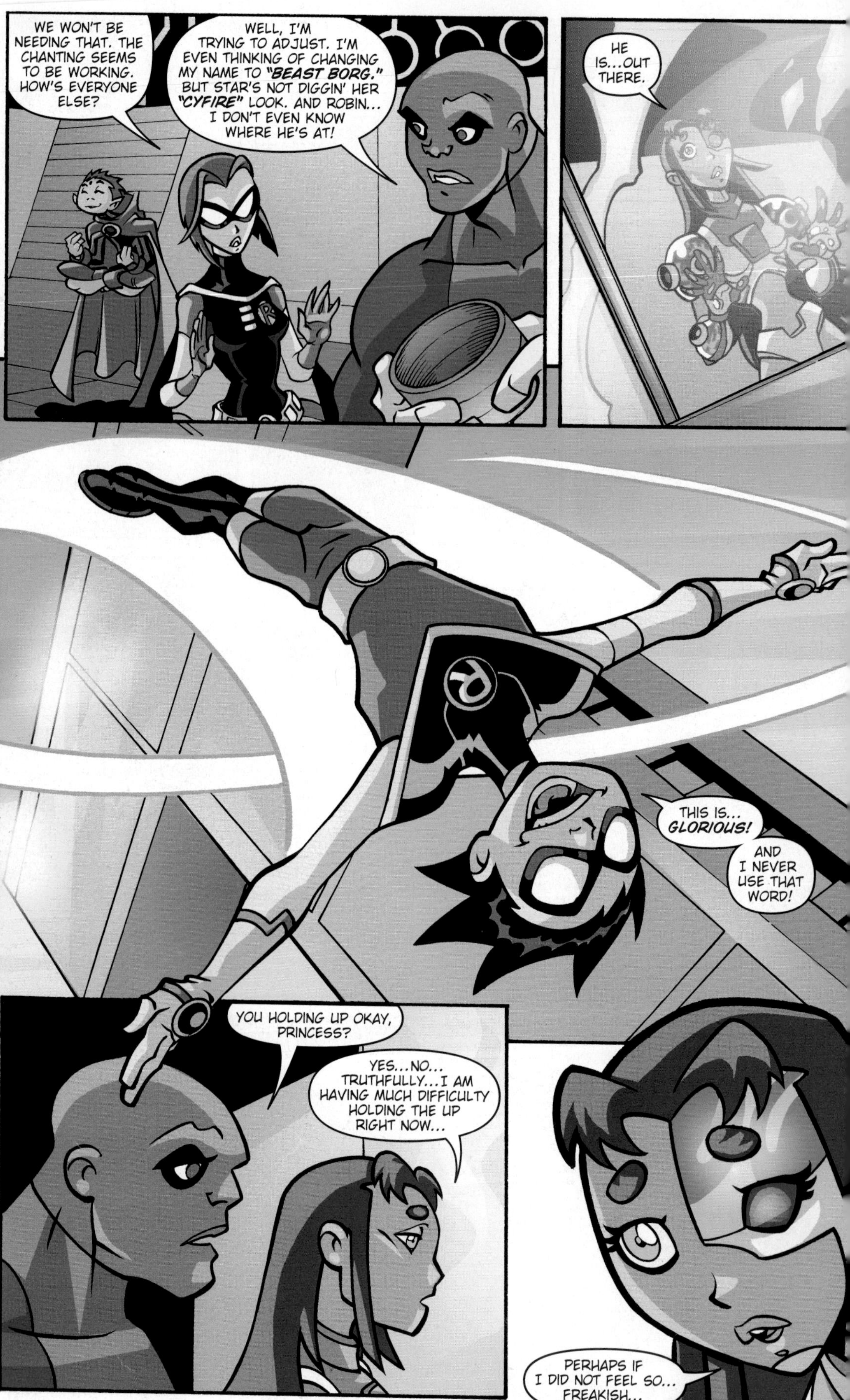
WE WON'T BE NEEDING THAT. THE CHANTING SEEMS TO BE WORKING. HOW'S EVERYONE ELSE?
WELL, I'M TRYING TO ADJUST. I'M EVEN THINKING OF CHANGING MY NAME TO "BEAST BORG." BUT STAR'S NOT DIGGIN' HER "CYFIRE" LOOK. AND ROBIN... I DON'T EVEN KNOW WHERE HE'S AT!
HE IS...OUT THERE.
THIS IS... GLORIOUS!
AND I NEVER USE THAT WORD!
YOU HOLDING UP OKAY, PRINCESS?
YES...NO... TRUTHFULLY...I AM HAVING MUCH DIFFICULTY HOLDING THE UP RIGHT NOW...
PERHAPS IF I DID NOT FEEL SO... FREAKISH...

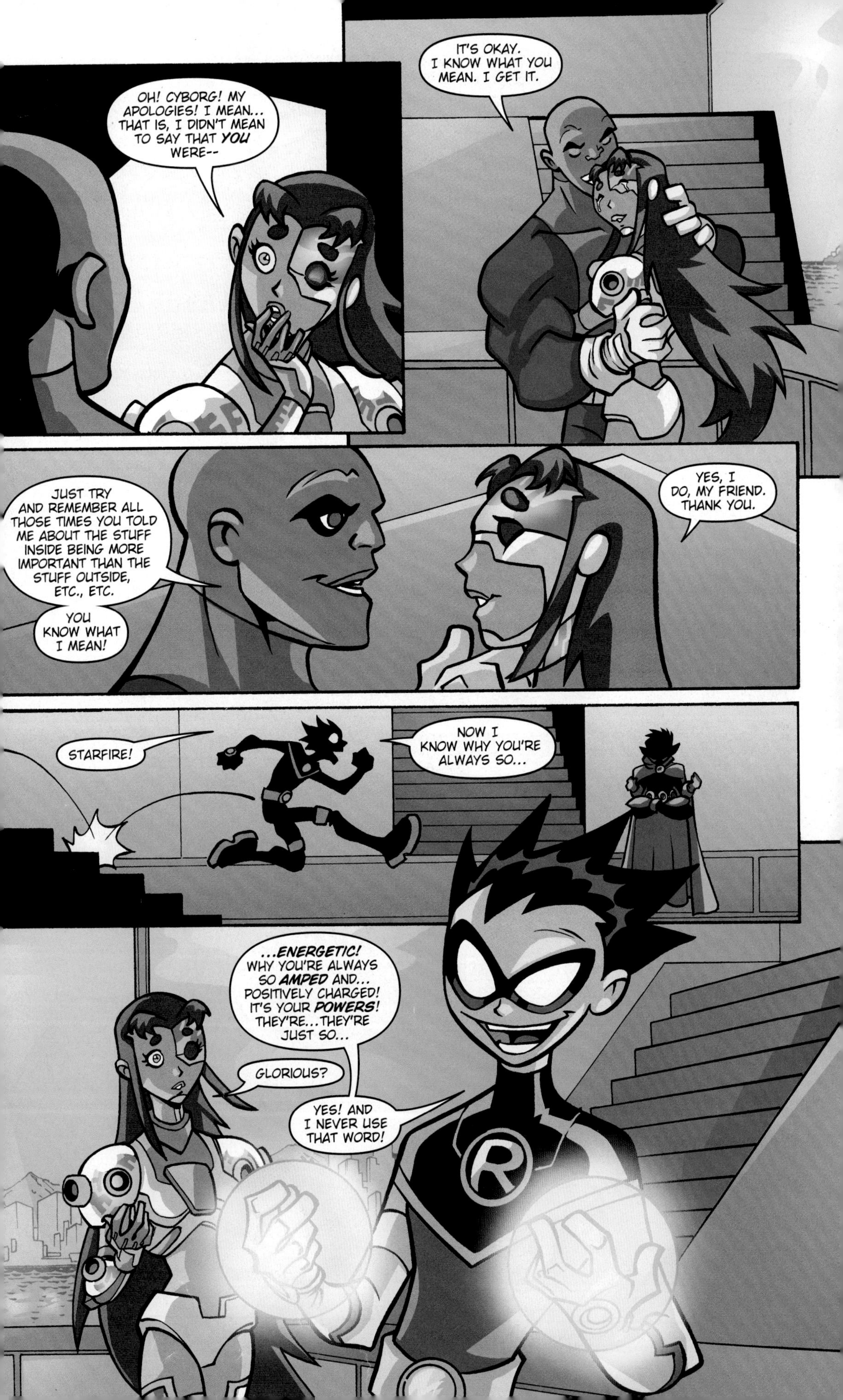
OH! CYBORG! MY APOLOGIES! I MEAN... THAT IS, I DIDN'T MEAN TO SAY THAT *YOU* WERE--
IT'S OKAY. I KNOW WHAT YOU MEAN. I GET IT.
JUST TRY AND REMEMBER ALL THOSE TIMES YOU TOLD ME ABOUT THE STUFF INSIDE BEING MORE IMPORTANT THAN THE STUFF OUTSIDE, ETC., ETC.
YOU KNOW WHAT I MEAN!
YES, I DO, MY FRIEND. THANK YOU.
STARFIRE!
NOW I KNOW WHY YOU'RE ALWAYS SO...
...ENERGETIC! WHY YOU'RE ALWAYS SO *AMPED* AND... POSITIVELY CHARGED! IT'S YOUR *POWERS!* THEY'RE...THEY'RE JUST SO...
GLORIOUS?
YES! AND I NEVER USE THAT WORD!

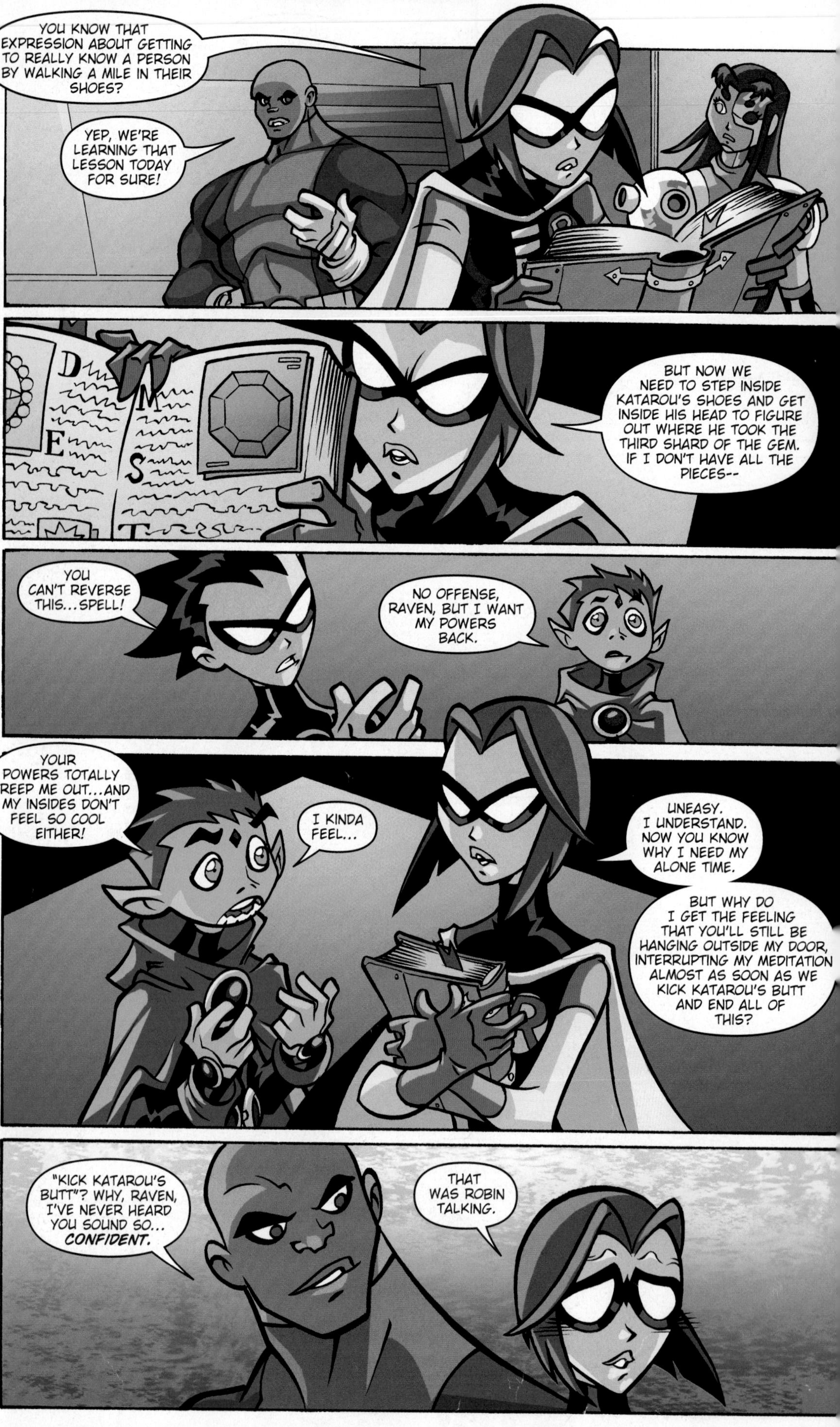
YOU KNOW THAT EXPRESSION ABOUT GETTING TO REALLY KNOW A PERSON BY WALKING A MILE IN THEIR SHOES?
YEP, WE'RE LEARNING THAT LESSON TODAY FOR SURE!
BUT NOW WE NEED TO STEP INSIDE KATAROU'S SHOES AND GET INSIDE HIS HEAD TO FIGURE OUT WHERE HE TOOK THE THIRD SHARD OF THE GEM. IF I DON'T HAVE ALL THE PIECES--
YOU CAN'T REVERSE THIS...SPELL!
NO OFFENSE, RAVEN, BUT I WANT MY POWERS BACK.
YOUR POWERS TOTALLY CREEP ME OUT...AND MY INSIDES DON'T FEEL SO COOL EITHER!
I KINDA FEEL...
UNEASY. I UNDERSTAND. NOW YOU KNOW WHY I NEED MY ALONE TIME.
BUT WHY DO I GET THE FEELING THAT YOU'LL STILL BE HANGING OUTSIDE MY DOOR, INTERRUPTING MY MEDITATION ALMOST AS SOON AS WE KICK KATAROU'S BUTT AND END ALL OF THIS?
"KICK KATAROU'S BUTT"? WHY, RAVEN, I'VE NEVER HEARD YOU SOUND SO... ***CONFIDENT.***
THAT WAS ROBIN TALKING.

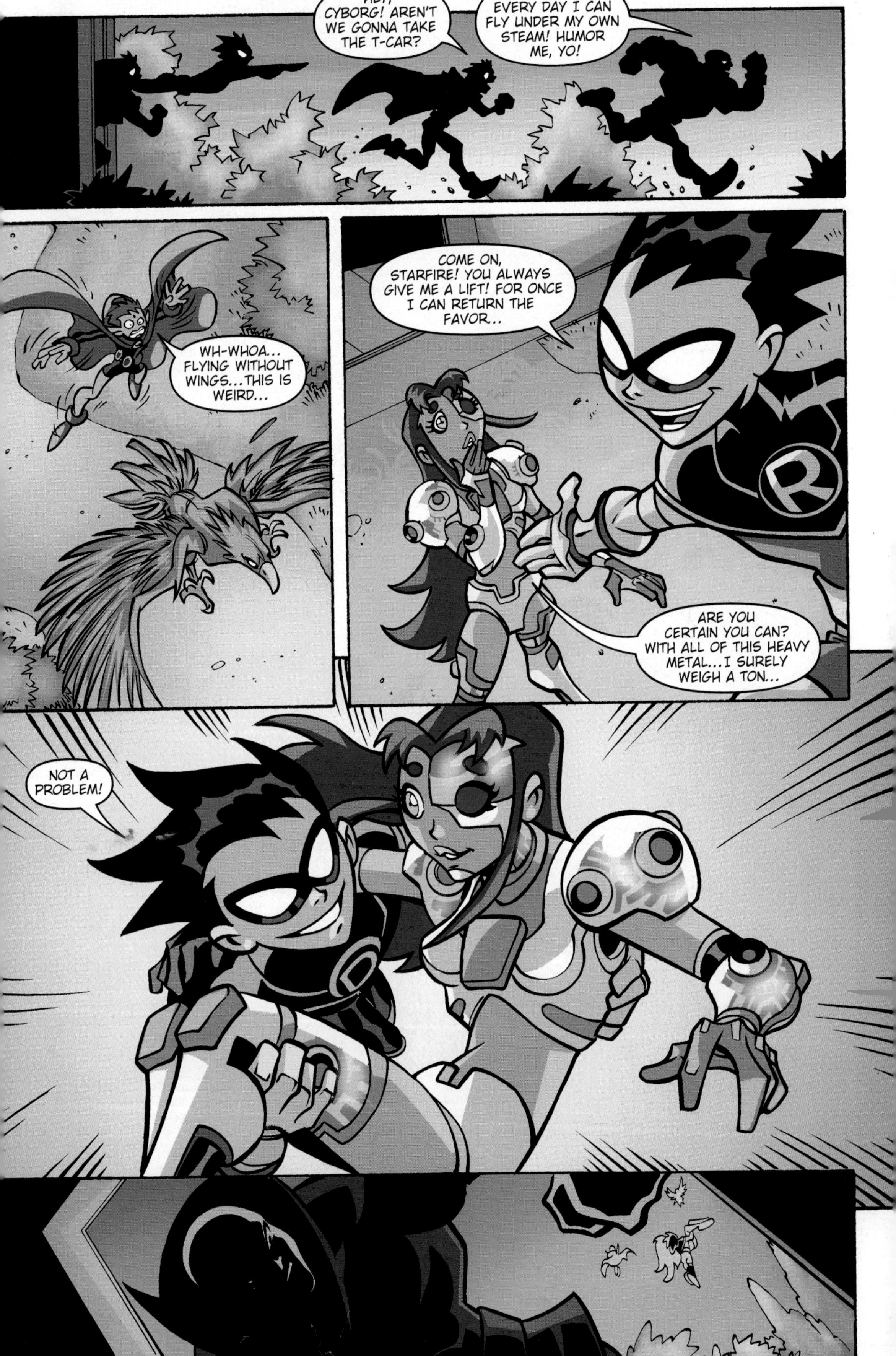
HEY, CYBORG! AREN'T WE GONNA TAKE THE T-CAR?
IT ISN'T EVERY DAY I CAN FLY UNDER MY OWN STEAM! HUMOR ME, YO!
WH-WHOA... FLYING WITHOUT WINGS...THIS IS WEIRD...
COME ON, STARFIRE! YOU ALWAYS GIVE ME A LIFT! FOR ONCE I CAN RETURN THE FAVOR...
ARE YOU CERTAIN YOU CAN? WITH ALL OF THIS HEAVY METAL...I SURELY WEIGH A TON...
NOT A PROBLEM!

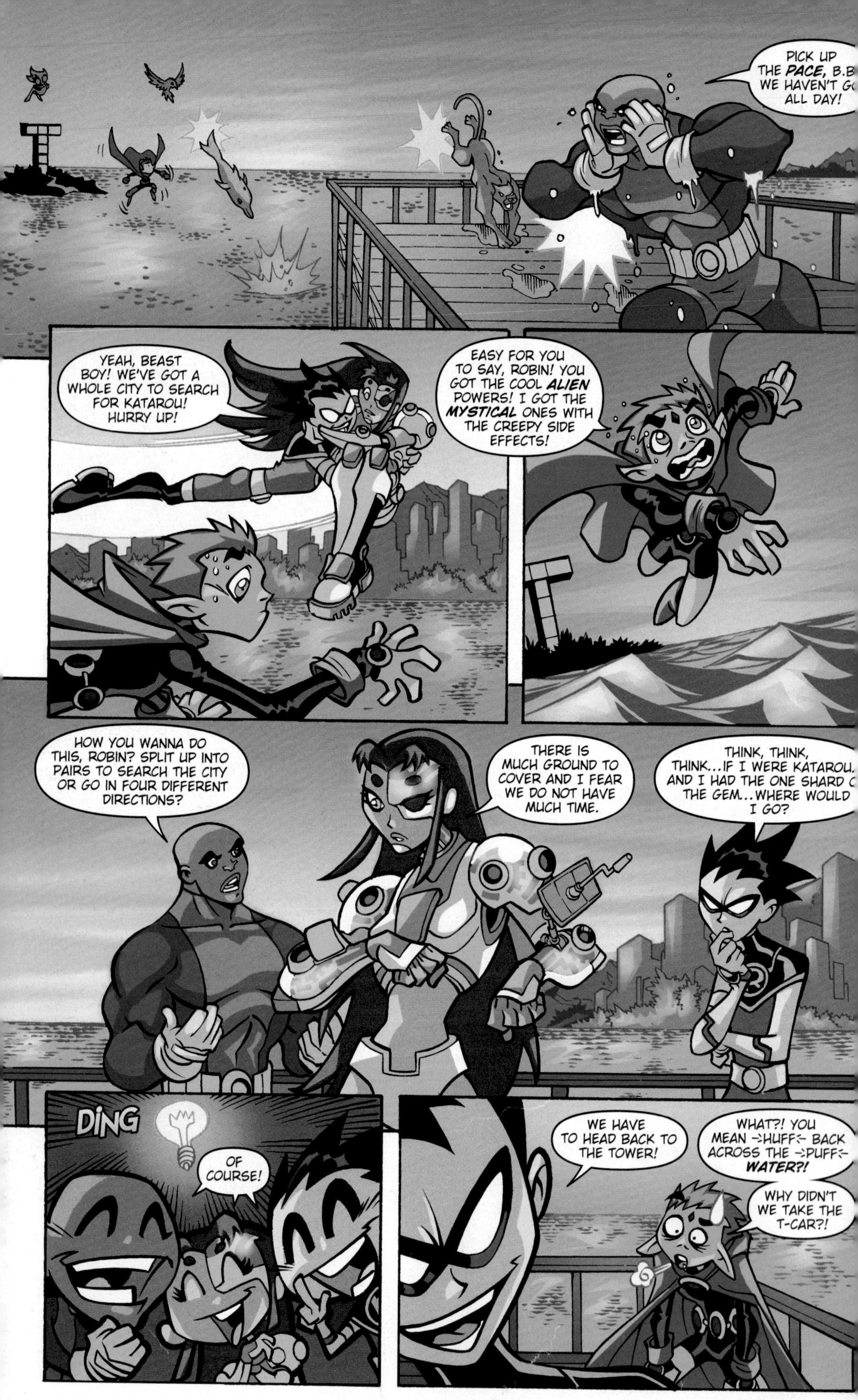
PICK UP THE PACE, B.B. WE HAVEN'T GOT ALL DAY!
YEAH, BEAST BOY! WE'VE GOT A WHOLE CITY TO SEARCH FOR KATAROU! HURRY UP!
EASY FOR YOU TO SAY, ROBIN! YOU GOT THE COOL ALIEN POWERS! I GOT THE MYSTICAL ONES WITH THE CREEPY SIDE EFFECTS!
HOW YOU WANNA DO THIS, ROBIN? SPLIT UP INTO PAIRS TO SEARCH THE CITY OR GO IN FOUR DIFFERENT DIRECTIONS?
THERE IS MUCH GROUND TO COVER AND I FEAR WE DO NOT HAVE MUCH TIME.
THINK, THINK, THINK...IF I WERE KATAROU AND I HAD THE ONE SHARD OF THE GEM...WHERE WOULD I GO?
DING
OF COURSE!
WE HAVE TO HEAD BACK TO THE TOWER!
WHAT?! YOU MEAN -HUFF- BACK ACROSS THE -PUFF- WATER?!
WHY DIDN'T WE TAKE THE T-CAR?!

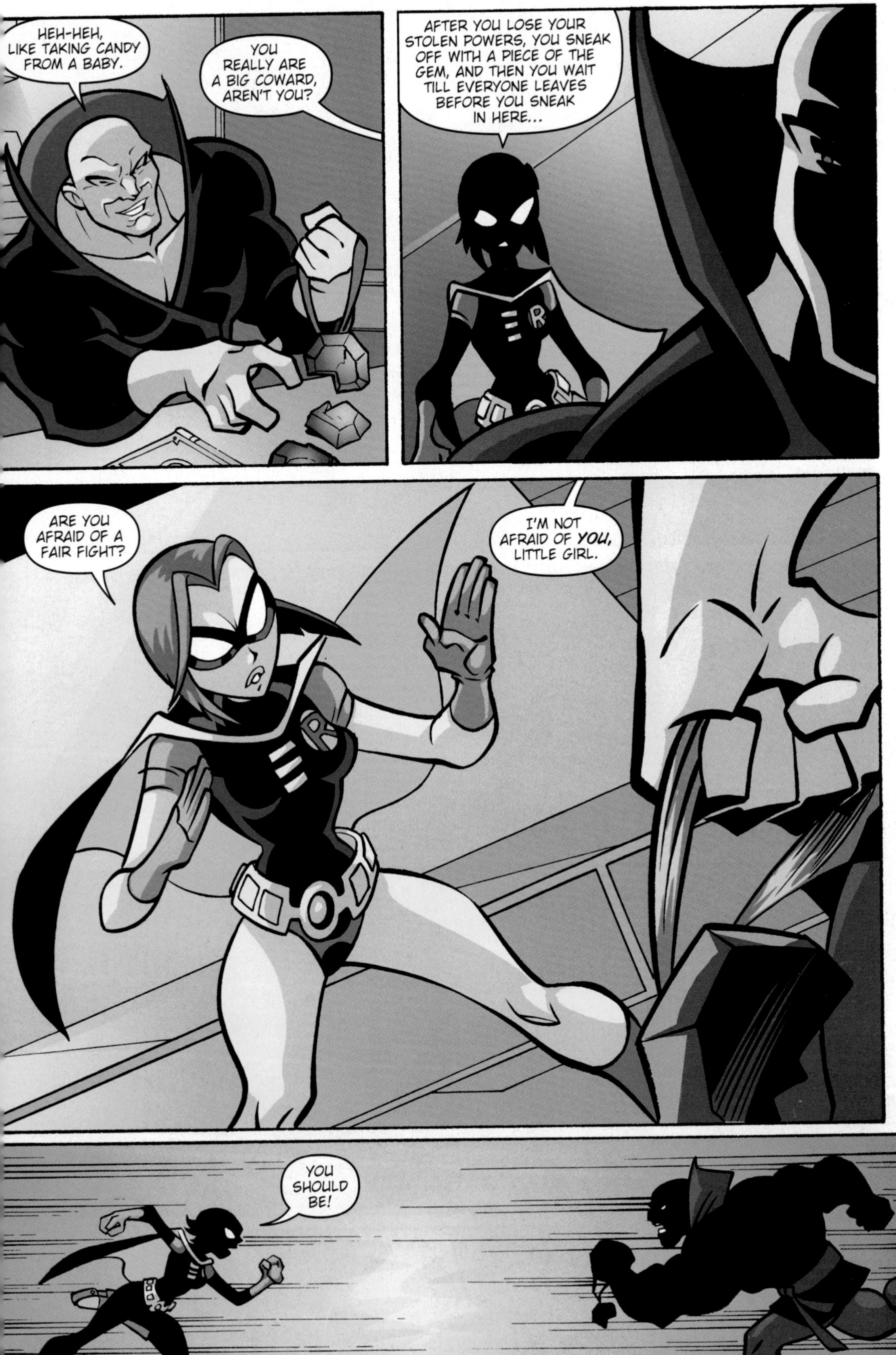
HEH-HEH, LIKE TAKING CANDY FROM A BABY.
YOU REALLY ARE A BIG COWARD, AREN'T YOU?
AFTER YOU LOSE YOUR STOLEN POWERS, YOU SNEAK OFF WITH A PIECE OF THE GEM, AND THEN YOU WAIT TILL EVERYONE LEAVES BEFORE YOU SNEAK IN HERE...
ARE YOU AFRAID OF A FAIR FIGHT?
I'M NOT AFRAID OF YOU, LITTLE GIRL.
YOU SHOULD BE!

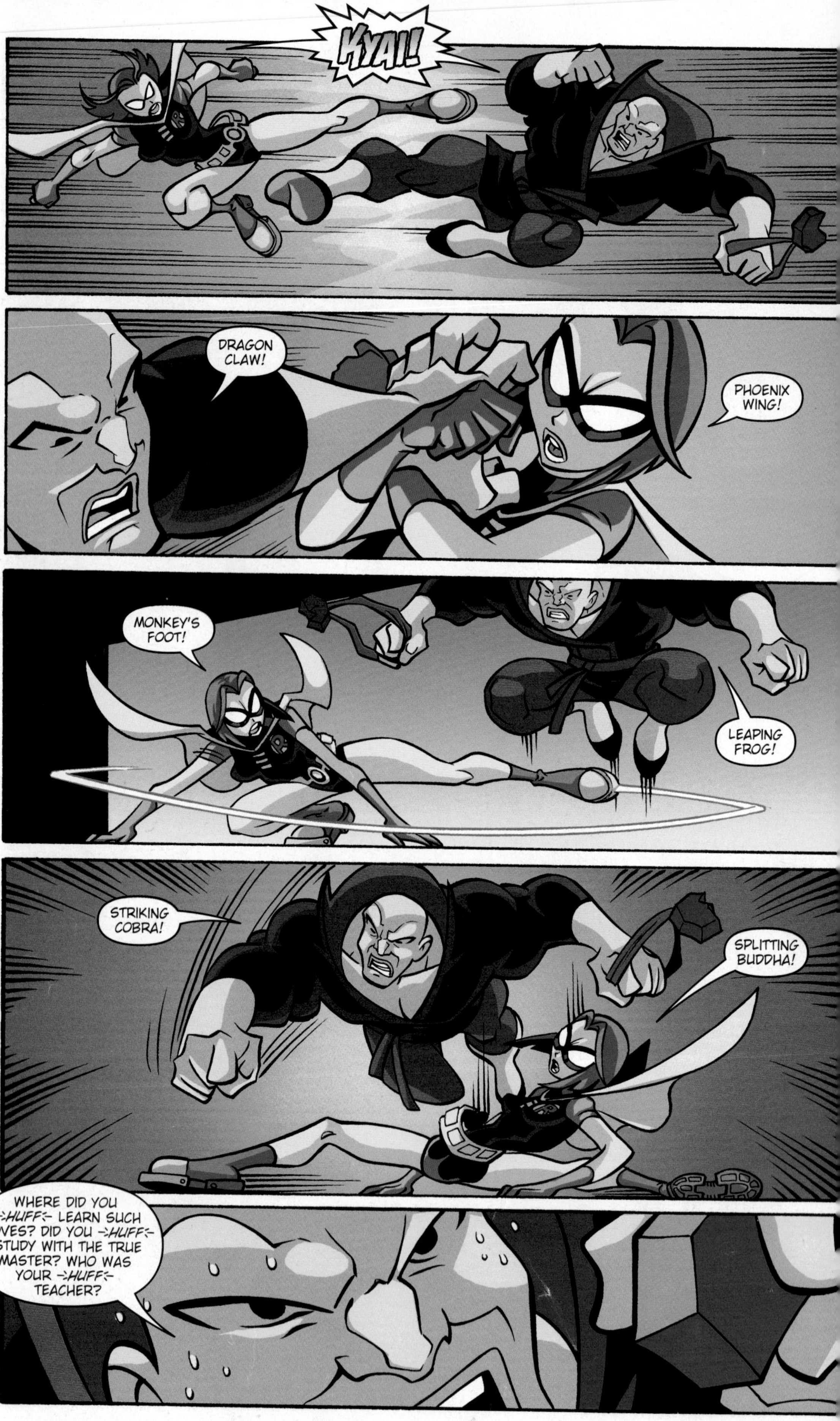
KYAI!
DRAGON CLAW!
PHOENIX WING!
MONKEY'S FOOT!
LEAPING FROG!
STRIKING COBRA!
SPLITTING BUDDHA!
WHERE DID YOU -HUFF- LEARN SUCH MOVES? DID YOU -HUFF- STUDY WITH THE TRUE MASTER? WHO WAS YOUR -HUFF- TEACHER?

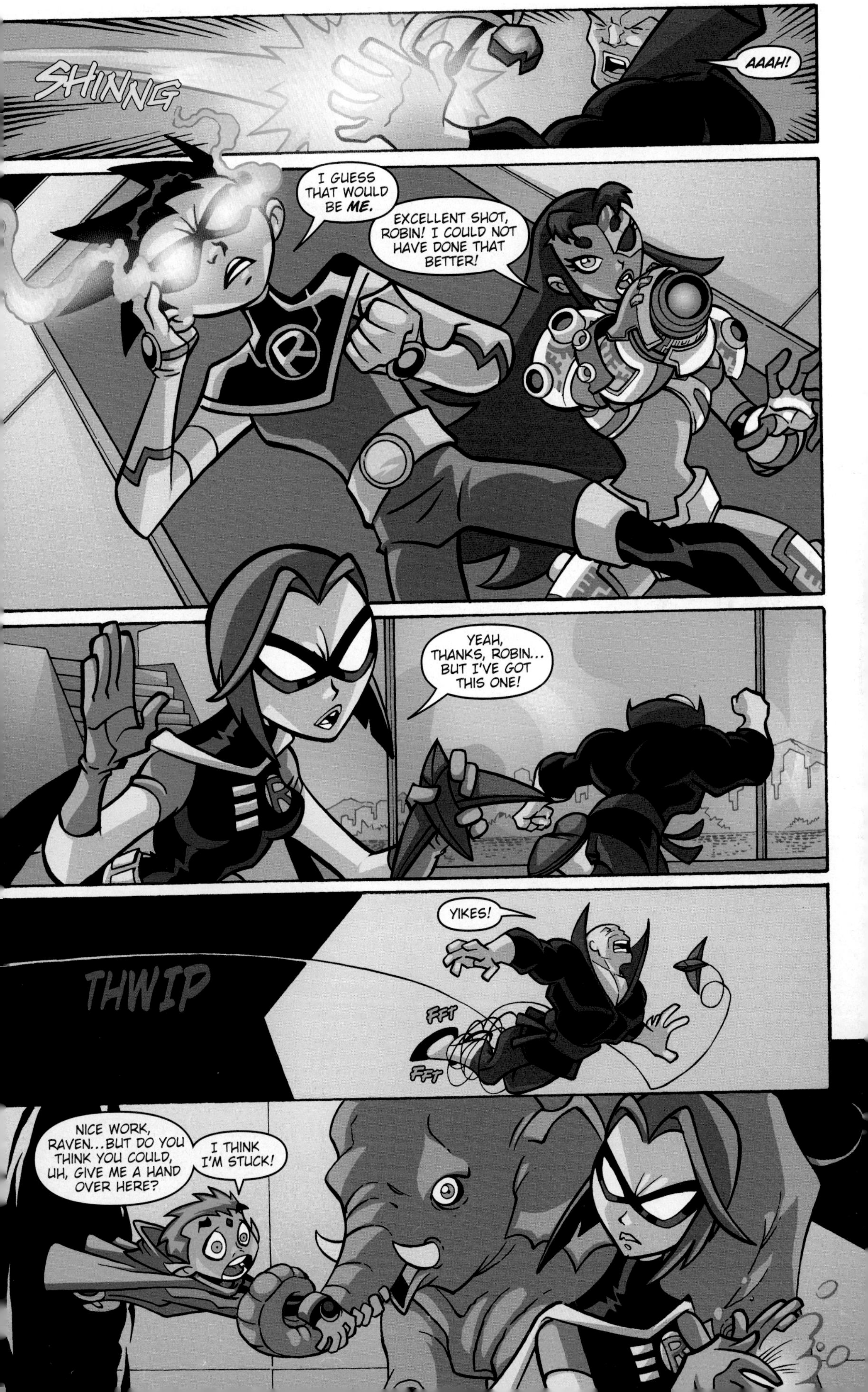
SHINNG
AAAH!
I GUESS THAT WOULD BE **ME.**
EXCELLENT SHOT, ROBIN! I COULD NOT HAVE DONE THAT BETTER!
YEAH, THANKS, ROBIN... BUT I'VE GOT THIS ONE!
THWIP
YIKES!
FFT
FFT
NICE WORK, RAVEN...BUT DO YOU THINK YOU COULD, UH, GIVE ME A HAND OVER HERE?
I THINK I'M STUCK!

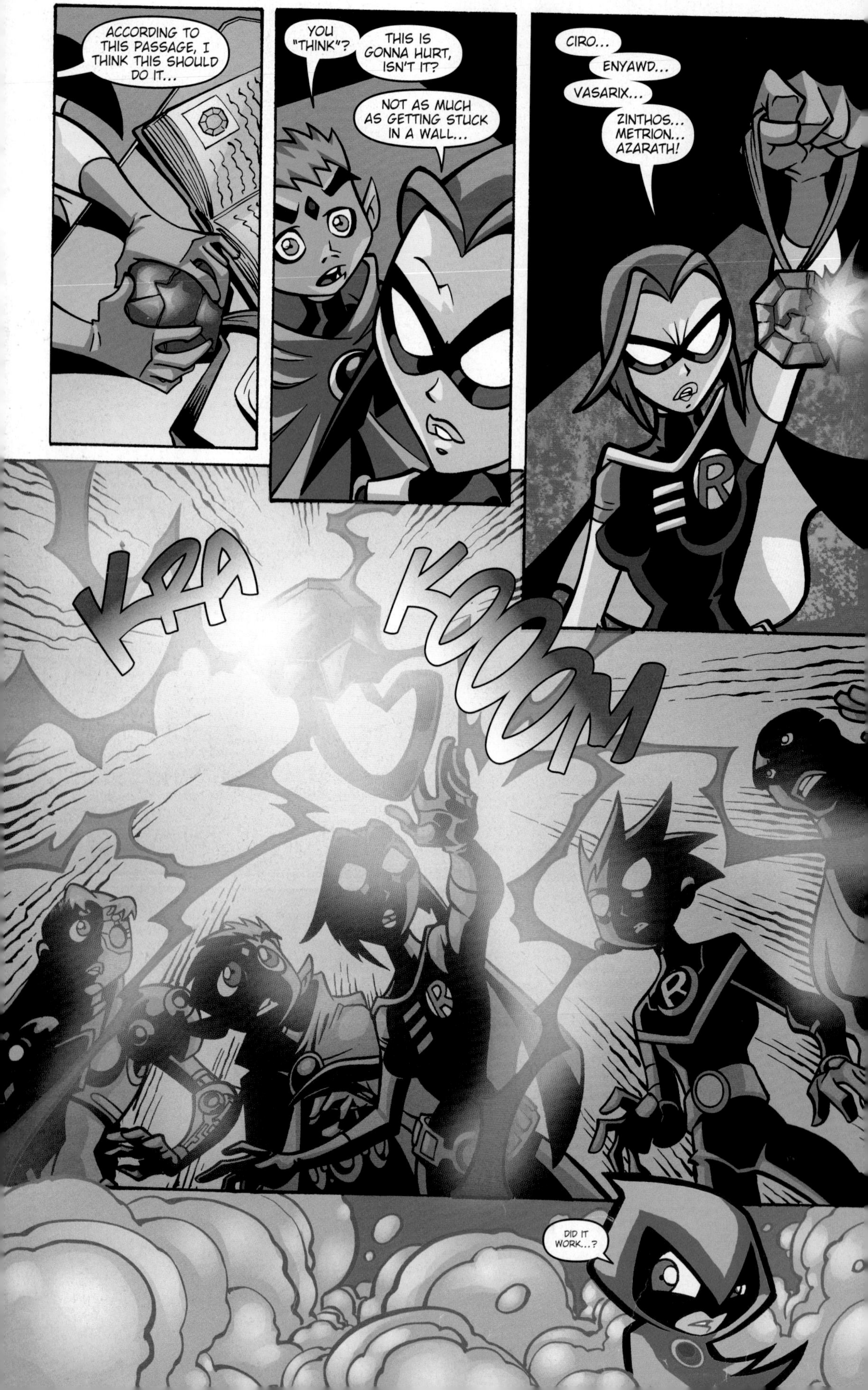

ACCORDING TO THIS PASSAGE, I THINK THIS SHOULD DO IT...
YOU "THINK"?
THIS IS GONNA HURT, ISN'T IT?
NOT AS MUCH AS GETTING STUCK IN A WALL...
CIRO...
ENYAWD...
VASARIX...
ZINTHOS... METRION... AZARATH!
KRA KOOOM
DID IT WORK...?

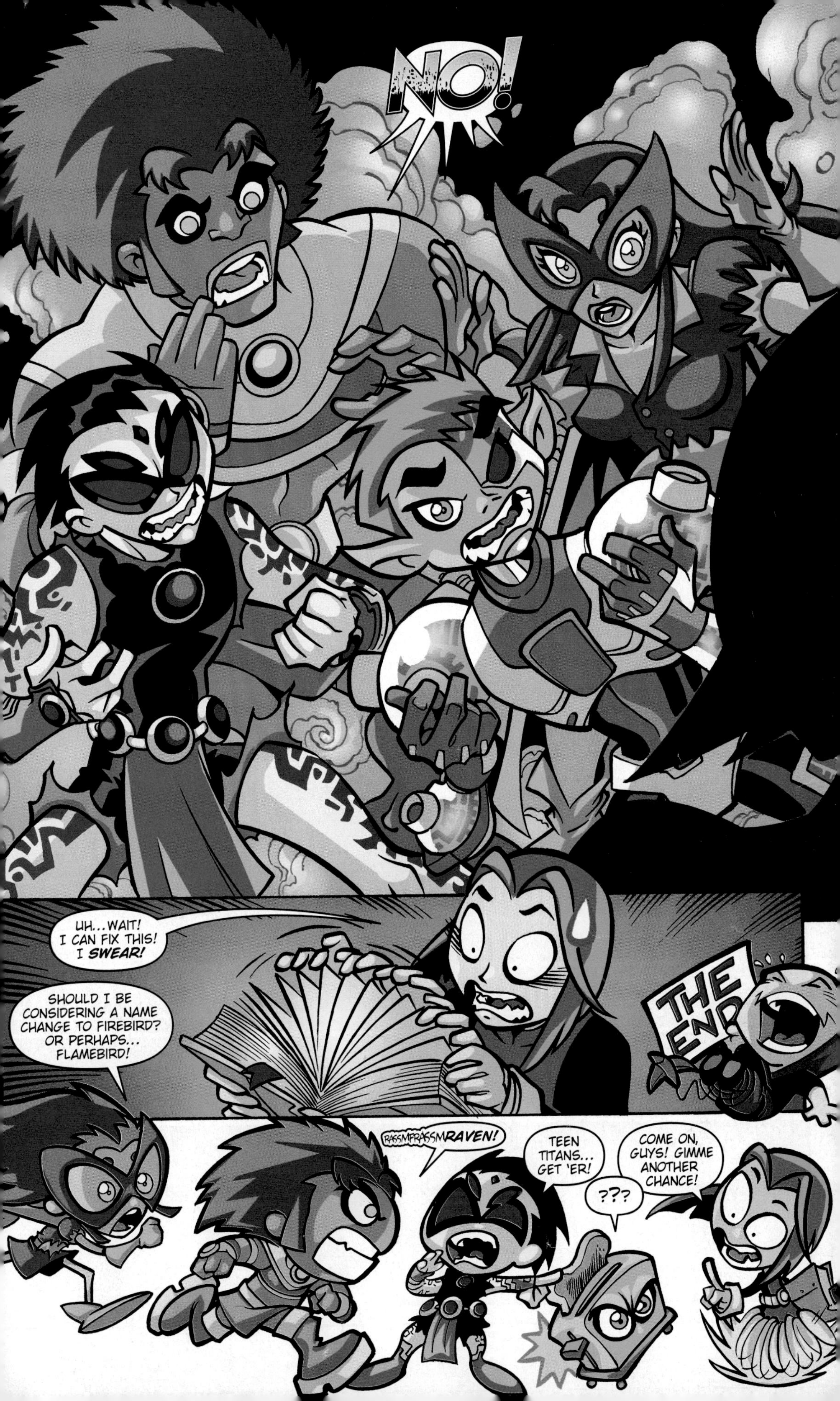
NO!
UH...WAIT! I CAN FIX THIS! I SWEAR!
SHOULD I BE CONSIDERING A NAME CHANGE TO FIREBIRD? OR PERHAPS... FLAMEBIRD!
THE END
RASSMFRASSMRAVEN!
TEEN TITANS... GET 'ER!
???
COME ON, GUYS! GIMME ANOTHER CHANCE!

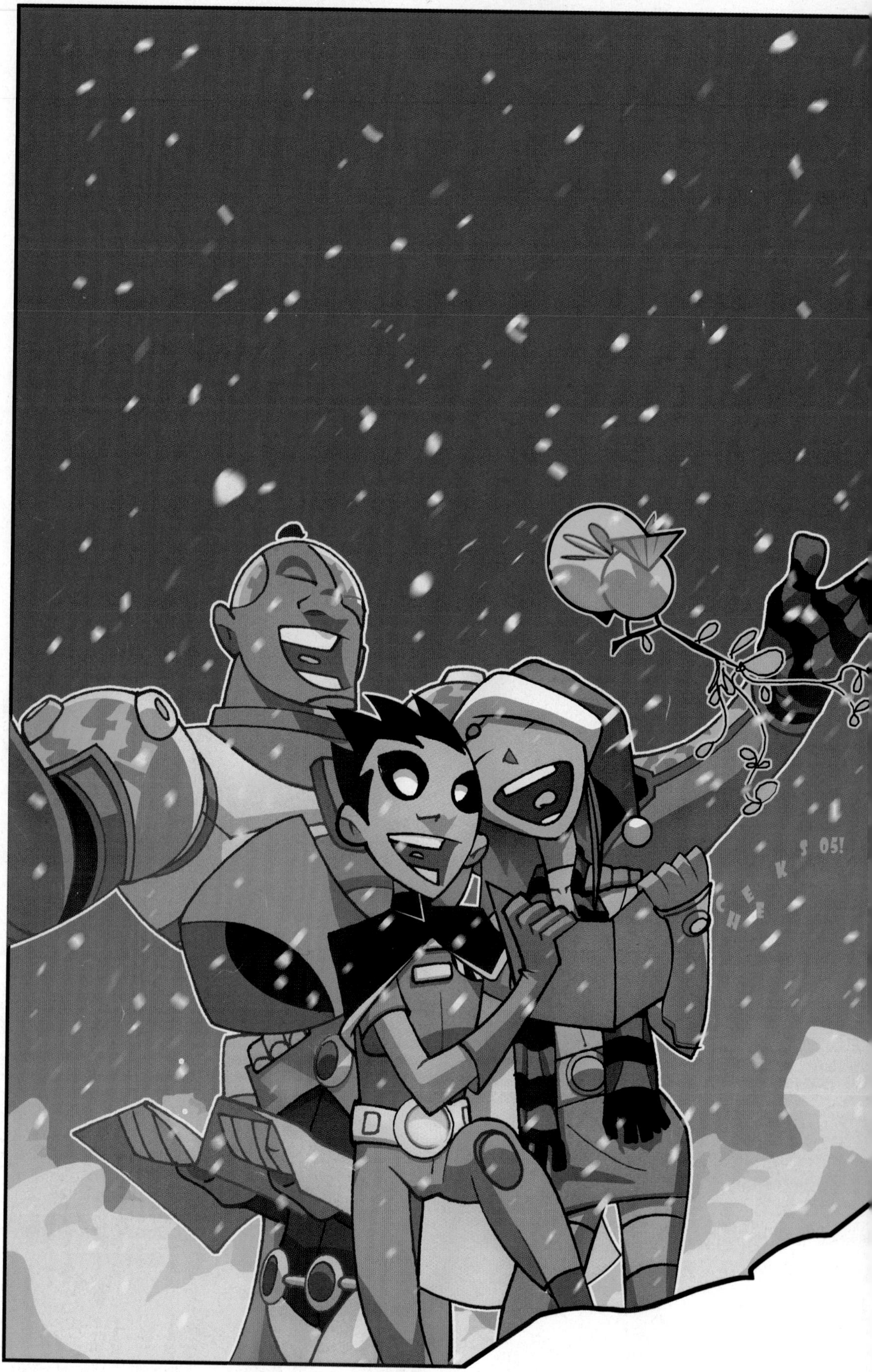
CHEEKS 05!

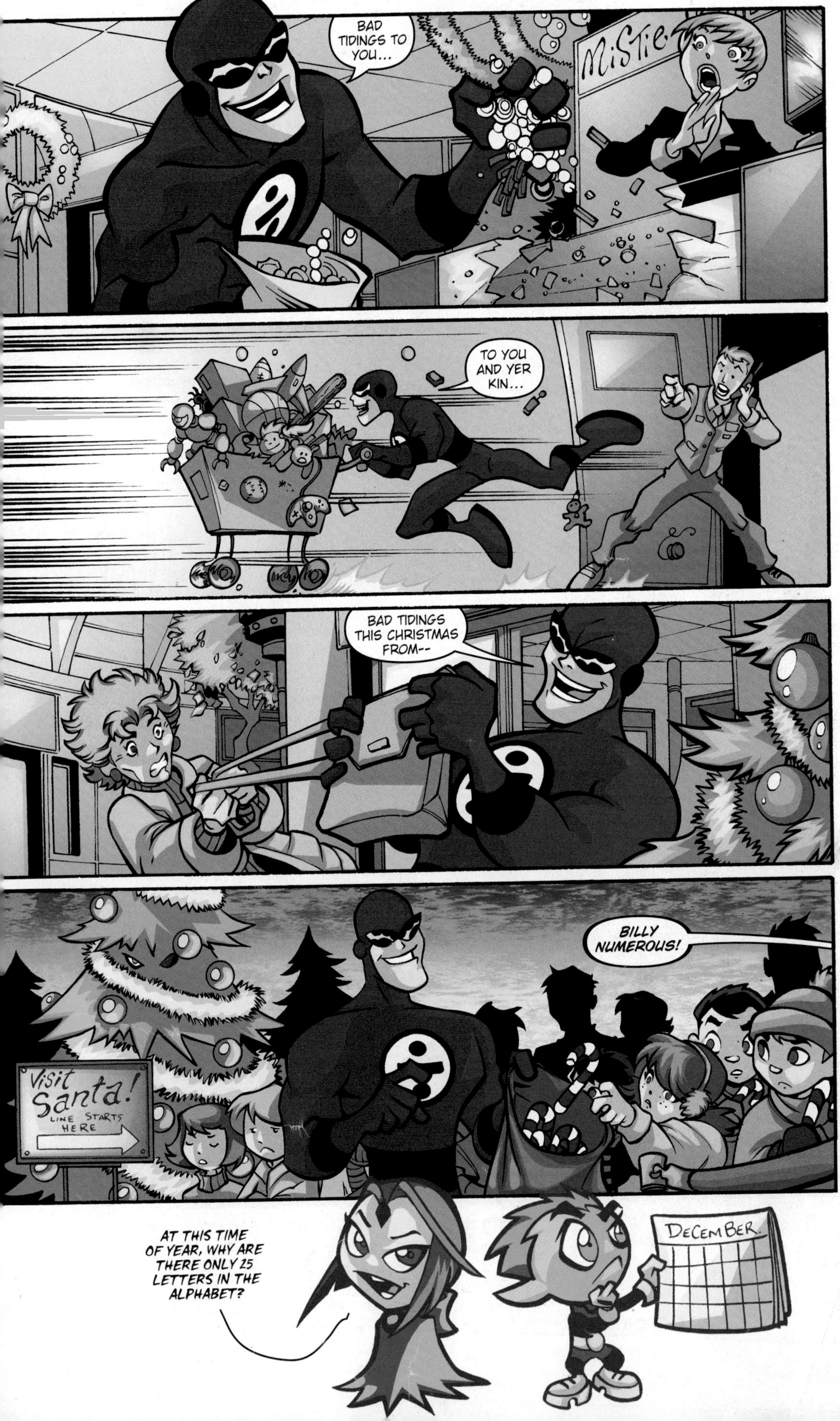
BAD TIDINGS TO YOU...
MiSTie
TO YOU AND YER KIN...
BAD TIDINGS THIS CHRISTMAS FROM--
BILLY NUMEROUS!
Visit Santa! LINE STARTS HERE
AT THIS TIME OF YEAR, WHY ARE THERE ONLY 25 LETTERS IN THE ALPHABET?
DECEMBER

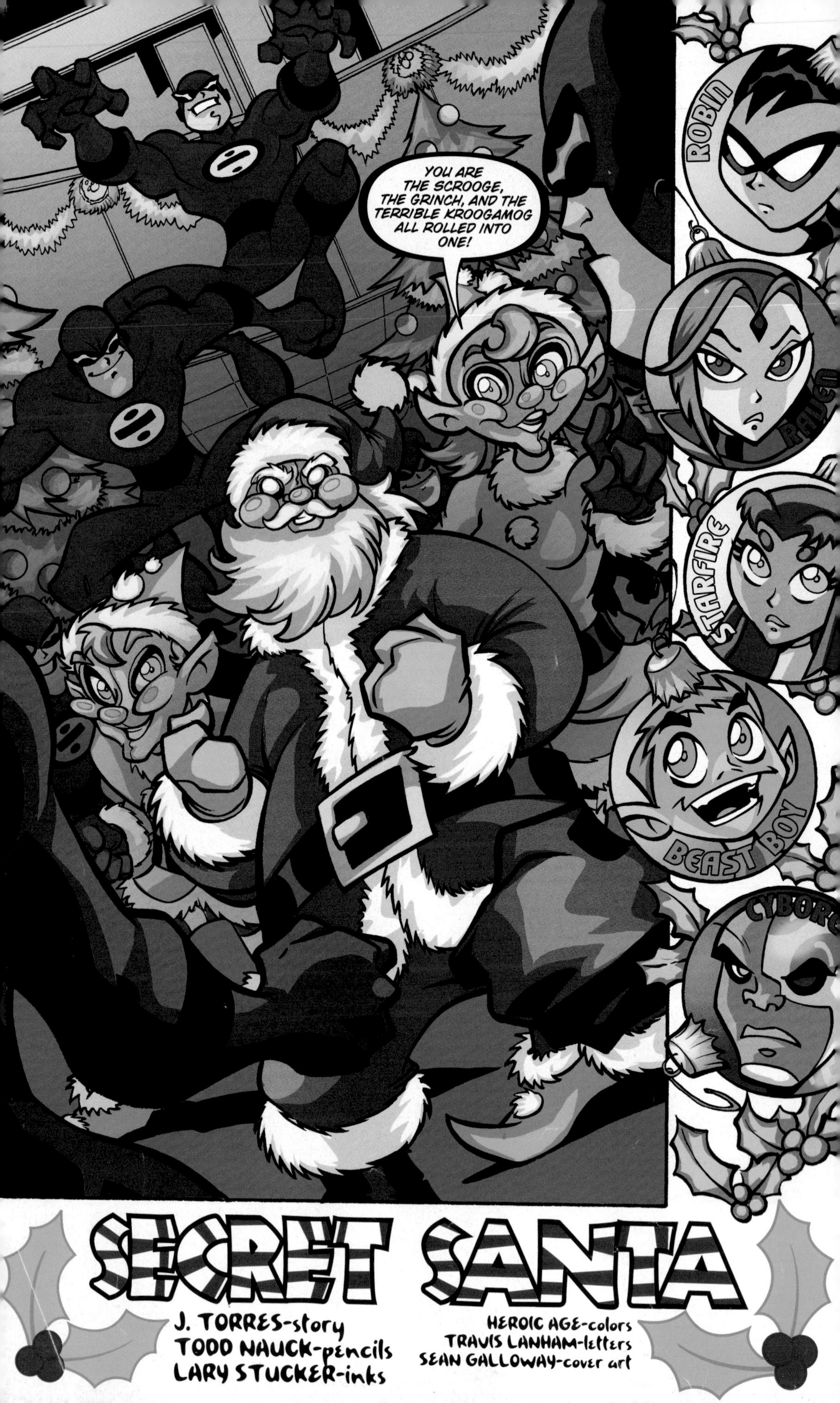
YOU ARE THE SCROOGE, THE GRINCH, AND THE TERRIBLE KROOGAMOG ALL ROLLED INTO ONE!
ROBIN
STARFIRE
BEAST BOY

SECRET SANTA

J. TORRES-story
TODD NAUCK-pencils
LARY STUCKER-inks

HEROIC AGE-colors
TRAVIS LANHAM-letters
SEAN GALLOWAY-cover art

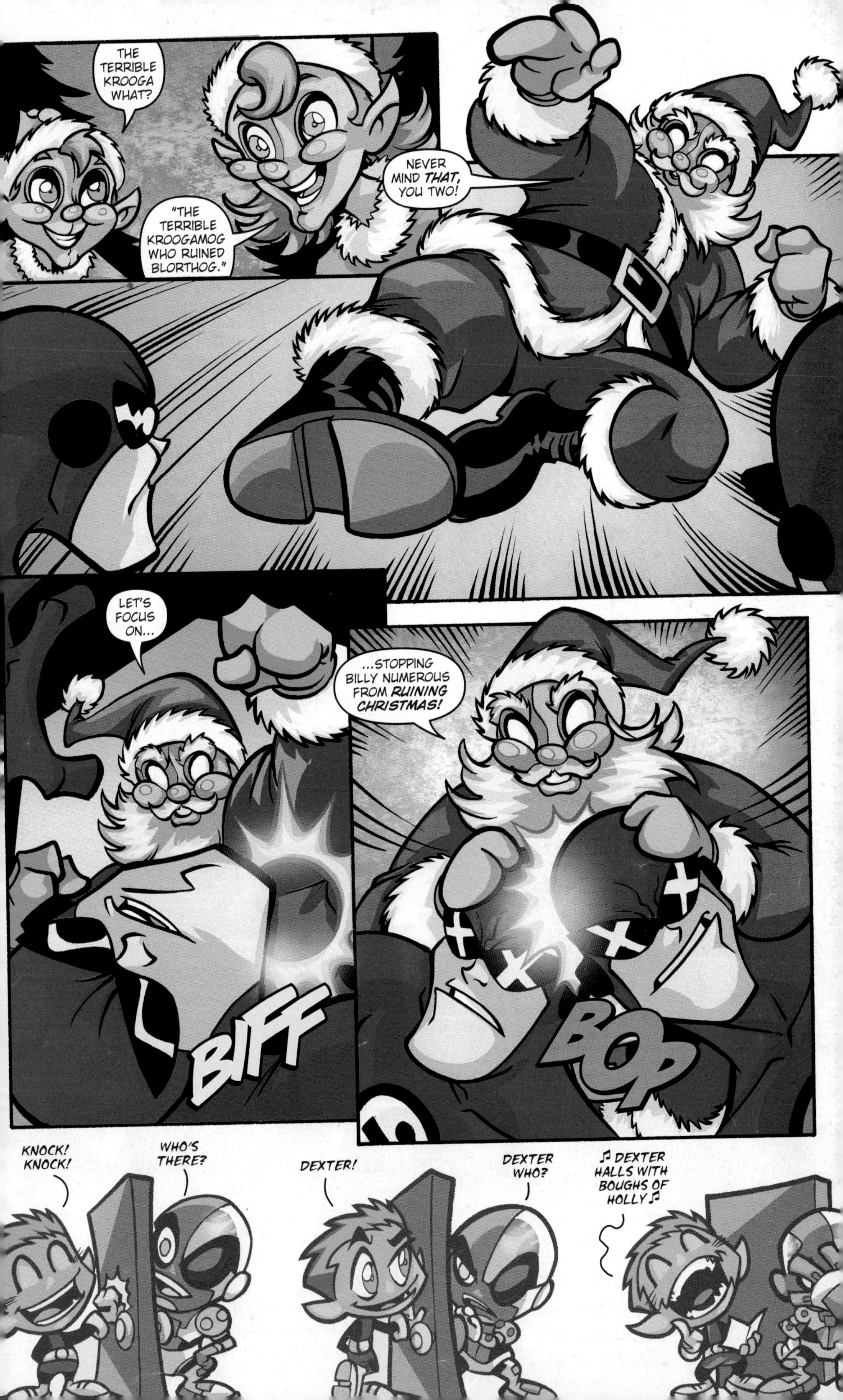
THE TERRIBLE KROOGA WHAT?
"THE TERRIBLE KROOGAMOG WHO RUINED BLORTHOG."
NEVER MIND THAT, YOU TWO!
LET'S FOCUS ON...
...STOPPING BILLY NUMEROUS FROM RUINING CHRISTMAS!
BIFF
BOP
KNOCK! KNOCK!
WHO'S THERE?
DEXTER!
DEXTER WHO?
♫ DEXTER HALLS WITH BOUGHS OF HOLLY ♫

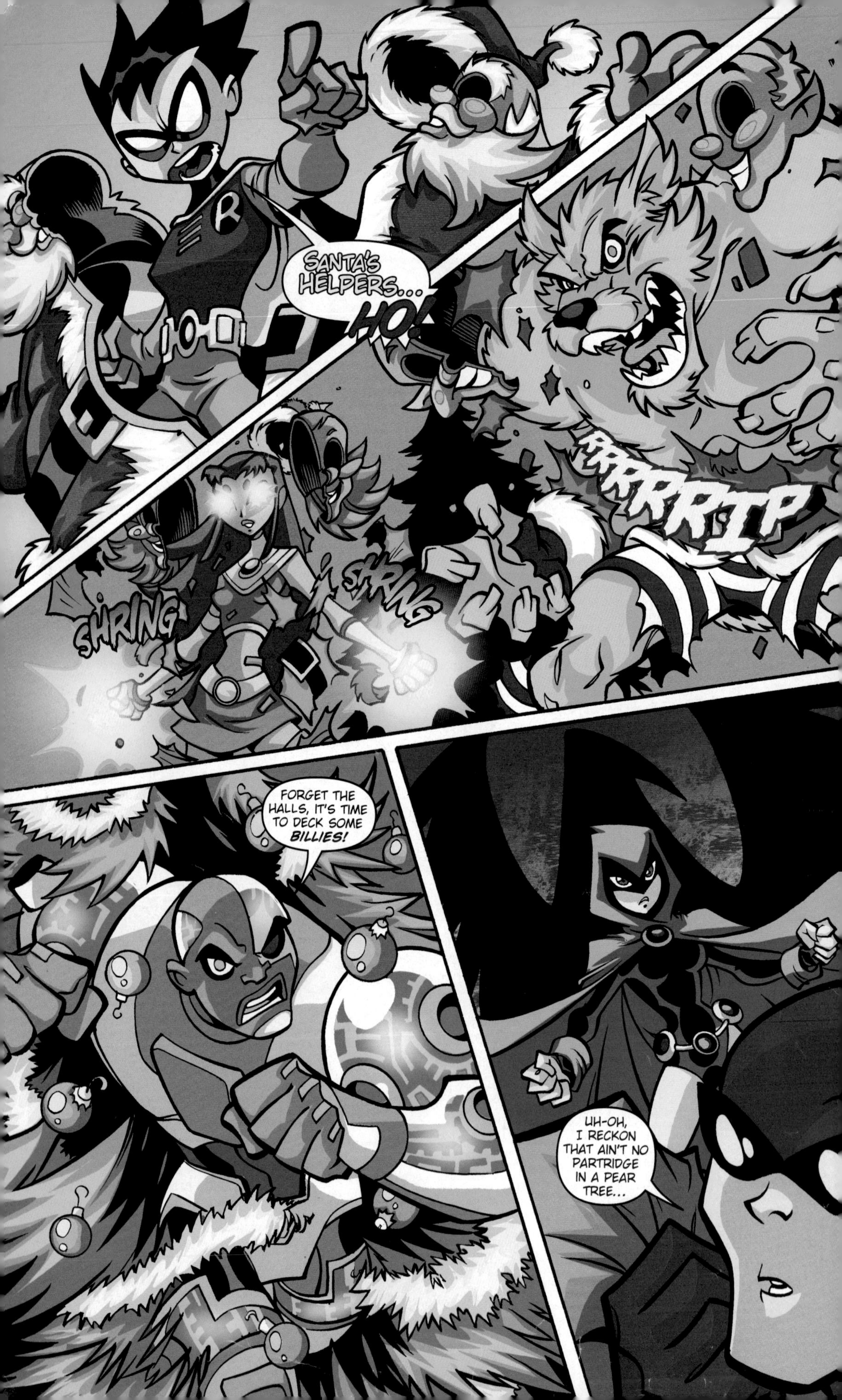
SANTA'S HELPERS... HO!
RRRRRIP
SHRING
SHRING
FORGET THE HALLS, IT'S TIME TO DECK SOME BILLIES!
UH-OH, I RECKON THAT AIN'T NO PARTRIDGE IN A PEAR TREE...

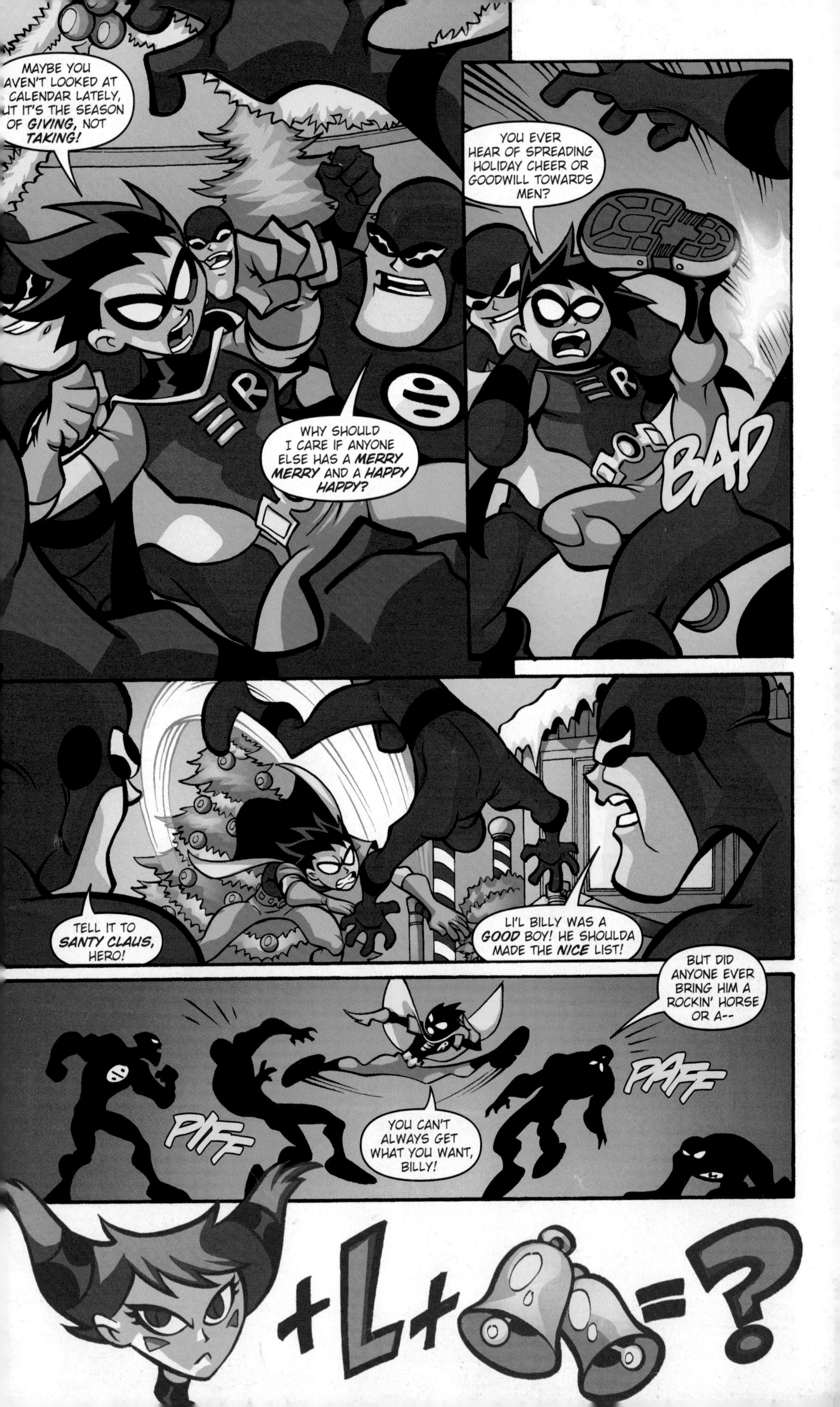

MAYBE YOU AVEN'T LOOKED AT CALENDAR LATELY, UT IT'S THE SEASON OF GIVING, NOT TAKING!
WHY SHOULD I CARE IF ANYONE ELSE HAS A MERRY MERRY AND A HAPPY HAPPY?
YOU EVER HEAR OF SPREADING HOLIDAY CHEER OR GOODWILL TOWARDS MEN?
BAP
TELL IT TO SANTY CLAUS, HERO!
LI'L BILLY WAS A GOOD BOY! HE SHOULDA MADE THE NICE LIST!
BUT DID ANYONE EVER BRING HIM A ROCKIN' HORSE OR A--
PFAFF
PIFF
YOU CAN'T ALWAYS GET WHAT YOU WANT, BILLY!
+L+ =?

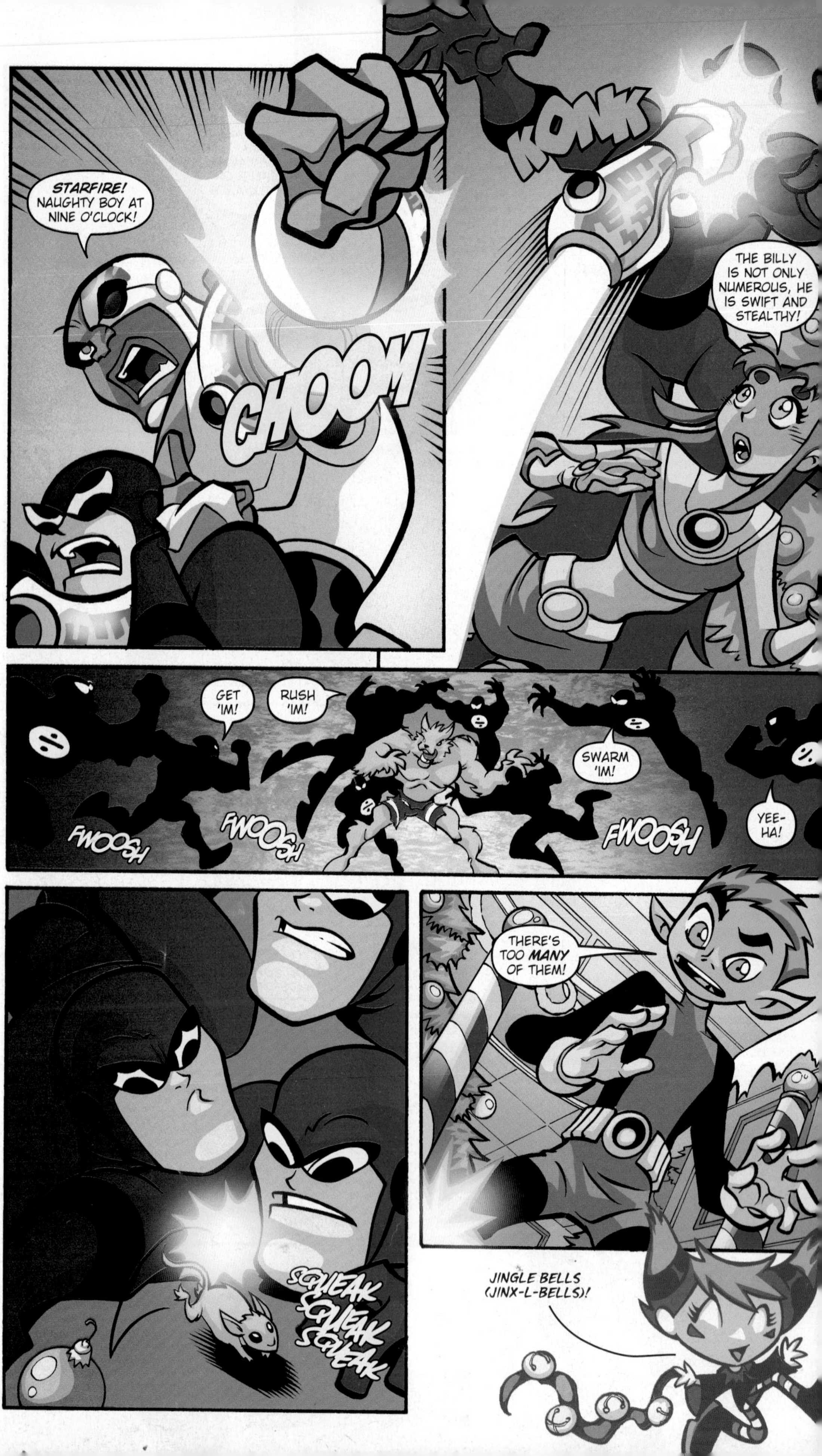
STARFIRE! NAUGHTY BOY AT NINE O'CLOCK!
CHOOM
KONK
THE BILLY IS NOT ONLY NUMEROUS, HE IS SWIFT AND STEALTHY!
GET 'IM!
RUSH 'IM!
SWARM 'IM!
YEE-HA!
FWOOSH
FWOOSH
FWOOSH
THERE'S TOO MANY OF THEM!
SQUEAK SQUEAK SQUEAK
JINGLE BELLS (JINX-L-BELLS)!

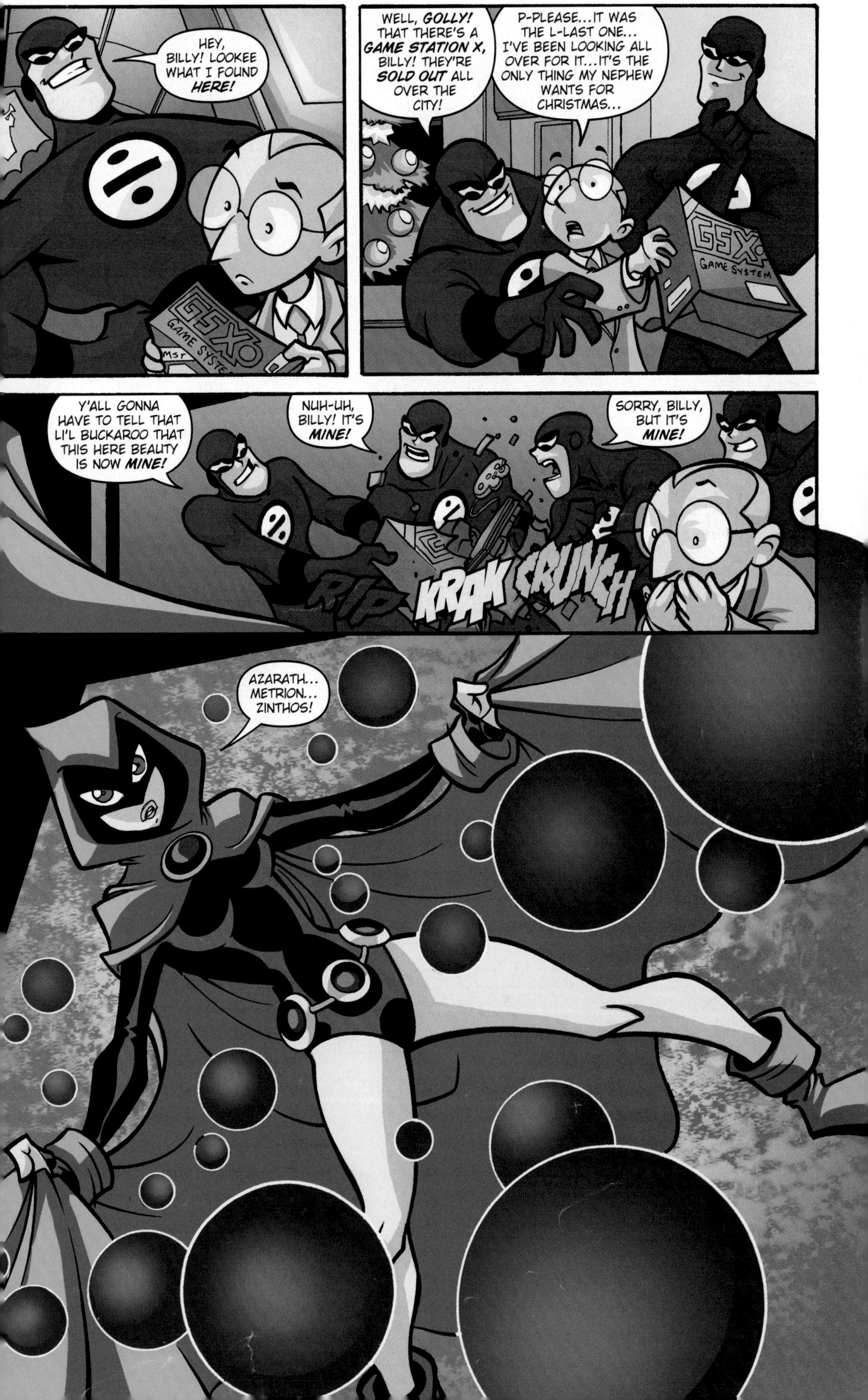
HEY, BILLY! LOOKEE WHAT I FOUND HERE!
WELL, GOLLY! THAT THERE'S A GAME STATION X, BILLY! THEY'RE SOLD OUT ALL OVER THE CITY!
P-PLEASE...IT WAS THE L-LAST ONE... I'VE BEEN LOOKING ALL OVER FOR IT...IT'S THE ONLY THING MY NEPHEW WANTS FOR CHRISTMAS...
GSX GAME SYSTEM
Y'ALL GONNA HAVE TO TELL THAT LI'L BUCKAROO THAT THIS HERE BEAUTY IS NOW MINE!
NUH-UH, BILLY! IT'S MINE!
SORRY, BILLY, BUT IT'S MINE!
RIP
KRAK
CRUNCH
AZARATH... METRION... ZINTHOS!

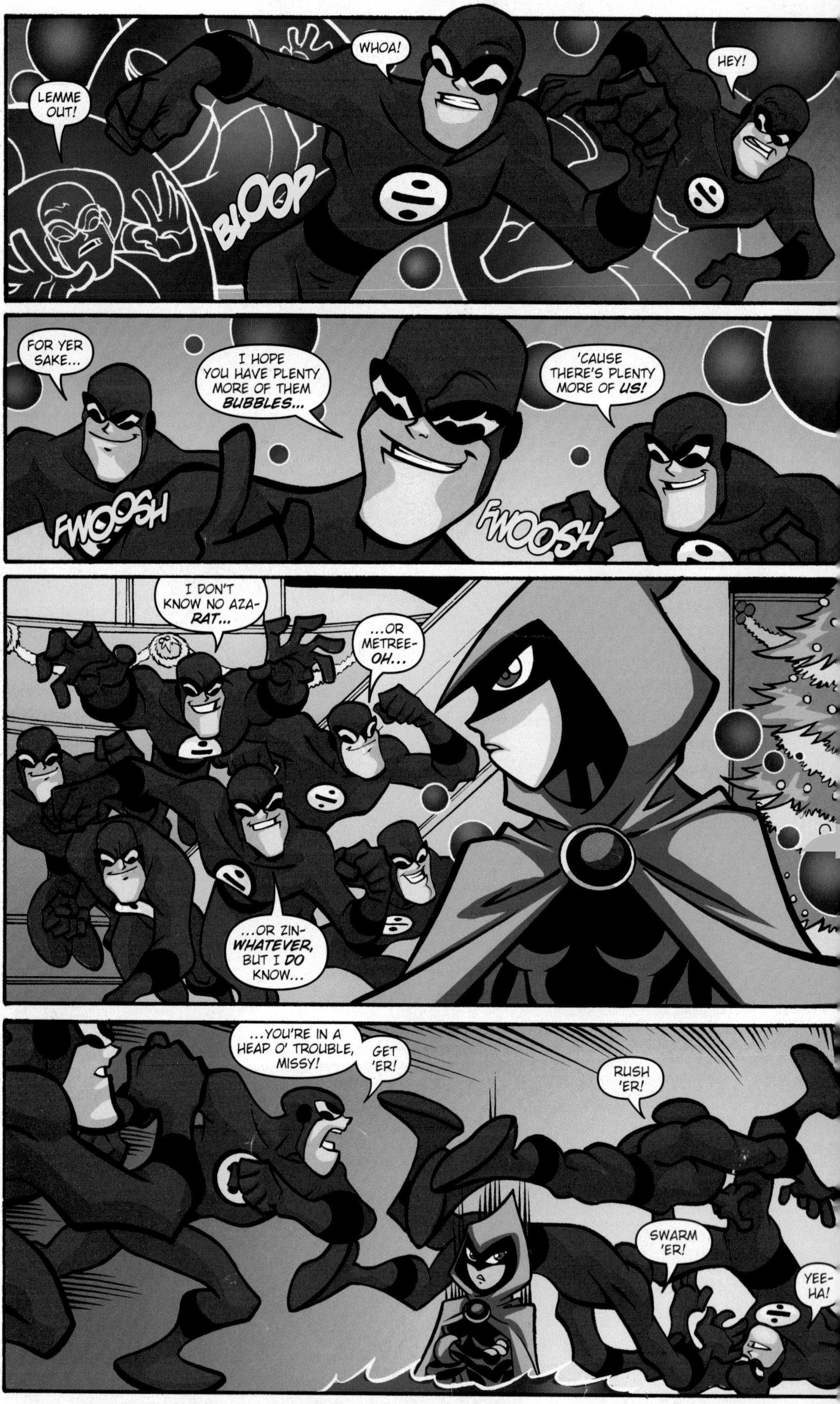
LEMME OUT!
WHOA!
HEY!
BLOOP
FOR YER SAKE...
I HOPE YOU HAVE PLENTY MORE OF THEM BUBBLES...
'CAUSE THERE'S PLENTY MORE OF US!
FWOOSH
FWOOSH
I DON'T KNOW NO AZA-RAT...
...OR METREE-OH...
...OR ZIN-WHATEVER, BUT I DO KNOW...
...YOU'RE IN A HEAP O' TROUBLE, MISSY!
GET 'ER!
RUSH 'ER!
SWARM 'ER!
YEE-HA!

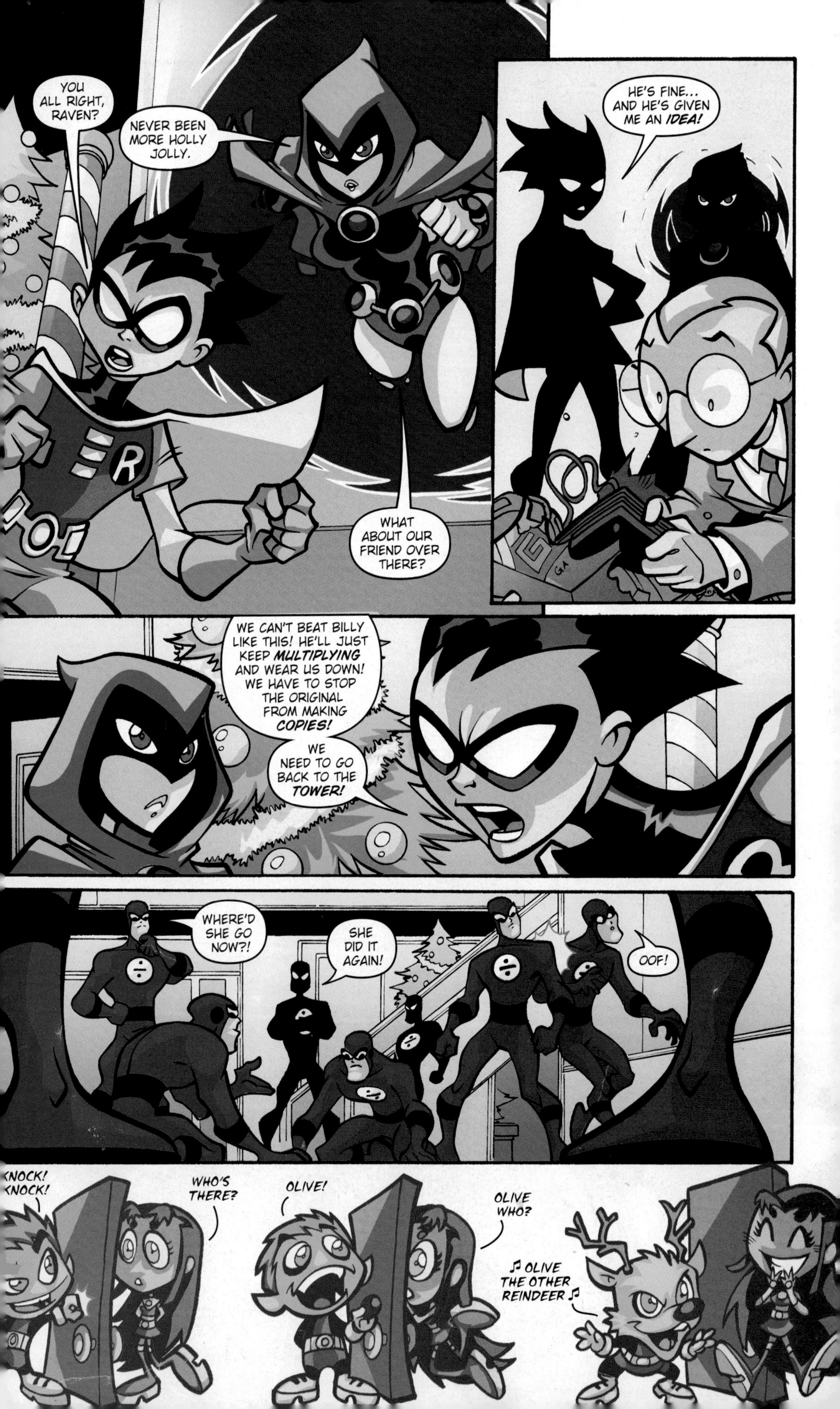
YOU ALL RIGHT, RAVEN?
NEVER BEEN MORE HOLLY JOLLY.
WHAT ABOUT OUR FRIEND OVER THERE?
HE'S FINE... AND HE'S GIVEN ME AN IDEA!
WE CAN'T BEAT BILLY LIKE THIS! HE'LL JUST KEEP MULTIPLYING AND WEAR US DOWN! WE HAVE TO STOP THE ORIGINAL FROM MAKING COPIES!
WE NEED TO GO BACK TO THE TOWER!
WHERE'D SHE GO NOW?!
SHE DID IT AGAIN!
OOF!
KNOCK! KNOCK!
WHO'S THERE?
OLIVE!
OLIVE WHO?
♫ OLIVE THE OTHER REINDEER ♫

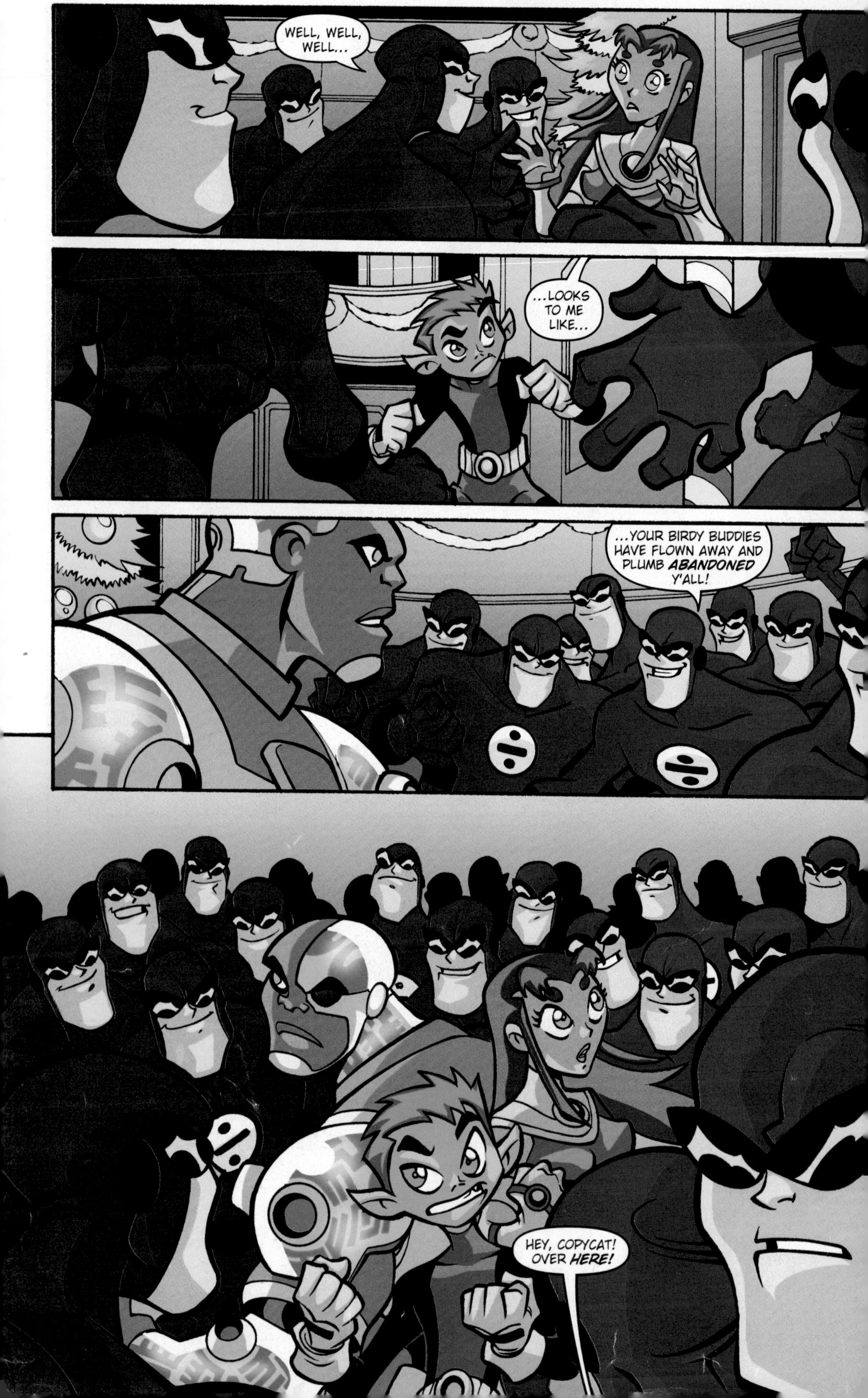
WELL, WELL, WELL...
...LOOKS TO ME LIKE...
...YOUR BIRDY BUDDIES HAVE FLOWN AWAY AND PLUMB ABANDONED Y'ALL!
HEY, COPYCAT! OVER HERE!

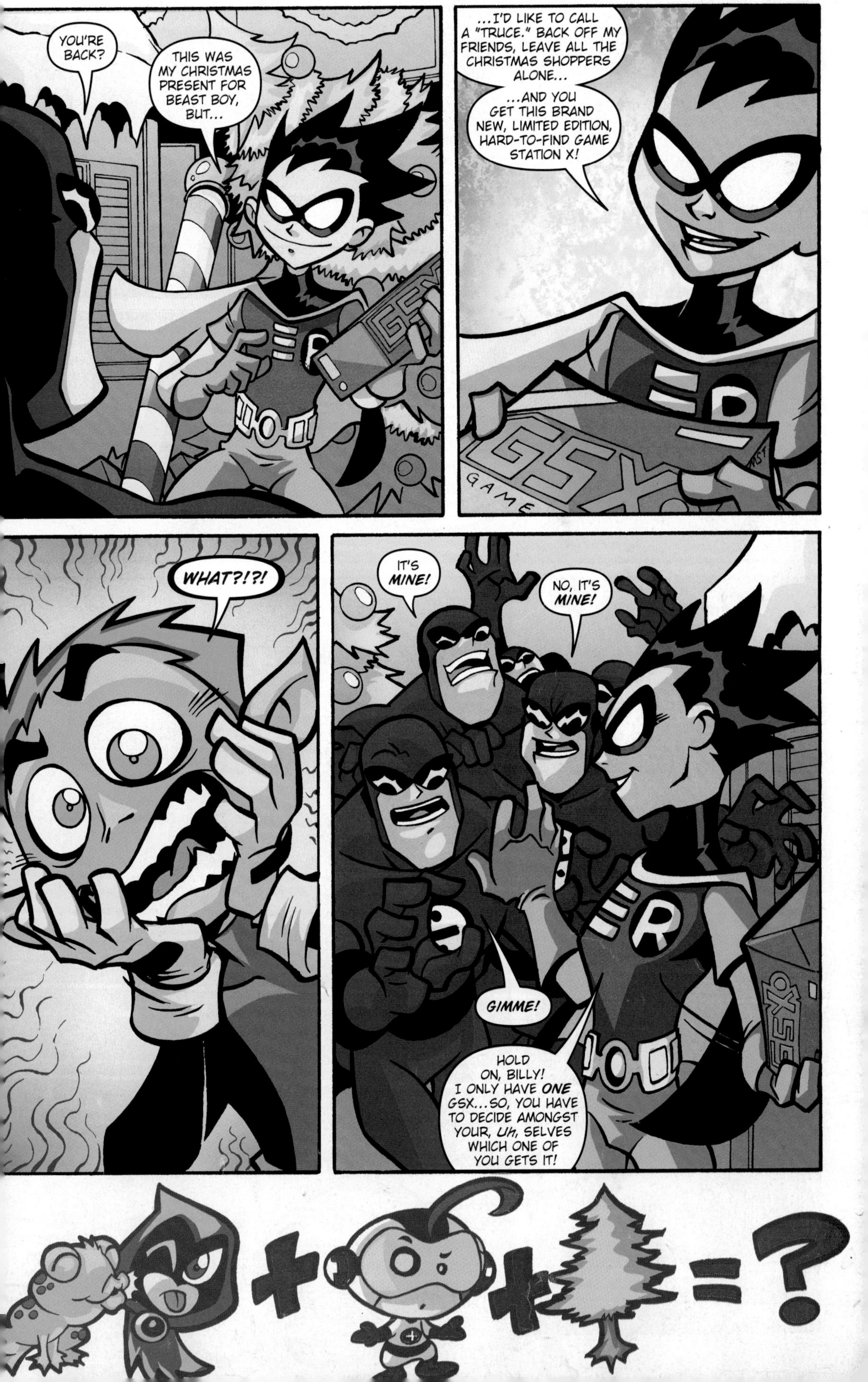
YOU'RE BACK?
THIS WAS MY CHRISTMAS PRESENT FOR BEAST BOY, BUT...
...I'D LIKE TO CALL A "TRUCE." BACK OFF MY FRIENDS, LEAVE ALL THE CHRISTMAS SHOPPERS ALONE...
...AND YOU GET THIS BRAND NEW, LIMITED EDITION, HARD-TO-FIND GAME STATION X!
GSX
GAME
WHAT?!?!
IT'S MINE!
NO, IT'S MINE!
GIMME!
HOLD ON, BILLY! I ONLY HAVE ONE GSX...SO, YOU HAVE TO DECIDE AMONGST YOUR, Uh, SELVES WHICH ONE OF YOU GETS IT!
GSX

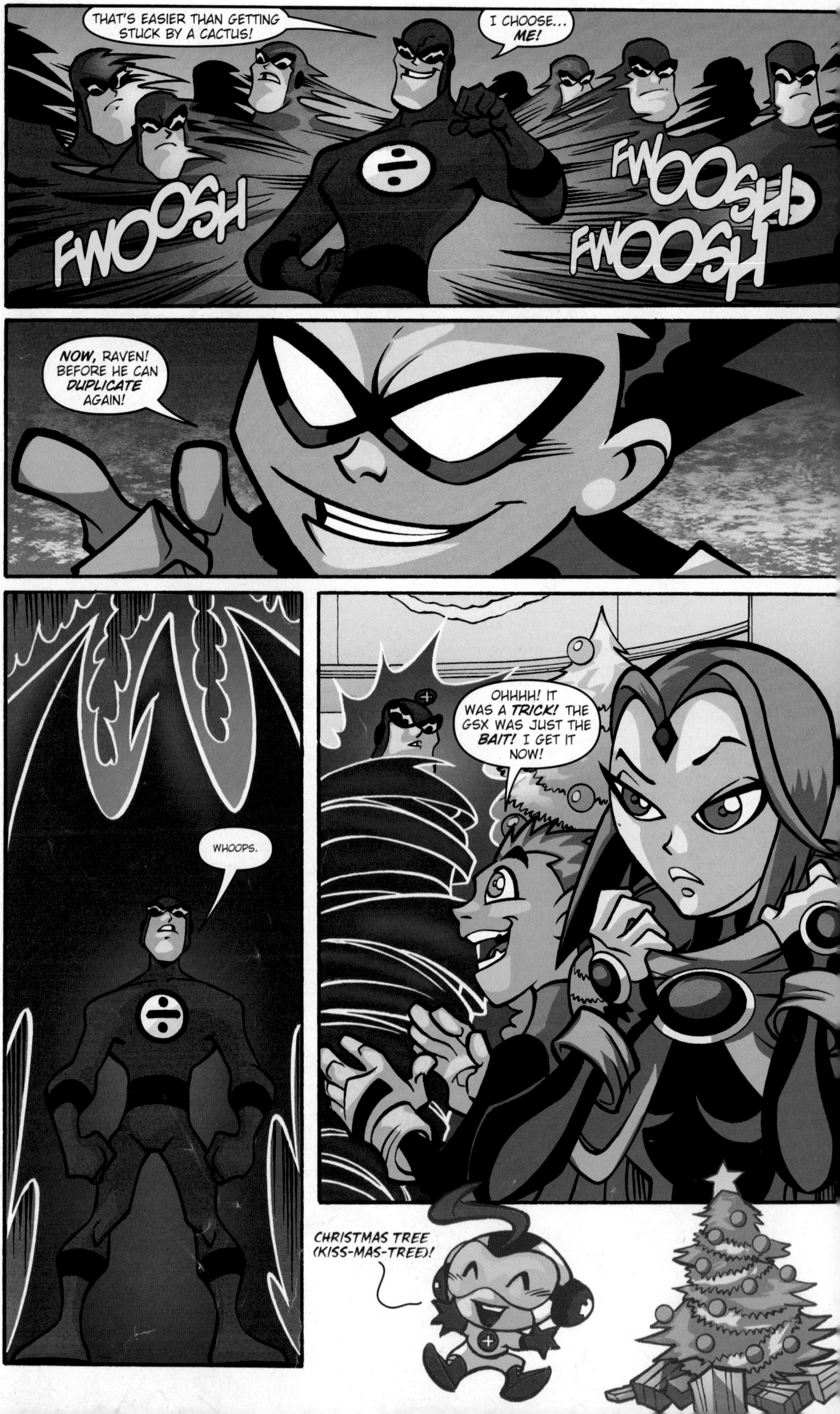
THAT'S EASIER THAN GETTING STUCK BY A CACTUS!
I CHOOSE... ME!
FWOOSH
FWOOSH
FWOOSH
FWOOSH
NOW, RAVEN! BEFORE HE CAN DUPLICATE AGAIN!
WHOOPS.
OHHHH! IT WAS A TRICK! THE GSX WAS JUST THE BAIT! I GET IT NOW!
CHRISTMAS TREE (KISS-MAS-TREE)!

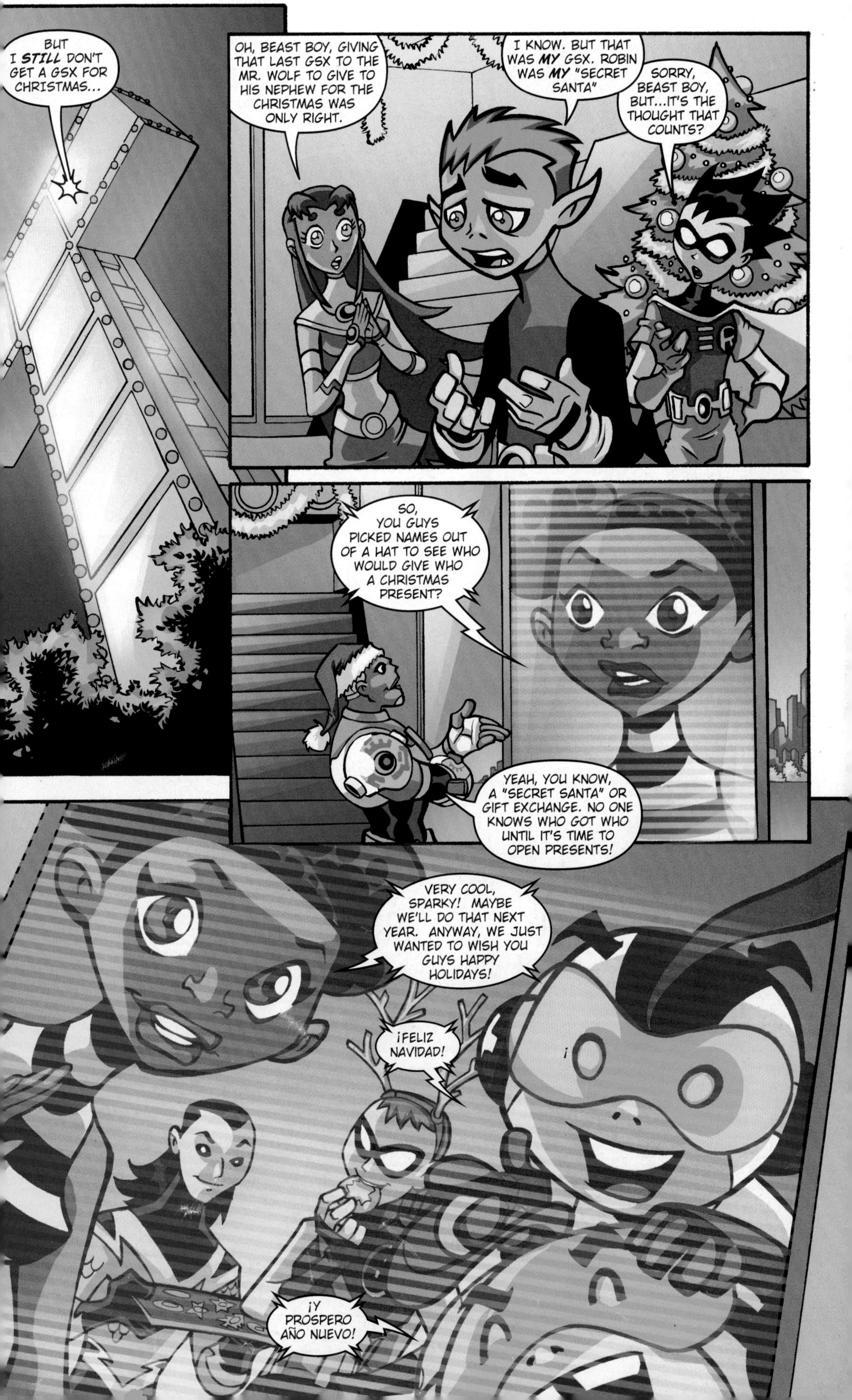
BUT I **STILL** DON'T GET A GSX FOR CHRISTMAS...
OH, BEAST BOY, GIVING THAT LAST GSX TO THE MR. WOLF TO GIVE TO HIS NEPHEW FOR THE CHRISTMAS WAS ONLY RIGHT.
I KNOW. BUT THAT WAS **MY** GSX. ROBIN WAS **MY** "SECRET SANTA"
SORRY, BEAST BOY, BUT...IT'S THE THOUGHT THAT COUNTS?
SO, YOU GUYS PICKED NAMES OUT OF A HAT TO SEE WHO WOULD GIVE WHO A CHRISTMAS PRESENT?
YEAH, YOU KNOW, A "SECRET SANTA" OR GIFT EXCHANGE. NO ONE KNOWS WHO GOT WHO UNTIL IT'S TIME TO OPEN PRESENTS!
VERY COOL, SPARKY! MAYBE WE'LL DO THAT NEXT YEAR. ANYWAY, WE JUST WANTED TO WISH YOU GUYS HAPPY HOLIDAYS!
¡FELIZ NAVIDAD!
¡Y PROSPERO AÑO NUEVO!

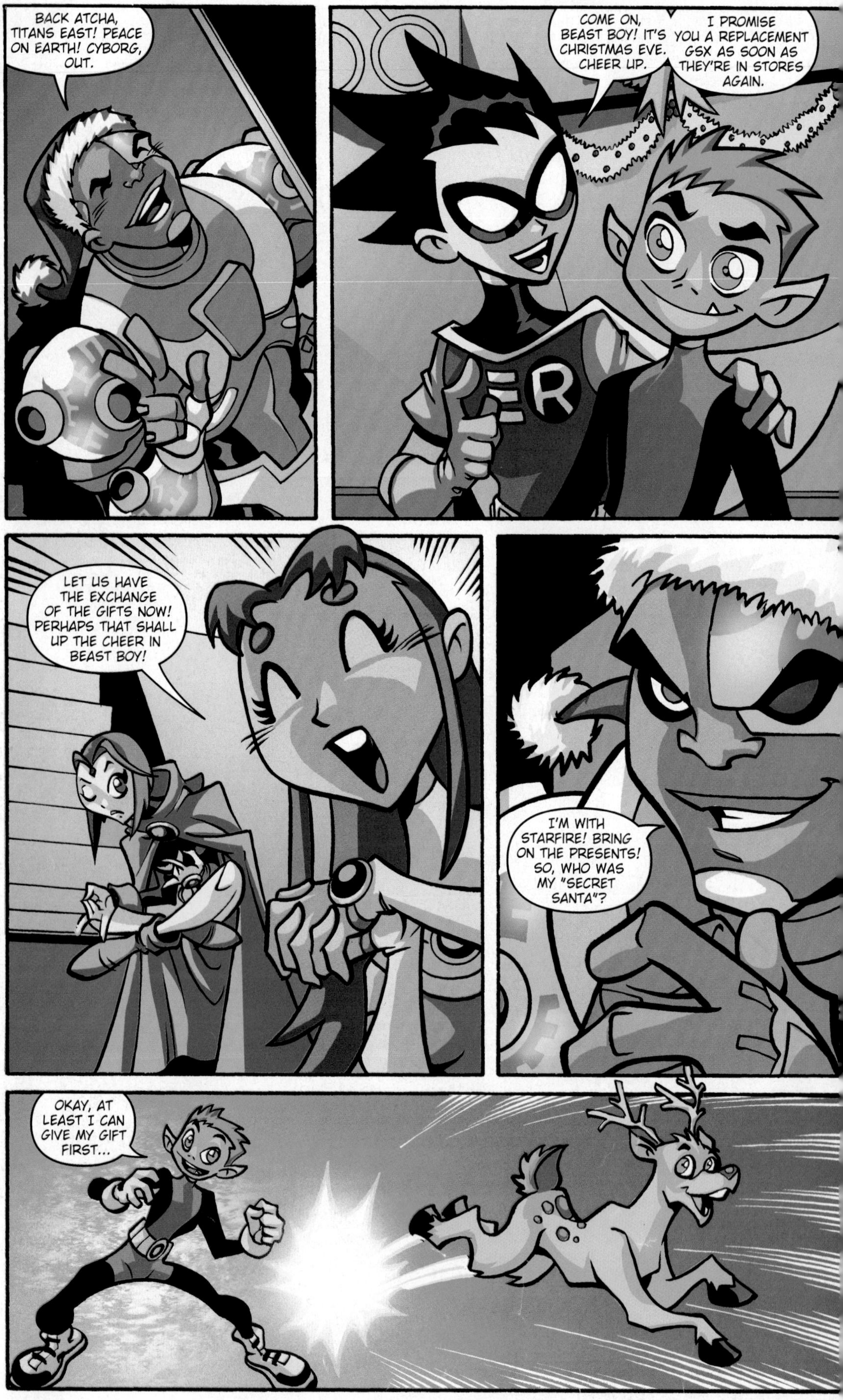

BACK ATCHA, TITANS EAST! PEACE ON EARTH! CYBORG, OUT.
COME ON, BEAST BOY! IT'S CHRISTMAS EVE. CHEER UP.
I PROMISE YOU A REPLACEMENT GSX AS SOON AS THEY'RE IN STORES AGAIN.
LET US HAVE THE EXCHANGE OF THE GIFTS NOW! PERHAPS THAT SHALL UP THE CHEER IN BEAST BOY!
I'M WITH STARFIRE! BRING ON THE PRESENTS! SO, WHO WAS MY "SECRET SANTA"?
OKAY, AT LEAST I CAN GIVE MY GIFT FIRST...

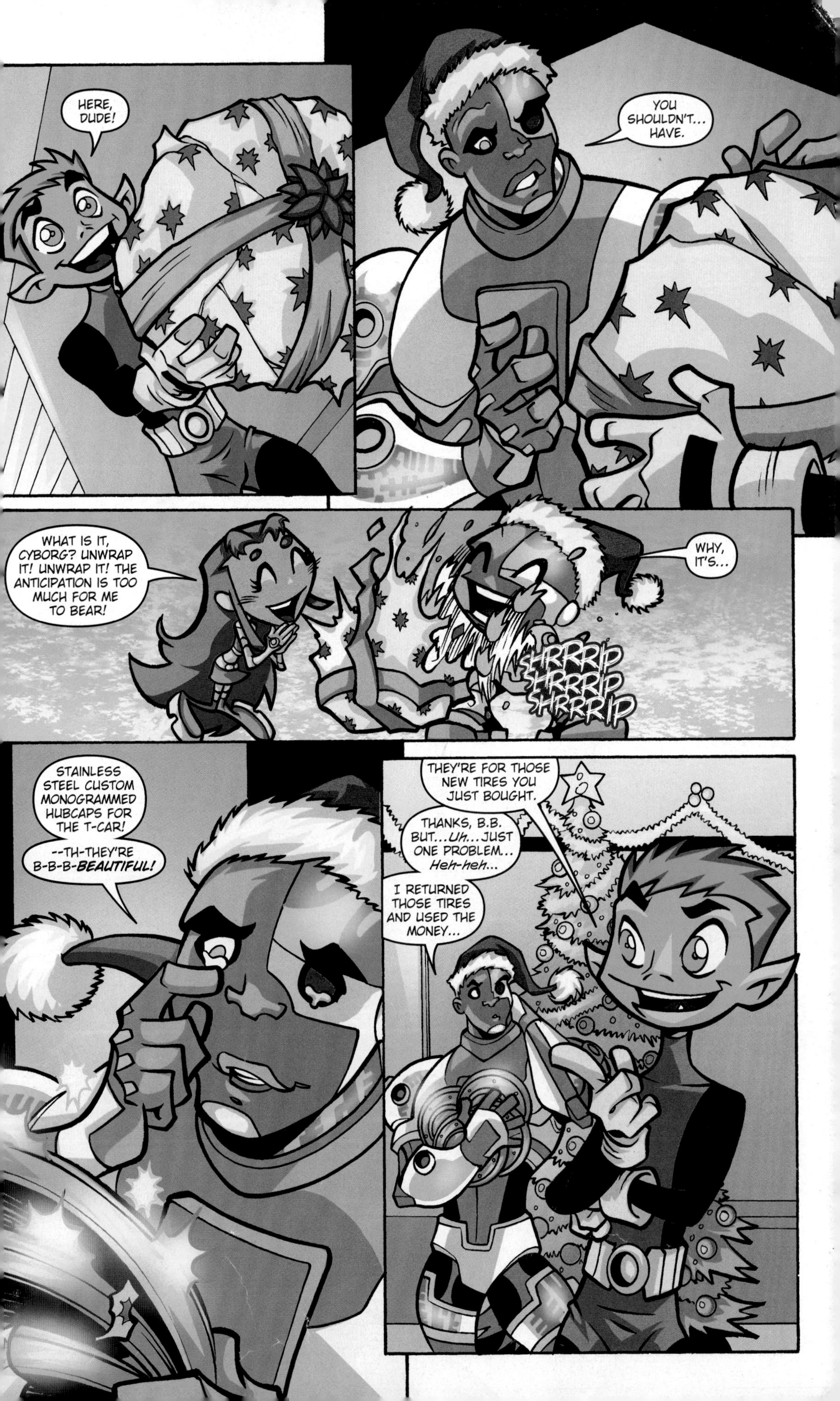
HERE, DUDE!
YOU SHOULDN'T... HAVE.
WHAT IS IT, CYBORG? UNWRAP IT! UNWRAP IT! THE ANTICIPATION IS TOO MUCH FOR ME TO BEAR!
WHY, IT'S...
SHRRRIP SHRRRIP SHRRRIP
STAINLESS STEEL CUSTOM MONOGRAMMED HUBCAPS FOR THE T-CAR!
--TH-THEY'RE B-B-B-BEAUTIFUL!
THEY'RE FOR THOSE NEW TIRES YOU JUST BOUGHT.
THANKS, B.B. BUT...Uh...JUST ONE PROBLEM... Heh-heh...
I RETURNED THOSE TIRES AND USED THE MONEY...

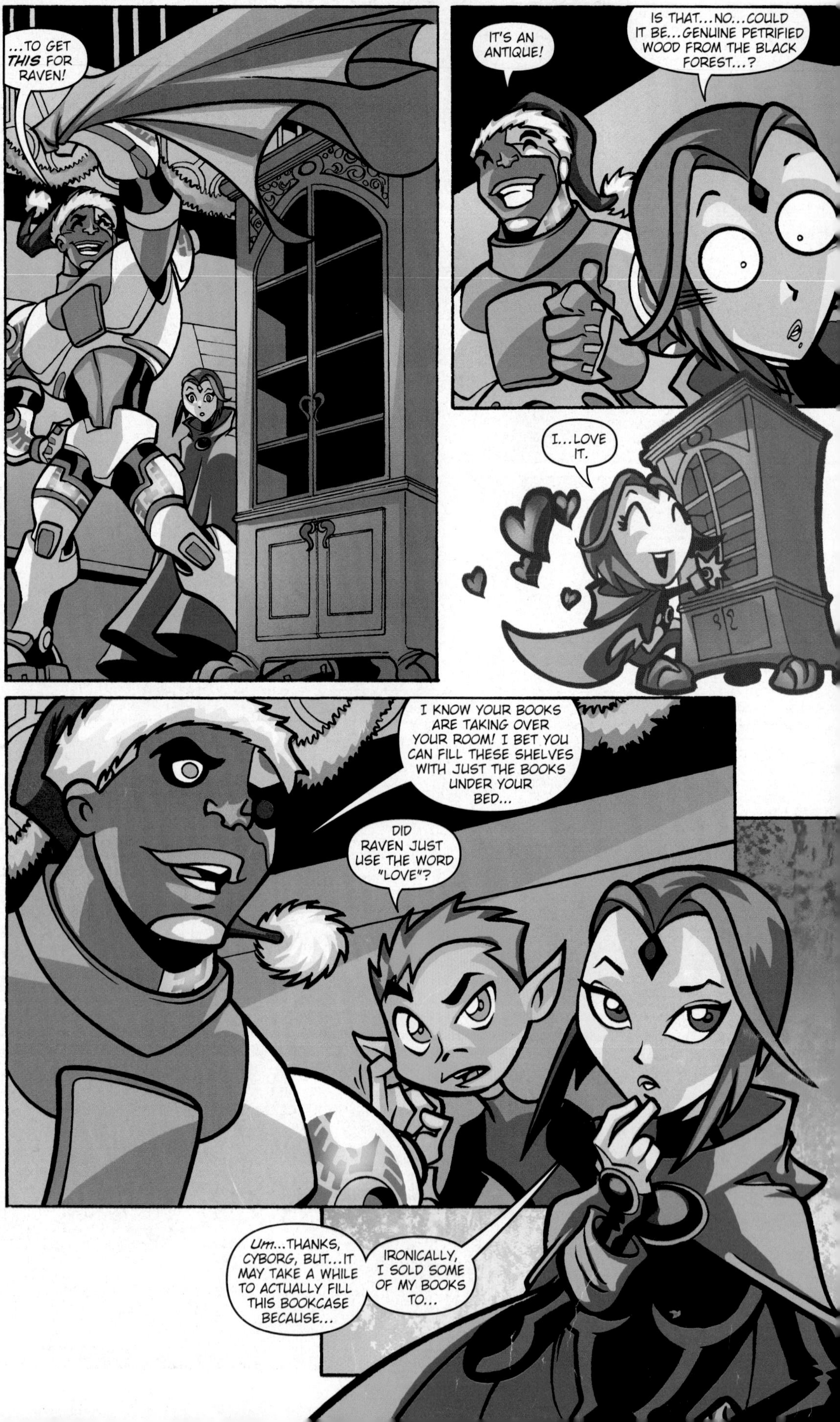
...TO GET *THIS* FOR RAVEN!
IT'S AN ANTIQUE!
IS THAT...NO...COULD IT BE...GENUINE PETRIFIED WOOD FROM THE BLACK FOREST...?
I...LOVE IT.
I KNOW YOUR BOOKS ARE TAKING OVER YOUR ROOM! I BET YOU CAN FILL THESE SHELVES WITH JUST THE BOOKS UNDER YOUR BED...
DID RAVEN JUST USE THE WORD "LOVE"?
Um...THANKS, CYBORG, BUT...IT MAY TAKE A WHILE TO ACTUALLY FILL THIS BOOKCASE BECAUSE...
IRONICALLY, I SOLD SOME OF MY BOOKS TO...

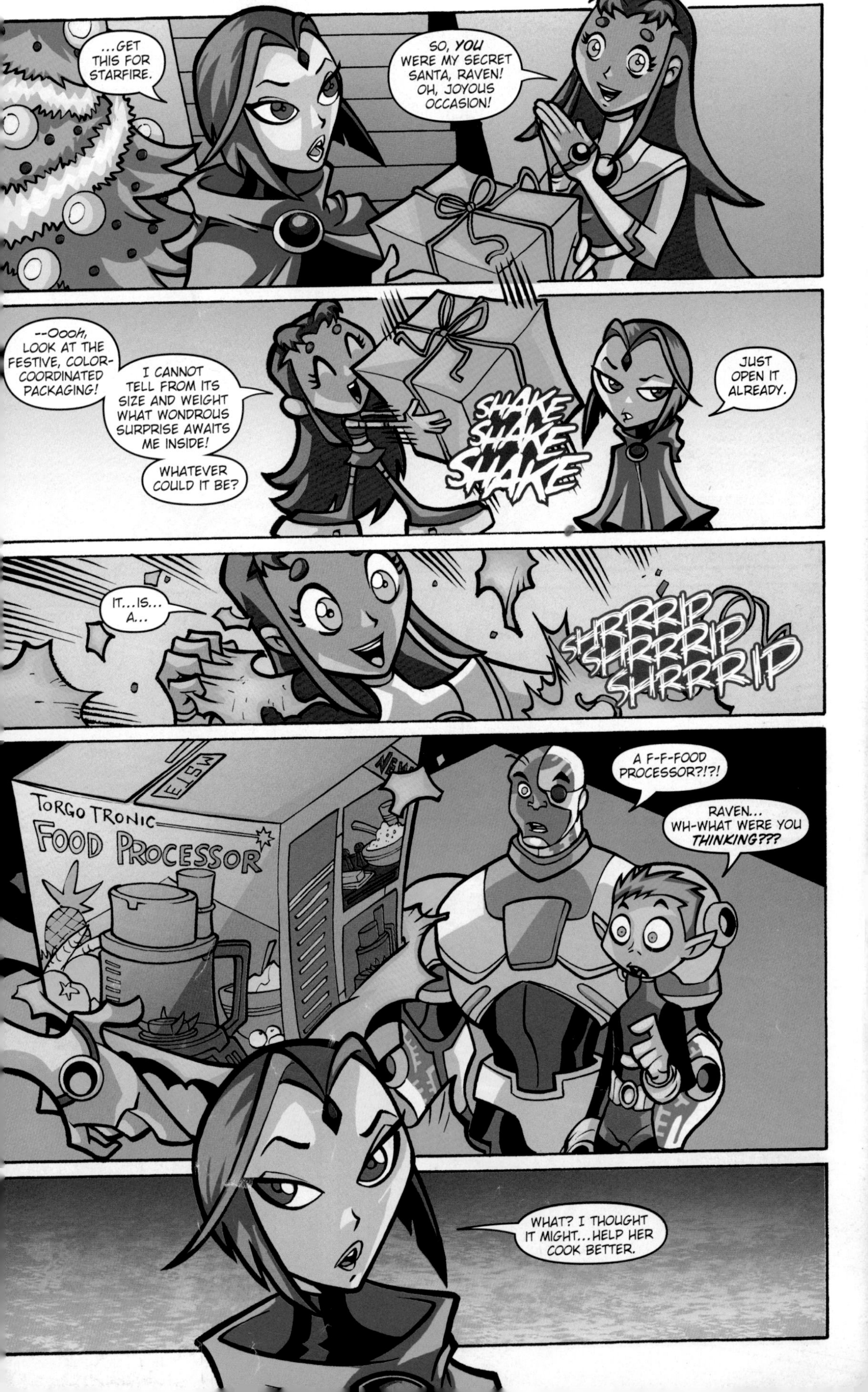
...GET THIS FOR STARFIRE.
SO, YOU WERE MY SECRET SANTA, RAVEN! OH, JOYOUS OCCASION!
--Oooh, LOOK AT THE FESTIVE, COLOR-COORDINATED PACKAGING!
I CANNOT TELL FROM ITS SIZE AND WEIGHT WHAT WONDROUS SURPRISE AWAITS ME INSIDE!
WHATEVER COULD IT BE?
SHAKE SHAKE SHAKE
JUST OPEN IT ALREADY.
IT...IS... A...
SHRRRIP SHRRRIP SHRRRIP
TORGO TRONIC
FOOD PROCESSOR
A F-F-FOOD PROCESSOR?!?!
RAVEN... WH-WHAT WERE YOU THINKING???
WHAT? I THOUGHT IT MIGHT...HELP HER COOK BETTER.

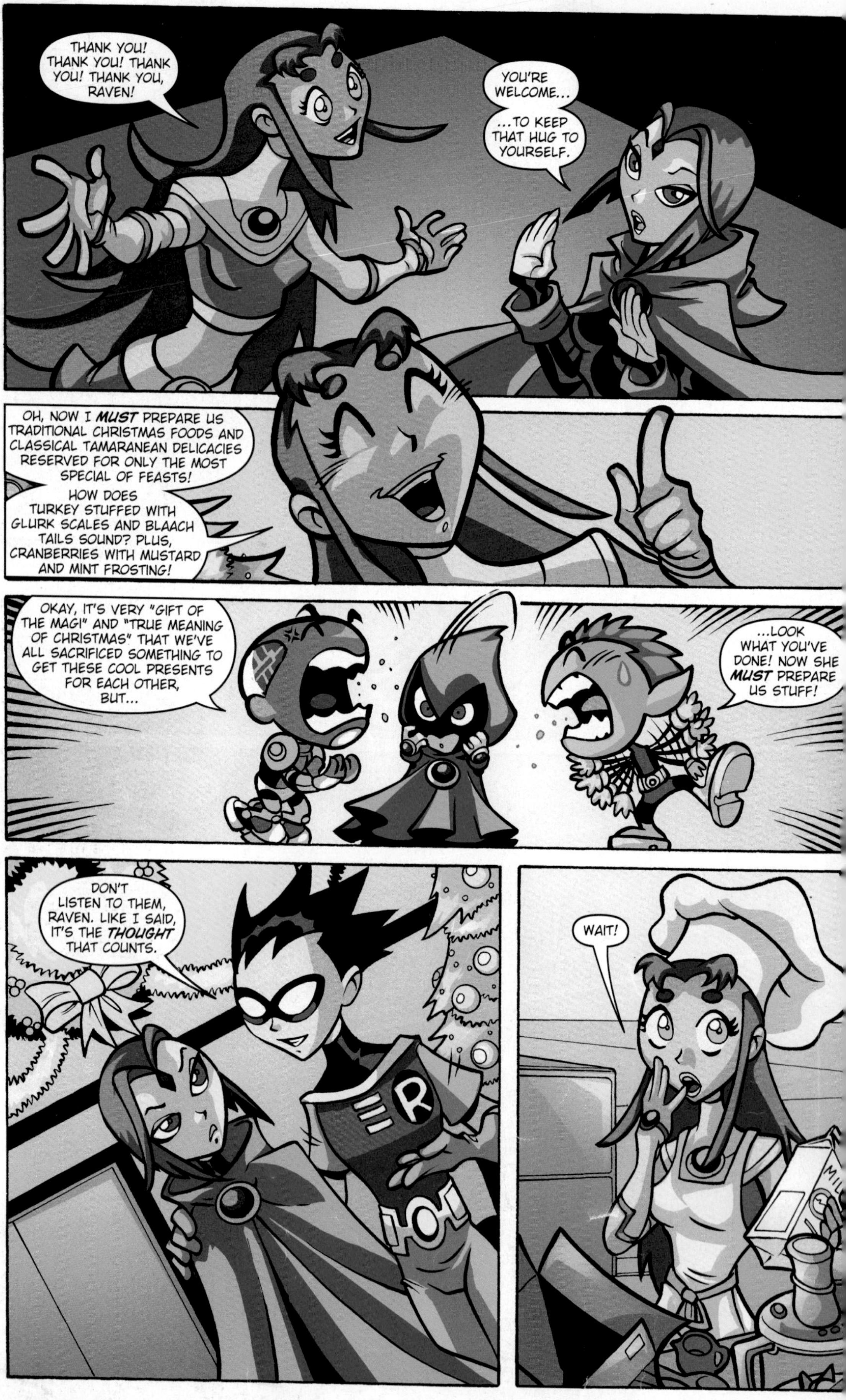
THANK YOU! THANK YOU! THANK YOU! THANK YOU, RAVEN!
YOU'RE WELCOME...
...TO KEEP THAT HUG TO YOURSELF.
OH, NOW I MUST PREPARE US TRADITIONAL CHRISTMAS FOODS AND CLASSICAL TAMARANEAN DELICACIES RESERVED FOR ONLY THE MOST SPECIAL OF FEASTS!
HOW DOES TURKEY STUFFED WITH GLURK SCALES AND BLAACH TAILS SOUND? PLUS, CRANBERRIES WITH MUSTARD AND MINT FROSTING!
OKAY, IT'S VERY "GIFT OF THE MAGI" AND "TRUE MEANING OF CHRISTMAS" THAT WE'VE ALL SACRIFICED SOMETHING TO GET THESE COOL PRESENTS FOR EACH OTHER, BUT...
...LOOK WHAT YOU'VE DONE! NOW SHE MUST PREPARE US STUFF!
DON'T LISTEN TO THEM, RAVEN. LIKE I SAID, IT'S THE THOUGHT THAT COUNTS.
WAIT!

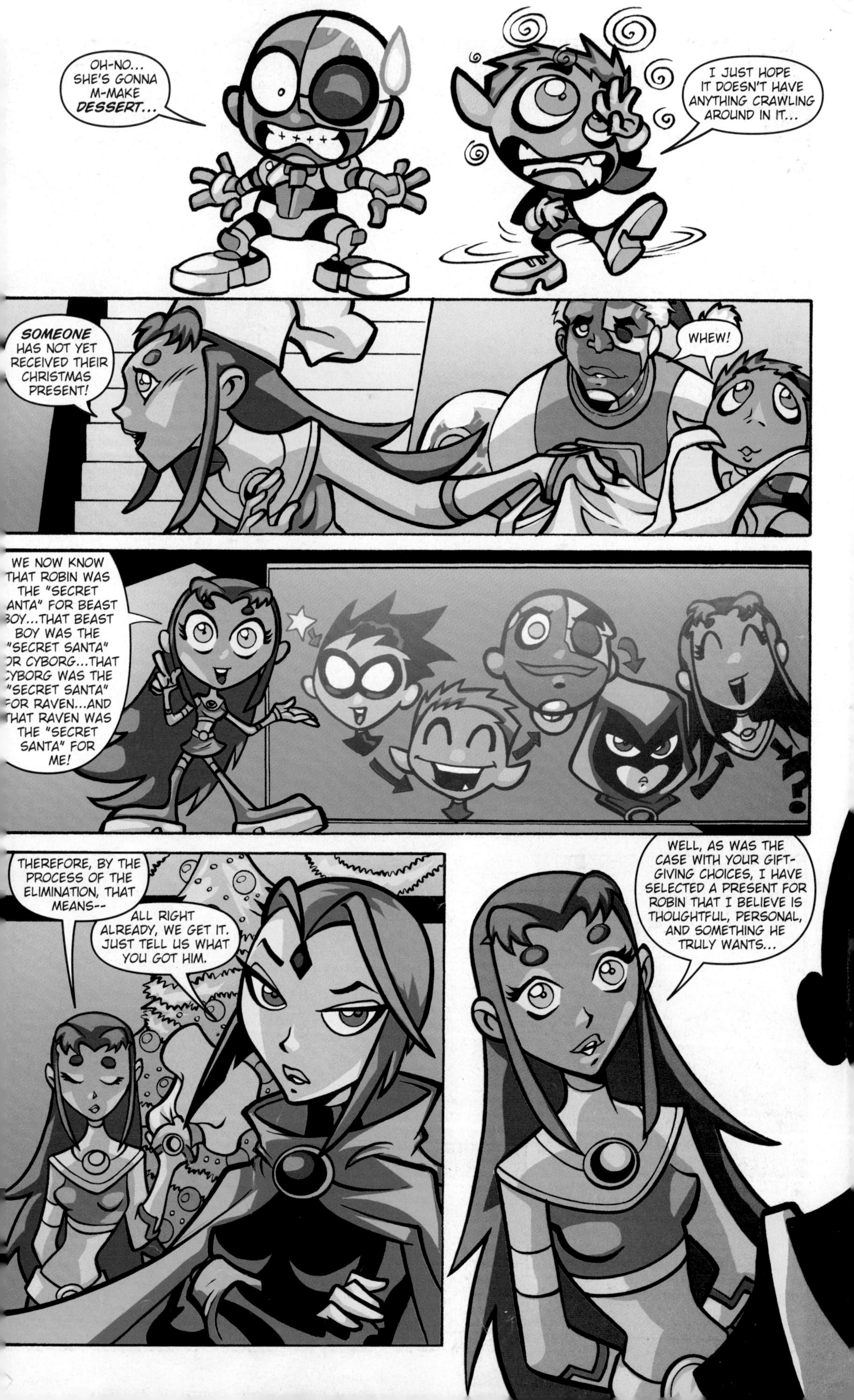
OH-NO... SHE'S GONNA M-MAKE *DESSERT*...
I JUST HOPE IT DOESN'T HAVE ANYTHING CRAWLING AROUND IN IT...
SOMEONE HAS NOT YET RECEIVED THEIR CHRISTMAS PRESENT!
WHEW!
WE NOW KNOW THAT ROBIN WAS THE "SECRET SANTA" FOR BEAST BOY...THAT BEAST BOY WAS THE "SECRET SANTA" FOR CYBORG...THAT CYBORG WAS THE "SECRET SANTA" FOR RAVEN...AND THAT RAVEN WAS THE "SECRET SANTA" FOR ME!
THEREFORE, BY THE PROCESS OF THE ELIMINATION, THAT MEANS--
ALL RIGHT ALREADY, WE GET IT. JUST TELL US WHAT YOU GOT HIM.
WELL, AS WAS THE CASE WITH YOUR GIFT-GIVING CHOICES, I HAVE SELECTED A PRESENT FOR ROBIN THAT I BELIEVE IS THOUGHTFUL, PERSONAL, AND SOMETHING HE TRULY WANTS...

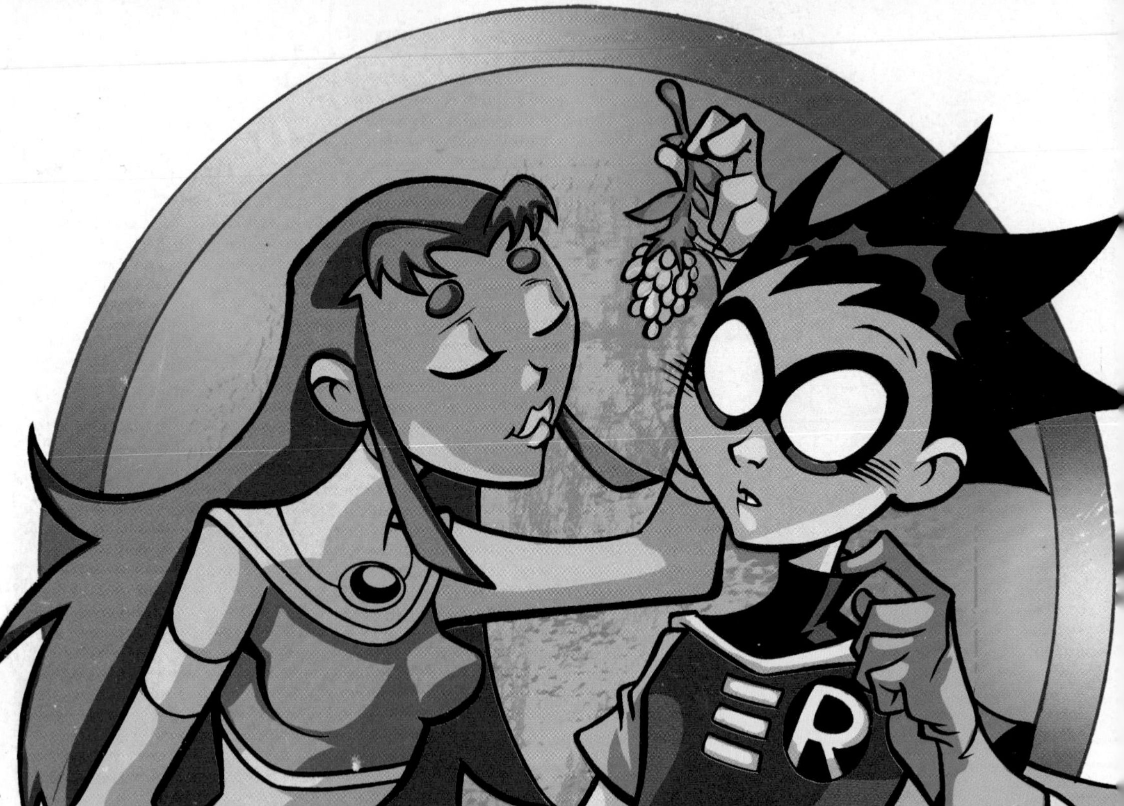

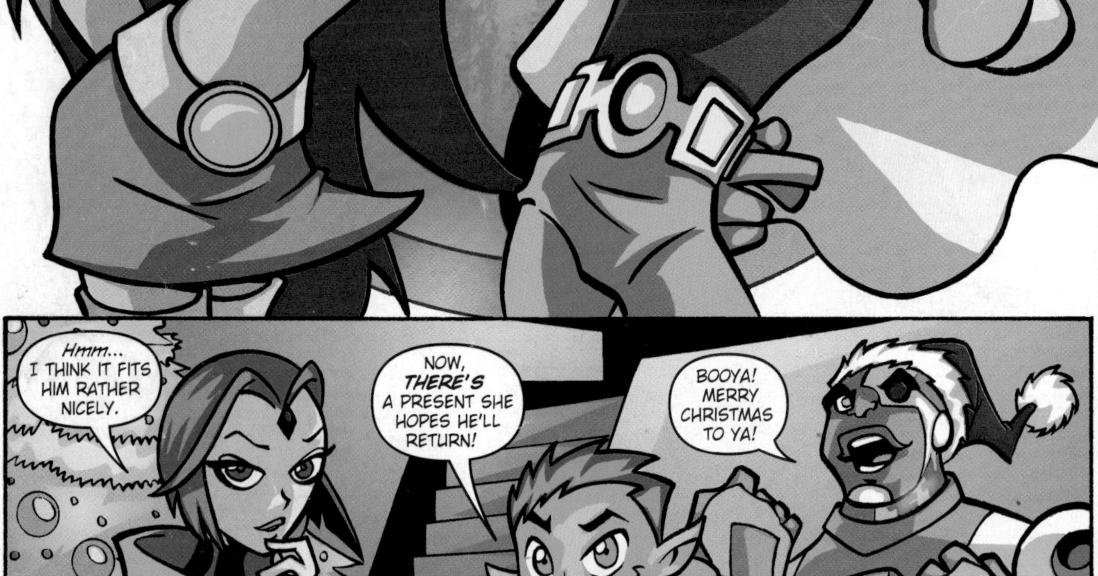
Hmm... I THINK IT FITS HIM RATHER NICELY.
NOW, THERE'S A PRESENT SHE HOPES HE'LL RETURN!
BOOYA! MERRY CHRISTMAS TO YA!
END

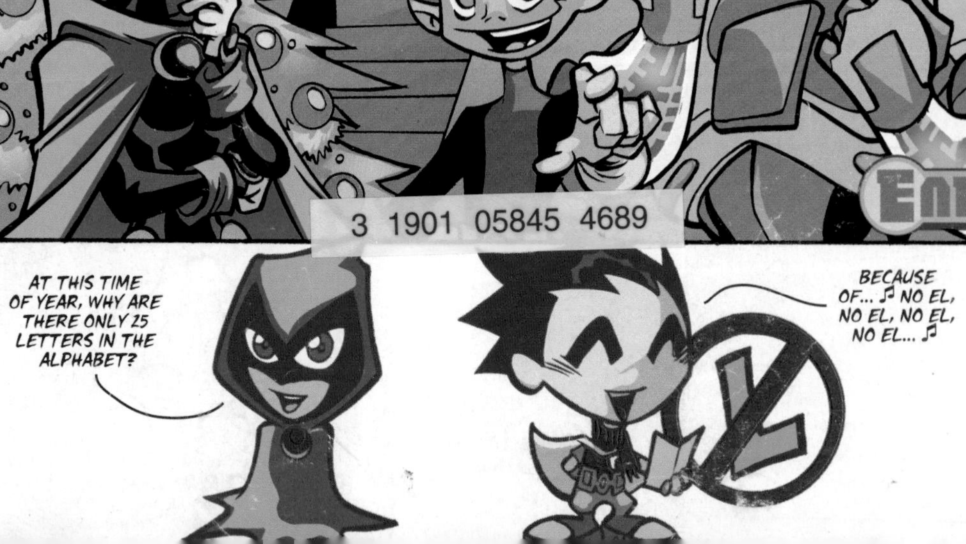
AT THIS TIME OF YEAR, WHY ARE THERE ONLY 25 LETTERS IN THE ALPHABET?
BECAUSE OF... ♫ NO EL, NO EL, NO EL, NO EL... ♫